BOOK THREE OF THE
MULTIVERSE ASKEW TRILOGY

AND NOW, TIME TRAVEL

CHRISTOPHER BRIMMAGE

THANK YOU FOR PURCHASING THIS BOOK.

To receive special offers, a free short story, and info on new releases, sign up for the Christopher Brimmage mailing list at cbrimmage.com

For Glen,
I miss you, too. If I could, then I would. In a second.

For Geraldine,
I love you in every timestream.

A NOTE FROM THE AUTHOR:

This novel (along with the previous two in this series) refers to different realities as "Earths." After receiving questions and criticisms about this naming convention, I felt it was time to explain myself. The choice to refer to different realities as "Earths" is definitely, totally, 100% due to following precedent set by Multiversal authorities. It was *not* a shortsighted decision made by an Earth-centric author during the writing of his first novel.

In fact, references to realities as "Earths" occur throughout this series because of a humanoid named Doctor Binglebramble Flambé. Dr. Flambé was one of the original Multiverse-Cartographers for the Bureau of Interdimensional Travel, serving the agency from around the time it was founded until his dishonorable discharge four decades later.

Dr. Flambé's home planet was called "Earth," and in his quintessential work for the B.I.T., *Multiverse Mapping & You*, he referred to all realities as "Earths." This naming convention was soon adopted as precedent throughout the B.I.T. as the organization incorporated Dr. Flambé's work into basic training documents and guidebooks to the Multiverse.

Following Dr. Flambé's dishonorable discharge from the B.I.T.—which is another tragic tale for another time—he entered the service of the Bureau of Time Travel as a cosmic cartographer, where he continued the practice of referring to realities as "Earths." The B.T.T. followed suit in adopting this naming convention.

Dr. Flambé devoted himself wholeheartedly to utilizing his Multiversal cartography skills to map as much of the Space-Time-Multinuum as possible, which he did until he was killed in the crossfire of the Quasar-Carnival Wars while demarcating the boundaries between the Feudal Age of Earth 7,300,112,008 and the Space Cowboy Age of Earth 45,222,143,555,888,001.

And that, as they say, is interdimensional-intertimeliminal history.

With the utmost sincerity,
Chris Brimmage

CHAPTER 1

A DIPLOMATIC MISSION

ALEXANDROS HO MEGAS—KNOWN as *Alexander the Great* if you reside on this author's Earth during this author's lifetime, and known simply as *Alex* to colleagues, friends, and indolent narrators—tilted to the right in his saddle to dodge an incoming fireball, which had a diameter twice as tall as he and blazed through the night like a hurtling meteor. It whooshed past his left ear and crashed into a member of his squadron.

Alex glanced over his shoulder and stared at the victim, a stocky teen whose name Alex had not yet learned. The teen moaned and struggled and kicked from beneath the flaming ball. Seconds later, the youth's muffled voice faded into silence.

Alex frowned as the stench of roasting humanoid flesh mingled with the fireball's sweet, caramelized aroma. This caramelized aroma existed because the fireball was no mere ball of fire. It had been formed from neither oil nor pitch nor anything else traditionally flammable that Alex had often encountered during his brief, wondrous time as King of Macedonia. It was instead a massive marshmallow approximately eleven feet in diameter that had been set ablaze by the enemy and launched in Alex's direction. It soon burned down to a crusty black shell atop the barbecued youth.

Alex nodded. He had been creeping across the battlefield toward the enemy to test the range of the enemy's mallowpults, and he had just found it. He marched his squadron back nearly fifteen feet and waited for the natives to loose another volley of the gigantic, flaming balls of sugar.

A dozen more of the gargantuan, flaming marshmallows arced high into the night sky and then crashed to the ground in front of Alex and his squadron. The marshmallows stuck in place, burning brightly atop the fluffy grass as they melted into gooey puddles. Alex squinted to stare past the flames, but they burned too brightly and left him with such night blindness that he could not see far beyond them.

Alex grunted and slammed his Phrygian-style helm onto his head. A red horsehair crest stood a foot tall from this shining golden helm and stretched in a straight line from the front of the helmet to the back. The helm clicked into place as clasps that extended from its bottom caught on clasps that rose from the top of his breastplate. This breastplate shone with gold and bore the angry image of a gorgon's face painted across its front. Alex reached a finger inside the helm and touched a tiny button just above his left ear. A pair of lenses made entirely from solid light appeared in the eye-slits of the helm. Through these lenses, all hints of night blindness disappeared, and he could see across the battlefield as though it were perfectly light out.

"Helmets on," barked Alex to his squadron.

The twenty-nine youths wearing uniforms that identified them as Bureau of Time Travel naval agents fresh out of basic training—skintight long-sleeve purple shirts, black leggings, black boots, black holsters, and B.T.T. badges over their left breasts that displayed a handless clock surrounded by a circular border embroidered with the words *"Time is on our side"*—retrieved small objects from their holsters that looked like pieces of folded, purple parchment. They each touched a button on the sides of these objects and waited for the devices to inflate into purple helmets, at which point they placed these helmets atop their heads and buckled straps beneath their chins to hold the helmets in place.

The youths looked like they were all wearing inflatable bicycle helmets. They reminded Alex of a B.T.T. Chief Security Officer named James Starley to whom he had reported many years ago. This officer had insisted on riding his confounded invention, a modified Penny-Farthing bicycle, everywhere he went—even on deadly missions requiring the utmost stealth. He concurrently insisted on wearing a bicycle helmet, which he claimed was invented long after his death but would have prevented said death if the objects had existed during his natural lifetime.

Hundreds of ululating shrieks erupted from the natives across the battlefield, and the memory of James Starley fled from Alex's mind. Alex stared at the savages and grinned, anticipation for the impending fight filling his heart.

"Activate Laser-Eyes," he ordered.

The purple-shirted squadron of youths tapped buttons near their temples, and laser-lenses stretched down from the fronts of their helmets to hover before their eyes. They let out a collective gasp as they stared across the battlefield. Alex scowled at their display of cowardice.

The ululating shrieks of the natives transformed into furious screams as they burst forth from the opposite end of the battlefield and sprinted toward Alex's squadron. They were bald humanoids with pale blue skin. There were several hundred of them, and they each hefted a gigantic wooden mallet as a weapon. On the left flank of this mallet-wielding infantry rode a hundred savage, blue-skinned cavalrymen. This cavalry bounced toward Alex's squadron atop giant marshmallows—riding these balls of fluffy sugar as though they were riding atop puffed, inanimate horses. A few dozen natives remained behind to load mammoth marshmallows onto the mallowpults, set the gigantic balls of sugar alight, and launch them toward the B.T.T. agents.

Alex shifted in his Gravitron Saddle[1], a device he had confiscated on a mission where he and the crew of the Bureau Time-Ship Unicorn Husker—the *B.T.S. Unicorn Husker* for short—had travelled to the 30th century of Earth 6,076 to ensure a peace treaty was signed between the native humans and a race of vampiric nebula clouds that sustain themselves by sucking atmospheres clean of nitrogen. Without the treaty, that particular timestream would have fallen into grave peril, and without the trusty Gravitron Saddle that Alex had commandeered during that mission, he likely would have fallen into the grave long ago—for the device was a

---

[1]A Gravitron Saddle is a hovering saddle that floats on pulsar beams. Its top speed in standard Earth 6,076-level gravity clocks in at 300 M.P.H., with capabilities of triple that speed in non-gravity situations. It is operated through handlebars that extend from its front that control its speed and cause it to vaguely resemble a flying motorcycle. An operator pairs these handlebars with Pulsar Boots, which—when toggled to the "*Saddle Ready*" setting—use pulsar beams that emanate from their base to create upward and downward momentum, depending on the direction the operator points them. The operator may place the Pulsar Boots in the "*Gravity*" setting to shut off the boots' pulsar beams and activate artificial gravity conductors in the boots' heels. So long as there is a large mass at which to aim one's heels, this is a most useful setting in the cold vacuum of space, because it allows a user to pull himself/herself down toward whichever object/mass he/she points his/her heels.

The Gravitron Saddle and its accompanying Pulsar Boots were invented by the famous cowboy-turned-engineer-turned-astronaut Victor Vakarov-Wu-Goldenblatt sometime during the 29th century on Earth 6,076 after an unsuccessful Bull-Slug ride in the Galactic Rodeo on the dark side of Oberon, the outermost moon of Uranus.

flying saddle that allowed Alex to traverse in and out of difficult situations at speeds and heights he never would have imagined during his natural lifetime.

Alex used his tongue to activate the communication toggle in his helmet so that his squadron might hear his orders no matter where he or they might roam in the looming battle. He cleared his throat, and the twenty-nine-remaining purple-shirted members of his squadron stood at attention. He ordered, "Agents Fourth Class, draw your Time-Phasers. Set them to a sixty-minute devolution."

The Purple Shirts seemed to gulp in unison. Then they unholstered their Time-Phasers from their belts and checked their settings. The Time-Phasers were petite, green ray guns with red rings circling around the barrels. They looked like toys with which Alex had watched children play aboard the B.T.S. Unicorn Husker, and in the hands of the Purple Shirts, they reminded Alex how young many of the Purple Shirts were.

Alex ignored this sentiment. Instead, he waited silently until the approaching natives had sprinted over halfway across the battlefield—a tactic he often employed to allow a less-disciplined enemy horde to tire itself and create gaps in its formation—at which point he gestured toward the incoming natives and screamed, "Attack!"

The Purple Shirts charged toward the blue natives. Alex sighed when three members of the squadron were immediately crushed and burnt to death by the next barrage from the mallowpults.

The remainder of the Purple Shirt squadron scrambled past the marshmallow-artillery fire and began shooting conical rays of orange light at the natives, who devolved into puddles of blue algae upon being hit. Alex frowned, for unlike his squadron of Purple Shirts, it was necessary for *all* the natives to survive this battle so that their leader might agree to sign a peace treaty with the Bureau of Time Travel. The natives would re-evolve back into their original, blue-skinned bipedal forms once an hour had passed, none the worse for wear other than the scarring pain of the devolution/evolution process. Thus, the natives would be entirely spared their losses from this battle, while the Purple Shirts' deaths would never be revenged—something which always nagged at Alex's conscience on diplomatic missions like this one.

Alex had no time to focus too deeply on his inability to avenge these newly deceased Purple Shirts, for he needed to provide cavalry support to the still-living members of the squadron before they were overwhelmed. Alex turned to his six fellow officers who had joined him on this mission. They were hovering in the air near him upon Gravitron Saddles of their own. These officers each wore a similar uniform to the Purple Shirts whom Alex had just sent into the fray, except where the Purple Shirts wore shirts colored purple, the officers wore shirts colored marigold. A similar marigold shirt covered Alex's torso beneath his breastplate, the difference between his and these other officers' being that their sleeves were solidly colored marigold, while his sleeves bore a single black stripe down their sides, indicating his rank as First Officer of his B.T.S.-class ship.

Alex nodded to the officers and said, "We ride behind the enemy and flank them from the rear. Set your weapons to sixty-minute devolution and follow me."

Alex glanced down at his holster. He wore a standard-issue B.T.T. holster around his waist, and in it was contained standard-issue B.T.T. equipment, including a Time-Phaser identical to the ones carried by the Purple Shirts. But being an officer had its perks, and in Alex's case, these perks meant supplementing his standard-issue equipment with weaponry that brought him comfort and confidence. Alex retrieved one such weapon from his holster—a metal cylinder that was approximately three-inches in diameter, ten-inches long, and wrapped in a grippy tape that Alex had applied to it years ago. Dials ran the length of one side. Alex twisted one dial's setting from an option that read *Permanent* to an option that read εξήντα. Then he twisted another dial from an option that read *Off* to an option that read *Mid-Range*.

Adrenaline raced through Alex as the cylinder vibrated for a few moments. Then it burst to life. An orange beam of light erupted from both ends of the cylinder to create a laser-Xyston, which was a laser-version of a twelve-foot long spear with a sharpened point on one end and a butt spike on the other. When Alex stabbed an enemy with either end of the solid-light spear, the enemy would be subjected to the same results as being hit by a Time-Phaser. This weapon allowed Alex to utilize the fighting styles that he had perfected in his natural lifetime before he had joined the Bureau of Time Travel. As a matter of fact, this laser-Xyston was an exact laser-replica of the type of weapon that Alex had implemented in his cavalry way back in Earth 6,076's timestream when he had conquered most of the world as the king of the most feared army on the planet.

Alex's fellow officers drew their Time-Phasers and followed him as he leaned backward and directed his Gravitron Saddle high into the air. The moniker *Boukephalas II*, which Alex had painted onto the sides of his Gravitron Saddle in neon orange reflective paint, shone in the moonlight. The group's saddles roared as they gained altitude, sounding like a chorus of deaf-tone demons singing the worst acapella concert ever. Alex and the officers flew up into the low-hanging clouds, flittered amongst them for a few moments, and then dropped behind enemy lines to the rear of the natives' mallowpults.

Alex leaned forward and darted toward a nine-foot tall blue man who was preparing to pull the lever on a mallowpult, which would launch one of the huge, flaming marshmallows into the midst of the Purple Shirts. Alex stabbed the man in his back. The laser-spear sank into the native's flesh nearly up to the handle. The man convulsed on its end and then melted into a puddle of blue algae.

Alex studied the mallowpult for a moment now that he hovered near it. It looked just like a catapult from Alex's Earth, but with a completely ridiculous payload. Alex stabbed the wooden base of the weapon with his spear, and the wood devolved into twisted, slimy, green vines. The giant flaming marshmallow flopped down atop the vines and burned them into nothingness. Alex smirked.

"Devolve the mallowpults and their crews, and then ride out to help our Purple Shirts," ordered Alex to his officers as he rode to the next mallowpult in the row, repeating the procedure with the next blue artilleryman. As he stabbed this native, he continued calling his orders, "And make a good show of it. We need to scare their leader into submitting to us."

As if on cue, an entirely new horde of thousands of blue-skinned natives burst forth from a nearby forest. Leading their charge was a massive, blue-skinned native wearing a glittering pink crown and riding atop the most grandiose marshmallow that Alex had ever seen.

Alex cursed. None of his sensors or scouts had discovered this group of flanking natives hiding in the forest, and the pre-battle intelligence briefing had indicated that there would be only a few hundred of the natives in total to subdue—the ones with which Alex's squadron was currently engaged—not a vast horde such as this one. Alex made a mental note to add a demerit to the permanent records of the pre-mission Holo-Scouting Deck scouts once he made it home from this mission.

Alex squinted at the thousands of incoming blue men and then barked into his communicator, "In case you haven't noticed, we have incoming from the north. Ricardo and Leif, set your Time-Phasers to automatic-shotgun-fire mode and provide suppressing fire from the ground. Draw them to your position, but withdraw and reset your attack from a safe distance if they get too close. The rest of us will take to the air and rain devolution down upon them whilst they are attempting to incapacitate the two of you. *Nobody* hit that individual with the crown. If he is devolved, then he can't sign our treaty."

"What about the Purple Shirts, sir?" asked Leif. "Should one of us break off and go assist them?"

Alex frowned. He replied, "Our mission is our top priority, and right now, our mission is at risk because of this surprise attack. The Purple Shirts must learn to stand on their own at some point. That point may as well be now."

And with that, Alex launched into the air, four of his six officers following behind. In midflight, he reached down to the handle of his laser-Xyston and twisted the dial from *Mid-Range* to *Long-Range*. The lasers emanating from his handle twisted shape so that he now brandished a laser-bow. When he felt sufficiently high above the incoming horde, he began loosing devolution-arrows formed from solid orange light down upon the thousands of flanking natives, careful to avoid landing one upon the blue-skinned male wearing the crown.

Minutes passed. Alex ignored the sweat dripping into his eyes. He continued devolving the natives.

More minutes passed. Soon, the threat of the surprise attack waned until it was not much of a threat at all. By Alex's count, he had devolved nearly two-hundred and twelve of the natives himself, while his fellow officers perched on their saddles near him had devolved about half that number each.

The enemy began to panic and was on the verge of routing, for the limited range of their primitive weaponry left them with no way to return fire upon the B.T.T. officers floating above them. Thus, *Victory* seemed prepared to bestow her metaphorical laurel wreath upon Alex, despite the surprise intrusion of this vast horde.

And then everything fell apart. A flash and a bang erupted from the ground in the middle of the marauding blue horde.

Alex screamed into his communicator, "Cease fire!"

Alex and the officers stopped firing into the crowd of natives as a man in a B.T.T. officer's uniform appeared amongst them from within a bright blue light. This man's uniform had two black stripes running down its sleeves, indicating his rank as Captain of his B.T.S.-class ship. He wore a domed maroon crown on his head, below which cascaded a few thick braids of curly black and gray hair that stretched all the way down his back, ending at his buttocks. His skin was dark olive in complexion, and a billowing beard flowed from his chin to his naval. He raised his fist in victory and called out in the natives' language, "I accept your surrender, King Blimpinny. I look forward to a treaty ensuring lasting peace between your people and our—"

A dozen gigantic mallets crashed down upon Alex's superior officer, Captain King Solomon. The Captain fell to the ground and screamed.

Alex cursed. He leaned down toward the Captain and jammed hard on his accelerator. He blasted the nearest blue thugs into puddles of devolved blue algae before landing next to his now-bleeding captain.

"Hmmph. Must've arrived a few minutes too early," muttered the Captain, his domed crown lying on the trampled grass beside him.

"Really?" asked Alex as he leapt onto the muddy grass next to his captain. "I hadn't noticed."

The king of the natives bounded over to Alex and Captain King Solomon, towering above them. The king raised his gigantic mallet for a deathblow.

Alex knelt, bowed his head, and yelled, "We surrender!"

*

The blue natives marched in a ring surrounding the Landing Crew of the B.T.S. Unicorn Husker. Firelight flickered from the torches that the natives carried. Alex sighed. He and the Landing Crew all had thick wooden clasps around their wrists that held their arms in place. Etchings of the natives bowing down in worship before gigantic marshmallows covered the manacles. Wooden chains linked the manacles to wooden bindings around each Landing Crew member's ankles. The ankle-bindings were connected to one another with another set of wooden chains, which were so short that the Landing Crew had to shuffle in little awkward steps to move.

Deep bass drums beat out a marching pace with which Alex and the crew struggled to match due to the short chains. At the front of the procession bounced the gigantic blue native with the crown. Every now and then, a bulging blue man nearly eight-feet tall—who Alex had surmised to be the crew's gaoler—would leap from the shadows with a torch in hand, gesticulate wildly without making a sound, and then either whack a Landing Crew member in the back with a gigantic mallet or spit a marshmallow in the victim's face.

As he had been trained, Alex walked nearly in the center of the herded Landing Crew, giving him protection as the second-most senior officer on this mission. Around him marched the six marigold-shirted officers, all of whom had thus far survived this mission, and around them in a protective ring shuffled the twelve remaining Purple Shirts who had not fallen in the battle. Alex glanced over his shoulder at the man waddling in the exact center of the B.T.T. herd, the man who was in the most-protected position, Captain King Solomon.

"My apologies, Alex," whispered Captain King Solomon. "It must've been the damned chronometer on the fritz again. We'll be OK, though. I have a plan."

The Captain winked and flashed a grin, and a few of his golden teeth sparkled in the torchlight from beneath his shaggy beard. Alex answered with an annoyed grunt, and then he faced forward. According to *this* captain, problems were never caused by his own error, but were always a malfunction in some other system outside his control. And then he always followed whatever mishap *he* caused with a convoluted plan to rescue the Landing Crew from whatever bigger problem replaced the original, much more manageable problem. Alex sighed.

Aside from releasing an occasional sigh, Alex remained silent for the remainder of the march, which lasted nearly four hours. The march ended when the group arrived at a village. Its outskirts were filled with dozens of farms growing a broad range of orange and yellow and indigo marshmallows. Ramshackle adobe shacks with thatched roofs formed a circle around a squat stone tower that stood atop a hill in the center of the village. Blue-skinned children stared with blank eyes from the shacks. A few dozen blond-haired females leaned out of doorways to watch the captives pass. These females did not only have blue skin, but instead had skin colors that ranged across every option of the rainbow. They stepped out of their shacks and began following the B.T.T. Landing Crew at a distance. Alex heard Captain King Solomon smack his lips and knew that the captain must be staring at the buxom blondes with lust in his heart. Alex sighed once more.

Soon, the group reached the squat stone tower in the center of the village. Its crenellations formed a shape in exact replica of the crown that stood atop the bouncing blue native at the front of the procession. The wooden doors that marked the entrance to the tower crashed open when two blue guards shoved them agape.

The procession moved inside, and once inside the tower, Alex could see a multitude of tapestries on the wall, all seeming to indicate how this blue group had suppressed orange and yellow and red and green peoples through conquest. On a dais in the center of the room was raised a squatty, blue throne. The four corners of the dais were upheld by sculptures of an orange man, a yellow man, a red man, and a green man, each kneeling in submission.

The blue-skinned native wearing the crown stepped off his gargantuan marshmallow steed and tossed it to a guard, who caught it and scrambled out of the tower with it in tow. The king then waddled up the stairs of the dais to the throne and plopped down on it with a heavy thud. He glowered at Alex and the Landing Crew of the B.T.S. Unicorn Husker.

The crowned native began gesticulating wildly and screeching at his captives in his native tongue, which sounded to Alex like a series of clicks and grunts and moans. The Universal-Translator-Flake in Alex's brain went to work, and the translation immediately clicked into place.

"King Blimpinny wants to know why we have attacked his people and created war with him," said Captain King Solomon, leaning over and practically shouting the words in Alex's ear.

Alex rolled his eyes. He glanced over his shoulder at his captain and frowned, for Captain King Solomon *knew* that Alex—like every agent in the B.T.T.—had a Universal Translator-Flake in his brain, so Alex understood the king's harsh words nearly instantly. The Captain's translation was completely unnecessary.

The Captain said, "Oh, don't give me that look. I *obviously* know you don't need me to translate for you. However, I'm setting the precedent to King Blimpinny that I must do so, for it shall cause him to underestimate our capabilities, and it shall buy me time—both of which I need for my plan to work."

Alex shrugged, not knowing how else to reply. Captain King Solomon winked at Alex and then shuffled forward out of the center of the Landing Crew. He stood alone before the native king. Captain King Solomon began gesticulating wildly and speaking in the natives' language. He barked. The native king barked back. Back and forth they went until King Blimpinny finally grinned and nodded.

The Captain returned to his crew and unnecessarily explained, "I explained the need for our treaty and the goods that it will provide to the king and his fellow natives. He became much friendlier when I explained that none of our weapons dealt lethal blows to his people and that they will have returned to normal by now. I recommended that he should send a squad back to the battlefield to retrieve those who fell to us in battle, because they are probably very confused. I then explained that there will be an alien species that enters this timestream three centuries in the future, and that King Blimpinny's cooperation is essential to the survival of his people and his Earth. He was receptive when I told him that if he sets the precedent for his people to live peacefully with the future-aliens this far back in the development of his people's culture, then it will prevent a war that would otherwise stretch across this entire timestream as well as the three nearest realities in the Multiverse, killing quintillions. I offered to open B.T.T. trade routes to here in exchange for our treaty, creating wealth for his people far beyond what they ever dreamed imaginable. That seemed to motivate him more than the number of lives that would be saved. Well, that *and* my revelation that if he cooperates, he will have the longest reign as king in all his people's history. By the end of our negotiation, he agreed to the treaty, but said he cannot sign it until we have completed his people's rites of covenant."

Captain King Solomon stared at Alex. Alex said nothing back.

Captain King Solomon whispered harshly, "Are you daft? Ask me a question! Make it *look* like we are having a discussion! My god, man, at least *try* and make my ruse to stall seem at least slightly believable."

Alex frowned. He then muttered the first question that popped into his mind, "And what do these rites entail?"

Captain King Solomon winked at him and said, "A sacrifice upon the Mallowpyre from both groups, followed by a trial by combat between me and the king. If I win, then it will prove to King Blimpinny that the gods are on my side and that the words I have spoken about the future are true. And then he will sign the treaty."

"Trial by *combat* between you and the king is extremely risky, sir," observed Alex. "He's nearly twice your size and probably a tenth your age. You'll be naming me as your champion, I presume?"

Captain King Solomon grinned, and then he winked once more. Alex sighed at all the winking. The Captain said, "Oh, no need, Alex. I planned for this eventuality in case our mission went awry, and we found ourselves in this exact situation. I wore a set of Discharge Undergarments beneath my uniform. I've been dragging out this translation-ruse so that the device can fully charge. I'm sure you figured out yourself that this device was the capstone of my plan, because otherwise the bulge in the rear of my uniform would have been a suddenly bulbous addition to my normally flat ass, and these last few moments would have been unnecessarily exposition-heavy."

A whining beep sounded from within the Captain's uniform. "That's my signal," he said. And with that, Captain King Solomon turned back to face King Blimpinny. He immediately accepted the terms for the rites of covenant.

*

The rites of covenant began at once. Everyone hastened outside, walked three times around the stone tower, and then followed a winding street that led away from the tower and toward a pyre upon which bright flames danced. The pyre was no wooden construct like Alex had frequently witnessed during his natural lifetime. Instead, it was a heaping pile made from hundreds of gigantic marshmallows that had been set aflame. The Mallowpyre was fueled by a continuous line of blue-skinned laborers who emerged from a nearby forest. They carried marshmallows that they tossed with great ceremony onto the fire, and then they returned to the forest to harvest more of these wild marshmallows.

The natives and the Landing Crew spread out to surround the Mallowpyre, and the sacrifice to the natives' gods began. A blue warrior stepped forward from amongst the natives. Carrying his mallet and a satchel full of tiny marshmallows, he approached the flames. He tossed both the mallet and the satchel onto the Mallowpyre, grunted a prayer, and then knelt with his head bowed to the flames. A throng of natives sprang forward, snatched the kneeling soldier, and hoisted him onto their shoulders. They cheered him and sang a hymn, and then they tossed him onto the Mallowpyre. He burned with a grin on his face.

Captain King Solomon turned to one of the twelve remaining Purple Shirts and said, "Your sacrifice will ensure this timestream's survival and will save countless lives. The Space-Time-Multinuum and I *both* give you our thanks."

"Wait, what?" asked the purple-shirted teen.

Captain King Solomon pointed at the Purple Shirt, and the blue natives sprang forth to snatch the youth. They unfastened his shackles and hoisted him up onto their shoulders. They sang another hymn while the young man screamed in terror. Then they tossed him onto the Mallowpyre.

"And now that we've fed their gods with a sacrifice, it will be my turn," said Captain King Solomon. He shuffled forward, and the natives freed him from his bindings.

King Blimpinny stood ferocious in the firelight, towering over Captain King Solomon at nearly twice the latter's height. A wooden mallet rested on the native king's shoulder, an enormous weapon with a head the size of Captain King Solomon's torso. Alex strained against his shackles, wishing that *he* could battle the native king in place of the aging Captain, who was more of a philosopher than a warrior.

Captain King Solomon and King Blimpinny bowed to one another. A trumpet sounded from the top of the stone tower. King Blimpinny bellowed a roar, raised his mallet high above his head, and charged toward the Captain. Meanwhile, Captain King Solomon stifled a yawn. He reached inside his right sleeve and tapped something.

A titanic bolt of lightning blasted from Captain King Solomon's uniform and crashed into King Blimpinny's ample belly. The native king immediately flopped to the ground in a fit of seizures. Captain King Solomon strode over to his prone opponent, wrested the mallet from his grip, and heaved it onto the Mallowpyre. He then placed his foot on the fallen king's chest and raised his fists in victory.

The surrounding natives squealed in disappointment. Captain King Solomon spoke in the natives' language, "This trial by combat is over. According to the rites of this covenant, your king will now sign our treaty."

The natives hissed and booed. Captain King Solomon produced a parchment and a small white tablet from his holster. He placed the tablet in King Blimpinny's mouth. It ended the seizures and revived the king. The king sat upright, beat his fists upon the ground, and barked a rage-filled bark at Captain King Solomon.

"Yes, it was a dirty trick," responded Captain King Solomon in the native tongue as he held the parchment out to King Blimpinny. "But I would do it again in a heartbeat before allowing you to wallop me with your mallet. And if you are now considering whether you might renege on the terms of our covenant because you are a sore loser, then let me offer you the following choice: you may sign to show me that the fate of this timestream is more important to you than your pride, or I can cut your children in half and split them evenly amongst your people."

Alex choked back a groan. Captain King Solomon's solution to every problem was to threaten to cut something of value in half—almost always children. It was apparently a negotiating tactic that had worked for him *once* during his natural lifetime before entering the service of the B.T.T., and he never missed an opportunity to return to its metaphorical well whenever he thought it would help him quickly attain a desired outcome.

King Blimpinny grunted. And then he nodded. Captain King Solomon placed the parchment in the king's hand, pricked the king's finger to produce blood, and then watched with a smile as the king signed. There would be peace in this timestream.

Captain King Solomon walked over to the Landing Crew of the B.T.S. Unicorn Husker. He pointed to a male and a female amongst the surviving Purple Shirts and said, "You two shall stay here in this timestream to ensure these natives abide by our treaty. You must be stalwart observers to confirm that they use the proper rhetoric about aliens in order to guarantee a future peace. If they do not, then contact me at once so that we can blockade their B.T.T. trade routes. Your descendants shall continue in your post after your deaths. In three centuries hence, the B.T.T. will return to reclaim them once it is confirmed that the threat we came here to prevent has been avoided."

The pair of Purple Shirts turned white with anxiety, but Captain King Solomon ignored this response. Instead, he strutted over to the throng of multicolored, blond-haired female natives that had surrounded the covenant ceremony. He put his arms around the two most buxom of them and said, "Now, let's go celebrate lasting peace."

The women giggled and began to walk away with him. Alex groaned at the Captain, because the Captain always followed a successful mission with what Alex could only describe as a Bacchanalia, but somehow even more hedonistic. And he *never* invited any of his fellow officers to join.

However, before the Captain could begin his celebration, a buzz rang out from every crew member's B.T.T. badge. From speakers embedded within the badges, a robotic voice declared, "Incoming transmission from Agent Arthur on Earth 6,076. All Landing Crew must return to the B.T.S. Unicorn Husker for emergency agent extraction!"

Alex grinned. The Captain's hedonistic celebration would have to wait. Alex tapped his badge and said, "First Officer Alexandros ho Megas to Officer Trixie. Mission complete. Jump us back to the ship at once. And please relay orders to Officer Groveland to collect our Gravitron Saddles from the battlefield for return to storage."

Thunder boomed overhead. Then a massive dirigible appeared in the sky. It consisted of an elongated, ellipse-shaped balloon that was easily the size of a major city. Thousands upon thousands of cables attached the bottom of the balloon to a gondola that was nearly as large as the balloon and shaped like an infinity symbol. A gigantic set of engines extended from the rear of the gondola, and these engines were as tall and wide as the gondola itself. The entire vessel was striped blue and white, though the stripes on the balloon were horizontal while the stripes on the infinity-symbol-shaped gondola were vertical.

A pale blue beam of light flashed from the underside of the ship and surrounded the Landing Crew of the B.T.S. Unicorn Husker. They were raised into the air by it, and then they dissolved into tiny particles.

They immediately reappeared atop a raised dais inside a cylindrical chamber on board the ship. Officer Trixie's head poked up from behind the controls to the Jump Chamber. Officer Trixie was a Cockatrice from Earth 82,202,444,121,003, which meant that she had the body of a two-legged dragon and the head of a rooster. This created the odd juxtaposition of a tiny, feathered head atop a gigantic, golden-hued serpentine body that—despite being curled as tightly as it could curl—occupied nearly every square inch of the Jump Chamber aside from the raised dais used for teleporting members of the Landing Crew. She wore the marigold shirt of an officer, though it was so small on her that she had merely stuck her head through the neck hole and allowed the shirt to dangle from her neck. She also wore a pair of reflective sunglasses, which allowed other crew members to look into her eyes without being accidentally murdered by her death stare, which was a natural defense mechanism amongst her species.

Officer Trixie crowed in delight to see the Landing Crew return. She waved at Alex with one of her two stubbly legs. Alex waved back at her and thanked her for the quick jump back onto the ship. She lifted a portion of her hindquarters to create a narrow path to the door, and the Landing Crew stepped down from the dais and ducked below her to the exit.

Alex and the Landing Crew exited the Jump Chamber. The Purple Shirts and the officers parted company in the hallway, with the officers rushing directly to the bridge while the surviving Purple Shirts dispersed to their cabins to recuperate. Upon arriving at the bridge, Alex took his seat near the helm in the First Officer's chair. Leif son of Erik from Earth 56,909 strode over and resumed his place at the ship's helm. 29333, the Communications Officer recently assigned to this ship, marched to her station and took her place there. Ricardo walked to the navigation unit and resumed his seat. Bagoo the Bog Ghost, the ship's Chief Security Officer, stood vigilant at his terminal near the back of the bridge as he had for the duration of the mission, for he was the officer who had remained behind to command the ship while Captain King Solomon and First Officer Alex departed it as part of this mission's Landing Crew.

Finally, Captain King Solomon sat down in the Captain's chair, a dispirited look on his face. He licked his lips a few times, his way of accepting and grieving the loss of his hedonistic celebration—the cost of fulfilling his duties as a safekeeper of the Space-Time-Multinuum. He pressed a button on the chair's right arm and said, "Chronal Date

4,890,888,546. Our mission: to seek out chronal anomalies and fix them diplomatically. The B.T.S. Unicorn Husker has completed a mission with the peoples of Earth 595,880 while awaiting an update from Agent Arthur on Earth 6,076. We have received his call and are now en route to his location. We skipped the native celebration festivities on Earth 595,880 in order to retrieve him."

The Captain released the button, and the recording stopped. He glanced over at Alex and said, "That's the most tedious part of this job, always having to provide that stupid oral record before we can actually *go* anywhere. Something to which you may look forward when you eventually command your own ship."

Alex shrugged. The Captain turned to the blond Leif son of Erik and said, "To Earth 6,076. Keep us at our current point in time."

Leif nodded, twisted the circular wooden helm, and then pressed a large red button. The stars and blackness of space outside seemed to slice into billions of tiny strips. They blurred together as the ship dove into them. Then they tangled together into billions of knots and undulated for what felt like hours. Then they untangled and transformed into the sky above Earth 6,076. Leif twisted the helm once more, and the mighty ship dipped downward toward the planet.

As the ship approached this Earth, Alex scowled at the scene looming outside the view screen. He hated Agent Arthur, and though he had not seen the bastard in nearly twenty years, the scene below reminded him why he despised the man. Agent Arthur was *supposed* to have absconded with the younger version of himself quietly and without causing alarm or alerting the natives to his presence, but on the street below was chaos frozen in time.

A billboard had been frozen in place as it was toppling over. Cracked pavement and random property damage peppered the street, and smoke billowed up from random small craters. And there in the middle of it all was Agent Arthur, wearing a blue bathrobe, flannel boxer shorts, and pink carpet slippers as he stood atop his hovering dolly. He waved at the B.T.S. Unicorn Husker like an idiot while next to him stood an enormous robot with drills for arms and at his feet lay his younger-self and a woman who looked identical to the ship's current Communications Officer, 29333.

"Officer Groveland, retrieve Agent Arthur and his companions from the Earth below," ordered Captain King Solomon into a communicator on his chair. "You may store them wherever is most convenient for you. I shall send a representative to retrieve them as soon as possible."

Blue light surrounded the waving idiot and his entire dolly. The man, his companions, and his dolly raised into the air. And then they disappeared.

Everyone on the bridge sighed, for Agent Arthur was once again in their midst.

CHAPTER 2

TIME UNBOUND

FOR THE PAST few minutes, Bureau of Interdimensional Travel[2] Agent 27142's entire body felt as though it were being pricked with pins. It was the exact feeling he got when his foot fell asleep and was just beginning to wake, only it spanned every inch of his body.

Despite the discomfort, Agent 27142 interpreted the feeling as a positive sign, because it was the first *new* sensation that he had experienced in nearly two hours. For nearly two hours ago, a version of himself from an alternate reality had ambushed him using a weapon that froze time. This ambusher had then absconded aboard a Bureau of Time Travel[3] vessel, taking with him the objects of Agent 27142's pursuit: an escaped prisoner who just happened to be yet another version of himself from an alternate reality *and* a robot with drills for arms, both of whom were directly responsible for the murder of Agent 29333—a fellow B.I.T. officer and the unrequited love of Agent 27142's life.

Agent 27142 attempted to wiggle his fingers. They moved. This would not normally be cause for rejoicing, but it was more evidence that time was now beginning to revert to normal, which meant that he would soon be free to continue his quest for vengeance against his escaped prisoner and the cursed robot with drills for arms. Because the B.T.T. was now harboring his prey, this quest meant he would need to blast his way through the time-policing agency to attain his vengeance. But making war upon the B.T.T. did not concern him, for he would destroy anyone and anything to

---

2 The Bureau of Interdimensional Travel—commonly referred to as the B.I.T.—is an oversight agency charged with regulating interdimensional travel, monitoring interdimensional trade, preventing interdimensional smuggling and illegal trafficking, collecting interdimensional taxes, serving interdimensional court documents, and policing Multiverse-level threats.

3 You met this organization in Chapter 1. If the type of work they do is still unclear, there is no need to worry. You will understand soon.

avenge Agent 29333.

"Finally, I can move," he muttered. He grew overjoyed when he realized that the words were not merely internal monologue. His lips had moved, and the sound had escaped from his mouth.

But then Agent 27142 frowned, because he remembered that time becoming unstuck *also* meant that the he would need to solve the lethal predicament that towered over him: yet another alternate-dimension-version of himself, this one a hostile god. This god was over nine-feet tall, had flames growing from his scalp instead of hair, and wore a cloak formed from the stitched-together hides of baby seals and white wolves. A necklace of severed ears hung from his neck, and a belt of thick rope hung suspended around his waist, attached to which were a leather pouch and tools made from obsidian. In his right hand he brandished a dagger with a serrated blade, which he had been on the verge of driving through Agent 27142's flesh before time had become frozen.

The god was also beginning to become unstuck in time, as evidenced when the god began blinking. His fingers began twitching on the green-furred cat's paw that served as the serrated dagger's handle. His flaming hair began dancing in the breeze.

This fiery, god-version of Agent 27142 laughed, a menacing cackle made even more terrifying because his left arm and the top left side of his torso had been melted off before time had become stuck. When time froze, the god had been in the process of using his godly powers to reattach the melted parts to the intact portion his body via gleaming strands of sinew that looked like angry red snakes.

The god said, "As I was saying before I was so rudely interrupted by that damned time-freezing device: it looks like a bad day for those who can't resurrect themselves."

A shrieking creak resounded above the god. The *Muse Electronics* billboard loomed overhead. This billboard normally stood erect across the street from Art's apartment, but it had been damaged during the mêlée prior to time becoming frozen and was in the process of toppling when time had halted. Its bulk eclipsed the sun and bathed Agent 27142 and the god in shadow. A second creak erupted from the billboard's gigantic pole, and whatever invisible strings were holding the damaged billboard aloft in the air began snapping. It slowly started to drop exactly as it had been dropping two hours prior, before it had been frozen in time.

The hand of the god's detached left arm was currently enclosed around Agent 27142's ankles, preventing the Bureau of Interdimensional Travel agent from rolling away to safety. Agent 27142 tried desperately to think of a solution to his predicament, but his mind went blank. He cursed as the precious moments ticked past. *"Think!"* Agent 27142 said to himself, only to frown in embarrassment when he realized that he had accidently screamed the word aloud.

He glanced from billboard to god to dagger. Then something clicked in Agent 27142's brain, and he remembered his saving grace.

"Henry! Help! Get me out of here!" yelled Agent 27142 to his companion, a sentient gourd who was currently being rolled by the god's nearly two-foot long, tattooed cockroach across the hot pavement and away from the danger zone of the falling billboard.

"Give me a moment," replied Henry the Jump Gourd—a Jump Totem[4] with the power to travel across dimensions who belonged to Agent 27142 because of a ruthless bit of thievery the agent had performed on a child—his melancholy voice so monotone that Agent 27142 felt a gnawing sense of boredom despite the dire situation that had enveloped him. Henry continued, "I'm in the middle of something here."

The god did not wait for Henry to help Agent 27142, instead slashing the dagger down at Agent 27142 in a ferocious arc, apparently intending to stab the agent before the falling billboard could crush them both. Agent 27142 twisted to his left just in time to save himself. He felt the dagger slam into his right shoulder—the exact spot where his heart had lain less than a second prior. The dagger cut all the way through his flesh, deflected off his bone, and scraped against the concrete below him. He screamed. And then he punched the god directly in the nose just as the billboard crashed down around them both.

---

4 Just in case you chose to skip the first two novels in this series: a Jump Totem is an object/animal/plant/machine native to an Earth (usually manifested as a sacred symbol) that is evolved to teleport between dimensions. These objects/animals/plants/machines allow their owners to legally travel interdimensionally for tourism or employment purposes, so long as the owner has followed protocol and obtained proper permitting from the B.I.T. before jumping. If caught dimension-hopping by the B.I.T. without the proper paperwork, punishment can range from a fine to a life sentence of hard labor in a penal dimension, depending on the severity and repetition of the infraction.

Screeching metal seemed to cry out in ferocious chorus from every surrounding angle. Chaos filled Agent 27142's world. The falling horizontal steel torsion bar smacked into the god, and the god was flung away in a rain of blood and gore.

Much to Agent 27142's dismay, however, the god's severed arm remained where it was instead of flying away with the rest of the god's body, and the arm's hand thus remained clamped around Agent 27142's legs. Agent 27142 immediately sat upright and attempted to pry his legs free, but it was to no avail. The god's fingers refused to loosen, and the agent could not escape.

The billboard hit the ground lopsidedly, with the steel torsion bar crashing upon the ground first to Agent 27142's left and then rolling toward him as the remainder of it hit the street. He glanced around in desperation. There! The manhole from which Agent 27142's enemies had emerged from the sewers before being whisked away on the B.T.T. ship. The manhole remained open, and if he were quick, Agent 27142 might be able to duck into it to save himself.

Agent 27142 attempted to drag himself toward it. But alas, the god's disembodied arm acted like an anchor, weighing him in place. He pulled his knees up to his chest and hunched with his head over his knees. He began tugging once more at the god's fingers.

And then he remembered that he had devices in his holster that could help free him from the hand. He felt like an idiot for allowing his desperation to cause him to forget them. He reached down to his holster for one of his brass pill-shaped devices—one of which he had used on the god before time had frozen to cause the god's arm to melt from his body.

But he ran out of time. With blinding speed, the world around Agent 27142 shrunk smaller and smaller. The cacophony of bending metal enveloped him, and then he could see nothing.

CHAPTER 3

COLLECTION FROM THE CARGO HOLD

CAPTAIN KING SOLOMON turned to Alex and smiled. "First Officer, I need you to make your way to the cargo hold at once."

The smallest of frowns curved downward across the edges of Alex's lips. "Why me, sir?"

Now it was Captain King Solomon's turn to frown. He arched an eyebrow at Alex and said, "I have known you to question an order only one other time, and that was when you were possessed by the time-displaced pirate-demon from Earth 90,009. Are you currently possessed by a time-displaced entity?"

Alex's frown grew as he thought, *I conquered and ruled the entire known world, while you lorded over a tiny backwater kingdom. I should be the Captain of this ship, and you should be my underling.*

Captain King Solomon seemed to sense Alex's thoughts. He tilted his head back and stared at Alex over his long, hooked nose. He looked like an overlarge falcon with a beard. The Captain said, "I understand your frustration in taking orders from me, especially when you feel the orders given are not worthy of your status."

"Sir, I never said tha—"

Captain King Solomon waved away the objection with the back of his hand. He said, "I would not ever claim to be a better strategist or tactical commander than you. But I *am* in command of this ship because the Bureau of Time Travel considers wisdom the greatest of virtues—while you display far too much brazenness, which the Bureau considers one of the worst vices. I have no doubt that you will make a fine Captain *someday* when you have matured, but for now, it would behoove you to use the time in my service to better yourself by suckling at the teat of my wisdom."

Alex furrowed his brow. Alex made a mental note to add the Captain's reference to his own teat to the ongoing backlog of inappropriate workplace behavior that Alex would someday be submitting to the Humanoid Resources Department. He replied, "Suckle at the *teat of your wisdom*? What does that even mean?"

Captain King Solomon furrowed his brow right back at Alex. The Captain said, "It means that you should observe my process for making decisions and implement it into your thinking. Try using your brains rather than your spear. Or don't, and I will instead cut you in half to teach you a lesson."

Alex sighed. As he thought back upon his time in service to this captain, he realized that the sagest insight he had ever gained was that if one strategy worked once, use it over and over and over again. Instead of commenting on the overuse of the Captain's bifurcation threat, Alex instead decided to comply, hoping it would speed this interaction along. He said, "Yes, sir. I will absolutely do that."

Captain King Solomon stared at Alex for a long, silent moment. Then he nodded and said, "Good. Good. Now head down to the cargo hold and escort Agent Arthur back here. Bring his companions, too."

"Yes, sir."

Before Alex could completely turn away and exit the bridge, Captain King Solomon said, "You should know that this particular errand does not exist merely to teach you humility—though that is a helpful byproduct. I have given you this duty because you and I both originate from the same Earth as most of Agent Arthur's companions. It will ease their transition into life aboard this ship to interact with one of *us* rather than with a humanoid from some other random Earth's timestream. And since I must create an entry into the Captain's Log before we can jump away from this moment in this Earth's timestream, I cannot embark on the errand myself without causing unnecessary delays."

Alex nodded as he spun on his heel and walked to the door. It slid open and he entered a long hallway, its walls made of metal painted beige and decorated with portraits of former captains and their first officers. Its floor was corrugated metal covered in thin carpet topped with a gripping material that prevented crew members from slipping and sliding across the floor in instances of the ship rocking when under attack. Alex passed a dozen crossways with hallways that extended into other parts of the ship, including the recreation room and the crew pub. About a quarter mile farther on, this hallway ended at a bank of cylindrical elevator tubes. The crowd waiting for a car stepped aside to allow their senior officer to cut to the front of the queue. An elevator opened, and five Purple Shirts stepped off. Alex and four Purple Shirts stepped onto the elevator car in their place. "Press Sublevel 6 for me," Alex ordered to no one in particular. A Purple Shirt obeyed.

The elevator zoomed downward. The plummet caused Alex's stomach to drop. He did not like the feeling, for it reminded him of the moment he was recruited into the B.T.T. He had lain ill in bed for eleven days at the palace of Nebuchadnezzar II of Babylon. On the morning of the twelfth day, as he stared up at the gilded ceiling, a light flashed above him, and he dissolved into nothingness. He reappeared somewhere new, and when he did, his stomach lurched so hard that he vomited. When he recovered himself, he found that he was standing before a panel of seventeen men, women, and assorted creatures. They sat on a wooden dais twenty feet above him and wore black robes that trailed all the way to the ground at Alex's feet. He noticed that his vomit had landed squarely on the pleated end of one of the robes.

One of the panel members—a pale man with corpse-blue skin—asked Alex if he would like to be healed and to join the Bureau of Time Travel, in whose service he would help protect the Space-Time-Multinuum from dangerous time anomalies. Otherwise, Alex's body would be returned to its rightful place in his own timestream, where he would die within hours.

Although Alex did not quite understand what a Space-Time-Multinuum was, nor why these divine creatures had chosen him to protect it, the offer seemed preferable to dying within the next few hours. Thus, he agreed to the deal.

And from there, Alex worked his way up the ranks from Purple Shirt to First Officer, surviving every challenge that came his way through a combination of luck, ferocity, and cunning. Compatriots lost or killed along the way were returned dead and broken and mangled to their proper timestreams, and their deaths were recorded in the annals of their Earths' histories as their Earths' timestreams demanded. Their service to the greater good was never known outside the confines of the B.T.T., their reward on average a few extra months of life.

Alex thought back on his long years of B.T.T. service, his mind's eye flittering amongst the memories of his many missions and campaigns. His time aboard the B.T.S. Unicorn Husker was his longest in service to a single ship—sixty-three years, not counting a nearly century-long side quest away from the ship that was the result of a Chronal-Dispersion-Shotgun disaster that occurred during a mission—and one in which he had started as a security officer reporting to the then-Chief Security Officer—a halfling named Barnabus "Brandywine" Buckle—and been promoted all the way up to First Officer.

Captains came and went. Many died on missions. But this current one, King Solomon—an officer with one hundred seventy-seven years' experience in B.T.T. service—had taken over duties twenty-two years ago, having been transferred from the captaincy of another ship that was lost in a battle at the end of the Earth 53,307's timestream. King Solomon had by now lasted longer than any other captain in B.T.S. Unicorn Husker history, and at times, Alex wondered if the gods were keeping King Solomon alive as punishment for some past misdeed of Alex's, forcing him to endure some odd purgatory consisting of constant lectures about the need for more wisdom.

The elevator jerked to a sudden halt, and Alex's thoughts experienced a similar jerk to the present. The other passengers on the elevator were staring at him, and he realized they were waiting for him to exit the elevator car. He stepped off into another long hallway. This one was identical to the one on bridge-level, except its walls were painted maroon and different portraits lined its walls. Alex followed the corridor until he came to the first crossway. He turned right. This hallway looped back in the direction from which he had just come, but it bypassed the bank of elevators and opened on a winding staircase. Alex descended this staircase to the cargo hold.

Chariots and carriages and cars and jets and rockets and hovering discs and twirling energy tornadoes and thousands upon thousands of other disparate modes of transportation lay stacked on shelves across the vast expanse of the cargo hold, all arranged in precise organized fashion according to timestreams and Earths by the Inventory Officer, Yardish Groveland.

Yardish was a black-haired female from Earth 8,808,763 with a gigantic unibrow, a wispy mustache, and a penchant for spreadsheets and organization. Her skills were tested and proven competent over and over as she speedily provided the Landing Crews with anything they needed every time a mission required specialized gear or localized transportation or disguises to blend in with the natives on whatever random Earth at whatever random point in its timestream was causing whatever random anomaly that needed to be resolved.

Yardish did not look up from her computer as Alex approached her. Instead, she raised one arm and pointed to her right, toward the far end of the cargo hold. Alex nodded his thanks and marched in the direction she had indicated.

His passed row after row of shelving that stretched out of view into darkness above. Robot arms dangled from the ceiling and flittered about, moving objects to other shelves or placing them on the ground in preparation for upcoming missions. Alex walked straight down the row for nearly a half-mile before finally reaching his goal.

Agent Arthur's hovering dolly floated above a raised metal square embedded in the floor. The square was about ten-feet by ten-feet and was deep cobalt in color. Each row in the cargo hold had one of these raised metal squares at its end. It was a Reintegration Transfer Conduit. When cargo was brought aboard the ship, it would appear atop one of these squares according to the location that Yardish felt was most efficient and appropriate, at which point the robotic arms dangling from the ceiling would dart down and move the cargo to its proper shelf. Alex sighed, wishing the robotic arms would have tucked the dolly holding Agent Arthur onto some shelf at the back of the cargo hold where it would never be found.

Agent Arthur lay on his side, asleep and snoring. Drool covered his cheek. Alex scowled at him. Next to the prone agent was the agent's younger-self, cradled in the arms of a woman who looked identical to the ship's new Communications Officer, 29333—an interesting woman who had been freshly promoted and reassigned to the Unicorn Husker due to heroic deeds aboard the B.T.S. Bumblebee Witch during its intervention in the Sentient Rock Rebellion of Earth 6,823,009,008,043.

And frozen in place toward the back of the dolly towered a gigantic robot. The twelve-foot tall behemoth had an oblong head with three radar dishes sticking out from its top, two telescopic red eyes, and a speaker embedded in its head beneath steel mesh in the equivalent location to where a human's mouth would sit. It had no neck that Alex could see. Instead, its cylindrical torso extended for five feet below its head, and large dials and knobs covered the front of its torso. Three huge wheels jutted out from below the robot's torso, and foot-long daggers extended from the spokes of each of these wheels. Large pipes formed the machine's arms, and these pipes each ended in an enormous drill. The robot's arms were so long and wide and thick that they reminded Alex of the king of Earth 7,099,443,201, whom Alex had met on a mission there to save its people from an impending Chronal-Hurricane originating two realities over. The people of that Earth were a race of gigantic gorilla-doctors who preferred surgically replacing their natural limbs with weaponry in order to wage war upon one another. Their king had replaced his forearms and hands with drills, and this robot brought to Alex's mind of a chrome version of that king.

Alex removed a rectangular device from his holster, tapped a few buttons on its top, and then set it down atop the hovering dolly. A bright green flash burst from it, accompanied by green smoke that smelled of seaweed salad pureed in balsamic vinegar. The younger Arthur and his female companion leapt to their feet.

"What the hell is happening?" demanded Younger-Arthur.

Before Younger-Arthur had the chance to wait for an answer, the side-effects of becoming unfrozen in time caught up to him. He and his female companion both collapsed, toppling back down into a prone position on the dolly. They rubbed their legs.

"What is happening to me?" demanded the female.

The robot did not move. Words emanated slow and slurred from its speakers, "[whir] Drillbot's gears feel – CLACK – feel rusted."

"I see that Agent Arthur failed to explain *anything* to you," said Alex. "That is no surprise. You are merely experiencing the discomfort of being unfrozen in time. It will pass momentarily. Nothing to worry about."

The two humans stared at Alex in confusion. He sighed. He had been speaking in his native tongue instead of this duo's, having forgotten to use the Universal Translator-Flake in his brain to adjust his speech to their language. It was a reminder of something he needed to do for them so that they might fit in more easily on this ship and not rely on others to translate for them. He glanced at the robot and asked, "Can you understand me?"

"[whir] Drillbot has – CLACK – Drillbot has universal translators embedded in his – CLACK – his programming."

Alex nodded. He removed from his holster two discs—not three, since the robot already possessed universal translator technology— the size and shape of fish food. He placed one on each of his index fingers and then squeezed his thumbs down atop them. A tiny jolt of electricity surged through his fingers to let him know the discs were now active. He frowned as he shoved his index fingers—and thus the discs—up the left nostril of both Younger-Arthur and the female. Once Alex removed his fingers from their nostrils, bolts of yellow electricity flashed from their noses. The smell of burning nostril hair filled the area.

Alex nodded once more, because the electricity meant that the Universal-Translator-Flakes—a species of tick from Earth 7,099,332,126— were burrowing up into the language centers of the duo's brains and finding homes. These creatures would feed off written, oral, and body language perceived by their hosts, and translations would instantly be defecated directly into their hosts' brains. The creatures were standard-issue equipment for every B.T.T. agent to allow communication with anyone in the Space-Time-Multinuum, and though these two were not agents, they were important enough to the B.T.T.'s cause to warrant issuing the Universal-Translator-Flakes to them.

Thus, now that the humans could understand Alex no matter which language he used, he repeated, "I see that Agent Arthur failed to explain *anything* to you. That is no surprise. You are merely experiencing the discomfort of being unfrozen in time. It will pass momentarily. Nothing to worry about."

Agent Arthur interrupted the moment with a loud snore. Alex reached out a finger and considered prodding Agent Arthur with it to wake him. He changed his mind and instead slapped the dolt across the face.

Agent Arthur jerked upright. "What the hell?" he squealed, holding a hand to the redness forming on his cheek.

"You were asleep on duty," said Alex.

"Well, yeah, because I was awake most of the night because I was excited to complete my mission. And then I was stuck here for, like, forever with these popsicles while I waited for someone from the crew to come meet me and sign me out of the cargo hold."

Alex frowned. "Well, I am here to do so. You and your companions are to come with me to the bridge. We will find a uniform for you to change in to along the way."

Agent Arthur rolled onto his rear end and then gently lowered himself from the hovering dolly. Younger-Arthur shrugged and did the same. They looked like identical frumpy toads, and loathing filled Alex's heart. Alex stepped toward them and jabbed a fist into each of their bellies.

Satisfaction filled Alex as an identical piggish squeal escaped each of their lips. The two Arthurs collapsed to the ground and groaned. As they tried to catch their breaths and writhed with identical pained wiggles, Alex grinned.

"Hey! That was uncalled for!" screamed the female. She hopped to the ground from the hovering dolly and steadied herself on its side. The robot's engines roared, and it leapt to the ground beside her.

Alex turned his back to them and began walking back the way he had come. He waved for the four to follow him.

"Lady," Alex called over his shoulder, thinking of how dry his shoes had been for the last twenty years, and how wet they were destined to become over the next few months, "you have no idea the annoyance and suffering and pain that those two will cause *everyone* around them. I'll guarantee that you'll want to do much worse to them before long. Now follow me."

They did.

CHAPTER 4

AN UNHOLY PACT

AGENT 27142 COUGHED for a solid thirty seconds. Thick dust floated inside his little cocoon of steel and canvas, making his eyes water. But that mattered little to him. He felt like the most fortunate B.I.T. agent in the Multiverse, for he had survived certain death through sheer luck.

He was sitting in the same position in which he had been sitting when attempting to pry the god's disembodied hand from his feet. The mammoth steel torsion bar lay across the exact spot his head had occupied before he had sat upright. Broken pieces of canvas and steel lay twisted and crumpled around him, but he had not been crushed to death. Granted, a jagged metal pole stuck out of his left thigh where it had impaled him, and he was quite certain that his right elbow had shattered, but at least he was *alive*.

He laughed in delight. But when he inhaled to laugh again, the dust filled his lungs, and he broke into a new fit of barking coughs. He reached into his holster and drew from it a small, round disc. He tapped an orange button on its bottom and tossed it into the air. It banged against the top of his metal cocoon, but instead of ricocheting and bouncing to the ground, the disc hovered in place. It began to glow, providing pale white light so that he could gain his bearings.

He found that there were few bearings to gain. He was curled in a tiny space within the jagged metal of the toppled billboard. The space was just long enough for his legs to curl before him so that his knees pushed into his chest and just tall enough for him to sit with his head hunched over his knees. Above him, the letters *M-U-S-E* were crunched together so they were nearly illegible.

Agent 27142 sighed. He winced as he reached up to the disc and tapped a blue button on its side. The disc buzzed and then released an arc of light from its top. The arc rotated three hundred and sixty degrees, momentarily blinding Agent 27142 as he stared into it. He rubbed his eyes with his palms and cursed his idiotic decision not to close his eyes. After a few moments, the blinding afterimages departed his vision, and he was able to see the output of his device. A three-dimensional model created from solid light now hung in the air below the disc, portraying a toppled and crumpled billboard lying on a street.

Agent 27142 winced once more as he reached up and spun the model. It turned in the air. He pinched his fingers and the image zoomed closer. He found his cocoon, and then he twisted the model to find the path of least resistance to freedom. He nodded. There appeared to be nothing that would collapse on him or shift in a deadly manner if he were to force himself out *that* way. The only impediment to that direction was the solid mass of steel, but a small problem like that would merely slow him down.

Agent 27142 reached down to his holster and pulled out another of his brass pill-shaped devices—the ones with the retractable spikes that heatlessly melt anything into which they are stabbed by rearranging the recipient's molecules—having dropped the one that he had been using in the fight with the god and losing it permanently when it was buried somewhere out of reach beneath the toppled billboard. He pressed the tiny button on this new device's side, and when its three petite spikes jutted out from one end, he stabbed the device up into the wreckage above him.

A portion of the billboard melted. It flopped down onto his head and then sloughed off to rest in a puddle on the ground. He frowned. Though the liquified metal and canvas were not hot, their weight was uncomfortable when it smacked against him. A gash about a foot deep and a foot wide now lay amidst the crumpled metal and canvas above him. He reached up into the gash and stabbed again. More melted steel and canvas poured down around him and collected on the ground.

Agent 27142 next stabbed the disembodied god's hand that surrounded his feet. As he kicked free of the melted appendage, he winced, because stabbing pain in his left thigh reminded him that a steel bar lay embedded there. He jabbed the pill's spikes into the bar. The bar melted away, and as it flowed out of his leg, Agent 27142 was left with a gaping hole in the now-unoccupied space. He could feel the color drain from his face as blood erupted from the wound.

He pulled from his holster a device that looked like a syringe-sized machine gun—particularly one known colloquially on Earth 5,999,234,007 as a *"Tommy Gun,"* a term he knew because he had confiscated one there on a mission to assassinate the matriarch of the Patronella Family after she decided to circumvent interdimensional law by smuggling cheap booze onto her Earth from other dimensions without registering the operation with the B.I.T. or paying the proper tariffs or filing the proper paperwork. He smiled as he recalled the delightful kick when he pulled the trigger on the confiscated Tommy Gun and the horrified look on the lawbreaker's face as she was filled with bullets.

But then pain shot through his leg, jerking his mind to the present. He grunted and pointed the barrel of the tiny machine-gun-shaped device into the opening of the wound. He pulled the trigger. The device's barrel flashed over and over in rapid succession, firing lightning bolts into his leg like a machine gun would fire bullets. Agent 27142's nose twitched at the smell of burning flesh, and when he finally released the trigger and pulled the miniature gun away from his wound, it was cauterized all the way through. He felt the wound's entry and exit holes with his fingers. Satisfied he had stopped the bleeding, he placed the miniature gun back into his holster and forced himself up onto his feet.

His head spun, but he could now manage a crouch in the space he had opened in the little cocoon. He checked the floating three-dimensional model to ensure that nothing had shifted during his melting of the wreckage above him. Satisfied that it had not, he stabbed with the brass pill once more, ducked his head as more metal and canvas melted around him to pool at his feet, and then found that he had torn into the wreckage enough that he could stand upright with only a slight hunch.

He smirked and began repeating the process over and over, always checking the three-dimensional model to ensure safety before stabbing. Before long, the pain in his elbow became too much of an encumbrance, so he pulled a cube of gel from a pouch on his holster and swallowed it. Later tonight, its aftereffects would force him into an exhausted, dreamless slumber. But right now, it numbed the pain in his shattered elbow and sent a burst of energy surging through him. He continued stabbing into the wreckage above, climbing up into it once he had melted his way high enough where climbing became a necessity.

Finally, after much stabbing and climbing and stabbing again, he stabbed one last time and felt fresh air dance across his face. He squealed with joy and realized that he was free. It felt like he had been working for days to ascend from the wreckage. He smirked when he glanced at his timekeeper and found that from start to finish, it had taken him only fifteen minutes to stab to freedom.

He climbed out of the gash in the wreckage and collapsed onto the top of the billboard's crumpled corpse. The disc floated out of the wreckage and hovered next to him. He tapped a black button on its side, and it fluttered down to his palm and powered off. He returned it to his holster, closed his eyes, and inhaled deeply. Freedom smelled delightful, though he could not help but note that it was accompanied by undertones of raw sewage.

"I don't know if *all* B.I.T. agents have horrible senses of smell—or if it's just you—but the tones of your inhalation indicate that you are entirely too satisfied with the stench of this neighborhood. This revelation is very disturbing to me," said a familiar monotone voice, breaking Agent 27142's concentration.

Agent 27142 opened his eyes and glowered at Henry, who was lying on his side and being rolled up on top of the wreckage by the tattooed cockroach. Behind the pair, on the concrete below, the god's corpse lay smashed and broken. Blood and organs pooled in a wide arc around him. The blood transformed into little rainbow-colored pixies that fluttered up into the sky. Agent 27142 chose not to respond to the Jump Totems, instead watching the oddly beautiful juxtaposition of the graceful pixies forming from the disgusting pile of gore.

"I hear sirens in the distance," continued the gourd. "On my home reality, those were signs of emergency vehicles approaching. We should probably get out of here before they arrive."

Agent 27142 looked away from the pixies and nodded. He said, "Yes, we'll need to jump to one of my safehouses so that I can heal."

He then pointed to the cockroach and said to Henry, "But first, we will need to dispose of the bug."

The bug reared up onto its hind legs. It flashed lightning between its antennae and spread its wings, revealing the entirety of the blue tattoos covering its body.

Henry squealed, "Don't say things like that to Beverly! She just saved my life. Besides, methinks disposing of her is easier said than done."

Agent 27142 glared at the gourd. Agent 27142 was unused to his orders being disobeyed.

Henry said, "To remind you once more, I have no eyes. So, if you are glaring at me, I wouldn't know it. However, I *can* smell emotions, and I can tell that you're full of rage and remorse over *something*. I would hope these emotions are your conscience punishing you for your heartless desire to murder this gracious, selfless, me-saving Jump Totem."

Agent 27142 said nothing. He refused to tell Henry the cause of his rage and remorse, refused to profane his lost love by saying Agent 29333's name to this apparently traitorous gourd and its new friend.

Henry interrupted the silence to continue, "You're supposed to be the strategist, but you're blinder than me. You wanted vengeance on your former prisoner and the robot, and you *almost* had it. Instead, you fought the god and let your true prey escape."

"Get to the point," spat Agent 27142.

"The point is that Beverly and her master had *no* desire to fight you. She told me as much while you were buried underneath this billboard. They merely want to use your former prisoner as bait to capture a cosmic pink bear. But now their bait has escaped them, leaving *both of you* bereft of your quarry. It seems to me that your goals are now relatively aligned."

Beverly rubbed her forelegs together. Henry continued, "She says she'll speak to her master about a partnership. She is over ninety-percent certain that he will partner with you to pursue your former prisoner and the robot, and he will almost certainly turn them over to you for punishment as soon as he has used them to capture the cosmic pink bear."

Agent 27142 scowled at the bug. Without taking his eyes from her, he waved his hand toward the crushed and broken corpse of the god. He said, "I take it none of you noticed the flattened body of her master. A little hard to team up with his corpse."

Laughter erupted behind Agent 27142. A shadow fell over him. He twisted and found the god towering above him, fully reformed. Agent 27142 glanced from the figure over to the corpse spattered across the concrete, and to his dismay found that the corpse was gone.

The god said, "You must be as stupid as the version of us that escaped.

I told you, I'm a god that resurrects."

Beverly rubbed her forelegs together, and her clicking sounded almost melodic. The god nodded. Then he said, "Seems ol' Bev thinks we should work together. She's been right more often than not, so I'm inclined to listen to her on this one. What do you say?"

The god held out a hand for a shake. Agent 27142 frowned as he took a few moments to think through his options. And then he held out his own hand. They gripped, and neither winced as the other squeezed tight.

Agent 27142 said, "Fine. I'll help you find my prisoner and the robot. You can use my prisoner to snag the pink bear. Then I get to kill them both with my own two hands."

The god smiled, but there was no mirth behind his eyes. The expression reminded Agent 27142 of a snake. The god said, "You have a much better handshake than our mutual prey. My name is Artheoskatergariabetrugereiinganno, but let's not stand on formalities. At least two written records refer to me as God-Art, so you may do the same. Now stand. Let's get you healed, and then we can go somewhere to discuss our next steps without the distraction of incoming emergency crews."

Agent 27142 raised himself onto his feet, and by the time he finished standing, music had filled the air around him and little hovering cartoon musical notes were floating from the god's lips and crashing into his shattered elbow, his wounded leg, and his longsuffering shoulder. This shoulder was the one in which the corpse of his former Jump Totem—an eagle issued to him by the B.I.T. way back when he had achieved his *officer* status—lay embedded beneath his flesh due to his unfortunate encounter a decade prior with the maw of a fifty-foot tall Cyclops.

Agent 27142 flinched in surprise and nearly fell over, but God-Art steadied him. A few moments later, Agent 27142 was completely healed, and his dead eagle was removed from his shoulder. The only signs of his struggle with the god were all the surrounding property damage and the dust that covered him from head to toe and the rips in his uniform.

Agent 27142 picked up Henry and ordered, "You and the bug—jump us to Earth 47,787. I have a safehouse there."

Beverly scrambled up God-Art's cloak and rested upon his shoulder. Lightning flashed from the two Jump Totems' antennae and then crashed into Agent 27142 and God-Art. Ambulances and fire engines turned onto the street just as the four of them disappeared.

CHAPTER 5

BUREAUCRACY, BUREAUCRACY EVERYWHERE

NORMAL-ART WATCHED THE blond man's curly hair bounce with each step he took, playfully pitter-pattering atop the shoulders of his marigold shirt. Normal-Art felt like he was watching a shampoo commercial. The idea of a commercial reminded him of home, and a deep sense of dread and longing filled the pit of his stomach. He just wanted to go home. Why did no one seem to care?

The blond man periodically glanced over his shoulder as he spoke, but Normal-Art had little desire to listen. He instead sulked silently and studied the random humanoid crew members that the group passed. Most of them wore shirts in some assorted shade of purple, though they passed a sporadic few with the same marigold color as their guide's. Many were human, and many more looked close enough to human to pass at a distance—ridged foreheads or black bowl cuts with pointy ears or rolling chins with segmented waves of cartilage. Many others, however, were bizarre creatures ranging in diversity from scuttling mastiff-sized spiders to ferocious spider-sized mastiffs, all of whom had stuffed themselves into purple shirts designed to cover more humanoid bodies.

After walking for entirely too long and ascending entirely too many steps and winding through entirely too many bends along the path, the quintet arrived at an elevator bank. A queue of purple-shirted individuals stood before it, but they seemed deferential to the blond guide and quickly ducked aside to let the group pass.

When the elevator car arrived, the guide ordered the car's current occupants to exit, and then he led Normal-Art and his three companions into the car. The guide glared at one of the Purple Shirts who had been at the front of the queue and who had begun stepping onto the elevator behind them.

"Um, I'll just wait for the next one, sir," she said as she backed out of the car.

The guide pressed the button to take the elevator car to bridge level, in doing so typing a command into the interface to override any other destinations previously given to the elevator car. Normal-Art's stomach twisted as the elevator shot upward. The guide began talking again, but Normal-Art continued tuning him out. He stared at his shoes for the duration of the ride. Then the elevator jerked to a halt. The guide disembarked and then gestured for his followers to exit. Drillbot, Ginny, and the robed, older version of Art stepped off the elevator car.

Normal-Art followed, but as he did so, he instinctively reached out his hand and pressed all the buttons on the control panel inside the elevator car. He smirked as they all lit up. Then he noticed a long queue standing outside the car, waiting to climb aboard. His smirk grew. He heard the new passengers yell out curses behind him as they entered the elevator car and saw what he had done. He quickened his pace away from the scene of his mischief.

After what felt like another hour of walking—but was likely closer to five minutes—the group stopped in front of something that looked like a vending machine embedded in a wall near a black door. The machine seemed to sense the group approaching, because it lit up with a circular pattern of neon blue lights that emanated from its center.

The blond guide turned to Normal-Art's older twin and ordered, "Use your I.D. card to get a new uniform."

Older-Art stared at his pink carpet slippers and muttered, "Umm, that may be a problem. I was in such a rush that I forgot my card. It's in my bathroom back on my home Earth."

"Isn't forgetting your card kind of impossible?" asked the guide.

Older-Art blinked. He replied, "N-No. Not so much. Not if you take it off, which you can do if you really want it off. I removed it one night when I was drunk and forgot to put it back on."

The blond guide sighed. "Fine. I'll procure you a uniform with *my* card. What size are you, Agent Arthur?" asked the guide.

"It's Art. And I'm an XL, with size thirteen shoes," answered Older-Art.

The blond guide leaned against the vending machine's glass, pressing his left pectoral against it until it beeped. The guide then leaned back and tapped a few buttons on a number pad that appeared on the screen. The neon blue lights turned green and the number pad disappeared. The screen then turned opaque and swirled as though a whirlpool had formed in its center. A few seconds later, the whirlpool changed direction, and a few seconds later than that, it spat a bundle of clothes into the blond guide's arms. A pair of black slip-on shoes flopped from the machine and landed atop the pile.

"Still Lavender?" asked Older-Art, staring at the color of the shirt. "Not that I *really* care, but I thought, y'know, with the job well done and all that, I would've earned a Violet promotion. Or an Orchid at the very least."

The blond guide shrugged and handed the bundle to Older-Art. "Guess not," he replied with a smirk. "Now put that on. And be quick about it. We're in a bit of a rush here, and you know the rule: agents aren't allowed on the bridge without wearing a B.T.T. uniform."

Older-Art pulled on the pants over his dirty boxers. They were form-fitting to his legs. He frowned as he pulled them up and the realization set in that they ended mid-calf. The pants looked to Normal-Art like Capri pants, and if Normal-Art's mom were around, she likely would have asked Older-Art when the flood's coming. But she was not around, so Normal-Art refused to think about what his mom would say.

Normal-Art then watched as his older-self kicked off his pink carpet slippers and slipped the B.T.T. shoes onto his feet. The older man's toes crumpled against the ends of the shoes. Normal-Art grew worried that they would pop out, but then he stopped worrying when they did just that and busted through the ends of the shoes.

Older-Art scowled. He then disrobed, pulled the shirt on over his head, and stretched it down as far as it would go. It covered the top of his torso and ended a few inches above his belly button. The sleeves ended just above his elbows. Obviously flustered, he stuffed his arms back into the blue robe and tied it to cover as much of his exposed body as he could.

Older-Art looked like an overweight, middle-aged dad dressing up in his child's clothing. He glared at the blond guide, who returned the look with an arrogant grin.

"You gave me the wrong size. Of everything," muttered Older-Art, stating the obvious.

"Oh, did I? I hadn't noticed."

Older-Art said, "Look, if this is about that shoe thing I used to do, can't we just let bygones be bygones? The last two decades *had* to be punishment enough for me."

"I still smell your foul odor in my nightmares. So no, we cannot *just let bygones be bygones*," replied the guide. He pointed at the door and continued, "Now move. The Captain is waiting."

Older-Art shoved his hands into the pockets of the robe. The guide walked to the black door, pressed his palm to a keypad next to it, and walked through the threshold when the door opened. Older-Art followed, Drillbot followed him, Ginny followed him, and Normal-Art, having nowhere else to go, followed her.

*

Normal-Art could not stop staring at the man's billowing salt-and-pepper beard. A few flecks of meat lay entangled in the bushy tangle of hair near the corners of the man's mouth, and Normal-Art was sure there must be years and years of similar crusty food hidden in the expanse from his chin to the end of the beard, down near the man's waist.

Normal-Art was so enthralled by the beard that he did not notice the man holding out a hand for a shake until the man waved the hand in front of Art's face and Ginny nudged Art in the ribs. Normal-Art jolted free from the beard's trance long enough to return the shake, but he was so distracted that he could only muster one of those clammy dead-fish handshakes.

The man with the beard removed his hand from the disgusting shake as quickly as he could, and then he said, "Welcome aboard the B.T.S. Unicorn Husker. I am Captain King Solomon."

The domed maroon crown atop the Captain's head bobbed up and down as he talked. His brown eyes twinkled when he mentioned his own name, and little crow's feet appeared in his olive skin near the corners of his dark eyes. The bright light of the bridge seemed to shine spotlights down upon his crooked yellow teeth.

"Hi, I'm Art," replied Normal-Art.

The Captain nodded. "I know who you are. Your older-self has been in my employ for decades. Isn't that right, Agent Arthur?"

Older-Art nodded. Then he said, "Yes. But for the bajillionth time, I go by Art. Arthur was my father."

The Captain stared at Normal-Art like he was supposed to be surprised or shocked or something at being in the presence of an older-version of himself. But Normal-Art felt none of these emotions, mainly because the older-version of himself had already informed him of who he was—thus giving him ample time to adjust to the concept—and because he had seen so many ridiculous versions of himself over the years that little remained that could shock him. Nevertheless, the Captain seemed intent on gazing at him until he reacted, so he forced himself to gasp.

This seemed to satisfy Captain King Solomon, so he turned to the other guests and shook their hands, too. He seemed much more satisfied with Ginny's firm handshake than he had with Normal-Art's, and he seemed even more satisfied when he gripped the end of Drillbot's diamond-encrusted drill in his hand. With a chuckle, he said to the robot, "I know of quite a few women in my harem back home who would be excited to meet you."

"[whir] Did your harem – CLACK – your harem require an extensive amount of drilling?" asked the robot.

Captain King Solomon guffawed and slapped his knee.

Drillbot said, "[whir] Did Drillbot say something – CLACK – something funny?"

Captain King Solomon patted the robot on the arm and replied, "That you did, m'boy. That you did."

Then Captain King Solomon turned to Older-Art. The Captain stared at the man with disgust etched across his face. He asked, "Agent Arthur, what is happening with your uniform?"

Older-Art stared at the blond guide with an accusing look and said, "It's just Art. And I lost my badge during my mission, sir. Had to rely on First Officer Alex to get me a new uniform out of the machine. Guess he must have *accidentally* typed in the wrong size."

Captain King Solomon frowned. He said, "In any case, you look ridiculous. We'll get you rebadged in a few minutes, and then you can get yourself a proper uniform. And then *never* show up here dressed like that again. Remember all our talks about dressing for the job you want, not the job you have? Well, right now you look like you want a job as a child playing dress-up in his mother's clothing. Is that the job you want?"

"No, sir," replied Older-Art, staring at his own feet.

Captain King Solomon nodded and turned back to Normal-Art. The Captain asked, "I take it First Officer Alexandros ho Megas caught you up on our situation and why we brought you on board?"

Normal-Art furrowed his brow. He responded, "Who?"

Captain King Solomon pointed to the blond guide and said, "First Officer Alexandros ho Megas. I sent him to collect you from the cargo hold because he and I are from your Earth's past. I thought it would help ease your transition aboard this ship."

Normal-Art looked at Captain King Solomon with a blank stare. He replied, "None of that sounds familiar."

Older-Art, Ginny, and Drillbot let out a collective groan. Ginny exclaimed, "Art! He said his name like eight times on the way up here, and he explained everything that's happening. And when you didn't seem to comprehend, he literally repeated it three times to you."

Normal-Art shrugged. He said, "Well, let's pretend that some of us weren't listening, and repeat it again."

Normal-Art's companions all groaned once more. Older-Art slapped Normal-Art upside the back of the head and said, "Dammit, why was I so…so *you* when I was younger? *You're* the reason why I'm in this mess."

Normal-Art glanced over at him. He said, "Don't blame me for your screw-ups. I didn't do anything to anyone. I just want to be left alone."

Older-Art replied, "Who else *should* I blame, you fool? You can *literally see* the person who you will become standing directly in front of you. You can *literally see* how your choices affect the both of us."

Older-Art nearly pulled out his own hair, but then he exhaled, inhaled deeply, and seemed to gain control of his frustration. He said, "I know this request is going to fall on deaf ears, but for both our sakes: please, please *please*, make *some* choices that benefit us. Don't be an idiot. Don't be like me when I was your age."

When Normal-Art did not reply other than to stare at his future-self, Captain King Solomon cleared his throat to grab the group's attention. "What's done is done," said the Captain. "Younger-Arthur did not listen to the First Officer, so we shall outline our situation once more so that everyone is caught up. Younger-Arthur, you have been brought aboard *the* premier ship in the Bureau of Time Travel fleet."

"What's *that?*" asked Normal-Art. The *Bureau of Time Travel* sounded familiar, and he could remember visiting their home reality seemingly an eternity ago, but he could not recall anything about the trip. He wondered whether being killed and resurrected so many times on the journey out of Hell had done permanent damage to his memory.

Captain King Solomon furrowed his brows. He answered, "A *fleet* is a group of ships that all serve the same cause."

Normal-Art sighed. This conversation was starting to remind him an awful lot of the ones he had with the mischief-god-version of himself. He muttered, "I obviously meant the *Bureau of Time Travel*, not the word *fleet.*"

Captain King Solomon replied, "Having spent time with you in the past, I can guarantee you that it was not as obvious as you think it was. Anyway, to answer your question: The Bureau of Time Travel is a regulatory agency that exists to resolve problems throughout *time.* We boldly venture into different points across the space-time-continuum within the Multiverse's different realities—a combination that we call the *Space-Time-Multinuum*— in order to ensure that the proper course of events takes place."

"So, you're like the B.I.T., but for *time,*" said Normal-Art.

"Yes, nearly exactly. Where the B.I.T.'s responsibilities lie in ensuring the safety of the third dimension, ours primarily reside within the fourth dimension. Without us, the B.I.T. would solve a problem only to have some time-traveling nutjob undo all their hard work."

"So, do you work with the B.I.T. a lot?" asked Normal-Art with a shudder. "Please say no. I hate those guys."

Captain King Solomon smiled and shook his head. He answered, "Oh, no. Think of us like two separate government agencies. Or even separate governments that have signed a treaty with one another. We don't interfere with their work and vice versa. As a matter of fact, most within their agency and most within the Space-Time-Multinuum do not even know of our existence. And that's how we like it, so we can ensure the proper course of events occurs with the smallest impact on everyday existence."

Normal-Art nodded. Then he glanced around the bridge and saw the person sitting near the front of the room at a station marked *Communications Officer*. She wore a marigold uniform similar to the ones worn by most of the other individuals on the bridge. However, her familiar scowl was identical to the one that Officer-Ginny of the B.I.T. would always display just before she tortured him.

He gasped and pointed to her. He all but screamed at the Captain, "Y-Y-You liar! You *are too* working with the B.I.T.! I would know that version of Ginny's face anywhere! She's B.I.T.! She tortured me for ten years! *And she loved it!* I want off this ship, now! Send me home!"

The Communications Officer stood, pointed back at Normal-Art, and yelled, "You didn't get anything you didn't deserve, you lawbreaking, lazy, rotten piece of backwater filth! You put the entire Multiverse in danger with your damned caper, and then you went and got *me* killed while I was fixing *your* mess!"

Captain King Solomon held up a hand to silence her. He grabbed Normal-Art by the shoulders and turned him so that he was no longer facing her. He said, "Arthur, please remain calm. You are needed to save the Space-Time-Multinuum, so I cannot send you home. But I did *not* lie to you. She was formerly employed by the B.I.T., but she no longer works for that agency. She changed agencies in the moment before her death."

"Huh?" asked Normal-Art.

"Ms. 29333 no longer works for the B.I.T., and I do not allow torture on my ship, so you have nothing to worry about from her on that end."

"*Ms. 29333?* Who's that?" asked Normal-Art.

The B.T.T.-Ginny sighed. "We spent a decade together, you fool. My name is 29333. Did you never wonder why Agent 27142 always referred to me as Agent 29333?"

Normal-Art frowned and pointed to his Ginny. He said, "Umm, I guess I always just called you '*Officer-Ginny*' in my head, since, y'know, you looked just like my Ginny, but in a B.I.T. officer's uniform. Also, who is Agent 27142?"

The B.T.T.-Ginny sighed even harder. She ignored his question about Agent 27142 and said, "Most of us are collected into B.I.T. service when we are babies. We're given a number as a name so that we are easier to track within the wider bureaucracy of the B.I.T. network. My name is 29333. In case you didn't notice, I never answered you when you called me any iteration of '*Ginny*.'"

Normal-Art shrugged. "I guess I don't recall that. It *was* kind of a long time ago."

29333 replied, "Well, it wasn't that long ago for me. And just so you know, I was under orders to torture you as frequently as I did. I won't say I didn't get some enjoyment out of it, but I *probably* wouldn't have done it as often otherwise."

29333 then pointed to Drillbot. She said, "In addition to all your other transgressions, you brought *that* beast into existence, and that beast is who killed me during my natural lifetime. Thus, *you* are directly responsible for my death. I'd say between my light torture of you and your terrible decision to create that robot, we're about even."

Captain King Solomon leaned over to whisper in Normal-Art's ear, "That's likely as close to an apology as you're going to get from her."

Normal-Art nodded to 29333. He said, "Umm, thanks for the apology, I guess?"

29333 nodded back, and then she sat back down at her station. She began checking the buttons and dials on her station, apparently done with this conversation. Normal-Art shrugged.

Captain King Solomon chimed in, "As I was saying, Arthur, we at the B.T.T. solve problems that would have negative effects on the Space-Time-Multinu—"

"Wait. How's she here if she's dead?" interrupted Normal-Art, pointing at 29333.

The Captain frowned. "I was *just* getting to that. I always forget how impatient you are. You see, we at the B.T.T. are recruited into service in the moments before our deaths. When the B.T.T. Humanoid Resources Department detects someone who may be a worthy agent, a Recruitment Commando appears in that person's timestream, brings them to the B.T.T. home reality on Earth 4 to appear before a Recruitment Council, and offers them a choice: return to their own timestream to die naturally, or be healed and serve the greater good until they die in service of the B.T.T. When they die in the B.T.T.'s service, their bodies—if one remains—are returned to the point in their timestream in which they would have died naturally. They gain longer life as incentive to serve our cause, the Space-Time-Multinuum gains an agent for the greater good, and nobody knows it ever happened other than those in the B.T.T.

"I am from your timestream," continued the Captain. "I am fairly prominent in your Judeo-Christian mythology as the wisest man to have ever lived, though I pride myself more on the fact that some of my bawdier poetry sits within the incredibly conservative temples within the Christian sects of your time period's religions. Next time you go to a Christian church, ask a pastor to discuss Song of Solomon Chapter 7. When I visit your time period, I love to do that. It's so much fun, for your time period is extremely prude."

Normal-Art frowned. "You ramble an awful lot, much like the mischief-god-version of me. I was glad to finally be rid of him. Please tell me you don't like to drone on and on and on like this every time you explain something."

Captain King Solomon's eyes turned cold and his beard twitched as he frowned. "I am *nothing* like that *beast.*"

Normal-Art shrugged. "Could've fooled me."

"Very well. If you want to bring that beast into this conversation, then I will dispense with the pleasantries. Most people would have liked to ask me some questions, maybe find out whether there is truth to many of the stories from which your reality's most prominent western religion is founded."

Normal-Art shrugged again. He said, "Sorry. I just don't care. Not the religious type."

Normal-Art jerked in pain as an elbow slammed into his back. Ginny whispered into his ear, "Art, be nice!"

Captain King Solomon smiled at Ginny. "I thank you for your manners, Ginny. But do not feel as though you should try to police Arthur's behavior. He will do what he will do, and then he will find himself stuck in another mess of his own making."

Ginny shrugged. Captain King Solomon pointed to the blond guide and said, "Arthur, this is First Officer Alexandros ho Megas. He is also from our Earth. You may know him as Alexander the Great, for that is how he is referred in your time period's history books. He is my right hand, and when it comes to battle, he is a tactical genius. He conquered our world before age 33, and then he came into the B.T.T.'s service as he lay on his deathbed."

Normal-Art smirked. "He conquered the *entire* world?" he asked.

Alex frowned. "Yes, I did."

"Even America? India? Africa?"

Alex's frown deepened. "Well, no," he acquiesced.

Normal-Art's smirk grew. He said, "So, you didn't conquer the entire world, then, right?"

"I conquered the *known* world," Alex replied.

Normal-Art felt another elbow from Ginny. He knew he should drop it and stop annoying these B.T.T. officers, but he had been forced aboard this ship when all he wanted to do was go home. He proclaimed, "By your logic, I know everything in the Multiverse, because anything I don't know doesn't count."

Alex's cheeks turned red. He pulled a tape-covered cylinder from his holster, and just before he twisted an ominous dial on it, Captain King Solomon reached out a hand and placed it on Alex's shoulder. "Calm down, First Officer. It won't do to devolve him. You know the Space-Time-Multinuum depends on him."

Alex glared at Normal-Art for a tense moment, and then he re-holstered the cylinder. He poked a finger in Normal-Art's chest and muttered, "You will make me miserable over the coming weeks. I may not be allowed to harm you, but just know that I will never forget your impudence."

Older-Art leaned over and whispered into Normal-Art's ear, "He's not lying about that. Please, just watch your mouth from here on out and don't start doing the thing with the shoes that you're going to scheme up soon. If you simply listen to me, then everything might go a lot easier for *you* than it did for *me*."

Alex grunted, "I doubt the fool has the self-control to prevent himself from becoming *you*. You didn't."

Captain King Solomon chimed in, speaking to Normal-Art, Ginny, Drillbot, and Older-Art, "Now, I want the four of you to go with the First Officer. He will get you licensed for time travel so that if you run into other B.T.T. agents on a covert mission, they can verify that you belong to this crew and thus will not assume you are a timestream-terrorist. He will then show you to your quarters so that you may get some rest before we embark on our mission. We will brief you on this mission at a later time. My patience with Younger-Arthur has worn too thin to do so right now, and I need a break from him to prevent myself from doing something I shall regret."

Alex shouldered past the four companions and exited the bridge. "C'mon," he barked.

Alex led Normal-Art, Older-Art, Ginny, and Drillbot down the hallway from whence they had come, but instead of following it all the way back to the elevator bank, they turned down a crossroad to their right. They climbed a set of stairs and came to a room with a long queue. It reminded Normal-Art of the Department of Motor Vehicles office in which he had worked before absconding with God-Art on the ridiculous caper to Earth 1,000,000.

Older-Art elbowed him and asked, "Remind you of somewhere? *Hey, Art, get back to work!*"

Normal-Art chose not to respond. He refused to reminisce with himself, not when all he wanted to do was to go home and be left alone.

Alex walked them to the front of the line, ignoring the faint protests of the Purple Shirts already queued. A woman with gray, curly hair and the thickest glasses Normal-Art had ever seen looked up from a stack of papers. Her uniform's shirt was teal rather than the purples and marigolds that Normal-Art had thus far seen aboard this ship. If he had cared to ask, he would have discovered that teal is the color reserved for the uniforms of career bureaucrats in the B.T.T.

"Wha'd'ya want?" she demanded.

Alex pointed to the group standing with him. He said, "These four need to get licensed for time travel, immediately. Captain's orders."

She looked them up and down. Then she pulled a two-foot tall stack of papers from beneath her desk and slammed them down on the countertop in front of Alex. She proclaimed, "Alright. They'll need to fill out the application in triplicate, and then I'll expedite the forms to get them badged today."

Normal-Art smirked. He remembered his old triplicate-trick from his job at the Department of Motor Vehicles, where he would instruct customers to fill out the same form three times if he did not feel like dealing with them. Alex, however, did not seem privy to this bureaucratic trade secret.

Normal-Art winked at the woman. He would never blow a fellow-government-worker's cover for being lazy. Instead, he picked up the stack of forms and walked over to a nearby desk, where he plopped down with a grunt. Alex and the remainder of Art's companions followed, sitting at desks nearby. Alex reached over to the forms sitting before Normal-Art and divvied them up so that each member of the group had a stack only half-a-foot high. Normal-Art began answering the questions on the forms, using the pen attached to a chain that lay atop his desk to do so.

The forms included typical basic identification questions, asking for name and city and home Earth number and timestream and occupation. When Art did not know an answer, he either called to Alex for help in the most annoying tone he could muster or made up an answer. These basic identification questions were followed by a huge psychological evaluation section for which Normal-Art merely wrote down the first ridiculous thoughts to pop into his head. These thoughts tended to be jokes and commentary pertaining to fecal matter.

Meanwhile, much to Alex's chagrin and Normal-Art's amusement, Drillbot could not fill out his forms because he had no hands, only drills incapable of picking up a pen. Thus, Alex transcribed the answers Drillbot called out, which took a ridiculously long time because Drillbot's speech was often interrupted when his gears seemed to clack against one another.

Finally, Normal-Art completed his forms in triplicate, though he wrote for so long that his hand spasmed with throbbing cramps. Ginny and Older-Art finished soon after, and following that, Alex finished filling out Drillbot's forms. Normal-Art noticed that toward the end, Alex had stopped asking the robot for answers and simply wrote in answers of his own.

Normal-Art glanced up and saw that the queue for the bureaucrat's desk had grown much, much longer. The old woman in the teal shirt—seemingly the only person working today—had not called any other customers to her station, instead waiting silently for Normal-Art and his compatriots to finish their paperwork.

Normal-Art led the group back to her station. He grinned at her and exclaimed, "Lady, I like your style!"

She did not smile back. Instead, she pointed to a rectangular square of teal paper that hung from the ceiling. She ordered, "Stand in front of that, one at a time."

They did so, and each member of the group had a portrait taken. Afterward, the woman took one of the completed triplicate forms from each of their stacks and dropped them into a machine that began scanning them. The other two completed sets of forms she dropped haphazardly into the bottom drawer of her filing cabinet.

The group stood in silence for nearly two hours. Normal-Art dozed on his feet, but then he jerked awake when the old woman's computer finally erupted with a loud *DING*. Four licenses materialized from the bottom of her computer screen and dropped onto the counter in front of her.

Normal-Art grabbed his. It looked nearly identical to the B.I.T. badge that God-Art had insisted he implant in his chest when they first met, but it contained more information. It had name, address, Earth number, year of origin, time period, timestream, a picture, and a circular B.T.T. seal, which consisted of a silver clock with no hands surrounded by a ring in which was inscribed the words, *"Time is on our side."* Every few seconds, hands appeared on the clock and spun around wildly in both directions.

Remembering the B.I.T. badge sent a chill down Normal-Art's spine. Then the method in which he had applied the B.I.T. badge flashed through his memory, and his heart dropped. He glanced over at Alex and Older-Art and said, "We're not about to do what I think we're going to do with these things, are we?"

"Wait, what does that mean?" asked Ginny. "What're we going to do with them?"

Alex ordered Older-Art, "Let's show her, Arthur. Help me put the license on your younger-self."

Older-Art smirked at Normal-Art. He said, "Unfortunately, licensing here works just like badging does for the B.I.T. You'll be OK. It'll only take a moment."

Normal-Art held up his hands in protest. He squealed, "No! Wait! I don't want to get licensed. Just send me home!"

Instead, Alex stalked behind Normal-Art and grabbed the bottom of Normal-Art's shirt. He yanked it off, exposing Normal-Art's relatively flabby torso. On his right pectoral, his B.I.T. badge stood in stark contrast to his pale skin. His gawking face stared out at the world from amidst the card embedded within the skin.

Normal-Art had no time to wonder *why* God-Art had chosen to resurrect him with the badge still intact before Alex grabbed his hands and held them behind his back. "Place the card on his left pectoral," ordered Alex.

Older-Art turned the B.T.T. license over in his hand so that Normal-Art's picture and identification information faced out. Then he touched the back of the card to Normal-Art's chest.

At first, Normal-Art felt only a slight tingling sensation. But then his skin began burning. It melted and engulfed the card. Much like the time that God-Art had badged him with the B.I.T. identification card, he tried to scream, but no sound left his mouth. The card popped out of his chest like a cartoon-heart and then slapped back down in place. It looked like he now had two badge-shaped nipples resting in his skin mere inches above his regular nipples.

His breath came in shallow puffs. The pain was too much. The situation was too much. The realization that he was yet again being whisked away somewhere he did not wish to go overwhelmed him. His head ached, and little multicolored lights began appearing in his vision. Seconds later, everything went black.

CHAPTER 6

NEW OLD EMOTIONS

GINNY FELT SOMETHING wrap around her leg. She threw back the blanket on her bunk and looked down. A pink tentacle had grown from the floor and had snaked under the blanket to grab her. It coiled around her right calf three times. It squeezed her until her tibia and fibula snapped. As the bones shattered, she screamed, but no sound escaped her lips. The broken bones tore through her skin, and the pink tentacle shoved itself into the bloody gashes in her skin. It found a vein, squeezed into it, and then followed the vein to her heart. Pink filled her vision. Hatred overwhelmed her.

Ginny awoke with a gasp. Sweat covered her body in rivulets. She threw back the blanket on her bunk and looked down. This time, rather than finding a pink tentacle advancing toward her, she found that her bed was so wet that it would not have seemed out of place in the murky abyss of some mermaid's underwater kingdom.

She felt her torso with her hand. She cried in relief as she confirmed that the skin was solid and that she had no hole permanently ripped through her middle, as she had for the ten miserable years that she had spent in service to the Pink One[5]. She cried even harder when she felt her

---

5 The Pink One is a cosmic incarnation of Death/Destruction. Ginny served the Pink One as its Right Hand of Destruction for a decade, during which the pair destroyed countless Earths. In exchange for Ginny's service, the Pink One spared Ginny's home Earth. The Pink One takes the form of a cosmic, pink teddy bear. Coincidentally, it is also a version of Ginny originating from the center of the Multiverse.

The Pink One is like the yin to the Blue One's yang. The Blue One is a cosmic incarnation of Life and was held in captivity alongside the Pink One on Earth 1,000,000 until being freed by Normal-Art in the novel *The Multiverse Askew*. After the Blue One was freed, it engaged in a cosmic war with the Pink One, during which Drillbot was the Blue One's most trusted general, pitting him against Regular-Ginny in cosmic battle after cosmic battle.

The Blue One also takes the form of a cosmic teddy bear, though it is blue. Coincidentally, it is also a version of Normal-Art originating from the center of the Multiverse.

eyes, confirming that she had two of them, and then she cried even harder when she rubbed a hand across each arm, confirming that they both remained covered in flesh[6].

She cried harder than ever when she realized that she felt *hope*, and that the emotion had not been immediately crushed in a deluge of hateful pink overflowing her heart. Her emotions were her *own*. She breathed deep her freedom and sobbed into her hands, for decades had passed since she had felt any emotion other than despair or pink-hued hatred.

She stood from her cot and glanced around the room. It was a small twelve-by-eight affair with a cot near the door, a nightstand for personal effects near that, a set of drawers on the opposite wall for clothing, and a lavatory at the back. There was a small lip rising from the floor that separated the lavatory from the remainder of the room, and she had tripped over the lip first time she strode through her room. But it was there to keep water contained in the lavatory without flooding the rest of the quarters, since the back four-by-eight section of the room was occupied by a sink with a mirror above it, a toilet, and a shower. A drain lay in the floor below the shower and a plastic curtain hung from the ceiling that she could draw across the lip in the floor to prevent water from splashing everywhere during showers.

Ginny walked to the bathroom, careful to step over the lip. The tile was cold on her feet, but she did not pay it any mind. She had felt infinitely colder temperatures in Hell. She walked to the mirror and watched herself cry. Eventually she was so overcome with her freedom that she could no longer cry. She instead had to laugh. She watched herself laugh for a while, the gap between her front teeth black in the overhead light and her snaggletooth poking out from beneath her top lip.

She glanced down at her body. Her B.T.T. license shone as the light hit her left breast. She laughed at the small portrait of herself on her license, for it displayed her with a ridiculous look on her face, caught somewhere between forming a smile and blinking—but either way totally unprepared for the teal-shirted bureaucrat to have snapped the picture as quickly as she

---

6 During the first novel in this trilogy, *The Multiverse Askew,* Ginny lost an eye, lost the flesh covering one of her arms, and was impaled by a magical onyx saber. These wounds remained unhealed until she was resurrected from the Ninth Circle of Hell by God-Art in the second novel in this trilogy, *The Endless War That Never Ends.*

did. Then she stared hard below the license, at the spot where her sternum met her belly. No gaping wound. She laughed until she cried once more.

Ginny and her Art and the older-version of her Art and Drillbot had been guided to their quarters after the licensing—her Art had to be carried by Drillbot because he had fainted—and were told by First Officer Alex that after their collective ordeal over the past decades, they would be given a fortnight to rest and adjust to life aboard the B.T.S. Unicorn Husker, after which they would embark on their mission to save the Space-Time-Multinuum. Alex refused to elucidate on what the mission would entail, but he answered most other questions from the group.

For the past three days since being guided to her quarters, Ginny had remained inside her room. The past three nights had played out identically to this one: some Pink-One-inspired nightmare invaded her sleep. In these nightmares, she was either killed outright, or she was returned to the pink fold through a massive act of violence, or she watched her home reality consumed in a fiery swath of destruction. Following whichever expression this nightmare chose to visit upon her, she awoke in a pool of her own making. And then she spent the rest of the day simply *feeling* whatever emotions she felt like feeling and watching herself in the mirror as the emotions rolled over her.

Before her experience with the Pink One, if she had stood outside herself and watched her behave as she was behaving now, she would have assumed that she had lost her connection to reality and needed to be sent to a mental ward. Instead, she continued staring at herself.

*

On the fourth day, Ginny finally left her room. She smiled and waved and said hello to every single person she passed in the crowded halls. Many did not reply, though many others smiled back at her, taken aback but delighted by her unorthodox, utter friendliness.

When a spider-creature wearing a purple shirt hissed back joyfully at her and then high-fived her with all eight of its arms, she rushed to find a private alcove in which she sat and cried with joy for twenty minutes.

She walked all over the ship this day, exploring everywhere her license gave her access. She saw the engines at the back of the ship, each of which rose over twenty-levels tall. She met Officer Trixie the Cockatrice in the

Jump Chamber, which was located on the top level at the aft-and-starboard corner of the ship. At the bottom of a staircase near the bridge, Ginny found the pub, which was gigantic and filled with crew members wearing an array of purple shirts, marigold shirts, and teal shirts. Ginny noticed that there was little intermingling between shirt colors. She shrugged, drank her first beer in over two decades, and coughed with every swallow as the bubbles tickled her throat. Feeling drunk from her single beer, she wandered the halls until she found the mess hall. She ate so much food that she ended up vomiting most of it back up. Her body could not yet handle the richness.

The following day, she decided to find Art's cabin. Though she had helped drop him off after he had fainted at the licensing, those first hours aboard this ship were such a blur that she could not recall where the cabin was located. She walked from her room to one of the touchscreen computer terminals that lay embedded in the walls of nearly every hallway on the ship. She tapped the black screen with her forefinger. Green letters appeared, spelling out, *"Identify yourself."*

Ginny shrugged and did what she had seen crew members do throughout her exploration of the ship. She leaned her left breast against the terminal so that she touched the screen with the spot where the B.T.T. license lay under her clothing. She felt a tiny jolt of electricity and jerked backward. She stared at the screen and realized that the jolt must have been a signal that the license had been read and accepted, for where the computer terminal had been mostly lifeless, it was now filled with menu options, each of which was displayed in a different color. She found a green tab that read *"Cabin Directory,"* and she tapped it.

A new page flashed onscreen and prompted her to enter a name. She typed in Art's full name and received back two cabin numbers and locations. She was confused at first, but then she remembered that the older-Art was the same person as her Art, so they would show up identically in the system.

Her life was made at least slightly easier when she read the details of each entry. The entry displayed original Earth and timestream numbers, as well as cabin and floor numbers. The Arts were both being housed on the same floor, Deck 8, the one above Ginny's. One's cabin number was fifty-six while the other's was seventy-five. She shrugged, logged off the terminal, and decided to check the lower cabin number first.

Ginny walked to a nearby elevator bank and waited her turn to enter. She disembarked on the floor above hers and walked through a hallway with cabins lining both sides. The numbers started at one on the left side of the hall and two on the right. Ginny came to the room on her right marked fifty-six and knocked. Embedded into the walls outside every cabin were small shelving units with plexiglass doors in which crew members placed their shoes before entering their quarters. She did not look inside this room's external shelving unit, or she would have saved herself a little time and noticed the older-Art's belongings: a pair of pink carpet slippers lying next to a pair of busted, undersized B.T.T. uniform shoes, which were lying next to a pair of larger, clean, unbusted B.T.T. uniform shoes.

The door zipped upward into the ceiling, and she found herself face to face with the older-Art. He arched an eyebrow and said, "Hey."

"Hey," she said back.

He smiled. "I'm trying to remember from my past which visit this would be. Have you visited my younger-self's cabin yet?"

She shook her head.

His smile grew wider. He said, "Then he's in for a treat. He won't realize it, because I was still an idiot back then, but he's in for one, nevertheless. I'll see you back here before too long."

Then he pointed down the hallway to his right. "He's in cabin seventy-five, down that way."

Ginny nodded. "Thanks," she said.

The door to cabin fifty-six shut in her face, and she turned to continue walking down the hallway. She reached the proper cabin and knocked on the door. No answer. She knocked harder. No answer. She slammed the heel of her palm into the space between the red numerals seven and five that were painted on the metal door.

Finally, the door zipped upward into the ceiling and her Art stood before her. He looked so unkempt that he could have passed for an unwashed panhandler on the street, if said panhandler were wearing nothing but ragged boxer shorts. A scowl was etched across his face. He said, "Are you deaf? I said who is i—"

Recognition hit him, and he cut himself off. "Oh," he said. "Hi, Ginny. I thought it was another B.T.T. person coming to bother me about eating."

Ginny smiled. "Can I come in?" she asked.

"I don't know, *can* you?" he replied with a smirk.

Ginny sighed. "You're so annoying. *May* I come in?"

"Yes, you may," answered Art, and he waved her inside.

Ginny's nose was assaulted by the smell of barbaric slovenliness. But the smell was one she had not experienced in years, and tears came unbidden to her eyes.

Art placed a hand on her shoulder. "You OK?" he asked.

"No, I'm Ginny," she replied.

Art sighed. He said, "You're basically one big dad joke, did you know that? But *really*, are you OK?"

Ginny nodded. "Yeah. More than I have been in years. You?"

Art shook his head. He replied, "No. I just want to go home. And nobody's listening. They should, like, rename this ship the B.T.S. Earless-Unicorn Husker."

Ginny broke into a fit of laughter. She guffawed and guffawed until she was sitting on the floor and tears were streaming down her face.

Art stared at her and scratched the back of his neck in confusion. He said, "Uhh, Gin, that was probably the most unfunny thing I've ever said. I wasn't even expecting a pity laugh. I said it mainly so you'd give me one of your annoyed sighs, because those are really cute and I haven't heard 'em in a while."

Ginny looked up at him and smiled. She said, "It's just been so long. So long since I've been able to enjoy even a terrible joke."

Art frowned. "That pink bear really did a number on you, didn't it?"

Ginny nodded, deciding not to mention that Hell had not been so great to her, either. Instead, she grabbed him by the hand and pulled him down on the floor beside her. He complained the whole way down about how cold the floor was, but she clamped a hand over his mouth to shut him up. When he finally ceased complaining, she asked, "What did you mean by what you said earlier—when you thought that I was somebody from the B.T.T. coming to bother you about eating?"

Art grinned. He answered, "I've got a plan, Gin. They said it themselves: they *need* me to save the Space-Time-Whatever. But I don't *want* to save it. I don't care. So, I've gone on a hunger strike in protest and am refusing to leave my room. If I'm really the key to saving everything, they can't afford for me to die on them. So, they'll have to let me go! You want to join me?"

She stroked his cheek with the back of her hand. If the B.T.T. needed him to save the Space-Time-Multinuum, they were not going to let him die of hunger, but they also were obviously not going to send him home, either. "You are such an idiot," she said. "But I missed you."

Ginny did not wait for him to say something to ruin the moment. She kissed him. More tears fell from her face as he kissed her back with his limp lips. She was quite positive that he was the worst kisser in the entire Multiverse, but even the worst kiss was better than anything she had experienced in as long as she could remember. She cried with joy. She stayed in his cabin this night.

Tonight, though, when she awoke from her pink nightmare naked and covered in sweat and terrified and panting and screaming about the Pink One, she at least was not alone.

Art rolled over to her, stroked her cheek gently until she calmed down, and said, "I think you wet the bed."

CHAPTER 7

ROBOTIC ANGST
AND ROBOTIC FOREGIVENESS

DRILLBOT FELT OUT of place on this ship from the moment he had rolled aboard. He was entirely too large. Whenever he rolled down a hallway, others often had to press themselves against the walls to let him pass. The blades jutting out from the spokes of his wheels had gouged scratches into many a wall in places where hallways narrowed, and he feared it was only a matter of time before he accidently cut through the fleshy legs of a crew member in some too-narrow passage.

The oily cherry atop the out-of-place-robot-sundae came during the B.T.T. licensing. After Art had screamed until he fainted, the older version of Art accepted his license with similar screams, though he had managed to remain conscious. Ginny received her license without fear and without a single cry of pain. She merely grimaced. Her expression caused vivid memories to flash through Drillbot's processors of the war that she and he had waged upon one another for a decade. His drills spun to life out of instinct.

Drillbot rolled forward and would have stabbed her to death in vengeance for his murdered love—the beautiful, ferocious Ginny Rex[7], whom Ginny had obliterated in battle—but Ginny glanced up, and her

---

7 Ginny Rex was a Tyrannosaurus-Rex-version of Ginny who was queen of her native Earth. Her attire typically consisted of a crown formed from gilded fangs, a blond mullet, a leather jacket, and a harness strapped to her back that held a pair of rocket launchers and a saddle, on which rode her trusty valet who operated the rocket launchers, an Ankylosaurus-version of Art named Artkylosaurus.

Ginny Rex and Drillbot fought alongside one another in service to the Blue One, during which time they fell in love. While serving the Pink One, Regular-Ginny permanently killed and disintegrated Ginny Rex.

fleshy eyes locked with his telescopic eyes.

Images of her while in service to the Pink One flashed into his processors, remaining there to allow an analysis comparing them to her present form. As he compared past-pink-blob-covered-Ginny with current-Ginny, Drillbot perceived none of the malice or anger or rage that had been constantly present in her eyes during their decade spent battling one another. Something about her present form elicited a sense of calm and kindness—the opposite of what he had encountered while she was the right hand of the cosmic entity bent on destruction of the Multiverse. He found that he could not bring himself to murder her, at least not without further investigation into who she had become and how responsible she had been for her actions while under the sway of the Pink One. He halted the spinning of his drills.

Drillbot's moment of rage and his decision for mercy had occurred over less than a couple seconds' time, so he glanced at the others in the group to see if any had noticed. None looked at him with the fear that would be present in their eyes if they knew that he had been about to murder one of them. He shrugged.

First Officer Alex stepped over and slapped Drillbot's license onto his torso. Drillbot had no flesh to melt over the license to hold it in place. The card merely tumbled away and clattered to the metal floor. Drillbot stared down at his portrait and noted that the license picture made him look rotund. First Officer Alex retrieved the card from the floor and slapped it on Drillbot's chest again, and again it fell to the ground. Alex frowned. He picked up the card once more.

"[whir] Drillbot does not – CLACK – does not think this is going to work."

Alex chewed on the end of one of his golden strands of hair, lost in thought. After a few moments, his eyes lit with an idea. He trotted back over to the old teal-shirted bureaucrat, chatted with her, and returned holding a second object in his hand. It was a red, heart-shaped magnet emblazoned with golden cursive lettering that spelled *Earth 3,434 is for lovers.*

Alex held the license against Drillbot's torso with one hand and placed the magnet atop the license with his other. It stuck in place. But a dull, throbbing pain developed in Drillbot's chest just below the magnet. If he were human, then the location of the pain would likely cause him to be concerned about a heart attack. Fortunately for Drillbot, he was not human, so he need not worry about such misfortune.

"[whir] The magnet causes discomfort to Drillbot. Is this – CLACK – is this license necessary?"

Alex furrowed his brows at Drillbot as though the robot had asked the stupidest question he had ever heard. "It's *absolutely* necessary," said Alex. "The license shows everyone that you are here legally, so they know not to detain you. It also gives you access to most levels of the ship, allows you to order food and drinks from the mess hall and the pub, lets you use the computer terminals in the hallways, and permits you to use the uniform machines if you need fresh clothing."

Drillbot frowned his version of a frown—his mouth-speaker retracted slightly, his telescopic eyes vibrated, and the radar dishes on top of his head wobbled. Drillbot stared down at his body. He needed neither food nor drink, his drills would not allow him to use a computer, and he was unlikely to fit into any uniform even if he desired to wear one. He felt like one of the robot-fish from Earth 103,522 flopping around outside one of that reality's many black oil-oceans. But he was a guest on this ship, and he did not think further complaints concerning the magnet-license-combo would get him anywhere, so he nodded acceptance and said nothing more about it.

On the first day following the licensing, he explored the areas of the ship to which he had access. He found that most areas which were off-limits to him were not off-limits because he was forbidden to enter them, but rather because he could not fit into them. He was so tall and so broad that there were many decks whose ceilings were so low or halls so narrow that he could not disembark from the elevator even if he ducked as low as he could possibly duck or contorted himself as much as he could possibly contort. He *could* have used his drills to tunnel his way through these hallways, but he refrained from doing so because his hosts might perceive such actions as rude and disruptive.

Before long, Drillbot stopped by Normal-Art's quarters to see if the man wanted to join him in exploring the ship, but his former master refused to answer the door, instead yelling in a whiny voice for whoever was outside to go away. Older-Art's snores could be heard echoing from within his cabin, so Drillbot decided to let the man sleep. Eventually, after he explored enough of the ship to feel satisfied for the day, Drillbot returned to his cabin and lost himself in thought.

Drillbot missed Ginny Rex terribly. The dull pain of the magnet was nothing compared to the deep, dark longing in his processors for the tyrannosaurus rex. When he was alone in his cabin, he spoke her name to the ether over and over. He replayed memories of her in his mind's eye. He could almost feel her scratchy tongue rub against his metal hide as he remembered her kisses. He could almost feel her tiny arms stroking his back as he remembered her spooning him.

And just when he was fully and completely lost in these memories, a knock on his door jolted his mind into the present, and the reality of Ginny Rex being dead and gone overwhelmed him.

Drillbot rolled slowly to the door and opened it. Standing in the doorway was Older-Art, a frown on his face. The man now wore a purple-shirted uniform that actually fit him. He said, "Drillbot, what's going on with you? You haven't left your room for four days."

Drillbot did the internal calculations and realized that Older-Art was right. He replied, "[whir] Drillbot did not realize that time had – CLACK – that time had passed by so quickly. Drillbot was – CLACK – was thinking."

Older-Art shrugged. "Dunno what you could be thinking about for four days straight. That would bore me to death."

Drillbot's eyes vibrated and his radar dishes wobbled. "[whir] Drillbot was remembering the one he loved."

Older-Art furrowed his brows. "Hmmm. I never realized you *could* fall in love." Older-Art looked Drillbot up and down before continuing, "Who's this lucky person? Or robot? Or, y'know, whatever you're into."

A short, nearly inaudible, pained screech emanated from Drillbot's speaker. Then he answered, "[whir] It was a surprise to – CLACK – to Drillbot when it happened. Drillbot did not know his processors possessed the capability for – CLACK – for attraction, let alone for love. Her name was Ginny Rex. Drillbot met her – CLACK – met her during the war, and it was love at first – CLACK – at first sight."

Older-Art frowned. He said, "Wait. Did you say her name was Ginny? Like, you fell in love with another version of *my* Ginny?"

Drillbot nodded. "[whir] She was the most beautiful, kindest, sweetest individual – CLACK – individual Drillbot has ever met. Drillbot would gaze into her reptilian eyes as long – CLACK – as long as time would allow between battles. Drillbot loved it when she would hold his drills in her – CLACK – in her tiny hands and press her gigantic body against his metal hide."

Older-Art arched an eyebrow. "Reptilian eyes? Tiny hands? Gigantic body?"

"[whir] She was the queen of – CLACK – of Earth 975,571."

Older-Art's eyebrow arched even higher. "OK. Well, that still doesn't explain the reptilian eyes and tiny hands and gigantic body."

Drillbot pictured her in his mind's eye. "[whir] She was the most beautiful Tyrannosaurus Rex in the entire – CLACK – entire Multiverse. Drillbot would sacrifice anything just to speak with her again. Her kisses would – CLACK – would leave Drillbot's processors roiling, her cuddles would – CLACK – would leave Drillbot in a peace he never knew possible, and her climaxes would – CLACK – would leave whatever dimension we were on quaking."

As Drillbot spoke of Ginny Rex, Older-Art's face transformed from pitying to revolted. He said, "Drillbot, maybe next time you keep that last part to yourself?"

Drillbot's telescopic eyes rotated as they focused on Older-Art's face. Drillbot petted the top of Older-Art's head with his drill. The gigantic metal appendage, however, was large and unforgiving, so Older-Art cried out in pain. Drillbot replied, "[whir] Drillbot will not. Mating is a natural – CLACK – a natural part of life. Ginny Rex was never ashamed, and Drillbot – CLACK – Drillbot will not dishonor her memory by being ashamed – CLACK – by being ashamed, either. Maybe if Art took better care of himself, he could – CLACK – he could find someone with whom he could mate."

Older-Art frowned for a moment, but then he seemed to remember something and smiled. He said, "Don't worry about me on that account, old friend. Someone's coming my way soon.

Older-Art continued, "But forget about *me*. I've gotta say, you're so much more layered than I ever thought you'd be. I mean, I created you on a whim with *literally* no planning."

Drillbot internalized the words, but his processors provided no proper response, so he nodded and stood in silence.

Older-Art frowned. He said, "Look, while you were sitting in here by yourself the last few days, my younger-self and Ginny got back together and are around each other *all the time*, which means I need somebody to hang out with. I can't watch them constantly fondling one other. I'm going to scream."

Again, Drillbot said nothing. He merely nodded.

Older-Art grabbed Drillbot by the drill and tugged on the robot. "C'mon," he said. "I've got an idea."

Older-Art tugged on the drill again, but Drillbot did not move. Older-Art said, "Look, buddy, I thought of something I want to show you. C'mon. It'll be a surprise."

"[whir] Drillbot does not feel like – CLACK – like leaving this room just now. Drillbot wants to be alone with his thoughts."

Older-Art frowned. "Look, just trust me, OK? I promise you that this will be the best thing you'll see on this entire ship."

Drillbot sighed. The sooner he appeased this fleshy being, the sooner he could return to his thoughts of Ginny Rex. He said, "[whir] Very well. Lead the – CLACK – Lead the way."

*

Drillbot followed Older-Art to an elevator bank, and after waiting in line for their turn, the duo took the elevator to the thirteenth deck. Once the elevator door slid open, Older-Art grabbed Drillbot by the drill and led him into the corridor.

The duo walked straight for a few minutes and then turned right down a side hallway.

CLANG! Drillbot's head crashed into a low ceiling. Though it did not hurt him, he sighed in frustration at yet another area with a ceiling too low for him to enter. Drillbot ducked as low as he could and rolled forward once more. He was still too tall. His wheel-daggers scraped into the wall, too, and he realized that even if he were *not* too tall, he would be too wide.

Older-Art stopped and looked back at Drillbot. "Sorry, buddy," he said. "I sometimes forget you're so big. We can find a different route."

Older-Art backtracked to a computer terminal set in the hallway from which they had just come. Older-Art pressed his chest against the terminal, and it sprang to life. He glanced over at Drillbot, smirked, and then leaned forward so that his body blocked the terminal from view and the surprise remained secret. His fingers flew across the screen, and a few moments later, he said, "Got it. It'll take us a bit longer, but we'll get there. You won't be disappointed, believe me."

Older-Art grabbed Drillbot once more by the drill and led him back the way they had come. They waited in line for the elevator, and when it was their turn, they took the car three decks below to the tenth deck.

They emerged in another seemingly identical corridor with a different color of paint on the walls. But this time, they followed the hallway much, much farther than the one on the thirteenth deck. By Drillbot's calculations, they were nearing the rear of the ship before Older-Art led them left down a side hallway to a thin, winding staircase. "I take it stairs aren't a problem for you?" called Older-Art over his shoulder.

"[whir] No."

Drillbot's motor roared and he sped up the stairs ahead of Older-Art, his processors adjusting his wheel mobility to account for the stairs. When he reached the top, he turned to watch Older-Art ascending the stairs. The man had an awed look on his face. Gouges and jagged metal lay in Drillbot's wake where his wheel-daggers had torn through the handrail supports when they narrowed too thinly.

Drillbot muttered, "[whir] Drillbot did not intend to cause this – CLACK – this damage. Drillbot apologizes."

Older-Art smiled. He replied, "No need to apologize to me. I'm all in favor of destroying whatever you want to destroy on this ship. The crew kidnapped *me*, so any opportunity for revenge without compromising the mission that will get me home is a job well done."

Older-Art led Drillbot down another nearly identical corridor. Crew members dodged out of their way and pressed themselves up against walls to avoid Drillbot's deadly wheel-daggers. The pair traveled down this corridor for nearly eight minutes. The corridor stretched farther on until it disappeared around a bend, but Older-Art stopped them when another staircase appeared on their right. This one was much larger and seemed to be a major thoroughfare on the ship, since it was covered in all manners of purple- and marigold- and teal-shirted B.T.T. agents rushing up and down it on seemingly important business. Drillbot and Older-Art joined the wave of people ascending the staircase.

The top of the staircase opened onto a huge atrium the size of a warehouse. In its center sat a behemoth of a fountain. The top of the fountain was shaped like a clock. Water cascaded from each of the numbers on the clockface and poured down onto a ring of hundreds of statues depicting humanoid individuals, each sitting in a chair that looked like Captain King Solomon's chair on the bridge. Drillbot recognized one of the individuals in the ring of statues as Captain King Solomon. The Captain looked much less dignified with water flowing across his face. At the base of the fountain lay an inscription in golden letters that read, *"Time flows across us all. Dedicated to the individuals who keep it flowing in the correct direction."*

Older-Art sighed. He said, "If you're wondering what this eyesore is, wonder no longer. I can tell you because I've asked before. Every time the ship gets a new captain, a sculpture of 'em is added to this fountain. This place is called *The Captain's Ring*—which isn't very clever, if you ask me— and it's the exact center of the ship. And that's yet another useless piece of information about this place that's clogging my brain when it *could* be filled with delightful episodes of whatever stupid show happens to be playing on my television back home."

Drillbot broke his gaze from the fountain and allowed himself to study the rest of the room. The scene behind the fountain reminded him of the home of the bee people on Earth 91,306. During the war between the cosmic pink and blue bears, it had taken the Army of Life quite some time to locate the Art and Ginny there to recruit into their army, since the entire Earth consisted of a gigantic hive occupied by nearly identical human-sized bees scrambling to-and-fro across its surface and through its depths.

The circular atrium at the center of the B.T.S. Unicorn Husker rose nearly eight decks tall, and hallways intersected the walls nearly everywhere Drillbot looked. Each hallway had a red number above it to identify the corridor. Wheeled ladders zoomed around the walls. Drillbot watched crew members type numbers into keypads attached to the base of these ladders and climb aboard. The ladders then lifted the crew members to the proper height and raced around the walls to drop them off at the corridor that corresponded with the numbers they had typed into the keypads.

Older-Art led Drillbot to a queue and they waited their turn, at which time Older-Art typed a number into a keypad, stepped onto a rung of the ladder, and instructed Drillbot to do the same. Drillbot frowned in annoyance. He had no feet with which to step aboard the ladder, so he instead hooked his arms around the rungs nearest him. As soon as he was in position, Older-Art pressed a blue button on the ladder. It lifted two floors into the air and then rolled around the wall until it reached a corridor with a red numeral forty-three above it. Another ladder zoomed toward them from the opposite direction, this one carrying a humanoid in knight's armor stuffed into a Purple Shirt uniform, and just when Drillbot thought they would crash, the other ladder leaned backward and passed around them.

Older-Art climbed off the ladder and entered the hallway. Drillbot swung from his perch and landed next to Older-Art.

"Nearly there," said Older-Art. He grabbed Drillbot by the drill and led him through this corridor for a few moments. They turned another corner and arrived at an intersection of three hallways, one of which was short and narrow. Drillbot realized the short and narrow hallway was the first one they had attempted to use, because as he zoomed in his telescopic eyes to see way back near its origin, he saw a Drillbot-shaped dent at its entrance and wheel-dagger-shaped scrapes in its walls.

"We're here," said Older-Art as the pair stood before a closed black door just beyond the intersection of hallways. Above it in green letters was written: *Holo-Scouting Deck.*

Before Drillbot had the opportunity to question what that phrase meant, Older-Art leaned against the license scanner to the right of the closed door. It chirped in response, turned green, and then the black door zipped up into the ceiling.

As the duo passed through the door, they entered a room with a single small lightbulb hanging down on a cord from above. The walls, ceiling, and floor were stark black with a grid-pattern of shining silver painted across them. When the door shut behind them, the robot experienced the sensation of both infinite space and claustrophobic confinement.

"[whir] What is this – CLACK – this place?" asked the robot.

"The crew uses this room to scout the locations of future missions," answered Older-Art. "The room retrieves a juncture in space and time. This allows the Purple Shirts to provide a recommendation on when and where the Landing Crew should appear within the timestream of whatever reality they're intending to interfere with. Years and years ago, back when I was first forced aboard this ship, I used this room frequently to look at my couch and remember how much I desperately wanted to be lying atop it and watching my T.V. Today, we can use it to bring to us your lost love."

"[whir] So how does Drillbot make it – CLACK – make it work?"

"Just say '*sprinkle Buns*,' and then the time, date, Earth number, latitude, and longitude that you want to see," replied Older-Art.

"[whir] '*sprinkle Buns*?' Drillbot does not – CLACK – does not understand."

Older-Art sighed. He said, "Yet again, here comes some information clogging my brain that I would rather devote to *literally* anything else: the first captain of this ship came from a family that operated a unicorn-dairy. They sold the milk across the Multiverse. *Sprinkle Buns* was the name of that captain's favorite unicorn. He named the ship's computer after her, and he named the entire ship in honor of his family's profession—a *unicorn husker* is apparently the colloquial term from his Earth for a unicorn-dairy farmer. From what I understand about the process, unicorn nipples have husks that you must yank off before they'll release any milk. People who do so for a living develop ridiculously huge forearms. The first captain is pretty easy to spot back in The Captain's Ring because his forearms are the size of a—"

Drillbot could wait no longer to retrieve a juncture in space and time that contained Ginny Rex, so he interrupted Older-Art by calling out the computer's name, followed by the time, date, Earth number, latitude, and longitude of the first time he met his love.

The silver stripes on the wall began vibrating, and then large wave patterns began flowing across them. It seemed as though the room was thrashing and rotating and bouncing. Pixels began floating from the black paint on the walls and filling the room. If Drillbot could become dizzy, he would have needed to shut his eyes at this moment to prevent nausea. But Drillbot was not capable of becoming dizzy, so he watched the change in scenery with awe. Older-Art, however, was absolutely capable of the sensation, so the shifting scene and floating pixels overwhelmed his senses. He began heaving his breakfast onto the floor, and then he collapsed. Drillbot caught him before he hit the ground.

A few seconds later, Drillbot found himself standing in a familiar jungle. The moon's light bounced off the surrounding leaves, creating a subdued tint to the vibrant jungle colors. Drillbot smiled his version of a smile, which manifested as his mouth-speaker vibrating on a nearly microscopic level, his telescopic eyes retracting about an inch inside his head, and the three radar dishes on the top left side of his head spinning slowly counterclockwise rather than clockwise.

Older-Art frowned and said, "I forgot to warn you about the shift. You need to close your eyes, or it causes severe nausea and dizziness. Forgot to shut my own eyes if it makes you feel any better."

Drillbot did not reply, instead setting Older-Art upon his feet. The man stood in place and put his hand on Drillbot's shoulder for balance. "You know where we are?" asked Older-Art.

Drillbot did not respond with words. Instead, he rolled forward. He passed between a pair of gigantic tree trunks and came to a familiar hill. He gasped when he looked up at its top.

Drillbot saw a still image from a moment in his past, only he was outside his body. At the crest of the hill stood a mirror image of Drillbot with a smitten look on his face. Drillbot smiled his version of a smile, remembering this moment and its significance in his life as the first time he had ever felt attraction. However, he then smirked his version of a smirk, for he had not realized before witnessing this moment from this vantage how *obvious* he had been about his attraction—an expression that manifested itself through his eyes telescoping outward, and in this case, his past-self's eyes were telescoped nearly a foot out of his face. Next to Drillbot floated the blue bear. The bear was missing the lower half of his body, and blue mist floated around him. His snout lay curled upward in a smile, and his pink teeth gleamed in the dim light.

A shadow lay across the Drillbot at the top of the hill, originating from the fearsome Tyrannosaurus Rex towering over him. Drillbot smiled when he looked at her. Ginny Rex, his one and only love.

Her dirty blond hair— short in the front and long in the back—hung below the crown of fangs that sat atop her head. The spikes on her jacket looked extra sharp in the dark hues of the moonlight. Her tail stretched out long and stiff behind her. Slaver was dripping from her dagger-like teeth. Artkylosaurus, her runty little Ankylosaurus valet, sat atop the saddle on her back, chomping down on his cigar and ready to fire the rocket launchers mounted to her sides if such an outcome was deemed necessary.

Drillbot raced up the hill. Older-Art called out something behind him, but Drillbot did not listen. Drillbot reached the feet of his lost love. He stared at the three ferocious toes on each of her feet and wanted nothing more than to massage the bottoms of those feet one more time.

Older-Art caught up to Drillbot. He stared up at Ginny Rex's terrifying visage. "That's *her?*" he asked.

"[whir] Yes."

Older-Art smirked. He muttered, "She must have a dazzling personality."

"[whir] The best. Isn't she – CLACK – isn't she the most beautiful creature you have ever seen?"

Older-Art frowned. "Sure, let's go with that."

Drillbot reached out his right drill and attempted to stroke Ginny Rex's face. But her skin felt limp and lifeless. He prodded it with his drill, and the drill passed through her. He pulled it out of her, and her skin popped back into place. Drillbot placed the end of his drill in her hand and pulled it down to his side to hold. But a flash of light erupted from her arm, and it disappeared in a blurry wobble. It reappeared back where it had been before he touched it.

Drillbot frowned his version of a frown—his mouth-speaker retracting slightly, his telescopic eyes vibrating, and his radar dishes wobbling to-and-fro. He spoke with a trembling voice, "[whir] What is this? Why can Drillbot not – CLACK – not interact with Drillbot's love?"

Older-Art frowned even harder. He said, "Sorry, old friend. This place is designed for scouting purposes. You can *see* anything at a single point in the Space-Time-Multinuum, but you can't *change* anything. You either pass through anything you touch too hard or try to move, or if you do manage to move it, it immediately reverts back to its condition right before you touched it—y'know, exactly where it was at the time and location that you ordered the computer to show you."

Drillbot wailed, "[whir] Why did you bring Drillbot here? This is – CLACK – This is torture!"

"I thought it might make you happy if you could at least *see* your Ginny."

Drillbot's radar dishes wobbled harder, his telescopic eyes vibrated faster, and his mouth-speaker retracted farther. His voice grew shakier as he said, "[whir] No. This is even worse – CLACK – worse than before. At least in Drillbot's memories, Drillbot was not merely a – CLACK – not merely a voyeur. Drillbot could interact with her."

Drillbot stared longingly at Ginny Rex's dagger-like fangs and reptilian eyes and flared nostrils. He wanted to hear her voice so badly that every gear in his body hurt. Seeing her again without being able to feel her alive in his arms was agony. He dropped his arms to his sides and muttered, "[whir] Get Drillbot out of – CLACK – out of here."

Older-Art called out to the sky, "*Sprinkle Buns, deactivate scenario.*"

The lush vegetation and the multitude of Arts and Ginnys in the forest around the duo melted and the pixels floated back into the walls. Ginny Rex and Artkylosaurus and the blue bear and past-Drillbot all collapsed into pixelated fragments that disappeared back into the walls. The hill upon which Drillbot and Older-Art were standing melted back into the floor.

Older-Art put a hand on Drillbot's shoulder. He said, "I'm sorry. I thought you would get some pleasure from this."

Drillbot said nothing in return. Older-Art led him to the door, and they exited. Older-Art led Drillbot back to the robot's room. Silence hung over the journey, a fog of sullen quiet into which Older-Art's sighs and grunts and apologies disappeared with no response from the robot.

When they reached Drillbot's room, Drillbot entered and shut the door behind him without inviting Older-Art in. Drillbot could hear Older-Art standing outside the door, his heart beating lonely thumps. Older-Art muttered another apology, and then he walked away.

*

Drillbot avoided Older-Art after that experience, doing so by staying in his room and losing himself once more in his memories of Ginny Rex. He did not answer the multitude of knocks on his door that came over the following days. Finally, one morning arrived in which knocks came and would not desist, no matter how many times Drillbot bellowed for whoever was without to go away.

He slowly rolled over to the door and opened it. Ginny stood on the threshold of his room. When she pursed her lips, the gap between her front teeth was visible. Drillbot wondered how much of one of his drills he could pass through it without touching either of her front teeth.

"I think you've been avoiding me," she said.

She *was* correct. He *had* been actively staying as far away from her as possible, because when he was in her presence, he needed to suppress his rage and his desire for vengeance lest he rip her apart.

When Drillbot did not respond, Ginny said, "Can't say I wasn't doing the same. But unless you're going to kill me to prevent it from happening, we're going to *have* to speak to each other sooner or later. I think we should get it over with *before* we're forced to work together on whatever mysterious mission the B.T.T. is planning to send us on. That work for you?"

Drillbot's drills activated as the sight of this woman filled him with rage. She stared at him with neither anger nor hatred, but rather acquiescence. She nodded and said, "I'm not going to try and stop you if that's what you want to do. Can't say I don't deserve it. But I'd rather you didn't."

Ginny ran her fingers through her hair and glanced at her own feet. Tears began falling from the corners of her eyes. She said, "I know that you despise me. I despise me, too. I'll never expect to be forgiven for what I did. And I would never ask for your forgiveness. But I want you to know that I *am* sorry. I was possessed by a power far greater than I could control. And now that I'm free of that power and can think for myself, I would trade places with the one I took from you if I could."

Drillbot stopped his drills. He rolled forward. "[whir] Come with – CLACK – Come with Drillbot."

Drillbot led her toward a nearby elevator bank. An elevator car arrived, and he cut to the front of the line. He ignored the protests of the queued Purple Shirts. Ginny followed him onto the elevator car. He said to Ginny, "[whir] Ginny has no idea how – CLACK – how Drillbot feels. Ginny took from Drillbot the thing he cared about more than – CLACK – more than anything else."

Drillbot slammed the point of his drill into the button for the tenth deck. The button smashed and cracked in half, but it lit up anyway. The Purple Shirts on the elevator gasped. The elevator car jerked into motion.

When the elevator opened onto the tenth deck, Drillbot exited. He led Ginny in silence, following the path that Older-Art had showed him to reach the Holo-Scouting Deck. Once inside the Holo-Scouting Deck, he called out orders to Sprinkle Buns. Pixels flared from the walls. Ginny leaned over and began heaving. Drillbot held her steady to prevent her from falling.

When the three-dimensional point in time was finally done forming, the Holo-Scouting Deck had transformed into the moment over a decade ago when Ginny had permanently murdered Ginny Rex. Drillbot fought every instinct inside himself, all of which were demanding that he rip Ginny apart.

He *needed* Ginny to experience this moment unencumbered by the Pink One. And he needed to see beyond her apologetic words, since words could easily be rehearsed or faked. He needed to see *how* she reacted when forced to confront what she had done. He would then allow his processors to analyze her emotions and determine whether mercy was truly the correct choice for her.

Ginny stared at the images in front of her with an expression mired in disgust and shame. Ginny's past-self was floating within her kaiju-sized pink blob, holding aloft a B.I.T. tank that she was firing into the resurrected half of Ginny Rex—the half to which the dinosaur's head was attached. Though she was in the process of being permanently eradicated, past-Ginny Rex was staring at past-Drillbot and mouthing something to him.

Ginny began sobbing. She asked, "What did the Tyrannosaurus Rex say to you?"

Drillbot moaned. Then he answered, "[whir] Because she did not make a sound and Drillbot had only her lips to read, it is hard to – CLACK – hard to tell for certain. Using deduction, Drillbot has narrowed it down to either '*I love you*' or '*Elephant*,' with an 85% likelihood that – CLACK – that it was '*I love you*.'"

Ginny stared at him. She asked, "How can you not be 100% certain that it was '*I love you*?' That seems pretty obvious."

Drillbot moaned again. Then he answered, "[whir] Because she – CLACK – Because she liked elephants. A lot."

Ginny glanced at her feet. She sobbed harder than ever into her hands. "I am so, so sorry."

Drillbot nodded. "[whir] Drillbot understands the logic that you were a puppet of the cosmic pink monster and that you had – CLACK – you had no choice in your actions. But the parts of Drillbot's processors that are not governed by logic are – CLACK – are filled with rage. Drillbot needs you – CLACK – needs you to see and understand what he sees *every* time he looks at you. Drillbot needs Ginny to understand how hard he must fight not – CLACK CLACK CLACK – not to kill Ginny when he is near her."

Ginny replied, "Oh, Drillbot. I picture this moment every time I look at you, too. And I feel shame and regret about it—and about the thrill I felt when I robbed you of the person you loved, for the pink in my veins made robbing you of this love feel *good*. Everywhere I look, I'm reminded of the terrible acts that I performed, and I relive them in my head over and over and over. Even when I sleep, I can't escape what I did. The Pink One invades my dreams every night. If you think I'm not scarred by my service to that beast, you are wrong. If you think I do not wish to change every choice I made over the past two decades, you are wrong. But I can't, and I will carry the shame with me for the rest of my existence. I am so, so sorry."

Drillbot allowed his processors to go to work. He studied her face and her body language. He analyzed the tempo of her heartbeat and the chemical composition of the scents that her body subconsciously released. Something within his emotional processors clicked into place, and he judged her remorse to be true. Though he still felt rage over Ginny Rex's death and hated the Pink One more than ever, the hatred for this current-Ginny standing before him flushed from his systems.

Just in case there came a time when he could not control his rage, he placed an internal, password-protected override order in his systems to shut down his drills if he intended to use them on Ginny. He nodded and said, "[whir] Drillbot knows. Drillbot has used his emotional profiling systems to evaluate your – CLACK – your reactions when faced with your most horrific deed, and Drillbot judges your remorse to be true. Drillbot can never forgive the Pink One, but Drillbot forgives – CLACK – forgives Ginny. Drillbot will do his best to restrain – CLACK – to restrain the urge to kill Ginny, but he can make no – CLACK – make no promises."

Ginny frowned. She replied, "But I didn't ask for your forgiveness. I don't deserve it. I was a puppet and I felt only hatred for a decade. But I *had* a choice to become that puppet—and to *stay* that puppet for so long. I was selfish, and I picked the safety of my own Earth above the rest of the

Multiverse. Above your love."

Drillbot rolled forward toward her. He put his heavy arms around her, and she collapsed under their weight. He did not mean to do that, so he picked her back up.

"[whir] Drillbot has thought about Ginny Rex – CLACK – Ginny Rex for nearly every second since her death. And Drillbot has concluded that – CLACK – that Ginny Rex loved Drillbot too much to want rage and anger and sadness to – CLACK – to consume Drillbot. Forgiveness is what – CLACK – is what Ginny Rex would have wanted. So Drillbot forgives Ginny, even if she will not accept Drillbot's forgiveness."

Drillbot watched Ginny stare at the hatred on her past-self's face for a while longer, allowing her to soak in the horror of the violence that she had enacted on Ginny Rex. Then he ordered Sprinkle Buns to return the point in space-time to its proper place and time. The room transformed back into its natural state of black walls with silver stripes.

Ginny turned to face Drillbot, tears continuing to stream down her face. She said, "My life feels like a terrible nightmare. I've woken up from this horrid dream, but every terrible thing I did inside that dream was true. I'm so sorry."

She hugged him. He hugged her back.

CHAPTER 8

WHEN HUNGER STRIKES ARE INEFFECTIVE...

NORMAL-ART LAY ON his cot in the darkness. He could not sleep. His stomach growled, and he stared at it with a combination of frustration and forlornness.

Ginny lay next to him and breathed on his neck with her warm breath. Claustrophobia overwhelmed him. He attempted to clamber silently over her and off the bed so as not to wake her, but he instead managed to tangle his legs in the sheets, and he tripped. He crashed to the cold, hard floor and yelped a curse. He glanced over at Ginny, expecting her to wake from the noise, but she continued tossing and turning and moaning and squealing, apparently ensnared in the pink tentacles of another nightmare.

This new development where she screamed in her sleep and sweated what he calculated to be gallons of sweat throughout the night was wearing awfully thin. He felt like he had been sleeping in a waterbed the last few nights, if only waterbeds consisted of regular mattresses soaked overnight in a salty bog. He had not showered since Ginny began sleeping in his bed, because he simply wiped away the wetness each morning and felt it was clean enough for his own approval.

He watched Ginny for a while. He strained within himself to feel *something* for her. He tried to tell himself that he loved her and that he had missed her presence when they had been apart, but really, he just missed her warmth because it helped him to fall asleep faster.

He held his breath and flexed every muscle in his body, hoping it would jumpstart some sort of feeling of affection or love for her, but all it did was make him lightheaded. It seemed like love for her *should* be there in his heart. After all, the Multiverse must have noticed some sort of cosmic connection between them, since the last couple decades seemed to have completely revolved around the symbolism embedded in their relationship. But maybe the Multiverse was wrong. It wouldn't be the first time.

He decided to leave her where she lay and continue his hunger strike where the B.T.S. Unicorn Husker crew could see him. He hurried into his clothes. Then he picked up the small scrap of cardboard box that he had found near the storage deck a couple days ago when on a walk with Ginny. He exited his chambers. In the light of the hallway, Normal-Art could read the message that he had written in marker across the cardboard's face: *NO HOME = NO FOOD = NO SAVING THE SPACE-TIME-WHATEVER!*

He plodded down the hallway toward the elevator bank. As he passed cabin fifty-six, the door zoomed up into the ceiling, and his older-self stood in its threshold, staring at him. Normal-Art pretended he did not see the man, and instead continued plodding.

Older-Art cleared his throat and stepped out of his cabin, quickening his pace to walk next to Normal-Art. "I remember this moment well," said Older-Art. "You're on the way to protest and flaunt your hunger strike in the face of this ship's officers."

Normal-Art ignored his future-self and walked in silence. Older-Art continued, "Please, for the love of whatever god you want to insert into this sentence, take my advice: just stop *now*. It's not going to work. All that's going to happen is that you'll get frustrated. And then you'll change tactics. But don't! *You're in soaked shoes* will cost you years of your life!"

Normal-Art scowled. Older-Art's advice made no sense. Normal-Art's shoes weren't wet, and even if they were, why would wearing wet shoes cost him years of his life? That was dumb. Normal-Art would have asked for clarification if he cared to hear it. Instead, he shrugged and walked faster.

Older-Art leaned against the wall and yelled after Normal-Art, "Listen to me! When the idea about the shoes pops into your head, drop it! For my sake as well as yours!"

Older-Art continued yelling, but Normal-Art did not feel like listening, so he quickened his pace and ignored the older man. He hated his older-self for kidnapping him and bringing him here, and every time he saw the older man, he became more and more annoyed.

Normal-Art arrived at the elevator bank and waited in the line, which was especially long at this hour. He poked a similarly queued Purple Shirt in the back and asked, "Hey, what's up with this line?"

The Purple Shirt turned around, and Normal-Art had to force himself not to gasp. The man had two noses and three eyes. The Purple Shirt seemed to sense Normal-Art's shock. The Purple Shirt barked, "Shift change," and turned abruptly away from Normal-Art without another word.

Normal-Art waited for what felt like hours but was instead probably only a dozen or so minutes. The hunger pangs in his belly made every tedious moment feel longer. He wondered how long it would take before all his flab faded away and he was left with a six-pack for abs. He stared down at his midsection and concluded that he probably had years to go before that would happen.

When it was finally Normal-Art's turn to enter the elevator, he sighed. He pushed the button for his desired deck and leaned against the wall as Purple Shirts crowded into the elevator around him. He felt a twinge of motion sickness as the elevator car jerked into motion, stopped, jerked again, stopped again, and so on. By the time he reached his desired floor, he nearly collapsed off the elevator car. When he entered the adjoining hallway, he steadied himself on the wall and waited until his lightheadedness passed.

He wound his way through a series of looping hallways and finally came to a ladder set in the floor. He scrambled down it to the mess hall, where hundreds of crew members were sitting at benches and eating breakfast. Purple Shirts filled most of the hall. Teal Shirts sat at a table near the entrance. And far at the back, Art saw his target: dozens of crew members wearing marigold shirts and sitting at a pair of tables. The tables on all sides of them had been left clear, which Art assumed was an intentional choice by the Purple Shirts to leave some distance between themselves and their commanding officers so that they could enjoy their meals in relative peace and privacy.

The buzz of conversation carried from every table. Normal-Art held his makeshift protest sign above his head and marched toward the back of the mess hall in the direction of the officers' tables. As he did so, he chanted, "Ding Dong! This is wrong! I won't eat! Until this fleet! Sends me home!"

None of the Purple Shirts seemed to notice him. None of them changed their conversations at all to mention him. None of them pointed at him or nudged their neighbors to take notice of him. Normal-Art frowned. He had hoped that at worst, he would have at least garnered some thumbs-ups or some nods of solidarity from these metaphorical plebeians at the bottom rungs of the power-scale on this ship. He had even fantasized that many of them, feeling frustrated by their lack of authority, would stand up to march alongside him.

Normal-Art reached the back of the mess hall and climbed atop one of the empty tables near the officers. He held his sign high above his head and screamed his chant as loud as he could. The officers turned to look at him, shrugged, and then returned to their conversations. Amongst the dining officers, Normal-Art noticed Captain King Solomon, First Officer Alex, and 29333. Captain King Solomon and Alex scowled in annoyance, but Art noted a hint of a smirk pass across 29333's lips before she mirrored the scowl of her commanders.

Normal-Art began marching back and forth across the tabletop as he chanted. He kept this up for a few minutes before a freezing rope appeared from behind him and clasped around his neck.

Between choking gasps, Normal-Art demanded, "L-L-L-Let me go! You can't harm me! I'm the key to saving the Space-Time-Whatever!"

The rope squeezed tighter. Frost formed on Normal-Art's skin. A chill entered his veins and coursed through his body. The smell of sulfur filled his nostrils. Cold breath enveloped his ear as a voice whispered into it, "Get down from there, eat something, and then come with me to my office. We must have a chat."

Normal-Art turned to face Bagoo, Chief Security Officer aboard the B.T.S. Unicorn Husker. Bagoo was a bog ghost, which was something Art did not know existed before coming aboard this ship. The bog ghost was pale blue and nearly transparent, except for his bright, scarlet eyes. Bagoo's face looked like it had been scratched from a burlap sack, with jagged nostrils and an overlarge, cartoonishly wide mouth. The top of his head rose to a drooping point. Tiny buzzing flies constantly zoomed in circles around his head. He wore a translucent, ghostly marigold officer's shirt upon his torso with a translucent holster around his center, in which sat his Time-Phaser and handcuffs and other assorted weaponry and tools. He had no legs, but instead floated in the air. Strips of what looked like bandages dangled from the bottom of his floating torso like tassels, one of which had stretched out to seize Normal-Art by the throat. Bagoo's arms were wide and looked like elongated balloons that had been overfilled with helium. They ended in thick hands shaped like mittens, with no discernable fingers other than a thumb and a long, skinny protrusion at their tips. Altogether, Bagoo reminded Normal-Art of a vicious cartoon ghost, but he refrained from mentioning that to Bagoo.

"L-Let's chat, then," answered Normal-Art. "B-But up here, where everybody can s-see."

The bog ghost's scarlet eyes morphed from scarlet to indigo and began swirling. As the bog ghost spoke, Normal-Art felt as though honey was being poured into his ears and covering his brain with sticky sweetness. And this honeyed feeling stood in stark juxtaposition with the voice of the bog ghost, whose tone was scratchy and transitioned from high-pitched screeching to low-pitched grunting throughout the course of every sentence like an incredibly disturbing and annoying series of waves.

"No, you will get down from this table," said Bagoo. "You will discard that pathetic sign, eat in sight of everyone in this mess hall, and then you will come with me to my office to discuss your behavior."

Normal-Art felt himself—his consciousness—being pulled out of his body. He hovered above his body and watched in helpless, honeyed numbness as his body obeyed the bog ghost's orders. His body clambered down from the table and threw aside the sign. The cardboard flipped end over end through the mess hall until it crashed against the back of the head of a burly Purple Shirt, who sprang to his feet ready to fight until he saw that Bagoo already had the perpetrator in custody, at which point the Purple Shirt sat back down with slumped shoulders.

Normal-Art's body walked to the buffet line, where it began thrusting dirty hands into the trays of food. The Purple Shirts who had been so intent on ignoring him before all stared at him now. Normal-Art's body grabbed a gigantic glob of scrambled eggs and slammed the gooey yellow mass into his mouth. Much of it ended up smeared across his face, but much of it also ended up tumbling down his esophagus. Normal-Art's body continued along the buffet line, grabbing fistfuls of bacon and sausage and a green mystery meat in the shape of a star and purple pudding and yellow honey, shoving everything into his gullet as he passed.

From his out-of-body floating perch near the ceiling, Normal-Art felt a satisfied sensation course through him, and his hunger pangs disappeared. A few of the Purple Shirts nearby began laughing. The one whom Normal-Art had hit with the sign laughed hardest. From his floating perch, Normal-Art wondered why.

And then he saw the yellow puddle forming at his body's feet. His body had apparently become so relaxed that it wet itself, though it seemed not to have noticed. It merely continued shoving food into its mouth. Bagoo scowled and decided that mealtime was over. He led Normal-Art from the mess hall and along the long route to his office outside the brig, which was located on the bottom deck in a secluded corner at the aft of the ship. Normal-Art's floating consciousness must have been tethered to his body, for he floated along just behind his body without even attempting to do so.

Squish-squish, squish-squish, squish-squish. Normal-Art heard his body's feet squishing inside his shoes as it staggered along the hallways and down the elevator and along more hallways. He found that with each step, he was floating nearer and nearer his body. Finally, without realizing that it had happened, he was back inside himself and marching alongside the bog ghost. His feet were wet and uncomfortable, and he was furious. He had not only been forced aboard this ship, but now he had been forced to eat, his hunger strike ended because of this cursed bog ghost's hypnotic meddling.

The *squish-squishing* of Normal-Art's feet in his shoes accompanied him as he crossed the threshold into Bagoo's office. And as Normal-Art listened to his shoes, his next ploy popped into his head with sudden clarity. He realized that his hunger strike tactic *had* been foolish. Ginny had been correct to criticize it. He was merely inconveniencing *himself* with it rather than those around him. And nobody else would take notice of his protest unless he inconvenienced *them*. He grinned.

He thought to himself, *I am brilliant! And I am hunger striking no more! I am now on urine strike!*

He decided at that moment that he would no longer be using toilets while aboard the B.T.S. Unicorn Husker, not until they granted him his freedom and sent him home. He would instead be spraying his displeasure wherever would be most inconvenient to the crew of ship. His fury was consumed by newfound excitement, and he knew that he needed to get away from the bog ghost as soon as possible in order to begin his new rebellion.

Bagoo sat Normal-Art down on a stiff wooden chair and then floated around to the opposite side of his gigantic wooden desk. He released the strip from around Normal-Art's throat. Warmth began filling Normal-Art's body once more. The frost on his neck melted. Normal-Art winced as cold droplets of water trickled down his back. The strip fell back to dangle below Bagoo, joining the dozens of other tassels hanging there.

A small, black nameplate lay atop the bog ghost's desk on which was written in silver block letters: *BAGOO THE BOG GHOST, CHIEF SECURITY OFFICER*. A framed picture sat on the desk nearby between the nameplate and the ghost's computer. Within the frame was a picture of Bagoo with his arm around a bog ghost that looked nearly identical to him, except this one had dark curly hair that rose into the air above it like kelp floating in the sea. In this bog ghost's arms was cradled a baby bog ghost.

Bagoo caught Normal-Art staring at the picture. The bog ghost nodded toward it. "My wife and kid," he said. "The photo was taken not long before the B.T.T. recruited me from my deathbed."

Normal-Art squinted. Bagoo chimed in before Normal-Art could ask, "Yes, bog ghosts can die. We're not actually ghosts. We're a species of clouds that live in swampy areas, where we eat algae and a certain type of fungus that grows within mud. Unfortunately, I ate the wrong type of algae while out foraging. My genetics predispositioned me to diffuse into nothingness upon digesting this particular variety of algae. Hence my deathbed recruitment into the B.T.T."

Normal-Art nodded. "Ok, sure," he said.

Bagoo nodded back. "We can't have you starving yourself," said Bagoo. "And we can't have you trying to incite a riot. We just can't, no matter how much you want to go home. We're a military operation, and to maintain a well-ordered ship, there must be discipline. Your protesting amongst the Purple Shirts *could* cause some of them to think that insubordination is OK, and if insubordination occurs, there is a chance that it could show up in the middle of a mission during which the fate of the entire Space-Time-Multinuum is at stake. That is too great a risk to allow you to continue such behavior."

Normal-Art fought a mischievous smile from crossing his face and stared at the bog ghost with feigned remorse. Finally, Normal-Art muttered, "You're right. I am ever so sorry."

The bog ghost nodded. He said, "I would punish you as I would any Purple Shirt who disobeyed B.T.T. protocol, but I have been forbidden from harming you by the B.T.T. Governing Council—no matter what ridiculous shenanigan you pull—because you are a guest on this ship and are needed in peak condition for a vital mission."

This time, Normal-Art could not prevent a smile from wedging the edges of his lips slightly upward. The bog ghost had just officially confirmed that Art could not be harmed *no matter what he did*, and it took everything in his power not to grin wider than he had ever grinned.

Normal-Art said, "Understood. You have my word that I will cease my hunger strike and that I will never attempt to *lead* anyone else into a protest ever again. May I go?"

Bagoo furrowed his brow and sighed. He stared at Normal-Art for a moment, and then he nodded. "Very well," he muttered.

Normal-Art stood and walked out of the office. Once out of view of Bagoo, he turned to a computer terminal on the wall. He logged in and searched for the cabin locations of all the officers on the ship. He giggled to himself.

As these officers slept in their cabins at the ends of their shifts, he would begin pilfering their shoes and urinating into them. His giggles turned into barking cackles, and he cackled so hard that by the time he finished, he had to sit on the ground to catch his breath.

Once he had himself under control, he hurried toward the nearest elevator bank. He needed to return to his room to begin strategizing this new round of mischief.

CHAPTER 9

IN THE MIDST OF THE BROCCOLI-PEOPLE

FIRST OFFICER ALEXANDROS ho Megas drank deep on what these natives referred to as mead. It was unlike any mead he had ever tasted. It consisted of the fermented blood of this people's enemies. Unfortunately, the people of this Earth consisted of humanoids made entirely from broccoli—gigantic stalks that walked on humanoid legs and worked with humanoid hands and had humanoid faces just below their puffy, bulbous florets—so the mead tasted like broccoli sweetened with extreme amounts of honey.

Nevertheless, Alex smiled. It felt good to be out on a mission again where he would have the opportunity to fight something. For each of the last few days, he had woken up to his shoes lying haphazardly in the hallway, their insides wet and musty. Someone had obviously been removing them from the device in which he placed them each evening when he retired to his cabin, this device being a glass disinfectant unit that lay embedded in the hallway wall outside of his cabin door.

Alex knew exactly who this *someone* was, and just the thought of the cur deflated the smile on Alex's face. The shoe-wetness indicated the phase of this time-loop marked by Arthur's urine strike. During the last repetition through this time-loop, Alex had been the Chief Security Officer—Bagoo's position now—and because of that position's duties aboard the ship, he'd had no opportunity to leave the ship when Arthur began urinating all over everything.

The directive from the B.T.T. Governing Council during the last few repetitions through this time-loop was that the crew was *not* to prevent Arthur from performing his urine strike and was *not* to punish him for it in any way. This directive had not changed. Thus, Alex was thankful that he had been promoted in the intervening period. Though First Officer status came with a multitude of additional stresses, every additional moment of stress was worth it to be able to escape Arthur's wake of chaos, if even for a little while. Alex planned to embark on Landing Crew missions such as this one as often as his duties would allow, passing as much time as possible off the ship and away from Arthur's stench until Arthur and his companions recovered sufficiently from their past ordeals to be ready for their upcoming mission.

Alex shook his head, hoping to shake loose the thoughts of Arthur so that he might concentrate on his mission. He glanced around the Long Hall, which was a gigantic wooden building similar in construction to many other realities' versions of Viking architecture that Alex had encountered during his years of B.T.T. service. At the far end of the Long Hall, he noticed a pair of the broccoli-men tossing a throwing axe back and forth. The action was so playful that had Alex not already been informed in his briefing dossier that axe tossing was one of the most popular children's games in this reality, he would have come to that exact conclusion on his own. Occasionally, one of the broccoli-men would flub a catch and the axe would slice through a finger. Green blood would spray on the ground, but within a few minutes, the wound would seal, the finger would begin regrowing, and the broccoli-men would resume their playful throwing of the weapon.

Alex sat at the place of honor on the high table, which was positioned on a dais seven-feet tall against the northern wall of the Long Hall. He squatted on a wooden bench that stretched the length of the table. Before him on the wooden table sat a meal that he had not touched. The meal consisted of a wooden bowl filled with dark brown sludge that resembled soft serve ice cream but smelled like cow manure.

To Alex's left, the king of the broccoli-people leaned down over his own bowl, sticking his green tongue into the mushy brown pile. A bulbous stomach grew from the king's center so big it would have been twice as large as Alex if Alex curled into a fetal position. The king wore a crown of leaves and a cloak striped green and brown. Hung on the wall behind him were the king's great sword—twice as tall as Alex—and the king's wooden buckler.

Four gigantic fire pits were dug into the ground, spaced evenly across the expanse of the Long Hall. The fires that blazed within these pits were large enough that their tops licked the wooden rafters, darkening them with black soot. Gathered at the tables below the dais were the king's subjects, a warrior clan that consisted of hundreds of broccoli-men with unkempt leaves growing from their faces in the shapes of beards. According to Alex's briefing, this band was a group of reavers known as the Brikings, who sailed along the coastlines and rivers of this Earth, pillaging and conquering anyone into whom they could sink their blades.

Alex respected their warrior prowess, but he disapproved of their lack of discipline and their utter nonchalance about the suffering they caused to their surrounding peoples. Unfortunately for the Brikings, a foul beast named Grundelflower had begun terrorizing them. According to the briefing dossier, Grundelflower crashed through the doors to the Long Hall every evening, killed as many warriors as it could kill, and then disappeared with their bodies, which it reanimated as albino ghouls that returned nightly with the beast to terrorize and murder the survivors.

Alex's briefing dossier from the B.T.T. Governing Council made it clear that if he did not put an end to Grundelflower, the king of the broccoli-people would be abducted and turned into one of these soulless ghouls three nights hence. The B.T.T. was intervening because the king happened to be such a world-class warrior that the soulless-ghoul-version of him would eventually conquer this Earth for Grundelflower. This circumstance itself would not normally cause the B.T.T. to interfere within a timestream, but if the B.T.T. did not act, then the ghoul-version of this king would eventually discover the means of both interdimensional travel and time travel through a highly illogical random encounter with a wayward interdimensional time-cruise ship that would accidentally sail into this reality centuries in the future. The cruise ship would be boarded and conquered by Grundelflower and the ghoul-king, at which point the ghoulish plague of Grundelflower would spread across multiple timestreams and countless realities.

Rather than interfere in the cruise line's business and distress its passengers by defending the ship at the moment when the incursion event was destined to occur, the B.T.T. Governing Council had decided that Grundelflower was the common denominator that should be eliminated in order to save septillions of lives and quintillions of dollars in time-cruise line profits.

The king finished slurping his meal and turned to Alex. The king smiled, a gesture that was rather off-putting, for the mouths of these broccoli-people consisted of jagged gashes that stretched across the center of their stalks. The king waved down at the dozen Purple Shirts who had accompanied Alex on this mission. The Purple Shirts were sitting at a table on the floor of the Long Hall, intermingling with the broccoli-people.

Then the king nodded toward Alex before he called out across the great hall, "Raise your goblets, my Brikings. These thirteen brave warriors have come to fulfill our prophecy:

> *When thirteen outlanders gather,*
> *Once more Grundelflower slathers.*
> *When the beast does attack,*
> *These thirteen shall strike back.*
> *Twelve brave soldiers shall fall*
> *To bring peace to this hall,*
> *But from these purple trav'lers doomed,*
> *We'll see bountiful spoils bloomed."*

Cheers rose from the crowd of walking, talking broccoli stalks. Many unsheathed their daggers and showed their approval by beating the tops of the wooden tables with their hilts. Alex smirked and glanced down at the dozen Purple Shirts. Most sat looking impatient or bored, but a few of them seemed to comprehend the king's prophecy. These sat shaking in fright.

The king continued, "Tonight, my Brikings, we feast as always. Eat your meals, procreate with your florets, and when Grundelflower comes, do *not* engage. Our guests have requested that honor this eve."

Cheers erupted ever louder, and then they grew louder still when dozens of slender broccoli-peoples wearing leather thongs and bras entered the Long Hall. These had a paler color to their skin and narrower facial features than the Briking warriors. They danced between the tables where the hundreds of Brikings feasted. Occasionally, these new entrants would lock eyes with a warrior and smile before displaying a vine that ended in a multicolored flower with petals of pink and yellow and turquoise. The warrior would then stand, bite the flower off the vine, chew it, dig a hole in the ground a few inches deep, spit the chewed flower into the hole, and bury it.

Alex leaned over to the king and asked, "What are they doing?"

The king grinned as he answered, "Mating, of course. Come morning, each of those buried flowers will have grown into a newborn baby warrior. As guests of honor, you have the privilege to mate with every female in our clan, and we shall raise your offspring as princes. Believe me, ugly traveler, when the flowers of these beauties enter your mouth, you shall experience pleasure as you have never known."

Alex frowned. He replied, "I must concentrate on my mission right now. I shall focus on the mating afterward."

The king shrugged. "After the battle, then."

Then the king grinned and snatched a couple females as they danced past. He bit the flowers from their stalks and moaned with pleasure. He said, "I shall not wait, for you never know what perils a night here may bring."

As the night wore on, the females accosted Alex and his Landing Crew over and over and over. None acquiesced, for B.T.T. bylaws prevented them from undertaking mating rituals until a mission was complete. Eventually, the fires in the great hall burned down to cinders and the native people began preparing for sleep, which they did by digging into the soft soil and burying themselves until only their faces and the tops of their stalks stood erect above the ground.

As the Long Hall drifted closer to total darkness, Alex checked his chronometer. He nodded, stood, and donned his armor. He retrieved his metal cylinder from his holster. He switched the pair of settings to *short range* and *permanent devolution,* and then he stared at the end of the device as the laser erupted from it. The solid light formed a forward-curving blade that was two-feet long—a perfect semblance of the *Kopis* that Alex had utilized in his army for slashing and lopping off limbs back in his Earth's timestream. The most astute of the Purple Shirts noticed his actions, so these nudged their fellows and began preparing themselves for battle. They placed helmets on their heads and unholstered their Time-Phasers.

Alex stuck out his tongue and used it to press a button in his helm that allowed him to speak into his crew's helmet receptors. He said, "E.T.A. of two minutes until tonight's attack. Switch Time-Phasers to *permanent devolution* and activate your Laser-Eyes. Good luck. Listen for formations as I call them. And try not to die."

Alex listened to the sighs of the Purple Shirts as he toggled on his laser lenses. A faint buzz hummed in his ears as the laser lenses appeared in the eye-slits of his helm. The dark hall lit up as though the sun itself had waxed within the confines of the walls. He walked over to his Gravitron Saddle and prepared it for the upcoming skirmish. Though the battle was to take place inside the Long Hall where one would expect infantry-style combat, Alex was a cavalryman at heart, so he would be using Boukephalas II to fly about the place and provide flanking support to his troops from the air.

Something suddenly smashed against the gigantic wooden doors to the Long Hall. The doors were at least twenty-feet tall and twenty-feet wide and opened in the middle. The only thing that prevented them from crashing open from the force of the blow was a wooden plank that lay wedged into clasps extending from the walls on either side of the doors, barring the doors from opening.

Two of the Purple Shirts gasped in surprise when the smashing against the door repeated. Alex would have made a mental note to reprimand them later, but the king's prophecy made it quite clear that there would only be one member of the Landing Crew returning home to experience a *later*, and Alex had a rather good idea of whom that would be.

The wooden shutters around the Long Hall began rattling. The king opened his eyes and frowned. He did not dig himself out from the ground. "Good luck," he called to Alex. "I'll be watching from here. And none of my Brikings shall intervene, just as our prophecy demands."

Alex nodded. The crash sounded once more against the wooden doors. One cracked at the top, but it held. The shutters on the window rattled again, and then another crash slammed into the doors.

Alex stared at his chronometer as the pattern repeated. *Got it,* he thought with a nod. He pointed at two of the Purple Shirts who were standing rigid with fright. He ordered, "You two, go to the doors and unbar them immediately after the next crash. Then open them on my mark."

Purpose seemed to drive their fright away. The two Purple Shirts nodded and sprinted to obey Alex. Alex continued, "The rest of you, Lambda Formation in front of the doors."

The remaining Purple Shirts formed the shape of an upper-case Lambda in front of the doors, with the point of the letter in the position farthest away from the doors. This would create a scenario where Grundelflower would bumble through the open doors and into the center of the group so that the group could attack it from all sides.

Meanwhile, Alex mounted Boukephalas II. He changed the setting on his Pulsar Boots to *Saddle Ready,* and then flew upon his mount up to the rafters of the Long Hall. He intended to fly forward and attack Grundelflower from above when it was engaged with the Landing Crew's Lambda Formation.

The crash rang out against the doors once more. The buried broccoli-people gasped. The walls rattled. The two Purple Shirts to whom Alex had given the order removed the wooden plank barring the doors. Alex counted to five. Then he barked, "Open the doors, now!"

The two Purple Shirts began pulling open the doors—one on each side because they opened in the middle—but the agents did not move fast enough. Alex sighed. Before the doors were completely ajar, a gigantic beast crashed into them with its shoulder. The doors swung the rest of the way open with such ferocity that the pair of Purple Shirts who were opening them were flattened against the wall. Blood sprayed from the agents like they had been transformed into a pair of grapes that had been smashed beneath the wheel of an oxcart. They died before they even had time to scream in surprise.

Since the pair of Purple Shirts had done half their job right, the doors did not slow the beast's momentum as the beast had expected it to, and it tripped and tumbled end over end. The creature rolled forward until it lay sprawled in the middle of the Lambda Formation.

Grundelflower began to sit upright. It was a gigantic humanoid cauliflower nearly the size of an Indian elephant. Its hands were larger than Alex was tall, its eyes were the pale color of snow, and out of its mouth grew gigantic fangs larger than Alex's laser-Kopis. It stared at the buried broccoli-people with hate. Then it noticed the Purple Shirts and grew confused. "What you?" it muttered in broken language.

"Attack," ordered Alex. All the Purple Shirts responded by firing their Time-Phasers into the thick body of the creature. It shrieked and melted into white goop.

The Purple Shirts cheered. Alex smiled. They had defied the king's prophecy by killing Grundelflower with nearly the entire group intact.

The king—still buried up to his face at the back of the hall—cleared his throat over and over until the Purple Shirts stopped cheering and looked over at him. He said, "Not to be the bearer of bad news, but that beast was actually but one of Grundelflower's children."

Alex frowned. Grundelflower's children had not been mentioned in the briefing dossier. The Purple Shirts seemed to metaphorically provide an exclamation point to Alex's confusion when they let out a collective, "Huh?"

The king frowned. He said, "You just killed Seedflower. He's a bit of an over-excitable oaf, but he's mostly harmless. Grundelflower generally uses him to announce her coming and to lay out her terms, though the terms are always the same: if we agree to sacrifice one of our own without putting up a fight, they leave with the single victim and allow the rest of us to live another day. Unless we're excessively drunk—which is not an uncommon occurrence—we usually agree to these terms, since Grundelflower is much bigger and scarier than Seedflower."

As if on cue, a gigantic albino face appeared in the doorway. The face was so large that it took up the entire threshold. It had facial features similar to Seedflower, but its eyes were wider set and its skin was even more ghastly white.

"Yoo-hoo! I'm ready for my sacrifi—" Grundelflower began to say, but it cut itself off when it noticed the gooey corpse of its son.

Grundelflower screamed in rage. Its face disappeared from the doorway. White hands the size of oxcarts reached into the doorway, gripped the wall, and jerked upward. The roof of the Long Hall ripped away, revealing the starry sky and a hundred-foot tall angry cauliflower. Grundelflower tossed the roof aside, and the wood went hurtling into the distance.

Grundelflower howled. Then it opened its mouth even wider, and its fangs shot from its maw like dozens of bolts loosing from a ballista that had somehow been enchanted to shoot multiple bolts at once. The jagged fangs crashed into the heads of many of the buried broccoli-people. The victims lost their green color, fading to the white hue of a cauliflower. Then they withered and became ghouls with ghastly fangs and pale white eyes.

These victims ripped themselves from the ground and screamed, "Feed!"

Then they leapt onto the Purple Shirts and the living broccoli-people alike, chomping into them and devouring them bite by bite. Eight of the remaining Purple Shirts fell under the onslaught of these ghoulish undead broccoli-people, while the last two found themselves smashed beneath Grundelflower's mammoth heel as the beast stomped its foot down upon them.

Alex scowled. Though the king had prophesied the deaths of the Purple Shirts, and though the B.T.T. Governing Council had seen fit to send Alex on this mission with exactly the number of crew to fulfill the king's prophecy, Alex had given himself a glimmer of hope that at least a couple of the Purple Shirts might return with him. With that now out of the equation, he sighed and sprang into action, jerking hard on the throttle of his Gravitron Saddle.

Alex flew higher into the air. The giant cauliflower-creature swiped at him. He dodged the blow, and then he continued evasive action as the beast launched another barrage of daggerlike teeth from its mouth. Most missed, though one scratched its way across Alex's breastplate before it caromed harmlessly away.

Alex zoomed round and round the creature in wide circles. It spun to follow him. He sped up, and soon he was flying in a circle so fast that the creature grew dizzy, tripped, and fell. Alex used this opportunity to leap from Boukephalas II and plunge his laser-Kopis into the beast's heart, or at least where he assumed the heart would be in such a foul creature. It screamed in pain and rage.

Then it devolved and melted into white goop. Alex leapt away before he could sink into the pooling liquid and drown. Boukephalas II swooped in below him, and he landed safely back in his saddle.

With Grundelflower dead, the zombified broccoli-people began shifting from withered whiteness back into their healthy green colorations. They cheered. Little baby sproutlings erupted from the ground and joined in the cheering. The king and the other Brikings unearthed themselves and cheered, too.

Alex landed Boukephalas II in their midst. He shut off his laser-Kopis and accepted their cheers with a bow. The females all leapt forward and began stroking his body. Dozens of flowers were dangled before Alex, and the king proclaimed, "Prepare for ecstasy, my new friend. Chew upon every flower and with each bite, feel more pleasure than you could possibly imagine."

Alex smiled and reached out to the first one, which was attached to one particularly buxom female.

A blue light flashed, and a bang erupted amidst the broccoli-people. By the time the light faded, Captain King Solomon had appeared on the scene. He clapped Alex on the back and said, "Great job, First Officer. As the Captain of our ship, I shall do my duty and oversee the victory celebration."

Alex frowned. "B-But I did the work," he complained.

"And I delegated it. Someday, when you are in my position, you will understand such heavy burdens."

Alex kicked the dirt and scowled. The Captain put his arms around a pair of the females. He began to nip on one of the flowers, but then he stopped himself. He turned to Alex and said, "Speaking of delegation, I need you to return to the Unicorn Husker right away. Instructions have arrived from the B.T.T. Governing Council. It's time to gather the Arthurs and continue the mission for which our ship was commissioned. You give the briefing, and I'll return after ensuring the proper celebration customs have been followed here."

Alex did not know whether to smile or to frown. On the one hand, his frustration with his captain threatened to overflow its metaphorical amphora, but on the other hand, the briefing of the Arthurs and the subsequent completion of their mission would relieve him of their annoying presence for a while.

He chose to smile. He tapped the B.T.T. badge on his uniform four times in quick succession—activating its communicator functionality—and said, "Officer Trixie, this is First Officer Alexandros ho Megas. Jump me back aboard the ship. And please relay orders to Officer Groveland to collect my Gravitron Saddle for return to storage."

And with that, blue light filled his vision and he reappeared on the ship with a newfound sense of hope.

CHAPTER 10

THE FIRST BRIEFING

THE ROOM IN which Drillbot stood lay in a side corridor a couple minutes' stroll from the bridge. The room was a large circle approximately twenty yards in diameter. Its shiny chrome walls reflected the overhead lights. A round, mahogany table nearly twelve feet in diameter sat in the center of the room. The table was surrounded by a few dozen black rolling office chairs. The position of the officer to which the chair belonged was emblazoned in silver letters across the back of each chair.

Each of the chairs had someone seated in it except for the one designated for the Captain. Though Drillbot knew that the Captain had left the ship to perform the native celebration duties with the broccoli-people following Alex's successful mission on Earth 48,333,241,111, the empty chair created a haunting absence amidst the surrounding crowd—which consisted of Drillbot, Normal-Art, Older-Art, and Ginny, along with nearly five-dozen Purple Shirts. Drillbot momentarily wondered if the empty chair foreshadowed something ominous, but then he remembered that he was a robot, and robots do not have the necessary coding within their programming to spot foreshadowing as it is occurring. Thus, he promptly ignored the notion.

Everyone present remained silent as First Officer Alexandros ho Megas called for silence to the silent room so that the briefing could begin. Alex gestured toward the center of the table and said, "Behold: Earth 8,669."

Everyone looked in the direction that Alex had indicated. Everyone then looked confused. Alex frowned. Normal-Art asked, "Does Earth 8,669 look like a table?"

Alex scowled. He replied, "No, it does not *look like a table.*"

He turned to his fellow officers and asked, "Why is the imaging machine not displaying Earth 8,669?"

29333 answered, "You have to turn it on, sir."

Alex's scowl grew larger. He muttered, "And *why* would I have to do that? It's always on when Captain King Solomon gives the briefings."

29333 shrugged and pointed at a blue button in the middle of the table. She said, "He gets here early and turns it on himself before everyone else arrives. It's that button there. He had it installed in the *middle* of this table so that we would all feel more equal. Or something like that."

Alex sighed. He looked like an undignified bug as he climbed up onto the round table and scrambled to its center to press the blue button embedded there. He sighed once more and then returned to his seat, all the while muttering curses under his breath. The metallic ceiling spread open, and a black cone emerged from the opening. The end of the black cone glowed blue, and below it an image formed of the planet Earth, though its continents all lay clustered together in one large land mass.

Alex cleared his throat and said once more, "Behold: Earth 8,669.

As he continued speaking, the image of the Earth zoomed in to focus on a large city at the jagged edge of a bay, "This is Herceg Novi, a bustling port city in this Earth's version of Montenegro. This city is one of this Earth's major sources of wealth. More importantly for us, this city is also the site of the infamous *Montenegro Bay Convention*."

At the mention of the Montenegro Bay Convention, all the Purple Shirts in the room hissed. Drillbot thought they sounded similar to robots releasing pent up steam. Alex waited until their hisses died down before continuing, "For our guests in the room who may not know," Alex waved a hand toward Drillbot, Normal-Art, and Ginny, "this convention unleashes one of the direst problems to ever face the Space-Time-Multinuum. In the B.T.T., we commonly refer to this problem as the Conspiracy of the Gods, or the C.O.G. for short."

The Purple Shirts hissed once more. As soon as their hisses began fading, one of the seated officers whom Drillbot did not recognize clarified, "Not to be confused with the much more interesting C.O.G.S., or Cost of Goods Sold. Or, if you were to originate from Earth 709,991—where gods are a commodity traded for currency—Cost of Gods Sold."

Alex glared at the woman. He said, "Officer Sprig, when I want the ship's Finance Department to interrupt my briefing with color commentary, then I will invite you to do so."

The officer melted under Alex's gaze—literally, because she was a sentient butter sculpture formed into the shape of a woman. "Y-Yes, sir. Just trying to h-help, sir," replied Officer Sprig, now a pool of liquefied butter contained within a marigold uniform on the seat of her rolling office chair.

Alex took a deep breath and said, "The C.O.G. occurred over a century ago within the timestream of Earth 8,669 when a nearly infinite cabal of gods assembled from across the Multiverse. The convention proceeded as these types of conventions are wont to proceed—networking events, orgies hosted by the gods of such things, catered lunches, et cetera, et cetera— but the power-hungry keynote speaker set in motion a plot that would ultimately destroy the Space-Time-Multinuum. This plot would prevent the Multiverse from creating new splinter universes, and thus would limit existence to universes that existed prior to the C.O.G.

"This is the part where it may get complicated for our guests to understand, so please pay close attention," continued Alex, staring at Normal-Art, who at this point was staring up at the lights in the ceiling and drooling with boredom. Ginny elbowed him, he squealed, and then he locked eyes with Alex. Alex nodded and continued, "The reason the C.O.G.'s outcome is so bad is that it prevents alternatives existing simultaneously in the Space-Time-Multinuum. So, when a major cosmic threat *succeeds* in destroying or conquering the Multiverse, following the C.O.G., there is no longer a second, equally infinite Multiverse that sprouts off from the existing Multiverse in which the cosmic threat fails. And given that the Multiverse is infinitely large and thus full of an infinite number of threats, it is only logical that if the C.O.G. is allowed to succeed, then there will *definitely* be a cosmic threat that ends the Multiverse—and thus all timestreams after that terrible moment in time—at some point, dooming us all.

Alex took a deep breath and continued, "To use an example our guests are familiar with: if we allow the C.O.G. to succeed, then when Arthur rescues the infamous cosmic bears from Earth 1,000,000, there would be no simultaneous reality where he fails. Without new splinter realities forming, the bears *are definitely out there* in the Multiverse, rather than remaining in a metaphysical state of being out there and not being out there. And thus, every reality and every timeline will eventually be affected by the cosmic bears' war as it continues to grow. This will be ultimately disastrous, for it will eventually envelop all existence. And this is but one example of the many cosmic threats lurking out there in the Multiverse.

Alex stopped for a moment to breathe before continuing, "Our mission is clear. We must send a Landing Crew to Earth 8,669 during the Montenegro Bay Convention, and we must prevent the gods from enacting the C.O.G. We will infiltrate the convention by disguising ourselves as minor deities from Earth 45,590,888, a reality that ceased existing a few moments prior to the convention taking place—and thus, there shall be no gods present from that particular reality to dispute our identities. At some point during the keynote speech, the speaker will provide instructions to the crowd on how to stave the growth of the Multiverse. We shall prevent the keynote speaker from finishing his speech. Through assassination.

Alex took another moment to breathe, and then he continued, "I will lead the Landing Crew. Accompanying me shall be Bagoo, 29333, Purple Shirt Squadrons Filbert and Kappa, as well as our guests: the Arthurs, Ginny, and Drillbot."

Older-Art spoke up, "It's just Art. And I know my protest will have no bearing on your decision, but I must protest, anyway. We are *not* trained for this type of mission."

Alex laughed. "Your Ginny and your robot-man led armies in a cosmic war for over a decade. That is training enough in my ledger. You and your younger-self unleashed one of the biggest cosmic threats of all time upon the Space-Time-Multinuum. You *will* join us for this mission, and you will help save everything in existence from the problem *you* caused."

Drillbot rolled forward. He proclaimed, "[whir] Drillbot does not – CLACK – does not protest his inclusion in this mission. Drillbot will – CLACK – will join willingly."

Alex nodded and presented a file folder stuffed wide with paper to Drillbot. Written in red letters on the outside of the folder were the words: *Mission Briefing: C.O.G. Prevention, Highly Confidential.* The robot touched the tips of his drills together to grasp it. Alex said, "I knew that you would, brave robot. You are always the first to volunteer. Here are further details concerning our mission. Please read these tonight."

Ginny stepped forward. She said, "If it will help make up for the damage I caused, then I'll help, too."

Older-Art shrugged, but then he stepped forward, too. He muttered, "Fine. Not like I have a choice, anyway. The sooner we get this done, the sooner I get to go home."

Alex handed them both file folders identical to the one Drillbot had received. Everyone began glancing around the room, searching for Normal-Art. The chair designated for the Captain began spinning in place. As the chair whirled round and round, Drillbot noticed that Normal-Art's face was hardened in a look of defiant mischief. When the chair finally came to a stop, all eyes in the room were set upon it.

Normal-Art sat in a puddle of his own making, which was quickly pooling so fast that it began cascading down to the floor and splattering upon the feet of those surrounding him. As he continued his self-proclaimed urine strike, a wide grin lay plastered across his face. "What's happening?" he asked. "I wasn't listening. You'll need to explain *everything* again. Or you could just send me home."

A chorus of groans filled the room. Alex sighed. He began the briefing once more.

CHAPTER 11

SOME THINGS ARE ONLY APPRECIATED WHEN REPEATED. AND REPEATED AGAIN...

THE LIGHT BOUNCED off First Officer Alex's brilliant golden hair as he restarted the briefing from the beginning. His voice filled the room, and something deep and basso underlying the man's squelchy tones filled Ginny with confidence. If someone asked Ginny to identify what about the man's voice stirred this feeling within her, she would have been unable to articulate it. If someone asked Alex to identify what about his voice stirred this feeling in others, he would have claimed divine lineage, battle experience, and the favor of the gods.

Ginny allowed Alex's honeyed words to wash over her, and she smiled. She glanced around the room and noticed that many of the Purple Shirts were doing the same. They looked hypnotized, like a gaggle of puppets. Alex locked eyes for a brief moment with a pair of Purple Shirts standing near the door, and then he ignored them as they swooned under his gaze.

As Alex continued to repeat the briefing, he pointed at a spot on the image of the globe that floated above the middle of the round table. While he was doing so, Ginny felt something wet splash across her leg. She looked down. What she saw dragged her from beneath the honeyed waters of Alex's charisma and back to normalcy. She felt like a fish that had been stabbed by a rusty hook and ripped from its underwater home. She scowled.

Ginny glanced from her leg over to Art. She shook her head in disbelief. Well, it was not quite disbelief, for she had long ago stopped disbelieving in anything. The emotion was more akin to shocked annoyance paired with exhausted frustration. Art had used his foot to push off the ground as hard as he could. He was spinning so fast in the Captain's chair—which he had moments ago filled with urine—that his yellowed discharge was spraying on those standing around him. A grin covered his face. He looked like he had transformed into the most disgusting water sprinkler that Ginny had ever laid eyes upon. She sighed. Her heart sank.

She could not believe that she had allowed herself to reignite a relationship with this scoundrel. She felt foolish. All the signs had been there from the beginning that he was the same selfish, disgusting man he had always been, the same jerk whose narcissism had chipped away enough of her self-confidence that she had been susceptible to the Pink One gaining a foothold in her heart and filling her with cosmic hatred. She thought that their common experience over the last decades would have bonded them in something deeper than what they had before they had been entangled in this decades-long adventure, but the reality of today's behavior was a stark bucket of cold water to her face.

She thought back over the last couple weeks. Art had never stopped talking about himself or his schemes. And while *she* had been metaphorically doodling their initials onto existence and surrounding those initials with hearts, *he* never noticed anything about her unless it inconvenienced him—like her night sweats. He never even realized that she had left to spend most of a day with Drillbot, and he never invited her to accompany him when he ran off to cause mischief. Everything was always all about *him*. And she realized with sudden clarity that she could not be a partner with someone who would *never* change or grow.

Alex glanced up from his briefing and scowled at Art. "Stop that," he ordered.

"Send! Me! Home!" replied Art.

Ginny noted to herself that Art did not demand for Alex to send "*us*" home. She frowned. He apparently did not even care if she and Drillbot and his older-self were left behind, so long as he got what he wanted.

Alex frowned. "Believe me, I would love to be rid of you. If it were up to me, I'd toss you from this ship at once, Space-Time-Multinuum be damned. But luckily for everyone in existence, I'm *not* the Captain of this ship, so it's not my decision to make."

Art shrugged. He said, "Then what do we need to do to make you the Captain? Do we need to revolt?"

Bagoo jerked higher into the air from where he had been hovering above his chair. He pointed at Art and bellowed, "Are you declaring mutiny, whelp? Are you foolish enough to ignore my warnings?"

Art sighed. Then he held up his hands in deference. He replied, "No, no, nothing like that. Didn't mean to imply mutiny. Just a homesick guy brainstorming how he can get home again."

Alex waved for Bagoo return to his seat. Alex said, "Calm down, Bagoo. As much as I would like to see you execute our guest for treason, we need him whole and intact."

Bagoo floated back down to his original position, mere centimeters above the seat of the chair marked for the ship's Chief Security Officer. Alex stared at Art in silence. Art stared back into Alex's steely eyes for a few seconds, and then broke the gaze to stare down at his own feet.

Alex said, "I will finish this time-wasting re-brief with no more interruptions. You will remain silent and you will stop being so annoying to everyone around you. And you will remove yourself from the Captain's chair. Now."

Art slowly nodded and then stood from the chair. Four Purple Shirts immediately strode forward from the back of the crowd carrying towels and spray bottles of what Ginny assumed was disinfectant. They used these to wipe clean the Captain's chair and the surrounding floor and any unfortunate spatter that had sprayed upon surrounding peoples' shoes or pants.

Ginny smirked. All that remained of Art's disgusting outburst were the wet pants that seemed to cling uncomfortably to his own legs. The four Purple Shirts had not bothered to clean Art.

Alex turned back to the floating image of Earth 8,669 and continued the briefing. As soon as all eyes were returned to the briefing, Ginny saw Art pull something from his pocket and crouch down on one knee. She saw that it was a tangle of thick shoelaces. She frowned.

A few hours ago, Art had snuck away from his room to find the Inventory Officer while Ginny was sleeping on his bed and embroiled in another pink nightmare. He had managed to finagle a large box of shoelaces from her. Ginny did not know how he had convinced the officer to hand them over, because as always, she had not been invited to join him. She sighed. He could be damned charming when he wanted to be. She sighed again. She had hoped that he would want to be damned charming toward her now that they were back together after so long apart, but such notions obviously did not matter to him. She sighed a third time as she watched Art begin his next round of mischief.

While the agents were distracted with Alex's briefing, Art moved slowly and silently around the room, tying the shoelaces around the ankles of the unsuspecting Purple Shirts—which he did instead of tying their own shoelaces together because a B.T.T. uniform's shoes form fit to an agent's feet rather than have laces. For each lace he wrapped around some poor, oblivious Purple Shirt's ankle, Ginny grew more frustrated and more disgusted with him.

She wondered why she *ever* thought the two of them made a good couple. She could recall no romantic dates or passionate trysts. Dread filled the pit of her stomach when she remembered how easily the Pink One had manipulated her frustration with him to turn her into a hateful puppet. She shuddered. If the Pink One ever got ahold of her again, the bear could probably twist the exact same knife as before to cause Ginny to do her bidding.

"I can't believe I was ever so stupid," whispered a voice in Ginny's ear.

She turned to see Older-Art leaning over her and smirking. Ginny whispered back, "Maybe I was just seeing what I wanted to see at the time, but when we were reunited after so long apart, I thought that he—well, *you*, I guess—had changed. That the events of the last couple decades had made him realize how much I matter to him, especially since our fates seem so intertwined."

Tears trailed unbidden down Ginny's face. She felt her cheeks flushing red. She did not *want* to feel this weak.

Older-Art reached out his hands to cup her cheeks. He whispered, "*He* is a fool. But *I* am not. I am a far different person than my younger-self, and *I* understand how important you are to me—to us. It's clear that the Multiverse has destined us to be together, Gin. But maybe the me of your time-period just isn't ready for *us* and isn't yet mature enough to put his own needs aside to be there for you. But if you give current-me a chance, I will not take you for granted as *that fool* has done."

Ginny leaned against him. She felt the softness of his midsection give against her weight. Something about it was comforting, like lying down on an old, overstuffed couch at the end of the day. He kissed her forehead. The phantom pink tendrils of doubt and hatred began to form in her heart, but when he kissed her forehead again, they retreated into the black depths from which they had appeared.

Ginny closed her eyes and enjoyed the weight of Older-Art's enveloping arms. It felt right, like maybe Older-Art's maturation was the missing ingredient in making their relationship work. The Multiverse obviously wanted *Art and Ginny* together, for they were both the centerpiece and the cause of the war that had ravaged across the Multiverse for over a decade. Ginny smiled. After a few moments, she realized silence had claimed the room. She opened her eyes and looked toward Alex, who was no longer pointing to the image above the round table. He now stood with his arms crossed over chest. He was staring at Normal-Art, who was standing once more and staring back at Alex, trying his hardest not to smirk at his own mischief.

Alex said, "And that about covers it. Any questions?"

Once again, Normal-Art said, "What's happening? I wasn't listening. You'll need to explain *everything* again. Or you could just send me home."

All the Purple Shirts in the room groaned, threw up their hands in exasperation, and immediately tripped. After falling onto the ground, they all began cursing at the shoelaces tied around their ankles. It felt to Ginny like she, Alex, Drillbot, and the Arts were all standing in an ankle-deep, writhing, angry, purple flood.

Alex stalked over to Normal-Art. He brought his face inches away from Normal-Art's and spat, "We had an agreement. You agreed not to interrupt me. You agreed to stop annoying those around you."

Normal-Art tried to back away. He tripped over a prone Purple Shirt. Ginny began reaching out a hand to prevent him from falling, but then thought better of it and let him fall.

Normal-Art looked up at Alex from the ground and replied, "A-A-And I held up my end of the bargain. I *didn't* interrupt you. I also agreed to stop being *so* annoying, *not* that I would stop being annoying altogether. I think we can all agree that a shoelace prank is much less annoying than pissing in a chair and then spraying it on people."

Alex bent over Normal-Art and shoved a finger against Normal-Art's chest. Normal-Art winced. Alex said, "But once again, you didn't listen to my briefing."

Normal-Art smirked. He responded, "That wasn't part of the deal. You never told me that I needed to *listen*. All *you* said was that I needed to stay silent so that you could finish the re-briefing, that I needed to be less annoying, and that I needed to get out of the Captain's chair. I did all three of the things you demanded."

Bagoo jerked high into the air and pointed at Normal-Art as he proclaimed, "Sir, if you will simply allow me to contact the B.T.T. Governing Council and explain our situation, I am sure that I can convince them to let me to mutilate this cretin!"

Alex scowled. He said, "You know them as well as I do. You know they will not change their stance once it has been decreed."

Alex shoved a thick file folder against Normal-Art's midsection. Art winced, and then he grabbed the folder. "Fine," said Alex. "I will repeat the briefing one more time. You *will listen*, you will annoy nobody, and you will not interrupt. If you do not comply, then I will allow Bagoo to mutilate you until all vestiges of your personality have been wiped from your brain, the B.T.T. Governing Council be damned."

Normal-Art remained silent for a moment. Then he nodded his assent. Alex repeated his briefing. This time, when he finished and asked if everyone understood, everyone nodded their assent—including Normal-Art. Alex dismissed everyone to leave, instructing them to read and study the file folders they had received before they departed on the mission, because it included more detailed information about the upcoming mission and the timestream to which they would be traveling.

Ginny turned toward the door. She watched the Purple Shirts file out—their ankles now untied. Drillbot followed them out the door, and as she stepped forward to follow the robot, Older-Art gave her shoulder a squeeze. He said, "You know where to find me," and then he walked away.

Ginny meandered through the exit. Normal-Art shuffled to her side and said, "I think I *finally* got through to them. I think they're *finally* beginning to understand how annoying I can be if they don't send me home."

Ginny looked over at him and scowled. But he did not even notice. He continued rambling about how great his mischief was playing out. She ignored him and walked silently beside him, a weird juxtaposition of numb frustration toward him and excitement about his future-self in the pit of her stomach.

When they reached Normal-Art's room, Art sprawled onto the bed and stared up at the ceiling. He began reciting ideas he had for more mischief. She said nothing to him, instead gathering her meager belongings before walking out his door.

Art did not call after her. He did not even seem to notice that she was leaving. She turned to her right and trotted along the corridor. She shrugged, the numb frustration in her gut fading and yielding completely to the fluttering tingles of excitement. She reached cabin fifty-six and knocked.

The door zoomed up to reveal Older-Art, who stood in a frilly robe with his arms crossed over his soft chest. He said, "Hey. This is the time you come to my door and I should be excited, right?"

She nodded. She removed her shoes, placed them in the disinfectant unit outside his room, and then darted inside. She shut off the lights.

After noting with a frown that age apparently did not in fact guarantee longer duration, she rolled away from Older-Art's sweaty body and promptly fell asleep.

When she awoke naked and covered in sweat and terrified and panting and screaming about the Pink One, she was once more not alone. The panic began to recede.

Older-Art rolled over to her, stroked her cheek gently until she calmed down, and said, "I think you wet the bed."

CHAPTER 12

FINALLY! THE COUCH!

"HOTFOOT, FLUSH THEIR shoes down the toilet, replace their coffee with decaf, spit in their coffee, complete the crossword puzzles in their magazines, get Ginny to show up on the bridge dressed like 29333 and have them argue over who's the real 29333, rub butter all over the floor just outside the bridge so the officers slip when they exit, get ahold of itching powder somehow and put it in the officers' underpants, draw little Hitler mustaches on the computer screens on the bridge so that when the officers bend over them to turn them on, they see the mustaches on their faces in their reflections and think that they're transforming into Hitler," said Normal-Art as he lay in bed. He felt a lot like the guy from that one movie who listed all the ways to cook shrimp, except he was listing ways to cause mischief that would annoy the crew of the B.T.S. Unicorn Husker until they sent him home.

He heard Ginny slink out of his cabin, but he was on such a roll brainstorming his next pieces of mischief that he refused to break his concentration to attempt stopping her. She would be back. She was likely just going for a walk to clear her head. She did that a lot, especially when he got in one of his "*listing*" moods.

Normal-Art continued listing his mischievous ideas for hours upon hours, starting over when he ran out. Finally, he dozed off, only to wake a few hours later and begin listing again. As he did so, he stared at the ceiling, which he often did to take his mind off the spartan décor of his quarters because they reminded him of his decade of confinement aboard the B.I.T. ship, the *B.S.S.C. Mimessiah*. And now that he was trying *not* to notice the similarities between his B.T.T. quarters and his cell on the B.S.S.C. Mimessiah, he could not avoid them. The uncomfortable cot, the tiny bathroom, the drab colors. He began feeling claustrophobic. He stood.

He glanced around the room and found a piece of paper and a pencil on the bedside table. He started to write a note to Ginny telling her to where he was going just in case she returned while he was gone, but now that he had started to write, the effort seemed too great. He dropped the pencil. She would figure it out. Probably.

Normal-Art pressed a button next to his door, and the door slid up into the ceiling, freeing him. He walked into the hallway and ventured toward the elevator bank.

Embedded in the walls outside every cabin door was a shelving unit. The door to each was clear, allowing for visibility inside. These shelving units were where every crew member was to place their shoes before entering their personal quarters. Once the door to the shelving units closed, disinfectant and sweet-smelling aromas enveloped the shoes[8].

To Normal-Art, the best part about the shelving units was that there were no locks on them. Apparently, the B.T.T. believed everyone in their service to have no use for mischief or personal gain, presumably because their duty was based on altruistic service to the greater good. As Normal-Art continued down the hall, he grinned at the ease with which this altruism allowed him to prank the officers. He noted Ginny's familiar pair of shoes lying haphazardly atop Older-Art's inside the shelving unit for cabin fifty-six. He shrugged and kept walking.

Normal-Art reached the elevator bank, waited in line, and then pressed the button for floor three. The elevator zoomed down, and when it came to a halt, Normal-Art trotted into the hallway. This floor held the officers' quarters. He consulted the computer embedded in the wall to remind him which cabins belonged to which officers. Then he walked to the cabin marked with a two, which was First Officer Alex's cabin. He cursed when no shoes sat in Alex's shelving unit. Alex must still be on duty.

Normal-Art continued down the hall until he found a cabin with shoes inside the unit. He looked at the number outside the cabin and noted that this was 29333's quarters. His heart leapt with excitement. This woman had

---

8 Normal-Art had been in the mess hall when Ginny had inquired for what purpose these shelving units were to be used. She had discovered that the Captain who had commanded the ship three captains prior to King Solomon had hated the smell of dirty feet so much that he had the units installed in the ship after encountering the technology on some random mission to some random timestream. This previous captain had made it a standing order for the crew to place their shoes in the units before entering their personal quarters, and none of the proceeding captains had rescinded the order.

tortured him for years. The small inconvenience he was about to unleash upon her feet was the *least* he could do to pay her back. He removed her shoes from the unit, set them on the ground, and promptly began urinating on them.

Her door zoomed up into the ceiling as he was midstream. "What the hell?" she squealed.

Normal-Art glanced over at her, grinned, and waved with one hand. "Hello," he said. "Nothing much to see here. Just a guy pissing on your shoes. Think of this as one of many installments in my payback plan for the years of pain you put me through."

"Stop!"

Normal-Art shrugged. "Can't," he replied. "I've already started going, and it hurts to stop."

29333 stalked out of her room and punched Normal-Art in the kidney. He screamed in pain.

"Did *that* hurt worse than stopping?" she asked.

"Yes!" he shrieked.

"Well, you have less than a second to cease urinating before I give you another."

Normal-Art frowned. He halted his stream and grimaced with discomfort. He stared down at her shoes. They glistened in the light of the hallway.

"Now pick them up and put them back in the disinfector," ordered 29333.

Normal-Art grabbed the shoes from the ground, opened the clear door of the shelving unit, and tossed them inside. When he shut the door, hissing sounds began emanating from the shelving unit as the disinfector went to work. Normal-Art wiped his hand dry on his shirt, and then he glanced over at 29333. She looked just like Ginny if a tiger had somehow climbed inside Ginny's skin and taken over the controls. Her eyes gleamed with predatory coolness. She smirked. Normal-Art could not shake the feeling that he was merely prey, and she was toying with him.

"OK, look, I'm just gonna go now, and we can forget this ever happened," said Normal-Art, backing slowly away and holding up his hands in deference.

She shrugged. Then she replied, "I didn't give you permission to leave."

Normal-Art stared down at his feet. "Ummm, OK," he said. "May I have permission to leave?"

29333 ignored his request and asked, "Why were you vandalizing my property? And why have you been a constant source of annoyance to those around you?"

Normal-Art frowned. He said, "Wait, what do you mean? I've made it abundantly clear *why* I've been so annoying since the moment I was kidnapped and brought aboard this stupid ship."

"Well, obviously you haven't been clear enough," replied 29333. "All *I* see is a guy tromping around this ship causing random acts of mischief. If Bagoo and Alex would only give me permission, I would have you sorted in but a few seconds."

Normal-Art's frown deepened. He nearly sobbed as he said, "I-I-I've been doing this so you all would get so annoyed with me, you'd s-s-send me home."

"Maybe you should have articulated that more clearly."

Normal-Art muttered, "B-But I protested. I-I-I made a sign and everything. And I constantly talk about not wanting to be here and how you all should send me home."

29333 shrugged. "OK."

Normal-Art's shoulders sagged. He slumped down onto the ground. He realized too late that he had slumped in the warm pool that he had created on the floor. He sighed, thinking of all the urine that he had wasted on the officers' shoes over the previous days and all the other brilliant pieces of mischief he had committed in vain, because the purpose behind them had not been understood. Then he moaned, "I just wanna go home. I haven't sat on my couch in over twenty years. I never *wanted* to get wrapped up in this mess. And all I've known is torture and pain for what seems like forever."

29333 frowned. She sighed, and the predatory look faded from her face. She replied, "It wasn't *my* choice to torture you, you know. Those were my orders. Granted, you were—and still are—the most annoying person I have ever met, so I probably enjoyed it more than I would have if you were merely some regular fool off the street. But I had nothing against you. You broke the law, so I was ensuring that justice got served."

"Could've fooled me," grunted Normal-Art.

29333 sighed once more. She stepped toward Normal-Art, and he flinched. She grabbed his arm and attempted to pull him to his feet, but he slid onto his back and used his bodyweight to resist her. He looked like a frumpy turtle stuck on its back.

"Oh, come on," she said. "Get up. I'm not going to hurt you."

"Y-You promise?" he asked.

She let go of him. She said, "You may think as many ill thoughts about me as you like, but when have you *ever* known me to lie to you?"

Normal-Art pondered for a moment the ten years he had spent with her. He could not recall a single instance of her being dishonest. She may not have always answered his questions to his satisfaction, but he could not say that she had *lied* to him. So, he used the wall to steady himself, and he stood. He said, "I'm up. Now what?"

29333 pulled on Normal-Art's arm and led him toward the elevator bank. Normal-Art noted that she stalked away from her room without putting on her shoes.

"Where are we going?" asked Normal-Art.

"To the one place on the ship that might make you happy. Maybe if you'd have seen this earlier, my shoes would be dry right now."

*

Normal-Art followed 29333 off the elevator when it opened onto the thirteenth floor. He followed her without speaking as they wound down a wide corridor and then turned down a low-ceilinged side hallway, which featured near its entrance an oblong dent in its ceiling and multiple scrapes in the paint on its walls. They followed this side hallway to its end and emerged where multiple hallways intersected. Directly in front of them stood a closed black door with green letters above it that spelled *Holo-Scouting Deck*.

29333 leaned against the license scanner to the right of the closed door. It chirped as it read her license, and then it turned green. The black door zipped up into the ceiling. She stepped inside. Normal-Art followed her. The door slammed shut behind him as soon as he finished crossing the threshold.

Once inside, Normal-Art's senses reeled. The room was black with a single light hanging down from the ceiling. Shining silver formed a grid pattern across the stark black walls, ceiling, and floor. The black walls felt like they stretched on forever, but the grid pattern brought a confining order to the infinence. Normal-Art felt overwhelmed by claustrophobia and agoraphobia all at once.

29333 said, "Sprinkle Buns," and then followed it with a string of numbers that Normal-Art could not follow. Then she closed her eyes.

The silver stripes jerked back and forth as they began vibrating and then began undulating like waves. Normal-Art grew dizzy. The room itself felt as though it were thrashing against the constraints of the silver grid. Pixels began rocketing from the wall and filling the room. The first layer created a scene that seemed like it was formed from 8-bit graphics. Normal-Art felt as though he had been engulfed in an old video game. But then the pixels kept coming. Then nausea overwhelmed him, and he collapsed onto the floor and became sick.

Afterward, he rolled onto his back and closed his eyes. A bare foot began nudging him in the side. He opened his eyes just wide enough to make eye contact with 29333.

"Sorry. Forgot to warn you to close your eyes," she said.

"Somehow I doubt that was an accident," he responded.

"Believe what you want," she replied with a shrug.

Something tickled the back of Normal-Art's neck, and the distinct smell of green grass filled his nostrils. He realized that he was lying on an overgrown lawn. He looked to his left and noticed the front of a familiar apartment building. He gasped in surprise.

He sat upright and wiped his mouth with the back of his hand. He glanced around. Across the street, the billboard for *Muse Electronics* rose high in the air. A blue Volkswagen Beetle was driving along the street. Something seemed odd about it, and after a few seconds of staring, Art realized it seemed odd because it was not moving.

"Hmm," he muttered. Then he spun around so he could face his apartment. As he soaked in its rundown façade, his heart filled with more joy than he had felt in a long, long time. But when his eyes locked upon the scene in front of his door, the joy curdled and made him want to vomit again out of sheer despair.

On the threshold of Normal-Art's doorway stood B.I.T. Officer 27142 and a mirror image of 29333, this one in a B.I.T. uniform. Like the car on the street, neither of them moved. Normal-Art grew confused, for he also saw himself standing in the threshold of his doorway. Agent 27142 was stabbing a tiny brass pill-shaped device into this other Normal-Art's pinky, and the pinky was in turn melting off this Normal-Art's hand.

Normal-Art squealed, "What the hell?"

29333 sighed. "Calm down," she said. "I didn't bring you here to frighten you. I brought you here because it's the only time that I ever experienced *this* place, and thus it was the only time that I could give to Sprinkle Buns to absolutely ensure we could experience the damned couch that you're always droning on about."

Normal-Art grimaced in confusion. He muttered, "Huh?"

29333 sighed more heavily. She answered, "This is the Holo-Scouting Deck. The room accesses a three-dimensional point at whatever confluence of space and time that you order it to access. I was feeling particularly nice today, so I ordered the room to retrieve a point in time when you would be able to enjoy the cursed couch that you never stop talking about. However, you'll need to walk *past* our past-selves to do so."

"So, I'm home? After all these years?"

"Well, yes and no. This device yanks a moment in time from its proper setting and temporarily places it in this room. This allows the Purple Shirts to scout said moment prior to embarking on a mission, returning the moment to its proper place once the scouting duties are complete. Nothing within the image that you see will even *know* that it was briefly displaced from time. Thus, nothing can actually move or change while we are here— but you *will* be able to revisit your place of residence as it existed at *this* particular point in time."

Normal-Art leapt onto his feet and grinned. He asked, "My couch? My T.V.? They're all here?"

29333 waved toward the door. She replied, "Go in and see for yourself."

Normal-Art all but sprinted toward the spot where his door used to be. He contorted his body to squeeze past the trio standing in the doorway and giggled with joy. The place was just as he had left it. Toward the back wall stood a mountain of pizza boxes. A few pairs of wild, golden eyes stared out from the dark cracks within, a remnant from the Blue One's visit to this apartment. The kitchen was messy and dirty. Spilled milk lay congealed on the ground near the coffee table. And in the center of the room sat the glorious, fluffy couch about which Normal-Art had dreamed for over two decades.

Normal-Art sprinted over to it and dove atop it. It felt a little more like putty than he remembered, but he basked in its contours, nevertheless. He rolled to face the television. A still image encompassed the screen, a picture of a familiar talk show where the host reveals to the guests who is the real father of the guests' children. In this image, the male guest was standing over the female, yelling at her. Little white letters spelled out, *"Lawrence is NOT the father,"* next to the talk show logo.

Normal-Art dug into the cushions and pulled out the remote. He aimed it at the television and pressed a button to change the channel. The remote squished in his hand. He relaxed his hand and the remote sprang back to normal. Nothing happened to the television. He pressed the button again. Again, the remote squished in his hand and nothing happened. He dropped the remote onto the floor. It dissolved and then reappeared with a flash of light where he had found it, poking up between two of the couch cushions. He stood and trudged over to the television.

He banged the top of the television with his palm. He frowned and looked over at 29333, who had followed him inside. "T.V.'s not working," he muttered.

29333 sighed. "I told you," she said. "You are at a *single* point in time. You will only see whatever image was on the screen at the *exact* point in the timestream that the computer retrieves."

Normal-Art nodded. He returned to the couch and sprawled upon it. Then he sat upright and pointed toward the frozen people in his doorway. "If this room is actually pulling a single point in time into itself, then couldn't I prevent the last two decades of problems by, I dunno, stabbing past-you and thus making it so that when this moment in time returns to its proper place, there's no one left alive to kidnap me?"

29333 smirked. She said, "Yes, you *could* do that. It might even seem cathartic to release some of the frustration you've got pent up inside you. But it won't make a difference. When we're ready to release this moment back into the wild, this room pulls apart the static image into its molecular building blocks and then reforms them in their proper place. Whatever you do to me and my former colleague would be erased once these pieces are returned."

Normal-Art kicked his feet up onto the coffee table. He said, "Well, if I can't take the easy way out, then I guess I'll just relax."

29333 sat down on the couch next to Normal-Art. She stared at him for a few seconds. Then she said, "You look so much like *him*, but you're so different."

"Like who?" he asked.

"Who else would I be talking about, you fool? 27142. My colleague from the B.I.T."

Normal-Art shrugged. He replied, "You act like that revelation is some sort of epiphany. You're the spitting image of Ginny, but you're totally different. You don't see *me* walking around stating the completely obvious."

29333 frowned. She said, "He was very rigid. Very angry. Very arrogant. But he was such a stalwart force in my life for so long that when I was first recruited by the B.T.T., I thought I would feel lost without him. And at first, I did. I felt like I was missing a limb. You get used to something for so long that when it's gone, you feel like a part of *you* is gone, too. But then time stretched on, and I realized that he was an awful prick to everyone around him—including myself—and that the part of me that felt like it was missing was no limb, but a malignant cancer that would have destroyed me if it had not been removed."

Normal-Art smirked. He said, "And this is where you tell me that even though he was terrible and was a horrible influence on you, you loved him anyway. Right?"

29333 scowled. "Are you daft?" she spat. "Of course not. I never loved him. How could anyone love that black hole of arrogance and bitterness? Hell, I never even liked him."

Normal-Art shrugged. He said, "Well, it was pretty obvious from observing it for a decade that he was in love with you."

29333's scowl deepened. She responded, "Don't even *remind* me. Did you know that one time when he was drunk, he came to my cabin and actually *ordered* me to love him back? It was pathetic."

"If you're in the mood to belittle that bastard, you'll hear no argument from me," said Normal-Art.

"You know I was only upholding the law, right? I had nothing against you."

Normal-Art shrugged again. He said, "You mentioned that. Having an attack of conscience, eh?"

Normal-Art pointed toward the television. He said, "That kind of thing ever starts happening to me, I just turn on the ol' T.V., and it takes those feelings and stuffs them deep, deep inside where they can't bother anybody."

29333 smiled. She said, "Well, T.V. has not really been an option aboard any of the ships to which I've been stationed. I usually rely on the physical act of coitus to keep myself distracted."

Normal-Art jerked up onto his feet and spun to face her. He promptly tripped over the coffee table and fell onto the span of carpet between the coffee table and the television. He gulped. "Huh?"

29333 guffawed and slapped Normal-Art's leg. She said, "Oh, don't get excited. I wasn't hinting that I wanted anything to do with *you*. You're not my type."

Normal-Art frowned. He realized that he was lying in the exact spot where God-Art had melted so long ago when he had attempted to gain infinite cosmic power by consuming the Blue One's heart. Well, if he were being honest with himself, *most* of the living room was the spot in which God-Art had melted, but Normal-Art was now lying near the epicenter. A couple feet away, circular burns in the carpet marked the spot where Normal-Art had been locked in a fiery cage. He shuddered at the memory. When he did so, his back rubbed across the carpet, and he felt a tiny jolt of static electricity. He frowned harder than ever.

Normal-Art glanced up at 29333. She smirked. And then she nodded as though she was somehow cognizant of the shock that he had just received.

Normal-Art shrugged and said, "Hey, if you don't mind, can we go to a point in time before the god-version of me showed up on my doorstep? This place is shoving too many bad memories into my face."

29333 nodded. She said, "Sure, just say the name of the computer, *Sprinkle Buns,* and then the time, date, Earth number, latitude, and longitude of the point in time to which you'd like to go."

Normal-Art frowned. "Ummm, I guess I could give a date and time, but there's no way I know the rest of that stuff."

"Wait, you don't even know your own Earth number? That's just sad—"

29333 was interrupted by a female robotic voice that seemed to emanate from all around the room. It said, "Officer 29333 and guest Arthur, First Officer Alexandros ho Megas has ordered you to meet at Officer Groveland's Inventory Requisition Station in the cargo hold at once to collect your equipment for the mission to Earth 8,669."

29333 nodded. "Thank you, Sprinkle Buns," she said. "We will be leaving now. Please shut down the Holo-Scouting Deck after we exit."

The sweetly melodic, robotic voice chimed back, "It is protocol for you to allow me shut down the program *before* you leave."

29333 scowled. She replied, "We have been called to a mission, and our orders were to move *at once*. We do not have the luxury of waiting for this place to shut down."

A noise that sounded almost like a *tsk* drifted down from the ether. The robotic voice said, "In that case, I'm noting it here in the computer log, so people don't blame me if something goes wrong."

29333 sighed. She muttered to nobody in particular, "We're on a ship whose sole purpose is to solve problems in the various timestreams throughout the Multiverse. Something will likely go wrong no matter what choice we make. That's why we average about one big adventure per week."

29333 did not wait for a reply from the computer, but instead led Normal-Art back out the front door of the apartment and over near the spot they had occupied when the Holo-Scouting Deck experience had begun. The air near them went fuzzy, and then a rectangular area about ten-feet tall disappeared and became a black door. It opened, revealing the antechamber where the three hallways converged outside the Holo-Scouting Deck door. 29333 and Normal-Art stepped through and returned to the regular confines of the B.T.S. Unicorn Husker. As soon as they did so, the door to the Holo-Scouting Deck shut behind them.

Normal-Art followed 29333 to the elevator bank. They cut to the front of the line and entered an arriving car. She pressed the button for Sublevel 6, and the elevator jerked into motion. A few moments later, it stopped, and the doors opened onto a corridor lined with maroon walls.

Normal-Art heard Sprinkle Buns' voice come from somewhere on 29333's uniform and warn, "Alert! Officer 29333 and guest Arthur, the Holo-Scouting Deck was unable to return *all* molecules from your visit to the past. Some have escaped on your persons."

Normal-Art glanced over to 29333 and asked, "Is that normal?"

29333 shook her head. "I've never heard of it happening. But judging by the sheer number of problems this ship deals with, I don't even know what normal would begin to look like."

Normal-Art felt a prick deep inside his skull. The sharp pain made him wince. Before he could stop it, his mouth opened on its own and began speaking, "Then I'm sure it's nothing to be concerned about."

Normal-Art slapped his hand over his mouth. "What the hell?" he muttered.

29333 stared at him with an arched eyebrow. "What's wrong?" she asked. Another sharp prick deep inside Normal-Art's skull made him wince once more. Again, his mouth opened, and words hurled unbidden from it, "Nothing. Everything's fine. Let's move."

29333 nodded and turned away. Normal-Art slapped himself in the face, hoping it would solve the weird issues in his brain. He stood silent for a moment. He did not feel another pain in his skull and his mouth seemed to be under his control again, so he shrugged and followed 29333.

*

By the time 29333 and Normal-Art arrived at Inventory Officer Yardish Groveland's desk, a gaggle of Purple Shirts was gathered around it in different phases of undress. Officer Groveland had handed each of them a purple toga, a wooden staff, sandals, and a purple wig. Nearby, Alex, Bagoo, Ginny, Drillbot, and Older-Art stood already dressed in costume. Drillbot, Ginny, and Older-Art wore costumes identical to those of the Purple Shirts—the only difference being that Drillbot looked even more ridiculous than the others in his—while Alex and Bagoo both wore marigold togas and wigs to match the colors of their officer's uniforms. The toga fell over Bagoo in such a way that Normal-Art could not even tell that the bog ghost had no legs.

When Officer Groveland noticed 29333 and Normal-Art approaching, she tossed costumes to them. The cold sterility of the organization within the cargo hold clashed with the unkempt nature of Officer Groveland's unibrow and wispy mustache, and Normal-Art found the juxtaposition oddly beautiful. 29333 immediately stripped and dressed in a marigold outfit identical to Bagoo's, while Normal-Art shrugged, stripped, and began donning the purple outfit he had been given.

The prick deep inside Normal-Art's skull stabbed once more. "What're these for?" he asked, his mouth yet again moving without his control.

Alex scoffed. "What do you mean?" he demanded.

Normal-Art tried to frown, but he found that he could not. He *knew* for what these costumes were intended. He had *actually listened* when Alex had repeated the briefing the last time. They were disguises for entrance into the Montenegro Bay Convention. But his mouth moved of its own accord, saying, "I don't understand why we're putting on these ridiculous outfits. What are we going to do in them?"

Everyone in the room groaned. Some grunts even rose from cages toward the back of the cargo hold where certain exotic animals were housed for exotic missions.

Alex glared at Normal-Art and muttered through clenched teeth, "You *told* me that you would listen."

Normal-Art tried once more to frown, and when his lips obeyed, he realized that he could control himself again. He stammered as fast as he could, "I *did* listen. Don't listen to me *now*. There's something wro—"

The prick jabbed again inside Normal-Art's skull, and then he slapped himself across the face. A grin appeared on his lips and hung there. His mouth once more moved without his consent and said, "Yeah, I was faking. I *said* I would listen, but I never said for how long. I stopped a couple seconds in. Please explain what's happening."

Alex grabbed Normal-Art by the throat and pulled him close so that their faces were mere inches apart. Alex grunted, "Fine. You will listen now, or I will murder you."

Normal-Art felt his head move in a slight nod.

Alex said, "I will give you the dumbed-down version, because I am tired of repeating myself. We are sneaking into the Montenegro Bay Convention. We'll be disguised as minor deities from Earth 45,590,888. We are going to prevent the *Conspiracy of the Gods* from putting the Space-Time-Multinuum in danger."

Normal-Art's mouth asked, "And how are we going to do that?"

Alex frowned. Then he said, "By causing assassinating the ringleader."

Normal-Art's mouth grinned even wider. His mouth asked, "And you think that will actually work?"

Alex squinted. His fingers danced on the metal cylinder dangling from his holster. "Why not?" he replied. "I've assassinated worse."

Normal-Art's grin somehow grew even wider. He wondered if he looked like a cartoon to those around him. His mouth said, "You're right. This sounds like a plan that will *totally* work."

Alex nodded. He barked, "I agree. Now finish getting dressed. We leave in fifteen minutes."

The pricks inside Normal-Art's brain disappeared, and Normal-Art found that he was under his own control again.

"That was weird," he muttered to himself. He heard laughter reverberate through his brain. He glanced at the other members of the group. None of them seemed to have heard it. He sighed.

CHAPTER 13

BACK TO EARTH 4

AGENT 27142 CLOSED his eyes as lightning engulfed him and teleported him off Earth 47,787. He opened them and glanced around the barrier between realities, which was simultaneously infinitely colorful and colorless.

Agent 27142 rode with Henry upon a bolt of lightning. Beside them, Beverly gripped a second bolt of lightning in one foreleg while using her other legs to drag God-Art through the barrier alongside her. Agent 27142 frowned and ground his teeth, because memories flashed through his mind's eye of the years that he had spent stranded in this bleak nothingness following his raid of the B.T.T. headquarters on Earth 4. He performed breathing exercises to calm himself, and after what seemed entirely too long, the group reached their destination, and the Jump Totems used their lightning to transition Agent 27142 and God-Art out of *The Barrier.*

They emerged from the lightning onto Earth 4 in the exact clearing where Agent 27142 had landed with his crew years and years prior. The purple sky shone overhead and clouds the color of blood drifted lazily across it. Agent 27142 glanced around the clearing, its expanse in shadow as the sun dipped behind one of the many mountains that formed a ring around it.

Debris filled the clearing, marking the site where Agent 27142 and his crew had done their damnedest to ensure the survival of the Multiverse. Broken boulders lay atop invisible shapes, which Agent 27142 knew belonged to the two cloaked shift-shuttles he had abandoned here after they had been crushed beyond all hope of functionality. Bits of bone and tattered B.I.T. uniforms lay randomly strewn about the clearing, unceremonious grave markers for Agent 27142's soldiers who had perished at the hands of the Cyclopes. A lizard shaped like a sundial skittered from one of the many skulls littering the ground. Agent 27142 squashed it with the heel of his boot.

God-Art whistled. He remarked, "This place has power. Or at least it used to. It feels like a sacrificial altar, but with old, dried blood on it."

Agent 27142 nodded. "It kind of is," he replied.

Agent 27142 explained to the god what had happened in this place all those many years ago. He told the god of the successful mission to steal the Stasis Bomb and the plot with the Moirai and the attack from the Cyclopes and the dead platoons and the narrow escape and the decade drifting through the expanse between realities. God-Art nodded along with the tale, his eyes gleaming most brightly when he heard of the Stasis Bomb.

Agent 27142 pulled a pair of goggles from his holster and put them on his face. He retrieved a second pair and held them out to God-Art. Agent 27142 said, "They'll let you see in the dark, and they identify the various creatures and traps we may encounter."

The god shook his head. "Don't need 'em," he said.

Agent 27142 began to return the second pair to his holster when Henry complained, "That's fine, don't bother offering me any."

"You don't have eyes, you fool," barked Agent 27142.

"Just because I don't have eyes doesn't mean I wouldn't appreciate the offer."

Agent 27142 sighed. He stretched the elastic band of his extra pair of goggles around the gourd. Then he pulled the cord back and snapped it against the sentient vegetable. Henry squealed. Agent 27142 smirked.

Agent 27142 led God-Art into one of the caves in the base of one of the surrounding mountains. Agent 27142 said, "There's an entrance into the B.T.T.'s headquarters at the back of this cave. There are booby traps to avoid, so watch your step."

Agent 27142 stepped gingerly through the cave, avoiding the booby traps. He passed rotting skulls, these belonging to his long-dead soldiers who Prisoner-Art had killed when he accidentally set off an Anachro-Mine. Agent 27142 frowned as he stared at the skulls. This Earth held the unmarked graves of his most loyal, most trusted soldiers. It was also the last place that he had seen his lost love, and the place responsible for his lost decade in *The Barrier*. He had hoped to never return here. But the return was necessary, for this was the one place he could think of that would provide intelligence on the ship in which his prey had escaped.

Agent 27142 bit the inside of his cheek and forced himself to concentrate on the task before him. Movement along the ceiling grabbed his attention, and as he glanced up, his goggles lit upon a snake that slithered across the ceiling with the end of its tail in its mouth. Little ringlets trailed behind it in the dust. Text scrolled across the goggles that identified the creature as: *Raalian Ring Snake, native to Earth 4. Diet includes Protian Sun-Lizards and Hourglass Pixies. Consume with caution: toxicity level 2—eat only if thoroughly cooked and if venom removed from mouth and tail.*

Agent 27142 shrugged and continued walking toward the back of the cave. He glanced over his shoulder and noticed God-Art standing next to an Anachro-Mine, staring at it. The god pursed his lips, lifted a foot, and began to drop it toward the trap. Agent 27142 spun on his heel, sprinted toward the god, and leapt. He jumped over the mine and collided with the god, bowling him over so they both lay sprawled on the ground, safely away from the mine.

"What the *hell* are you doing?" demanded Agent 27142.

"We're on the home reality of the organization that polices the Multiverse's timestreams," responded God-Art. "The mine looked different than any I have seen before. I figured it might warp time somehow, so I was curious."

Agent 27142 slapped his own forehead and groaned, "Seriously? At least when our stupid alternate-self set one off, he didn't do it on purpose. Next time simply ask me what a random trap does, and I will *tell* you. Or wear the goggles I offered you, and you can read all about it."

God-Art stood, brushed the dust off his robes, and nodded. "Very well. Next time I will ask. So, what does this mine do?"

Agent 27142 stood and dusted himself off. He said, "It's an Anachro-Mine. When tripped, it creates a weaponized time anomaly by retrieving random creatures at the most stressed and angry points in their lives. I lost many good soldiers to one of these mines the last time I was here."

God-Art nodded at the explanation and asked no further questions about the device, so Agent 27142 continued toward the back of the cave. God-Art followed close on his heels. Agent 27142 sidestepped multiple Anachro-Mines and eventually reached the stone wall at the rear of the cave. A familiar stone dial protruded from the rock.

Agent 27142 turned to the god and said, "This entrance will get us into one of the sub-basement warehouses of the B.T.T. When we escaped the last time I was here, we fled through this door and left some dangerous creatures on the other side. They may still be lurking there."

"What kind of creatures?" asked God-Art.

"Treendians. A species of sentient trees who use gigantic mallets as their primary method of attack. A bunch of wooden crates turned into them as part of the B.T.T.'s security system."

God-Art nodded. He said, "Shouldn't be a problem for us."

Agent 27142 furrowed his brow and asked, "And how can you be so sure?"

"If they're tree-people, then I'm not worried. Trust me. I hardly broke a sweat when I killed the god of the tree-people on my Earth. He was my cousin, Leaf Ping-Pingson, and I wanted to use his magical roots for a stew. While I'm on the subject of ol' Leaf, there's a funny story about how he was formed. My uncle, Ping-Ping, was walking through the woods one day when he noticed a nymph bathing naked in a rain puddle. What you need to understand is that my uncle was about the ugliest lout you could ever imagine. Well, when the nymph saw him, it fled and managed to escape, but not before ol' Ping-Ping's blood—and at least one other thing, if you catch my drift—had risen. So, he turned to the first thing he could find, which just happened to be a gnarled old maple tree. And Uncle Ping-Ping procreated for years with that thing, up until the woodland creatures formed a union and ran him off. Leaf was spawned from his seed not long after. Leaf was a rather annoying cousin, too, always luring people and creatures up into his limbs so he could stare at their genitals. Now, when I heard about this behavior, it gave me a great idea for an enchanted stew tha—"

"Does this damned long-winded story have a point?" demanded Agent 27142.

God-Art shrugged. "Yes, of course."

Agent 27142 stared at the god. "And it is?"

God-Art sighed and said, "Well, the point is that I can handle sentient trees. No need to worry about Treendians."

Agent 27142 scowled and said, "Then just say that next time and leave it at that. I don't need to hear you recite an entire novel about it."

Agent 27142 began twisting the stone dial back and forth in a pattern he had memorized long ago. On the last twist, a loud CLANK erupted from within the stone wall and it opened, revealing a dark warehouse with row upon row of wooden crates stacked on high shelves. Many empty spaces marked places where crates *should* be sitting, but these crates had been transformed into Treendians during Agent 27142's last visit here. But Agent 27142 saw no sign of the Treendians, who had been looming just inside the door when Agent 27142 had left over a decade ago.

Agent 27142 whispered, "Hmm. I don't see any Treendians, nor do I see the crates from which they had formed. Maybe they revert to their crate-forms when they're no longer presented with a threat? And maybe they did so before they managed to return to their proper places on the shelves?"

God-Art shook his head. He replied, "Hmm. Possible, but I think not. I sense multiple enchanted presences similar in nature to my cousin. I will lead the way."

"OK. But be careful. There are laser tripwires that set off the traps that turn these crates into the Treendians. One wrong step and we'll have to deal with more of them."

God-Art nodded. "Noted," he said. "Then the crates are the problem."

"Well, no, not exactly," replied Agent 27142. "The creatures that form from the crates are the problem."

"That's where you're wrong. The crates are ammunition for the defenses. Just wait here a moment. And hold Beverly. I will handle this."

God-Art grabbed Beverly from her perch on his shoulder and handed the bug over to Agent 27142. At the safehouse in which Agent 27142 and God-Art had restocked and planned over the past few days, Agent 27142 had added another holster to his belt. This additional holster had been large enough that he was able to perch Henry in it, so Henry currently resided there, strapped to Agent 27142's belt. But there was no additional space *in* the holster to add Beverly, so he set the bug on top of Henry.

"Well, this is humiliating," muttered the gourd.

God-Art stepped over the threshold and into the warehouse. And then chaos ensued.

A gigantic tree with a red amulet in its center and blue and yellow war paint covering a face carved into its trunk dropped from the ceiling. It landed squarely on top of God-Art, crushing the deity and spraying his bright blood everywhere. Agent 27142, Beverly, and Henry simultaneously gasped in surprise.

A half-dozen additional Treendians dropped from whatever perch on which they were hiding up near the ceiling and landed next to the first. The first Treendian stepped off God-Art's crushed body. Its companions began making a series of ululating clicking noises from their mouths. They then proceeded to take turns using their car-sized mallets to smash both God-Art's corpse and the fluttering pixies that formed from his blood. Soon, where God-Art's body had been lay a mass of bloody pulp that resembled a disgusting side dish of mashed potatoes doused in entire bottles of ketchup.

Agent 27142 sighed and muttered, "This is exactly why I never delegate."

He unholstered the new Scatter Gun pistol that he had picked up from his safehouse and took aim at the first Treendian that had dropped from the ceiling. He clicked off the safety and pulled the trigger. Lightning leapt from the tip of the pistol and connected directly between the Treendian's ferocious eyes. It yelped and disintegrated. The group of Treendians stopped toying with God-Art's corpse and glanced over at the source of the lightning. They seemed to notice Agent 27142 for the first time, and expressions of murderous excitement appeared on their carved faces. Each raised its mallet above its head and began stalking toward Agent 27142.

But then God-Art's head reformed from the squashed, bloody, unidentifiable mess on the ground. The god winked at Agent 27142. Then flames reappeared from the god's scalp. God-Art sucked in a large breath, shut his eyes, and an expression appeared on his face that made it look like he was grinding his teeth with exertion.

The flames on God-Art's head erupted. They launched from his head and formed into a giant phoenix. The phoenix breathed fire onto the Treendians, and they dropped their mallets and began running in tight little circles as they screamed in agony. Agent 27142 looked from the phoenix down to God-Art, whose head was now shiny and bald. The god's pupils were dashing left and right and up and down, and whichever way he jerked them, the phoenix lurched through the air in that direction. The god used the phoenix to burn every single crate in the room.

Agent 27142 screamed at the god, "Hey! Don't let the fire get out of control! We still need to get *through* this place without burning ourselves to death!"

The remainder of God-Art's body reformed from the bloody pulp. The god said, "I obviously wouldn't have used fire if it was going to impede us or harm us. I'm a god of mischief, not a god of stupidity."

There was something oddly disturbing about having a conversation with a person whose pupils were darting every direction, but Agent 27142 ignored the sentiment and said, "OK, then why don't you go ahead and show me *how* it won't be a problem so that we can get moving before every B.T.T. agent in the building swarms this sub-basement."

Flames had spread to fill the entirety of the room behind God-Art. God-Art shrugged. He spun on his heels and began walking forward into the flame. "C'mon," he said. "Stay near me and you'll be fine."

The god raised his hands into the air, and a bubble formed within the flames. Agent 27142 entered the room and shut the secret entrance behind him. He crept as close to God-Art as he could. The pair shuffled forward at a pace as near to a sprint as they could muster while the warehouse around them burned. They passed by the smashed and rotting corpses of Agent 27142's long-dead soldiers, many of which were naught but gray skeletons that were in the process of blackening due to the spreading flames. Agent 27142 opened his mouth to warn the god not to activate the laser tripwires, but he shut it when the god tripped the first one. All that happened was the trap in the ceiling shot conical ray beams into nearby crates, but these crates were already burning, so any Treendians that formed from the process merely came into existence, screamed a death cry, and burned into oblivion.

The pair reached the back of the warehouse. Agent 27142 sighed and thanked his lucky stars that the computer terminal that sat next to the elevators had not yet been engulfed in the spreading flames.

Agent 27142 sat at the computer terminal and turned it on. It booted up. He typed the override password that he had learned long ago from the B.I.T. High Commander's classified documents. Then he tapped the icon marked *Crew and Passenger Manifest Search*. He typed Prisoner-Art's full name and home reality number into the search function as fast as he could. Two entries popped up. But both said they were aboard the same ship, so he shrugged.

Agent 27142 informed God-Art, "This lists our prey as aboard the B.T.S. Unicorn Husker. But the ship is not *at* this point in time. It is currently in the past. We will need to steal a ship from the B.T.T. to pursue it."

God-Art nodded, his pupils still darting around as they guided the phoenix. "OK. Let's do it," he said.

Agent 27142 accessed a database of ships docked at the B.T.T. headquarters and typed more commands into the computer. He said, "And here we go. There's an unmanned transport ship up on floor eighty-eight. Just finished routine maintenance and the crew has been granted R&R for the next three days on one of this building's paradise floors."

God-Art pressed the button to call an elevator car. Then he said, "Let's get moving."

The phoenix flew down from the ceiling and perched on the god's head, where it sank back into his scalp, reverting to his regular flaming hair. The fire behind the god continued spreading through the warehouse, and the aftermath of the chaotic destruction shone across the god's face as disturbing, flickering highlights.

A beep let the group know that the elevator car had arrived. Agent 27142 made a mental note that he probably should not trust the maniacal-looking god. But since necessity had made them the oddest of bedfellows, he swallowed his reservations and walked onto the elevator. God-Art joined him.

*

The elevator car jerked to a halt on the eighty-eighth floor. The door opened. Agent 27142 and God-Art stepped off the car. The elevator bank stood in the exact center of this floor. The room was a gigantic circle that spread out in a radius that must have been at least a half-mile wide with a ceiling that must have been a good eighty-feet high.

This place was one of the B.T.T.'s many docking floors. Ships of all shapes and sizes filled the expanse of the room. The outside walls were all open to allow ships to land here, where they could dock and unload cargo, reload cargo for trade, and fly away again to the vast expanses of the Space-Time-Multinuum. There was constant movement, and it would be easy to get lost in here or to creep about without being noticed.

Luckily for Agent 27142 and God-Art, the latter was just what they were looking to do. They crept from the elevator and turned right. They followed a narrow path between a small fleet of ships shaped like the numeral four. Then they ducked left between a long, skinny ship in the shape of a snake and a wide ship that looked like a silver pancake.

They continued winding and creeping for a good twenty minutes until they finally approached the ship for which they had been searching: a twenty-by-thirty transport ship shaped like a numeral eight. The ship was painted neon green, and orange letters on its side spelled *Mama's Gangrene*. Agent 27142 tapped a button on a black pedestal rising from the floor near the ship. A hiss sounded from the side of the ship, and then a door opened in its side and a ramp descended to the ground.

Agent 27142 and God-Art ascended the ramp. They passed through a short corridor that opened onto a small cantina. Off to one side of the cantina lay an ordering counter with pictures of all kinds of fried foods. Spaced evenly across the bulk of the room were tables with benches attached to them. The lights were off, and the room seemed cold. Embedded along the walls were rows of rifles and pistols hung inside locked cases.

God-Art walked over to a case. His finger transformed into the shape of a key, and he jammed this key-finger into the lock where a key would go. He wiggled it. The lock disengaged, and God-Art opened the case. He plucked a rifle from its home and examined it. Then he noticed something embedded in the wall.

"Hmmm," he muttered. He tossed the rifle aside, and then he performed the same key-finger trick with a safe that lay in the wall.

God-Art retrieved a palm-sized object from the safe. It was a silver device in the shape of an eight. God-Art said, "And what do you do, little thing?"

The readout on Agent 27142's goggles appeared: *Unidentified device. Molecular residue surrounding it indicates that it can somehow affect time. Recommend staying a safe distance away, a full two realities over if possible.*

Agent 27142 ignored the useless readout since it did not have the functionality to adjust to his classified-level access and thus could not identify the object. His mind shifted back to the classified documents through which he had scoured when he had first achieved high enough classified access within the B.I.T. to learn of the B.T.T.'s existence.

As though he were reading from a teleprompter, Agent 27142 said aloud to God-Art the text he had memorized from the classified tomes, "That device is a *Timeflow Gun*, not to be confused with a *Time-Phaser*, which is a standard-issue B.T.T. device that freezes time or devolves or evolves opponents. The *Timeflow Gun* is much more powerful. It allows agents to reverse or fast-forward time in a given area—target range as large as an entire reality or as small as an appendage on a person. In addition, there are toggles that allow the user to send an object to a particular location across realities *and* backward or forward in time. However, the *Timeflow Gun* was discontinued, and the remaining few in service are issued only to the highest-ranking medical officers for use in healing the Space-Time-Multinuum's most important individuals. This is because the device operates by borrowing time from the endpoint of the Space-Time-Multinuum, and the B.T.T. discovered that this catastrophic endpoint was moving earlier with each use of these devices."

Agent 27142 walked closer to the device and studied it more closely with his goggles. The goggles returned no serial number. Agent 27142 continued, "Judging by the fact that this one was tucked inside a safe that was inside a locked cage, coupled with the fact that it has no discernible serial number, I'd guess that it came into this ship's possession illegally."

God-Art shrugged. He replied, "Or this is a medical vessel."

Agent 27142 said, "Sure, that's possible. But it's unlikely given the gigantic cargo hold indicative of a transport ship and the lack of obvious medical equipment. Oh, and also the fact that this ship was labeled as a transport ship in the B.T.T.'s databanks. But I guess there remains a *microscopic* chance that this ship is a medical vessel."

"Anything is equally possible when you're with me," responded the god.

Agent 27142 sighed and then cleared his throat. He pointed toward a ladder at the rear of the room. He muttered, "Sure. Whatever you say. Let's move. We're in a bit of a hurry."

God-Art nodded, and the pair stalked up the ladder. They found that it exited onto the bridge. Agent 27142 sat in the pilot's chair. His fingers flew across the instruments and the ship's engines roared to life. He pressed a button to shut the entrance on the side of the ship and raise the ramp. Once that was done, he grabbed the controls and jerked back on them. The ship lifted from the ground.

Agent 27142 steered it toward the exit. A voice crackled over the radio, "*Mama's Gangrene,* you are not yet scheduled to depart. Your hold has not yet been fully restocked for your next missi—"

Agent 27142 jerked the radio knob until it squelched off. He jammed the accelerator and the ship lurched forward, launching out into the bright purple sky.

Agent 27142 began toggling devices on the dashboard. After testing a few of them, he found the one for which he was looking. As he twisted this one to the left, the readout atop the dash indicated that he was changing their destination to the past. Before Agent 27142 could engage the button to initiate the jump, God-Art grabbed his wrist.

"Wait," said God-Art. He was still holding the small eight-shaped object and staring at it. "We need to make a quick stop first."

"But if we don't leave *now*, we may not have the luxury of doing so later."

God-Art smirked and gestured toward his surroundings with the back of his hand. He said, "Oh, please. The B.T.T. is a joke. They were never able to stop me in the past, and there's no way they'll be starting now."

God-Art pointed toward a spot on the ground far below and said, "Set the ship down there. We will be quick. It'll be worth it, I promise."

"You know that's where we *appeared* on this reality, right? Why would we want to go back there? It's going to be swarming with B.T.T. agents at any moment—if it's not already."

God-Art sighed. He said, "Trust me. I've got a plan."

Agent 27142 shrugged and turned the ship toward the cursed valley that had played such an instrumental role in shaping the last decade of his life. He frowned, feeling like his life had become a series of concentric circles surrounding this damned clearing.

CHAPTER 14

A FUNNY THING HAPPENED ON THE WAY TO THE CONSPIRACY OF THE GODS

IT FELT LIKE the magnet that was holding Drillbot's B.T.T. license to his chest had expanded all over his body. A tingling sensation burned through his torso and limbs and gears and rotors.

And as quickly as it began, the feeling ceased. Drillbot found himself standing in a forest, when before he had been standing in the Jump Chamber aboard the B.T.S. Unicorn Husker with the other members of this mission's Landing Crew. Trees towered over him with trunks so wide that it would take him at least a couple seconds to drill through them. A light breeze blew through the forest, causing flowers of orange and yellow and blue and magenta to dance amongst the surrounding foliage. Birds twittered overhead, and bees buzzed from flower to flower. A light layer of grass and dark mulch covered the ground. Drillbot zoomed in his telescopic eyes and watched an ant fight against the odds, pulling to some unseen lair the carcass of a dead insect probably twenty-times its size.

Drillbot allowed the serenity of nature to wash over him. The breeze frolicked across his metallic hide. The birdsongs delighted his processors. The subtle vibrations of the buzzing bees pollinated the hope that lay nearly dead beneath the closed petals of his steel heart. And then one of the Purple Shirts sneezed and ruined the moment. Drillbot jerked his head around to glare at the young man. But the young man apparently could not read Drillbot's annoyed expression, because he waved at the robot rather than wetting himself in fright.

Drillbot sighed. The logical part of him knew that the peaceful moments never last long anyway. Thus, he could not begrudge the young Purple Shirt for ruining it so abruptly, especially since the youth seemed ignorant of the frustration he had caused. So Drillbot waved back at the kid, and then he turned to face First Officer Alex.

"Alright," said Alex, "we've got about a ten-kilometer hike ahead of us, and we've no time to waste. Stay on the trail and ignore any native fauna you may see lurking as we pass.

As you all know from reading your briefing dossiers," continued Alex in a tone that belied little faith in the statement as he stared at Normal-Art, "there are dangerous creatures stalking this wilderness, and we will not be slowing down our cosmically important mission to rescue *anyone.*"

"Yes, sir!" called all the Purple Shirts in unison. Drillbot noted that Normal-Art instead called out, "Except me!"

Drillbot shook his head. The crew should never have let his former master know how important he was to the success of this mission. It was just enough leverage to make the man dangerously careless.

Drillbot shrugged and occupied the defensive position at the rear of the Landing Crew. Alex led the group along a worn trail that promised to climb over a high ridge and then snake back down into a valley that jutted up against the sea, ending at their destination: the bustling port city of Herceg Novi.

"Why'd we have to land so far away from the convention?" asked Normal-Art. Drillbot noted an odd but subtle squeal underlying Normal-Art's speech. This squeal was also present when Normal-Art asked his annoying questions in the cargo hold. Drillbot stared at his former master and frowned his version of a frown, wondering if this change in speech pattern signaled another incoming round of annoying mischief.

Drillbot heard the Purple Shirts near his former master groan. One of them said, "If you had read your briefing dossier, you'd know that we landed way out here to prevent as many of the convention-attending-gods as possible from detecting the teleportation residue from the *Husker.*"

"That's dumb," replied Normal-Art, the subtle squeal still there. "I guarantee that at least one of them already knows of our presence. We're all doomed, I'd wager nearly anything on it."

The Purple Shirt did not reply. That meant Normal-Art had no quip with which to respond in turn, which meant that the rest of the group could hike in relative peace.

The group of two-dozen Purple Shirts, Alex, Ginny, 29333, Bagoo, Normal-Art, and Older-Art walked in silence, everyone using the staffs from their costumes to support their weight as they began the ascent high up onto the rocky ridge—well, everyone but Drillbot, for he had been given no staff because he had no hands with which to carry one. The trail transitioned slowly from grassy mulch to barky brown soil to dusty rock as it began winding back and forth up a seemingly endless series of switchbacks. Before the group completed two of the switchbacks, Normal-Art collapsed. He lay on his side, panting.

"I – huff – have – huff – to – huff – take – huff – a – huff – break," moaned Normal-Art, his voice normal once again. Drillbot would have frowned at this development, but Normal-Art's panting huffs caused Drillbot to worry that his former master might be about to have a heart attack.

Drillbot sent word up to Alex that the group needed to stop and take a break. Alex marched back down the line and stood over the prone Normal-Art. He nudged Normal-Art in the ribs with his foot and ordered, "Get up. We don't have time to waste."

Normal-Art shrugged and said between huffs, "Can't."

Alex frowned. He pointed at four of the Purple Shirts and said, "You four will take turns ferrying him on your backs."

The Purple Shirts waited to groan until Alex had returned to the front of the line and was well out of earshot. Then the biggest of them gripped Normal-Art by the armpits and roughly hauled the lout off the ground. The Purple Shirt then hefted Normal-Art over his shoulders into a fireman's carry and trudged forward.

The group eventually reached the top of the switchbacks and emerged onto a rocky outcrop that overlooked a bay far below. Drillbot's sensors indicated that he was over four thousand feet above sea level. At the confluence of the bay and a wide river lay a sprawling city, overgrown with houses and parks and towering buildings. The roof of each building was capped with dusty brown ceramic tiles, and the façade of each building was painted white.

In the center of the city rose the biggest building that Drillbot had ever seen, despite his spending a decade hopping from reality to reality fighting in an infinite war. The building's shape was reminiscent of an arena, but it stretched so high into the air that Drillbot could not see the top even when he telescoped his eyes as far as they would go. Its outside seemed to consist of different styles of temples and amphitheaters and theaters and sporting complexes stacked one upon another. The exterior of the bottom layer was covered in an array of Doric columns, Corinthian columns, and sculptures of gargoyles and mythic beasts. This bottom layer was painted white to match the façades of the surrounding buildings in Herceg Novi. The next layer was stark black marble, the next green tile, the next purple velvet. The changes corresponded with the different building styles that were stacked one atop another, creating a jumble of colors and cultures that stretched high into the sky until they disappeared out of sight.

Somebody let out a stunned whistle. Drillbot realized that it was Older-Art. Alex furrowed his brows at the man, and Older-Art replied with a shrug, "I didn't pay enough attention to appreciate its scale the first time I saw it."

"What is it?" asked Normal-Art, the underlying squeal returning to his voice, this time a little stronger.

Drillbot glanced over at Normal-Art. The Purple Shirts assigned to ferrying him had set him on the ground as they gazed up at the infinite building. They let out a collective awed breath at the sheer scale of it. Normal-Art, however, merely shrugged after looking up at the building for a couple seconds.

Alex sighed. Then he screamed, "It! Was! In! The! Briefing! Dossier! That! I! Gave! You!"

Normal-Art screamed back, "I! Obviously! Didn't! Read! The! Stupid! Files! That! You! Gave! Me! So! Explain! It! To! Me! Now!"

Alex grunted. He rubbed at his temples. He muttered, "It's an Infinity Vortex. It has retrieved the courts and arenas and gathering places from the nigh-infinite pantheons within the Multiverse who accepted their invitations to this convention. It stretches unto infinity now, but it will split apart after the convention ends and each will return to its proper Earth. It's where the Conspiracy of the Gods will be set into motion.

Alex continued, "We must hurry. If the vortex has been summoned, then the cocktail hour has begun, and the convention will soon be underway. The B.I.T. will respond to this threat in about ninety-six hours, and as we know from the history of the Space-Time-Multinuum, that will be too late."

Drillbot watched Normal-Art. The human stared down at the ground—obviously not listening intently to Alex's explanation—and his eyes went wide when he noticed a cute, neon green bunny on the ground, its ears flopped to the side and its eyes gigantic and wide. The little mammal nuzzled up against Normal-Art's leg.

Drillbot let out a tiny gasp when he realized what was about to happen. "Well, look at you," whispered Normal-Art. "Aren't you just the cutest little thing?"

"[whir] Don't!" warned Drillbot, but he was too late.

Normal-Art bent to pet the bunny. As soon as he touched it, the bunny melted and contorted and wrapped around Normal-Art's arm. It formed into a neon green tentacle and lifted Art high into the air.

The tentacle's owner revealed itself. Its top half was a ferocious brown grizzly bear nearly twenty-feet tall. Instead of legs, eight octopus tentacles stretched from the bottom of its torso, each a different color and each with the image of a different cute animal occupying its end.

Drillbot's internal processors fired, and his mind brought to bear the information about native flora and fauna from the briefing dossier: *this creature is known as a bearopus—this one specifically belonging to the grizzly variety. Its diet consists of fish, fruit, children, and travelers. Numbers of wild bearopi have dwindled to near extinction in recent years, but the native scientists have bred them in captivity and have begun releasing them into the wilderness outside Herceg Novi. Their numbers are now steadily increasing and are expected to soon grow high enough for the species to exit its distinction as an endangered species. The bearopi are fiercely territorial but are known to wander into cities in search of food when nourishment is scarce in their native habitat, making meals of entire elementary schools before emergency crews can respond and return any trespassing creatures to the wilderness. Because they are endangered, it is illegal to kill the animals.*

Drillbot willed himself to stop scanning the file from his memory banks. He brought his mind back to the present. He heard Alex scream at Normal-Art, "I told you *not* to interact with the native fauna!"

Drillbot launched into action, gunning his engines and roaring headlong toward the maw of the beast, which was mere inches from tearing into Normal-Art's flesh. The purple wig atop Drillbot's head fluttered in the wind like a battle standard.

As Drillbot reared his drills back to drive them into the beast's flesh, a conical bolt of orange light flashed past his head. The bolt slammed into the bearopus's torso. The beast flailed and screamed. It dropped Normal-Art, and then it melted into a pile of brown and yellow goop.

Drillbot screeched to a halt. He shrugged and glanced over his shoulder. Alex stood holding a metal cylinder from which stretched a bow formed from solid light.

Alex nodded and said, "Drillbot, I appreciate your courage, but I *did* order everyone—including yourself—not to interact with the fauna. This beast in particular, which you were about to unceremoniously drill apart, is destined to lead the bearopi of this forest in revolt against the peoples of Herceg Novi, who have mistreated these beasts for years and don't realize that these beasts have become sentient. As a matter of fact, at this bearopus's orders, one of the species has managed to get a tentacle with a human-shaped image on its end elected to government office, and then managed to pass legislation to protect the bearopi, which has given them enough freedom to breed higher numbers unmolested so that they might eventually fight back. This revolt will cause a helpful distraction for the B.T.T. later in this timestream. So, please follow my orders in the future, because they do have a *strategic* purpose."

Drillbot frowned his version of a frown. "[whir] If this bearopus was – CLACK – was so important, then why did *you* just – CLACK – just kill it? Is the end result not the same as Drillbot killing it? Is the manner of its – CLACK – of its death important?"

Alex tsked. He replied, "Oh, Drillbot. I thought you of all people here would put the pieces together. I *didn't* kill it. I used my weapon to *devolve* it. I set my weapon so it will return to normal—albeit a little confused—in a half-hour."

Drillbot nodded. He said, "[whir] Drillbot understands. We should – CLACK – we should move, then. So we can be far away when it returns to its original – CLACK – its original form."

Alex nodded. "Right you are," he said. Then he pointed to the Purple Shirts who had been carrying Normal-Art. "Pick that bastard back up, and if one of you drops him or lets him do something foolish again, then so help me gods, I will execute you myself."

The Purple Shirts scrambled to obey. Drillbot took another awed look at the colossal building that grew from the center of Herceg Novi like it was a redwood tree amongst a field of tiny wildflowers. Then he rolled forward to continue the mission.

*

As Drillbot rolled across Herceg Novi's uneven cobblestone streets, his vision bobbled and bounced. If Drillbot were capable of motion sickness, he would likely be feeling it right about now.

The streets were packed with citizens bustling about to work and to play, and Drillbot often had to dodge to prevent his wheel-daggers from slicing their legs from their bodies. The group passed all manner of shops as they hurried toward the middle of the city where the Infinity Vortex stood. Each pavilion they passed contained hundreds of people crying out their wares and bombarding the group with cheap trinket after cheap trinket. Drillbot noticed a shop selling shoddy, plastic dinosaur toys. They reminded him of Ginny Rex, and he shuddered with sadness.

As they neared the center of the city and reached the marble stairs leading up to the entrance of the Infinity Vortex, they passed a cart selling little clay sculptures of a familiar figure with fiery hair.

"Wait! I have to get me one of these!"

Everyone groaned and turned to look at Normal-Art. He was leaning over from his perch on the shoulders of one of the burlier Purple Shirts and grabbing one of the figurines from the stand.

Everyone's groans turned to gasps. Apparently, nobody had noticed a new change that had happened to Normal-Art's body sometime during the remainder of the hike here, for everyone had been doing their best to ignore him and his increasingly annoying behavior. But a second neck and a second head had sprouted from his right shoulder. The second head looked just like Normal-Art's own, except its eyes were black, its skin was pale blue, and flames rose into the air from its scalp rather than hair.

Normal-Art seemed confused. He asked, "What? Why's everyone staring at me?"

29333 pointed to the second head on Normal-Art's shoulder. She said, "Look to your right."

Normal-Art slowly turned his head to the right, and immediately screamed.

"There's no reason for *that*," responded God-Art's head. People on the street turned to gawk, but since they had all recently experienced an infinitely tall building sprouting up from the ground in the center of their city, this development seemed relatively minor. Thus, they all continued about their business.

Normal-Art screamed again. God-Art shook his head. "You should stop screaming," suggested the god.

Normal-Art stopped screaming just long enough to gasp, "What the hell? Where did you come from?"

"Well, my father was a god of wisdom and battle. One day, as he was strolling to the market, he noticed a fissure in the southern hemisphere of the planet. Though he was a god of wisdom, that didn't mean he wasn't extremely stupid. But to be completely fair to him, this was a long time ago, back before anyone was really all that smart. Anyway, my father went *wild* on that crack—if you know what I mean—and nine years later, I popped out of it."

Normal-Art groaned, "That's not what I meant, and you know it."

"Oh, you must've meant that you want to know where I came from when I appeared on your shoulder," said God-Art. "Well, you should have been more specific. The answer to *that* is simple. Some of my molecules hitched a ride on you when you meandered through them in that contraption on the B.T.T. ship that retrieves a three-dimensional moment in time. Just enough of them attached to you for me to resurrect myself here and now. After all we've been through, you *really* should have known to stay away from that place if you didn't want me showing up. Also, the B.T.T. should consider simple hologram technology rather than physically displacing a moment in time and bringing it aboard a ship. It would prevent surprising developments like this.

"Anyway," continued the god, "I reformed inside your skull, and then I burst forth from a pore in your shoulder. It's funny: everyone believes that you didn't listen the last time that the buffoonish blond briefed you on your mission because you're normally such an annoying buffoon. But you *actually did* listen to him! But *I* didn't because I wasn't yet attached to you, so I pulled some levers in your brain and made you pretend you didn't know anything. And then I kept doing it the whole way here because it was *fun.*"

"I *knew* it!" yelled Normal-Art. "I knew that something was wrong. I kept asking about the briefing without being able to control it. I thought at first maybe I was just addicted to annoying everyone around me, but it kept happening, and I couldn't stop it. At least now I know that it was just some stupid god controlling my body, and not me going crazy!"

Everybody in the group who had hands slapped themselves on their foreheads in dismay. Alex moaned, "This *isn't* an improvement to the situation, you dolt! If that god-version of you is here, then it means our mission is foiled before it even begins."

God-Art grinned. He pursed his lips and whistled. Atoms whirled and swirled, and a miniature gray tornado formed on the ground. It rose about eight feet into the air and then disappeared. In its place stood God-Art's body, only it was headless. The body's arms reached out, grabbed the god-head growing from Normal-Art's shoulder, and ripped off the head. Blood sprayed from the base of the head in all directions. As it rained down onto the cobblestones, it transformed into tiny pixies. The pixies darted one by one over to kiss God-Art's cheek before fluttering away.

The body slammed the head in place atop its neck, and God-Art stood re-formed before the group, wearing his usual outfit—his cloak made from the stitched-together hides of baby seals and white wolves, his necklace of severed ears dangling down to his belly button, and his belt made from rope on which hung his pouch, his serrated dagger with the hilt formed from a green tiger's paw, and his obsidian tools. The god's grin widened.

"Oh, Alexandros ho Megas, you have no reason for such harsh words," said the god, placing both hands over his heart. "Look, I might be a right bastard at times, but I want to help."

Alex furrowed his brow. He asked, "And why would you want to do that?"

The god said, "Because I've listened to you, and I've learned the error of my ways. Look, if I don't stop this conspiracy that *I* put into motion, if I don't help prevent the cataclysm that the cosmic bears will unleash upon every reality in existence, then I'm as good as responsible for the Multiverse's eventual downfall."

Alex's brow-furrowing deepened. He replied, "And *why* would that concern you now? Surely past-you understood that the end of the

Multiverse might be a possibility if you proceeded with your conspiracy."

"Yeah, well, past-me didn't *truly understand* what I might be causing. Your briefing details made me realize that if the Multiverse is ended, then I'm ended, too, because we're *all* ended. That's bad for me."

Alex responded, "So, helping us is ultimately about helping *yourself* rather than helping the infinite people you would murder if you caused the end of the Multiverse?"

God-Art frowned. "I guess so," he said. "But helping infinite people is an added benefit, wouldn't you agree?"

Drillbot rolled forward and pressed the tips of his drills against the sides of the god's skull. He warned, "[whir] Do not trust – CLACK – trust this god. He will betray us. We should kill – CLACK – kill him, and then kill him again when he – CLACK – when he resurrects. Over and over, until the mission is complete."

God-Art held up his hands in supplication. He said, "Drillbot, you are much fiercer than I remember you. May I make a suggestion? Let me help on a trial basis. At the first sign of betrayal, *then* move forward with killing me. This plan you're enacting has so many opportunities to fail, having a god on your side may be the difference between success and failure."

"Do it, Drillbot. Get rid of him," barked Regular-Ginny.

The god glanced at her with murder in his eyes. The hostility disappeared almost as soon as it appeared, and he once more feigned supplication. Drillbot noticed it, though. He began to power on his drills.

Alex placed a hand on Drillbot's shoulder. "No," said the commander. "The god is right. It is in *his own* best interest to help us, and the B.T.T.'s files on him are clear: if we can trust one thing, it is that this creature will serve his own interests above all others. Strategically speaking, that is an advantage for us. We shall accept his help."

Ginny and Normal-Art gasped in surprise and then scowled with disgust. Drillbot groaned and then lowered his drills.

Drillbot warned the god, "[whir] Drillbot will be watching you – CLACK – watching you."

God-Art smirked. He replied, "Sure. Whatever you say, Drillbot."

Alex nodded. Then he spun on his heel and strode up the steps, entering a doorway in the side of the Infinity Vortex. God-Art spun on his own heel in mocking mimicry and followed. Drillbot followed close behind, readying his drills to spring into action at a moment's notice. He had a bad feeling about what was to come.

CHAPTER 15

INTO THE CONVENTION

GINNY ASCENDED THE marble steps. Her thighs burned, sore from the long hike to get here. She scratched the top of her head, trying to dig her fingernails deeply enough into her purple wig that she could relieve the itching it caused on her scalp.

The pit of her stomach was filled with dread. This anxiety was rooted in two causes: one part caused by her poor acting skills, which she was confident would cause her to flub at an inopportune time and lead to the Landing Crew getting caught, and the second part caused by her distrust of the god-version of Art, who had reappeared on the scene a few moments ago.

She swallowed hard and continued her ascent up the steps. Her feet followed just behind the Purple Shirt's in front of her, who must have been following just behind the Purple Shirt's in front of him, and so on. As a matter of fact, people must have been walking up these marble steps in this same pattern for a long time, because they were worn and bowed inward. She wondered how long attendees had been gathering for this godly conspiracy.

She glanced up. Every inch of the building's façade was covered in sculptures of gargoyles or gods or mythological beasts. As she neared the door, she realized that it was no exception. The stone around the door was shaped like the wide, angry face of a toad, the threshold an open representation of its mouth. Ginny felt odd as she stepped past its lips and into its gullet. After all she had seen and experienced, she would not have been at all surprised if the sculpture came alive to swallow her whole.

Once past the threshold and inside the Infinity Vortex, Ginny and her companions came to a grand staircase that led down into a massive atrium. The atrium's walls were the same white marble as the exterior of the building and its ceiling was so high that when Ginny looked up, she could not see its top. Concession stands lined the walls offering all manner of divine fare, ranging from mashed ambrosia to bottled incense to charred oxen-fat wrapped around thigh bones to flagons of mead. Lines had formed in front of the many stands, and Ginny scowled when she witnessed how gods queue: they twist their lines back and forth and up and down to create sigils. Before Ginny was given the opportunity to ignore the behavior and move on, God-Art leaned over to the Landing Crew and whisper-yelled, "They stand like that to channel protective wards. Many of these gods represent opposing forces. They're vulnerable in line, so they stand in such a way that allows them a modicum of safety. Normally they could count on a truce to keep them safe, but every pantheon's trickster god is present at this conference. And those guys should *never* be trusted."

Alex replied, "We know. All of this was in the briefing dossier. Now stay silent!"

God-Art winked at Ginny. She shuddered and looked away. Gods of every shape and size had filled the atrium. She saw a pair of green-skinned giants who were so tall their faces disappeared out of view and a black rabbit wearing a top hat and a muscular male in a toga with a storm cloud covering his face and a giant spider and an angry man with long blond hair carrying a gigantic hammer and a one-eyed man with a bronze helmet and a buffalo wearing a colonial-era powdered wig and a baby fluttering around on tiny wings and a man with rainbows for nipples and hundreds upon thousands more gods with equally odd physical features.

Throughout the atrium, potted plants dotted the landscape. On closer inspection, Ginny realized these were not placed at random, but instead formed more sigils. Some of the plants were blossoming fruit bushes, while others were withered and dead. One gigantic god with a gray beard and a name tag that read, *"Hello! My Name is Yahweh!"* stood next to a gigantic tree from which dangled apple-like fruit. He handed out the fruit to passersby. A sign at the base of this tree's pot warned that this was *The Tree of The Knowledge of Good and Evil,* and that demigods and half-gods should refrain from partaking.

There was so much divine oddness to observe that Ginny could have stood there and stared at the scene forever. When she turned to make just such a comment to Older-Art, she realized that the Landing Crew had continued walking without her and was now down the stairs, through the atrium, and over near the entrance for Section 42, the section for which the Landing Crew had tickets.

Ginny cursed as she ran to catch up to her group, dodging between gods and pots and queues and stalls. She caught up to them as they reached the entrance to Section 42. Alex pulled a wad of tickets from a fold in his marigold toga and handed the tickets to the usher who stood at the entrance. The usher was an old, wizened man who chewed on his lips as he took the tickets from Alex. He hummed a happy little tune as he flattened the tickets and counted them.

As the usher ripped each ticket in half, a small rainbow launched from its end and crashed down to the floor next to the usher. It looked like someone had taken a bulldozer to the floor where the ends of the rainbows crashed. Ginny leaned over and chanced a glance into the hole. She could see no bottom. Before Ginny could ask, Alex leaned over and whispered in her ear, "The weight of nearly an infinite number of rainbows crashing to the floor in the same spot. That's the problem with these damnable enchanted tickets. Nobody thinks about the unintended consequences. I bet whatever city is on the opposite side of the world is having a really bad day right about now."

The usher handed the stubs back to Alex, who handed one to each member of the Landing Crew. The group began walking forward, but the usher raised a hand to stop them. He said, "You're one short."

God-Art grinned, dug into the pouch that hung from the rope he used as a belt, and produced a ticket stub. It looked nearly identical to the stubs that Alex had just handed to the Landing Crew, but older, dirtier, and even more wadded. The god arched an eyebrow at the usher and said, "Mine's already been torn. I entered this theater a *long* time ago, left, and now I'm back."

The god turned and winked at the Landing Crew. Every single member sighed. The usher joined them in sighing, and it sounded as though a choir of angels had all become jaded at the exact same moment.

The usher replied, "Alright. I take it you're another of them gods of time or illusion or whatever. I done seen enough of yer kind today to know there's no point in trying to understand what's happening here. The presentation starts in half an hour. Now move along, the lot of you."

The usher waved the group through, and they walked past him and toward the arena proper. They ascended a flight of stairs. Ginny felt a weighty sense of history and importance to these stairs, and she noted it was the same feeling she sensed the time that her father had taken her to see a game at Wrigley Field when she was a kid. People had poured their energies into that place and had turned it into one of symbolic importance. *Gods* had done the same to this location, and she could not help but feel the palpable weight of this significance as it coursed through the building around her.

The group reached the top of the stairs and emerged into the arena. Ginny had never heard anything like it. The voices of a nearly infinite number of gods rang out all around her. Though the gods were merely engaged in small talk, their small talk was on a divine scale. Ginny felt every atom inside of her vibrate. It tickled and hurt all at once. She traded expressions between laughing and wincing.

Then she glanced around her, and all her senses became overwhelmed by the sheer size of the arena and the insignificance she suddenly felt about herself. Outside of this building, the Infinity Vortex seemed mesmerizing, but at the same time, it was something her mind could at least theoretically wrap itself around—it was a building with a bunch of interesting design quirks that was so tall it disappeared into the sky. However, as she glanced skyward *inside* the building, it felt like the building was both wrapping itself around her so she could not breathe and heaving her upward into infinity. The blood drained from her face and her legs buckled out from under her.

Before she could collapse to the ground, Older-Art caught her and steadied her. He said, "Whoa there, Gin. Sorry, I forgot to warn you not to look up. Gives you a sense of vertigo, like when you're standing at the edge of some ridiculous height and there's nothing to keep you from falling. But, y'know, upward.

Older-Art jerked a thumb toward Normal-Art and continued, "All in all, I'd say you're handling it better than I did the first time."

Normal-Art had collapsed onto the ground and was lying in a pool of his own drool. His hands were clinging desperately to the steel struts that held the nearby bleacher-style seats in place. He was staring upward and muttering something unintelligible.

Older-Art said, "Look down at the ground or straight across to the other side of the arena. Just never up, and you'll be OK."

Ginny steadied herself and nodded. She and Older-Art turned to Normal-Art and helped him off the ground. Older-Art grabbed the back of Normal-Art's head and forced it to look down at the ground. Normal-Art began to recover himself, and after a few moments, he agreed to walk under the condition that he could hold onto Older-Art so that he wouldn't fall away into the sky.

Older-Art assented. Normal-Art hugged him from behind, and they walked through the auditorium looking like a spooning couple, passing pantheon after pantheon until they arrived at the section of bleachers that contained their seats. Oddly enough, Ginny noted that none of the pantheons remarked about how odd the Arts' behavior seemed. She shrugged. *Guess there's plenty of weird in your life when you're a god*, she thought.

The group's seats were located near the center of the arena, though really every seat seemed to be at the center of the arean since it was shaped into a circle. Alex, Drillbot, God-Art, 29333, Older-Art, Ginny, and Bagoo sat on one row while the Purple Shirts occupied the next few rows directly behind them. Ginny sat in the rightmost seat with Older-Art on her left. Normal-Art sat to Older-Art's left and leaned his head onto his older-self's shoulder, complaining of a headache. God-Art sat on Normal-Art's left, a grin plastered to his face, and Drillbot occupied the next space over. Alex sat next to Drillbot, 29333 next to Alex, and Bagoo hovered inches above the leftmost seat.

To the left of the group sat a pantheon of gorilla deities. Their leader was a giant silverback wearing an amethyst crown, an ivory monocle, and a violet cloak with ornate, jeweled coconuts woven into the fabric. He was surrounded by a harem of over a dozen females who were in a constant state of feeding him and gently rubbing his shoulders. He held in his hands a few dozen leashes, each of which was attached to the neck of a tiny male gorilla sitting on the row below him. Each gorilla had branded into its arm a different symbol ranging from a wheel to a compass to an anchor to a plow to a paintbrush.

When the patron god of this pantheon noticed God-Art, a look of confusion passed over his face and he called out in a voice lispier than any Ginny had ever heard, "Ho, Artheothkatergariabetrugereiinganno. What art thou doing up here in the thtandth? Aren't though thuppothed to be on thtage?"

God-Art shrugged. "I'm supposed to be in a lot of places. Don't you worry, Goraxula. You just ensure your kids stay leashed. We can't afford for your pantheon to go through its perennial rebellion and culling, at least not until everything's finished here."

The gorilla grunted and then nodded. He said nothing else, instead frowning and staring hatefully at the smaller gorillas on the leashes in front of him. Ginny glanced over at Alex, Bagoo, and 29333. None of them seemed to have heard God-Art's suspicious exchange with the gorilla-god. She was just about to call it to their attention when voices thundered to her right.

When she looked in that direction, she saw a god lying prostrate on the ground. He wore a light blue tunic, gladiator-style sandals, and golden bracelets on his arms. His skin tone reminded her of someone from one of her reality's Arab countries. There was nothing remarkable about his appearance other than the fact that he wore a gigantic dead fish as a hat and his head and hands had been severed from his body. His beard grew in curls and would have stretched all the way down to his naval if his head were attached to his neck.

He stared up at the god closest to him and all but screamed, "When will you ever get over yourself and stop picking on me! I made a *single* mistake. Eons ago! And *you won* in the end! There's no reason to continue treating me with such indignity!"

The god sitting before him looked exactly like the one with the Yahweh name tag out in the lobby. As a matter of fact, this one also had a name tag that described himself as Yahweh. Ginny wondered if this was the same version as the one that she had seen outside, or a different one from a different Earth. The conundrum made her head hurt.

Yahweh scowled, and his voice boomed, "Thou disgraced *me* after thou captured me, putting me on display for all the gods of Mesopotamia to see. And since I overcame thee from that indignity, thou knowest my decree: any time we are gathered with other gods, I shall do the same to thee."

A man who looked a little over thirty years old with curly brown hair and red hands sitting to Yahweh's right leaned over and put a hand on Yahweh's shoulder. It left red handprints when he removed it. The young man said, "C'mon, Papa. That's enough. Calm down and allow the

Philistine to heal himself. He's learned his lesson dozens upon dozens of times by now."

Yahweh grunted. He seemed to consider the young man's words for a few moments, and then a grin appeared on his face. He nodded and patted the open spot on the bleachers next to him—the one between him and Ginny—and said, "Jesus, thou are right. Thou pleasest me as always, my son. Dagon, reattach your head and your hands and sit next to me!"

A light flashed around Dagon, and when it disappeared, the god was whole. He stood, brushed himself off, and sat between Yahweh and Ginny. The fish on his head smelled so rotten that Ginny had to fight the urge to vomit. She noticed that fish entrails were braided through the god's long, curly hair, and she gagged.

Normal-Art was apparently feeling better, because he took that moment to lean over to Older-Art and Ginny. He pointed at Dagon's head and muttered, "Holy in the front, party in the back, am I right?"

Normal-Art grinned and held out a hand for a high five. Nobody smiled or even made the vaguest effort to oblige him. Normal-Art responded by saying, "Get it? A mullet is a kind of fish, and that guy's wearing a fish on his head. And it's also the name of a terrible haircut. And there's that one phrase that people say about the haircut: *business in the front, party in the back*. And I changed the saying so that it referenced the god and his fish-hat. Nobody thinks that's funny?"

And nobody did.

TREACHERY SOMETIMES ISN'T AS BAD AS YOU THINK

DRILLBOT DISCOVERED THAT sitting on a bleacher seat is uncomfortable. Since he was not designed to sit in chairs, he found that when he did so, he was forced to lift his wheels so that they dangled out in front of him. He felt like a screwdriver that someone was trying to use as a hammer—awkward and out of place and not quite living up to its purpose.

Drillbot glanced over at God-Art. God-Art sat to his right, studying his surroundings and grinning a grin that stretched the entire width of his face. Most of the gods on the way to their seats had waved to God-Art or muttered ominous-sounding words or acted like they were teens meeting their celebrity idol for the first time—well, the latter was at least how Drillbot had overheard one of the Purple Shirts describe it; Drillbot had no real concept or experience with celebrity, so he had merely nodded and agreed.

Drillbot frowned his version of a frown, his mouth-speaker retracting slightly, his telescopic eyes vibrating, and his radar dishes atop his head wobbling. It had become extremely obvious from the moment the Landing Crew had entered the Infinity Vortex that God-Art would *not* be blending into the background like their mission demanded. The god's body language indicated that he was fine with such an outcome. Alex's, however, indicated an obvious sense of anxiety.

Actually, when Drillbot played the past few minutes back through his internal processors, he realized that the description of Alex was not *quite* true. As Drillbot studied Alex's image in his memory banks, he noticed that there was a weird discrepancy in the officer's body language. He visibly shook on the outside as though he were anxious of the attention that God-Art was bringing to the Landing Crew. He frowned a lot and wiped his brow and yanked at his toga's collar, just as one would expect a nervous human to do. But when Drillbot zoomed in on the images, he noticed no glimmer of sweat on Alex's brow. And Alex's heartbeat had not grown faster, as would be expected in a human experiencing extreme anxiety. And the nervous moans Alex kept uttering did not register the same high-pitched note that seemed to accompany every human's nervous moan, the note right up at the front of the moan that falls outside the range of human hearing. Drillbot frowned harder at this conundrum, his mouth-speaker retracting even farther, his telescopic eyes vibrating even harder, and his radar dishes atop his head wobbling even faster.

Drillbot decided to ask Alex about this discrepancy in his behavior. He whispered to Alex, "[whir] Why are – CLACK – why are y—"

Alex gave a nearly imperceptible shake of his head and Drillbot halted his question. The robot's frown intensified. He decided not to press the question, instead placing a calendar reminder in his system to ask Alex about the behavior later.

Drillbot altered his gaze and studied the crowd. He began passing the time by scanning the crowd for different iterations of the same god. He had reached over a thousand versions of the god sitting two spots to Ginny's right, Yahweh, before feedback squelched through the entire Infinity Vortex. Many of the gods in the crowd held their hands over their ears. Just as many shrugged. Just as many called out curses. Just as many called out poetic verses full of lusty joy. Drillbot counted at least a dozen whose heads exploded.

All eyes turned down toward the stage on the ground in the center of the arena. A bipedal god wearing a cloak stitched together from dead baby seals and dead white wolves stood in its center. His scalp burned with glowing flame. It was God-Art.

Drillbot turned to face the God-Art to his right. This version of the god wore a sheepish expression on his face. He said, "Look, there's nothing to worry about. I've heard your point of view. My past-self was wrong, and we've got to stop him to preserve the Space-Time-Multinuum—and thus, all of existence. You have my word. I shall give you my assistance."

Ginny, Normal-Art, and Drillbot all began speaking at once to protest about accepting this god's word as any sort of guarantee. But Alex interrupted them and said to God-Art in a nervous, shaky squeal, "I-I-If you pledge to us your honor and give us your word, then that will be good enough for me. P-Please, this is our *only* opportunity to save the Space-Time-Multinuum. I beg you to think of all the lives that are at stake—your own amongst them!"

God-Art ran his fingers over his heart in a motion that resembled the letter *X*. He replied, "You got it. Cross my heart."

Alex and the other officers of the B.T.S. Unicorn Husker nodded. None of the Purple Shirts dared to say anything.

Past-God-Art on the stage held a conch shell to his lips and blew into it. The shell glowed neon pink, its end erupted with rainbow-colored flames, and the entire world seemed to shimmer. The same squelching feedback noise from a few moments ago crashed caromed more through the confines of the Infinity Vortex. This time, it hushed the crowd completely.

Past-God-Art puffed up his chest and blew once more into the shell. This time, rather than producing a squelchy feedback noise, the action caused Past-God-Art's voice to fill the expanse of the Infinity Vortex. He proclaimed, "Welcome, all ye holy ones. Thank you for heeding my call and for your cooperation in this vital plan. As most of you already know, I am Artheoskatergariabetrugereiinganno from Earth 49,652.

The god took another breath and continued, "We have a grand opportunity lying before us. The Multiverse is ever expanding. And every time the damned place expands, our power relative to the size of the Multiverse shrinks. And that's a problem. As a matter of fact, the Multiverse has expanded to create a nearly infinite number of new universes since I began speaking, and from there expanded into yet another infinite number of universes, and so on. Infinity is constantly raising itself to the power of infinity.

He continued, "And now we have a chance to stop this madness. We can put a cap on infinity and begin the process of increasing our powerbase. And how we do so shall be simple."

The gods in the crowd either hissed with doubt or cheered with excitement. Past-God-Art reached down and grabbed the end of a chain lying on the stage near his feet. He tugged on it, and a hulking creature nearly twice his height emerged from the shadows. The opposite end of the chain was wrapped around the creature's neck and torso, leaving only its face and the bottom halves of its legs exposed. It shuffled toward Past-God-Art's position on the stage. It resembled a gigantic baboon, but with flowing silver hair extending from its chin and thick, round spectacles over his eyes.

Past-God-Art sucked in more air and blew again into his magical conch shell. The air shimmered, and a gaseous ball containing thousands of seemingly random mathematical symbols exploded from the end of the conch. The gaseous ball zoomed skyward, flying past Drillbot until it disappeared into the air high above. Then it exploded like a firework.

Past-God-Art continued, "We shall use math! I must reiterate my thanks to the pantheons who donated your patron gods of mathematics and physics and engineering to this fine cause. This creature standing next to me—Dr. Divine Baböönfacé from Earth 494,809,111—was the first to crack the code to our problem, and he deserves your thanks.

Past-God-Art continued, "We have discovered that it is but a matter of us deities collectively and simultaneously placing a replicating wave function into a single molecule in the atmospheres of our respective skies. These wave functions shall spread like a virus to every reality in the Multiverse, and soon, we shall have no more pesky, new realities splitting off from our own. Our powerbases will *mean* something again, rather than being but a drop within an ever-multiplying infinity-bucket.

"In two hours hence," he continued, "following our networking session, I shall reveal to you the mathematical function that we shall use and the time at which we shall enact our grand scheme. So, get to mingling. Get to know your fellow gods a bit. Make some new friends, some new allies, some new enemies."

And with that, Past-God-Art removed the conch shell from his lips and silence filled the auditorium. Past-God-Art spun on his heel and began to walk toward the exit at the back of the stage. He tugged on the chain, and the baboon-like creature followed.

Godly voices began filling the silence as the surrounding gods delved into networking. To his right, Drillbot heard Ginny stammer nervously in conversation with Yahweh, Jesus, and Dagon. Drillbot ignored her, for much to his chagrin, he realized the numb feeling from the magnet that held his B.T.T. identity in place below his toga was simultaneously growing larger and sliding up his torso.

Drillbot glanced at God-Art and noticed that the god was muttering to himself, staring at Drillbot, and slowly sliding his finger upward through the air in front of him. Drillbot jerked his right drill toward the god, intending to stab him into oblivion.

But just before his drill connected with God-Art's clavicle, the magnet zoomed up into view from beneath Drillbot's toga and stuck squarely to Drillbot's forehead. It had grown seven times its original size and eighteen times as thick. As Drillbot scanned it, he realized its molecular makeup had also changed. Before his sensors could tell him just what this change entailed, Drillbot's thoughts went from coherent to a jumble of ones and zeroes that he could not translate. Greens and magentas filled his vision, and every straight line he could see went jagged. Voices around him slowed and morphed together. He could see nothing, hear nothing, understand nothing.

*

When Drillbot's senses returned to normal, he found that he was lying on his side with Older-Art standing over him. The older version of his former master must have yanked the magnet from Drillbot's head, for Drillbot witnessed the older man using both hands to toss the now-gigantic object aside. It clattered across the ground.

Drillbot's head ached. The ones and zeroes in his processors began returning to their proper places. But they were definitely being slow about the process, and it seemed like they kept bumping into one another.

"Are you alright?" asked Older-Art.

Drillbot repositioned himself so that he was upright. A string crafted from intestines and dozens of putrid, severed ears lay on the ground around him. He must have accidentally snagged the god's necklace of severed ears and ripped it from the god's neck, but he could not remember doing so, for he could remember nothing of the last few moments but black nothingness. He frowned his version of a frown, for he was confused.

Drillbot heard Alex scream from a few feet over, "Drillbot, the damned god has betrayed us, and *you* just let him escape! Kappa Squad, we're out of time! Initiate the assassination! Now! Before the damned past-version of the god can leave the stage!"

Drillbot attempted to respond to Older-Art, but all that came out was, "[whir] CLACK CLACK CLACK CLACK CLACK."

Drillbot turned his head to watch half of the Purple Shirts produce scoped rifles from within their togas. They altered the settings on the sides of the guns to *permanent*. Then they all turned and began sprinting to different spots in the auditorium, scrambling past the networking gods to find locations on the bleachers that would allow the perfect vantage for a sniper shot.

Alex grabbed Drillbot by the arm and pointed toward the nearest exit. "Down there. Now."

Every member of the Landing Crew not currently hurrying to assassinate Past-God-Art—Alex, Bagoo, 29333, the Arts, Ginny, Drillbot, and the Filbert Squadron of Purple Shirts—scrambled toward the exit. Drillbot chanced a glance down at the stage and noticed that Past-God-Art had not yet departed it. A few burly gods carrying war hammers and sickles had appeared on stage and were talking with him and the spectacled beast he held chained at his side. Drillbot shrugged and moved with the Landing Crew toward the exit, crushing a few of the severed ears as he rolled past. None of the gods surrounding the Landing Crew seemed to notice or be concerned with their panic.

Once outside the exit, Alex pointed to the left and they darted down a side hallway. "Stop," he ordered. "29333, erect a sound shield."

29333 produced a small disc from her holster, dropped it to the ground, and stepped on it. Blue light fountained from its top and formed a sphere around the group. 29333 said, "Done, sir. No sound's getting in or out."

Alex nodded his thanks to her. Then he turned to the Landing Crew. He muttered with a smirk, "I thought that damned god was *never* going to escape us."

Drillbot tried to speak, but he could still only produce CLACKs. Ginny seemed to pick up on what he was trying to ask and said, "Wait, you knew the god was going to escape?"

Alex nodded. "Of course. We needed him to. Him escaping is our diversion."

Ginny placed her hands on her hips and scowled. "And when were you going to tell us?"

"Well, now. Obviously. The god who stowed away on our mission is now scrambling off to warn his past-self of our intent to assassinate him, which will in turn prevent the assassination altogether."

Ginny frowned. She replied, "But the *entire reason* we're here is to assassinate him. We were told in the brief that we're supposed to alter this timestream by killing him, which will prevent him from releasing the mathematical equation that will destroy the Space-Time-Multinuum."

Alex smirked. He said, "Well, the brief wasn't entirely true. Besides, if you *really* think about it, you'd realize that's a dumb plan. He's a god who resurrects himself pretty much at will. If our *true* solution was to assassinate him, he'd simply reform himself and eventually repeat this damnable conspiracy at some point in the future."

Ginny's frown deepened. "But—"

Before she could continue speaking, Alex interrupted her, "But nothing. We don't have much time. The members of Kappa Squad were not informed of our deeper plan. They truly believe that they are up there preparing to assassinate the god. But they are actually all about to be brutally murdered when the god warns his past-self and the alarm goes up. So, we must ensure their sacrifices aren't in vain by sneaking backstage and doing something much *subtler*: we must alter the math in the god's equation ever-so-slightly. We shall alter it so that his math succeeds in preventing new realities from branching off of existing ones—because if this is not the case, then there would be a reality out there where *we* fail, rendering our work moot—but then gets coded to immediately run an imperceptible counter-virus to cancel his equation's effects. And we must make this change so that he and all the gods gathered here *think* his plan succeeded completely and *believe* they've won."

Ginny frowned. "That doesn't make sense," she said.

Finally, Drillbot's processors seemed to click back into place. He found that he could control his fine motor skills and that he could speak once more. He responded, "[whir] Yes it – CLACK – Yes it does. It is perfectly – CLACK – perfectly logical."

"How so?" asked Ginny. "I'm trying to understand, but all this time travel stuff hurts my head."

Drillbot replied, "[whir] The Purple Shirt assassins are the lives that we are – CLACK – we are sacrificing to save the Space-Time-CLACK-Multinuum. First Officer Alexandros ho Megas could not reveal the – CLACK – reveal the *true* plan to us earlier because he and the B.T.S. Unicorn Husker crew engineered for Former-Master-Art to be possessed by God-Art, and First Officer Alexandros ho Megas needed to create a – CLACK – create a convincing charade to fool the mischief god into believing his past-self's plan works so that – CLACK – so that the god would believe he bested the – CLACK – the B.T.T. and thus never attempt to – CLACK – to replicate it. Drillbot would wager that only the Captain, First Officer Alexandros ho Megas, Bagoo, Older-Art, and 29333 knew the – CLACK – knew the true plan. And now, because God-Art thoroughly believes that we are here to assassinate his past-self, neither of them will be watching for a flank attack on his – CLACK – on his math."

Alex nodded. "You know, for a robot, you're pretty intuitive."

"[whir] And for a – CLACK – for a fleshy bag of meat, you are pretty – CLACK – pretty intellig—" Drillbot began to reply before realizing that he was speaking to nobody, because Alex had already spun on his heel and sprinted down the hall. The remainder of the Landing Crew had followed close behind him.

Drillbot sighed.

CHAPTER 17

THE CUTEST LITTLE CANNON FODDER

AGENT 27142 STEPPED off the ship with God-Art. As soon as they were off, God-Art raised his hands above his head and began making noises that sounded like ululating moans. The ground began vibrating, and then vines sprouted from it. The vines grew rapidly, twisting high into the air and then stretching themselves over the ship, covering it in a thin layer of curled greenery.

"What are you doing?" asked Agent 27142.

God-Art smiled. He answered, "Cloaking our ship. It will register to anyone searching for it as a patch of thick grass."

"How?"

"Magic, obviously."

Agent 27142 sighed. "I hate magic," he said.

God-Art shrugged and then stalked over to a set of bones. They poked out from underneath a gigantic boulder that lay in the clearing.

"One of yours?" asked the god.

Agent 27142 stared at the heap of weathered carcass, which included a crushed skull and four horse-legs, the bottoms of which were stuck beneath the gigantic gray boulder. A B.I.T. badge lay nestled amongst the bones like a golden necklace embedded in a rat's nest. Agent 27142 picked it up and stared at it. He said, "Affirmative. Member of Squadron Ampersand. Crushed to death by a Cyclops following our raid on the B.T.T. headquarters."

God-Art nodded. Then he cupped a hand in front of his mouth and whispered something into it. The words transformed into a powder that fell from his mouth and into his hand. He smirked and flung the powder at the boulder that lay atop the bones. The powder hit the boulder and then spread across it. The boulder began shaking. It transformed into thousands of butterflies that rose up into the air in a great swarm.

Agent 27142 nodded as five more carcasses were revealed beneath the boulder. He recalled watching these six soldiers being crushed as he was tossed into the maw of a Cyclops, and he shuddered.

God-Art twisted a dial on the silver eight-shaped device. Then he aimed it at the first pile of bones, the one that included the horse-legs. God-Art squeezed the trigger.

A green blast of conical light burst from the silver object's end and enveloped the broken bones. They began to glow. Then time within the green light reversed. Color came back to the bones. Then the gradual decay of muscle and organs began reversing, reattaching to the bones in a matter of seconds. Finally, skin and hair reformed, followed lastly by the dead agent's uniform.

A puzzled B.I.T. agent now stood where only bones had been seconds before. It was a centaur named Agent 4040404—referred to affectionately by his fellow troops as Not-Found. He had hollow cheeks and a long face. A ponytail of black hair stretched from the back of his head to his waist, where his human torso ended. His lower half was a horse with chestnut fur and a tail so long that it dangled from his rear end to flutter upon the ground. Agent 4040404 roared in confusion and reared up on his hind legs.

Agent 27142 grabbed God-Art by the hem of his cloak and demanded, "What the hell are you doing?"

God-Art shrugged. "What does it look like I'm doing?" he asked.

"It *looks* like you're bringing my dead soldier back to life."

"You *are* a perceptive one."

Agent 27142 sighed. He replied, "Why? We are in a hurry, and these soldiers were not chosen to accompany me here because of their intelligence or initiative. I chose them because they followed orders without questioning me. They were disposable lackies—trustworthy and loyal lackies, but lackies nonetheless."

Agent 27142 did not deign to glance at Agent 4040404, for he did not care if his assessment of the agent affected the agent's emotions.

God-Art smirked. He gestured with the small device in his hand and said, "Then the *why* should be pretty obvious. We're about to embark on a dangerous journey, and I would rather send disposable lackies into danger ahead of me, since dying and resurrecting myself is not always fun. And I'm sure you would prefer to do the same, since you do not have the ability to resurrect yourself."

Agent 27142 strummed his chin for a moment as he thought. Then he nodded. He said, "Understood, and I cannot dispute the strategy. Carry on."

God-Art nodded back. "Glad we can agree on something."

God-Art turned and began walking to the next pile of lifeless bones that had been revealed beneath the gigantic boulder. Before the god made it more than a step, Agent 27142 grabbed the back of his cloak.

"Wait a second," demanded Agent 27142. "Something's bothering me. The B.T.T. is an invisible organization. Anything about them is classified in my agency, and you must reach a relatively high status to even gain knowledge of their existence. When did *you* encounter B.T.T. agents, and how did you live to tell the tale?"

God-Art shrugged. "Long time ago. When I hosted the Montenegro Bay Convention on Earth 8,669. The B.T.T. tried to stop me, and they failed."

Agent 27142 let out a low whistle. "*The Conspiracy of the Gods*?" he asked. "That was *you*?"

God-Art nodded. "Guilty."

Agent 27142 scowled. He proclaimed, "Then you realize that once we have successfully achieved our mutual goals, I will need to detain you for this crime."

God-Art smirked. "You're welcome to try," he said, moving into position to continue resurrecting dead soldiers.

The centaur roared once more and stomped his hooves on the ground. Dust kicked up below him. "Where am I?" he asked.

"OK, you've got my attention," muttered Agent 27142. He walked over to the centaur and placed a palm on the creature's flank. "Calm down, agent. Everything is OK."

Agent 4040404 screamed, "What is happening? I do not understand!"

Agent 27142 replied, "You were dead. We brought you back to life to help with a mission of dire importance."

"What? No!"

Agent 27142 frowned, making a mental note to punish Agent 4040404 later for insubordination. "What do you mean, '*No?*'" he demanded.

The centaur replied, "I was at peace, sir. I was a stud in my people's heaven. I mated with cosmic foals to create centaur-angels—sometimes hundreds a day. And you ripped me away from that, sir!"

Agent 27142's frown deepened. "Then this is unfortunate for you," he said. "But you made a vow to the B.I.T., and your services are still needed."

Agent 4040404 frowned. He squealed, "But I died doing my duty. I'm supposed to be free."

"Nothing in the vow you took mentions *freedom* upon death," replied Agent 27142.

The centaur's shoulders sank, and tears streamed from his eyes. "But I was finally happy, sir."

Agent 27142 shrugged. "Your happiness is not my concern," he said. "We have a mission. If you perform your duties admirably, then when we are finished, I may be convinced to allow you to commit honorable suicide to return to your centaur-heaven."

The centaur's shoulders slumped even further. "It doesn't work like that. I have to die bravely in battle."

Agent 27142 shrugged once more. He responded, "Then there's nothing I can do, except promise you that you *will* see battle again. Hopefully, you shall die taking many of the enemy with you."

Agent 4040404 frowned and nodded. "Fine," he muttered. "Since I've no other option."

Agent 27142 glanced away from the centaur to find that God-Art had already reversed time on the other five corpses that had been trapped under the boulder. The god had somehow also known that three more soldiers had been crushed to death under a separate boulder near the entrance to the cave that housed the Moirai. The god had already removed this boulder and had resurrected the three corpses beneath it. The god smirked at Agent 27142 before disappearing into the cave.

Agent 27142 cursed. The resurrected soldiers stood in states of confusion and anger and glee, some having been returned from oblivion, some from heavens, and some from hells, each depending on his/her/its own home culture's interpretation of the afterlife. Agent 27142 stalked as quickly as he could over to his resurrected soldiers. He walked amongst them, reassuring those that needed reassurance, threatening those that needed threatening, and coaxing those that needed coaxing. Soon, he had the revived soldiers following him through the cave after God-Art, welcoming back more dead comrades each time the god resurrected them.

*

"Had three more soldiers that disappeared into these surrounding caves," said Agent 27142. "Was pretty obvious at the time that something in there ate them. I'd recommend that we leave them dead."

"You got that right, mate," replied God-Art. "We'd have to sift through entirely too much mythological fecal matter to find them. And since we're just going to use them as disposable lackies, anyway, I'd say they're shit out of luck."

Agent 27142 followed God-Art out of the cave with a reformed Squadron Ampersand at nearly full strength—sixteen in all. Aside from the three soldiers who had been eaten in the cave's tunnels during the search for the Moirai and the one soldier who had defected from the B.I.T. and run away to retrieve Cyclopic reinforcements at the Muse's behest, God-Art had resurrected all of them in a matter of minutes.

God-Art then led the group out of this cave and into the cave on the other side of the clearing—the one in which the secret entrance into the B.T.T.'s compound was located.

On the way to the back of the cave, the god used the *Timeflow Gun* to resurrect the ten Squadron Umbrella soldiers who had been killed by the Anachro-Mine. Upon reaching the back of the cave, the group stood once more before the entrance to the B.T.T. compound.

God-Art put his ear to the wall, listened for a moment, and then turned to Agent 27142. The god said, "I hear B.T.T. agents in there. Lots of them."

Agent 27142 frowned and replied, "Then we don't open the door. Squadron Twelve and the remainder of Squadron Umbrella will just need to remain dead."

God-Art guffawed. He proclaimed, "Please. I told you: I can handle the B.T.T. Give me a moment to prepare, and on my mark, open the door as quietly as you can."

Agent 27142 shrugged. God-Art sat on the ground and began whistling onto the dirt. It rose into a miniature tornado that floated in front of him. He then dug his arm into the pouch that hung from his belt. He retrieved a ball of snow as large as a mammoth. A freezing wind crept across the cave. The god tossed the snowball into the miniature tornado, and even though the snowball was much larger than the tornado, it disappeared inside. The tornado's color transformed from dusty brown to dazzling white.

"Now," said God-Art.

Agent 27142 input the combination and opened the entrance as silently as he could. Once open, he spotted dozens and dozens of purple-shirted B.T.T. agents carrying fire-retardant equipment. They were spraying the room to put out the flames that God-Art had earlier left burning in the room. Dozens upon dozens more were trudging through the room, scanning the scene with handheld equipment that appeared to be some sort of DNA detector with screens that featured chronal and geolocation information. The two agents nearest the entrance were currently using their devices to scan a footprint that God-Art had scorched into the floor of the warehouse.

Before any of the B.T.T. agents even realized anything was amiss, God-Art blew upon his tornado. It erupted into the warehouse and bounced from one agent's head to the next, encircling each head just briefly enough to apply a thin mask of snow to each agent's face. Screams resounded from each agent for a few seconds before they each collapsed into deep, pained slumbers.

"What the hell did you just do?" asked Agent 27142.

God-Art replied, "On my home-reality, I was given the duty to bring sleep to my pantheon's subjects. I did so by using snow from atop my mountain fortress. It overwhelms your pain receptors until you pass out. I keep tons of it in my pouch for cases such as this."

The god did not wait for a reply from Agent 27142. Instead, he sprinted into the warehouse and used the *Timeflow Gun* to resurrect the ten dead members of Squadron Umbrella and the thirteen dead members of Squadron Twelve that had been killed a decade ago by the Treendians. The group exited the warehouse through the secret door in the wall, and Agent 27142 shut it behind them.

As the group walked back toward the entrance of the cave, God-Art noticed something. His heels skidded to a halt on the dirt floor of the cave. Agent 27142 stopped, too, expecting that some new threat had just been exposed.

Instead, Agent 27142 watched as God-Art crouched next to a set of fossilized bones embedded in the wall. The last few times that Agent 27142 had been in this cave, he had been so focused on his mission that he never noticed fossils entrenched in the cracked cave walls.

As Agent 27142 stared at the bones of the creature, blue letters appeared in his goggles and informed him: *BeavBok, sentient creature native to Earth 798,098. Resembles a combination of a beaver cub and a baby chicken, but it has the intelligence of a humanoid. Would advise against eating, since its meat is high in copper and there are myths warning that the creature's spirit will latch onto your soul and slowly devour your sanity if consumed.*

"Looks like it must have died long, long ago," said God-Art. "I'm going to see if this gun will reverse a death this old."

Agent 27142 shrugged. He readied his Scatter Gun pistol to defend himself just in case this idea went awry. He said to God-Art, "The goggles say the creature's race was sentient. I'm aligned. Give it a shot."

God-Art aimed the business end of the *Timeflow Gun* at the bones and squeezed the trigger. The green light enveloped the bones, and a few dozen seconds later, a three-foot tall beaver with a chicken beak instead of a snout stood before God-Art and Agent 27142. The beaver was male, had black fur, two humongous teeth drooping from the tip of his beak, and a gigantic, flat tail. He wore a puffy blue parka and held a spear twice as long as he was tall.

God-Art stared at the creature for a moment, and then he began laughing.

"What's so funny?" asked Agent 27142.

God-Art shrugged. He replied, "I kind of expected something like this to happen right about now. Within the thematic construction of this adventure, this is the point in a trilogy where a creator would introduce an incredibly cute—albeit deadly—creature in order to sell toys."

Agent 27142's face was a mask of blankness. "I don't understand," he said.

God-Art shrugged again. "I wouldn't expect you to," he replied.

The creature noticed God-Art and Agent 27142 and interrupted them by falling to his knees. He bowed to them and cried, "My saviors! It was prophesied that a pair of twins would one day save the BeavBoks!"

"Who—or what—are the BeavBoks?" asked God-Art.

The creature raised a fist into the air and began to speak, but Agent 27142 cut in before the little creature had the chance to reply, saying, "If you'd have used the goggles that I offered you, then you'd already know."

God-Art swiveled his head toward Agent 27142 without moving his body, creating a ghastly scene where his head faced backward while his body continued facing the creature. The god scowled as he said, "I'd rather have it from the creature's lips. Those B.I.T. contraptions don't often tell *both* sides of the story."

The god spun his head back around to face the fuzzy little creature and said, "Go on, little one. You were just about to tell us about the BeavBoks."

The little creature grinned, flashing his tiny, jagged back teeth. He said, "Yes, yes, yes. Me and a few of my kin were brought to this Earth by the B.T.T. But soon after we arrived, the B.T.T. genocided our people, wiping from existence all who remained on our home reality. Me and my kin were supposed to be ambassadors to the B.T.T., but after our peoples were murdered, we were instead kept as artifacts in a B.T.T. zoo. Me and my kin were kept alive because our images sold merchandise to the B.T.T. children. One of my kin was a prophet, and after he received a message from the gods, he proclaimed a powerful prophecy about a pair of twins who would save my peoples. My kin believed the prophecy would come true in a matter of days. I disagreed. I escaped and found this cave to await our saviors. I hid here until I-I-I..."

"Until you died," finished God-Art for him, since it became clear that the BeavBok had just realized that he had died.

"Wait, if I'm dead, then how am I here right now?" he asked.

God-Art smiled. Mischief glimmered behind his eyes. "*I* brought you back," he answered. "We're going to fight the B.T.T. Want to join us?"

The little BeavBok squealed in delight. He danced in small looping circles while twisting his hips as though he was spinning a hula hoop around his waist. "Of course! Of course! You've got Tick-Tick's spear for your cause!"

Agent 27142 smiled. "We welcome you to our service," he said.

God-Art looked over at Agent 27142 and said, "I think we have revived all your soldiers that are easily revivable. We should leave before the B.T.T. manages to pierce the glamour that I put over our ship."

Agent 27142 nodded. "Then let's go."

Agent 27142 felt a tug at the hem of his pants. He glanced down to see the little beaver-creature yanking on his pant leg. Agent 27142 scowled. He did not like being touched by people below his station. The only exception he would happily make would be for Agent 29333. "What?" he spat.

Tick-Tick did not seem to notice the scorn. He replied, "Well, sirs, I'm sure that the people on my home Earth would like to join you in your fight against the B.T.T., if you have the time to resurrect them."

Agent 27142 and God-Art looked at each other. A hungry look flashed between them. They both silently and simultaneously mouthed to each other, *We need all the disposable lackies we can get!*

Agent 27142 patted Tick-Tick on the head and said, "We would *love* for your people to fight with us."

Agent 27142 and God-Art all but sprinted back to the ship in excitement. The resurrected soldiers—twenty members of Squadron Umbrella, thirteen members of Squadron Twelve, and sixteen members of Squadron Ampersand—and the lone BeavBok ran to try and keep up. God-Art waved his hands at the greenery camouflaging the ship. It melted away. Everyone scrambled aboard the ship.

God-Art, Agent 27142, and Tick-Tick made their way to the bridge. Tick-Tick muttered his Earth number to the pair. Agent 27142 lifted the ship off the ground and engaged the jump drive. The ship vibrated and jerked forward. Cosmic spots filled the view screen. A green arc of light burst from the nose of the ship and sliced a hole in the sky. The ship entered the barrier between realities.

Neither of the Arts had warned Tick-Tick to take a seat and fasten his safety belt. As the ship jerked forward, the momentum knocked Tick-Tick backward. He fell down the ladder at the back of the bridge and down into the hold with the soldiers.

God-Art laughed. Things were starting to look so good for the pair that Agent 27142 could not refrain from laughing, too.

CHAPTER 18

FOILED

"HALT! WHO GOES there?" demanded a behemoth of a man with thick blond hair, ruddy cheeks, and crooked, yellow teeth.

The man's voice held such weight behind it that Normal-Art felt every bone in his body vibrate. He already needed to urinate, and the vibrations made the sensation grow exponentially worse. He nearly moaned, but a well-timed elbow in his stomach from Ginny knocked the wind from him and stifled any moaning. The Purple Shirts behind him grabbed him by the shoulders and prevented him from toppling over in pain.

The man stood at the end of the hallway, guarding the door that allowed access into the backstage area of the convention. Normal-Art cleverly deduced this fact because of the sign above the man's right shoulder that read, *Backstage Area: Production Crew and Pleasure Deities Only.*

Alex nodded to Bagoo. Bagoo bent his head low, and as he raised his head back up, his ghostly, translucent shape shifted, taking on the form of a beautifully ethereal woman. He floated toward the massive guard.

"May we pass?" asked Bagoo in his best imitation of a female voice. "We are pleasure deities from a pleasure Earth, and we have must *thank* Artheoskatergariabetrugereiinganno for the boon that his plan has bestowed upon our pantheon."

The behemoth arched an eyebrow. "So, you're here for the networking orgy, too, eh?"

Bagoo nodded.

The behemoth frowned and said, "Being the patron god of guarding things is the worst gig in all of godhood. I *never* get to participate in the fun stuff. Go on in. Follow the signs, you can't miss it."

Then he grabbed Bagoo by the upper arm. His frown deepened. He muttered, "Just, y'know, maybe send somebody out for ol' Heimdallr at some point."

"I'll see what I can do," replied Bagoo. He swept past the guard and waved for the Landing Crew to follow him. Alex nodded, and the Landing Crew marched forward, having hung back toward the end of the hall in case anything went wrong with Bagoo's charade.

The group entered the backstage area and descended a flight of stairs. They entered a long corridor. Every few feet hung a piece of poster board with the message "*Networking Orgy This Way*" written in bold calligraphy. Below the words lay an equally bold arrow and pictures of humanoids engaging in acts of utter depravity.

"Sir," called a Purple Shirt with a smirk as he stared at one of the signs, "if you need any of us to infiltrate the networking orgy, I'll volunteer myself as tribute."

Normal-Art began to chuckle, but he stopped short when he realized nobody else was amused. Alex scowled. He replied, "Son, if I wanted you to try and amuse me, I would have informed you in your briefing dossier. Keep your mouth shut unless you have something to say that's pertinent to the mission."

Normal-Art shrugged his shoulders and patted the kid on the shoulder. He whispered, "Don't mind him. He has no sense of humor. *I* thought it was funny."

The group continued walking. Soon, they passed the open doorway marked for the orgy. The moans emanating from within were staggering. Normal-Art was nearly knocked off his feet, so he stopped for a few moments to gawk at the carnal acts. He noticed that between moans, the gods screamed out their own names and occupations within their pantheons. He realized this because they were all wearing name tags while copulating. He shrugged. Gods were weird.

The group walked on for another few minutes before intersecting with a hallway to their right. It ended in darkness. However, the darkness was interrupted when a flickering light appeared in the distance.

Alex sighed. He pointed at Normal-Art and said, "And that will be the god-version of you. He will have just divulged our assassination plot to his past-self and will now be on his way to the networking orgy."

Alex turned to two of the Purple Shirts, one of them the guy who had volunteered to join the networking orgy. "Distract the god," ordered Alex. "We need a few more minutes to complete our mission. So, stay alive for at least a few more minutes to buy us some time."

The pair drew their Time-Phasers and twisted a knob on them. They gulped, nodded at the group, and sprinted away to confront God-Art. Before the remainder of Landing Crew could sneak away to complete the mission, the pair promptly disobeyed Alex. Fire erupted at the end of the hallway and engulfed the duo, killing them before they even had time to scream. Normal-Art shrugged. *Better them than me*, he thought.

"Dammit," muttered Alex. "I ordered them to buy us some time, not to die immediately!"

The fiery flicker moved toward the group from the darkness. The god attached to it giggled. "Oh, B.T.T., I am impressed with how quickly you managed to escape the arena and how tenacious you are to enter these backstage catacombs in search of past-me. The fact that you are so willing to throw away your lives to ensure my past-self's assassination is flattering, especially when you *could* have escaped to live another day—unlike those of you who were caught in the arena. Having lived through this experience in my younger days, I can assure you that my past-self is now hiding somewhere you shall *never* find him. And considering that I don't recall interacting with you lot at *his* point in my history, I'd say that means you die before making it to your target. Congratulations on dying in vain."

"Nooooooooooo! We failed!" screamed Alex. "We were the best hope for the Space-Time-Multinuum!"

Normal-Art nodded, impressed by Alex's acting ability. He resisted the urge to clap at the performance.

"But this current interaction between us has left me puzzled," continued God-Art, completely ignoring Alex other than to point at the man. "Why would you send a mere pair of pups down this hallway to kill me after you wasted an entire squadron in the arena trying to assassinate past-me? I am deserving of at least a squadron myself. And you, one of the greatest strategists in the history of Earth 6,076, *must* have known that."

The god continued approaching. Normal-Art could see his face now. It looked like the god was silently working through some complicated equation in his head. Something seemed to click in place, and the god grinned. He remarked, "Oh, because you just wanted to slow me down. You did not actually *want* them to stop me. And why not, I must ask?

The god strummed his fingers across his chin and continued, "Hmmm.

I thwarted your snipers in the arena while *you* ran. And now I'm back here after having reported to my past-self every facet of your mission, which you *voluntarily* divulged to me when I was in my slothful alternate-dimension-self's body. I'm starting to think that you knew I was inside him and that you *wanted* me to escape, to find my past-self, and to tell him everything I know about your plot. And then you *wanted* to make it seem like you were still giving an effort by sending those pups to attack me. That meager assault was obviously a distraction, but a distraction for what purpose? What would *you* be searching for back here? Oh, wheels within wheels."

The god grinned. Then he answered his own question, "Oh, I get it. I know exactly what you were trying to do. Clever. And you would have gotten away with it, if only you had sent more of your whelps down this hallway to meet their doom."

Alex glanced over at the Landing Crew. Normal-Art thought he recognized panic in the officer's eyes. Art knew that someone needed to act—and fast—or the B.T.T. would never complete its mission, and he would never get to go home. So, he shrugged and decided that the actor may as well be himself.

Normal-Art turned to the Purple Shirts behind him and improvised. He grabbed the nearest one and began slapping the agent over and over and over. He squealed, "You cowards! We could have killed this bastard-version of me! We could have completed our mission and I could have finally been sent home! But *noooooo*, you were too frightened to attack him when ordered! Instead, you let your two friends—one of them funnier than you could *ever* hope to be—rush to their deaths, all alone!"

Normal-Art shoved the kid onto the ground. Then he turned back toward God-Art. God-Art's grin was gone. Normal-Art could only hope his display had been enough to throw doubt on the god's deduction.

But alas, the god shook his head. He said, "Art, you are a terrible acto—"

God-Art never finished the sentence. Instead, Normal-Art snatched a device that was definitely *not* a Time-Phaser—though Art was too inobservant to notice the difference—from inside the toga of the Purple Shirt whom he had been slapping. He aimed it at God-Art's chest and pulled the trigger. Dozens of magenta spheres flashed from the barrel and crashed into God-Art. They melted into the god's torso.

"Hey! A direct hit!" exclaimed Normal-Art, beaming with pride.

The god frowned. He said, "You absolute fool! All you accomplished was sending a tickle of indigestion through my tummy. But now I'm angrier than ever, and instead of simply murdering you, I am going to flay you alive and sew your skin onto my cloa—"

But then the god's threat was interrupted when he exploded into billions of tiny dots that flashed magenta before disappearing.

Alex turned to Normal-Art and demanded, "What the hell did you just do?"

"Well, it was obvious that he was onto us," replied Normal-Art. "So, I took initiative. You weren't doing so, so somebody had to."

"What the hell did you just *do?*" repeated Alex.

"I-I shot the god-version of me with one of your agency's stupid guns that devolve things. And I stopped him. And now we can complete our mission uninterrupted. And to be honest, we should have done that in the first place when he appeared out of my neck."

"That's not a Time-Phaser, you fool. If you'd have read your briefing dossier, you would have known!"

"Huh?"

Alex pointed at the Purple Shirts surrounding Normal-Art. He said, "This squadron of Purple Shirts has three engineers attached to it. And engineers *do not* carry Time-Phasers. They carry a modified version of B.I.T. weaponry that spreads molecules across the Space-Time-Multinuum, which they normally use when they need to clear out a lot of mass really quickly without sending the entire mass to a single different place in time. It's called a *Chronal-Dispersion-Shotgun*, and they do *not* use such a tool on a god who specializes in resurrection!"

Normal-Art glanced down at the gun. Now that he studied it a bit more, he realized it was shaped much differently than the Time-Phasers. It looked like a numeral two with a thin barrel poking out of the base. When looking at the knobs, there were settings for *Past, Present, Future,* and *All-Molecule Dispersion,* whereas Time-Phasers had knobs that determined the timing of its effects and whether something needed to be devolved or evolved or frozen in time.

"What setting is that gun on?" demanded Alex.

"Looks like it's set to *All-Molecule Dispersion*," replied Normal-Art.

Alex sighed a furious sigh. "Do you realize that you just sent the god's molecules careening across the past, present, *and* future?"

Normal-Art responded, "And in doing so, I got him out of our way. Now let's finish our mission so that I can be sent home to my couch."

Bagoo screamed in rage, "You fool! Don't you understand how what you did could be a bad thing to do to a god of resurrection?"

Normal-Art took a moment to think, and then he said, "No, not really."

Older-Art slapped him upside the back of his head. He said, "His molecules sent to the past can reform in the past and then warn his current-self that our *actual* plan is deeper than a mere foiled assassination attempt."

Bagoo also slapped Normal-Art upside the back of the head and screamed, "Exactly! We are good and truly screwed."

Older-Art smirked. He said, "God-Me once told me about something called a *deus ex machina*—something unexpected that comes out of nowhere to save the hero of a story. What would you call something that comes out of nowhere to completely screw the heroes? *Deus sex machina?* If so, I feel like that's what we've just experienced."

Alex strode forward. He slapped both Older-and Normal-Art across the face. He ordered, "Be quiet so the real heroes can hear themselves think."

CHAPTER 19

GATHERING FURRY RECRUITS

AGENT 27142 STEERED the ship toward the surface of Earth 798,098. Blocky brick factory buildings with dozens of gigantic chimneys seemed to cover every square inch of the ground, stretching into the distance and past the horizon. "*Horizon*" was a generous term, since thick clouds of black smog billowed from the chimneys with such ferocity that visibility was difficult more than a few hundred feet ahead.

Tick-Tick leaned over Agent 27142's shoulder and stared out the view screen. The creature gasped and then let out a moaning wail. He cried, "What happened to my home?"

Agent 27142 sighed. The bridge had been much more serene when the BeavBok had fallen below decks. Agent 27142 asked, "What do you mean?"

Tick-Tick's voice grew faster and higher-pitched as he replied, "It was forests and streams and wildlife. This is wrong. All wrong."

God-Art shrugged. He said, "Well, look on the bright side. With all this smog, I bet the sunsets now are more beautiful than ever."

Tick-Tick cried.

A voice over the ship's intercom interrupted Tick-Tick's cries, "Incoming Infinity Transport Ship, identify yourself and state your business here."

Agent 27142 glanced over at God-Art. "What do we say?" he asked the god.

The god smirked. "You are in luck," he replied. "You are in the presence of the best mischief god in the history of the Multiverse. Let me handle this."

The god leaned down, pressed the intercom button, and exclaimed, "This is Infinity Transport Ship callsign 8888888888888888888888, and we are here to inspect factory number sixteen for possible chronal incursions from a space-time-rat infestation."

The god released the button. The voice over the intercom immediately replied, "That was complete gibberish. HQ sent word of a stolen Infinity Transport Ship with your exact energy signature. Prepare to be boarded."

Agent 27142 looked over to God-Art and muttered, "Wow. I am *very* impressed with your mischief. Far and away the best in the whole Multiverse. *Now* what do we do?"

The tops of two nearby factory buildings retracted. Dozens of ships shaped like the numeral four launched into the sky. They began to open fire with bolts of purple energy. Agent 27142 jerked the stick and jammed the throttle, initiating evasive action. Tick-Tick said something, but Agent 27142 ignored the creature and concentrated on dodging the incoming barrage from the hostile ships.

The ship shook as a purple laser bolt crashed against its side, a direct hit from one of the incoming hostile ships. Purple crackling tendrils swept across the view screen. "OK, I was being sarcastic before, but I could seriously use your help here. *Now* what do we do?" demanded Agent 27142.

God-Art shrugged. "I suggest we listen to our new friend," he replied, pointing at the BeavBok.

Tick-Tick screamed, "Forget *resurrecting* my people! Use this ship to go back in time! Let's gather them *before* they're genocided!"

Agent 27142 called over his shoulder, "Fine! When were you taken from this planet?"

Tick-Tick screamed the answer. Agent 27142's fingers danced across the console, typing in the chronal destination. Then he engaged the time jump. The ship vibrated and jerked. Cosmic spots appeared in the view screen. A green arc of light burst from the nose of the ship and sliced a hole in the sky. The hole immediately began shrinking, and the ship surged through it before it closed.

Tick-Tick apparently had not learned his lesson from the last jump. He had neither taken a seat nor buckled himself in, so he tumbled backward and fell down the ladder to the area below decks where the resurrected soldiers were seated.

Agent 27142 heard Henry's laughter emanating from the seat behind God-Art, where the gourd and Beverly were harnessed safely. "Did the creature fall again?" asked Henry. "Oh, I do love slapstick comedy!"

God-Art smirked. "But why?" he asked. "You don't have eyes to see it."

Henry's laugh merely grew louder. Agent 27142 and God-Art joined in. Then Agent 27142 realized how cartoonish and ridiculous they all must have seemed with their choral laughing, so he stopped. The others realized it, too, and awkward silence soon filled the bridge.

Then the ship arrived at the intended date in the past and reappeared above Earth 798,098.

*

Agent 27142 steered the ship toward the surface of Earth 798,098. Lively forests of pines and elms and sequoias with gigantic branches seemed to cover every square inch of the ground, stretching into the distance and past the horizon. "*Horizon*" was a generous term, since thick flocks of black birds billowed from the tree branches with such ferocity that visibility was difficult more than a few hundred feet ahead.

Tick-Tick leaned over Agent 27142's shoulder and pointed toward a sunny spot in a clearing near the confluence of two streams. "Put 'er down over there," said the BeavBok.

Agent 27142 nodded and landed the ship in the soft, dark mud. As soon as he finished powering down the ship, Agent 27142 unstrapped himself and Henry, placed the gourd in the empty gun holster on his belt, descended the ladder into the ship proper, and followed a hallway to the aft of the ship. He pressed a button on the back wall, and it fell backward, tumbling to the ground to form a ramp. Agent 27142 descended to the bottom of the ramp.

Hot air and humidity crashed across his face. Sweat formed on his brow. The darkness and shadows of the forest seemed to loom over him on all sides like a pack of predators. He smiled. Showing a predator any sort of trepidation was an easy invitation for attack.

Lying scattered amongst the underbrush and between living trees were dozens and dozens of felled sequoia trunks with radii easily thrice the length of the ship that Agent 27142 had just exited. Their ends were conical and showed signs of tooth marks.

Hundreds of pairs of golden eyes appeared amongst the darkness of the forest. As the owners of these eyes stepped forward into the meager light of the clearing, Agent 27142 noticed they were all attached to BeavBoks. Many wore brown and green hooded cloaks while many more wore holsters made of woven fur in which metal objects with ominous red buttons gleamed. Each carried a spear or a bow and arrow. All weapons were trained on Agent 27142.

God-Art and Tick-Tick descended the ramp and caught up to Agent 27142.

"Brothers! Sisters! Elders! Younglings!" screamed Tick-Tick. "After all these years, I am returned. How I have missed you!"

Agent 27142 did not understand how to read BeavBok facial expressions, but he was rather certain that the looks the creatures were sending Tick-Tick's way were quizzical at best, utterly confused at worst.

After a long moment of silence, one of the BeavBoks stepped forward. This one had black fur streaked with gray and a wooden stump in place of its right leg. It wore a golden shawl wrapped around the top of its head, and stitched into the front of the shawl was a bright crimson letter *C*.

"Captain Hump-Hump!" cried Tick-Tick. "How I have missed your sage advice."

Hump-Hump frowned. He said, "Cousin Tick-Tick, you left with the B.T.T. agents but a few seconds ago. Why are you back?"

Hump-Hump then gestured toward Agent 27142, God-Art, and the B.I.T. soldiers who had now descended the ramp. He continued, "And who are these strangers?"

Tick-Tick slapped his own forehead, realizing his conundrum. Tick-Tick replied, "Don't worry about them. I need to see President Clearland at once. I am here to prevent the most terrible catastrophe you could possibly imagine."

Hump-Hump hobbled toward Tick-Tick and raised his bow and arrow so that the arrow was aimed squarely at Tick-Tick's forehead. Hump-Hump said, "The creatures wearing the purple shirts warned President Clearland not to allow that to happen. They said that we must detain anyone who arrives to warn us of impending doom."

"But *they* are the ones who are going to cause the catastrophe! Of course, that's what they'd say!" screamed Tick-Tick.

Hump-Hump furrowed his brow. The point of his arrow drooped ever so slightly toward the ground. "Explain yourself," he commanded.

"I've come from the future! Our people get genocided because of the B.T.T.!" screamed Tick-Tick. He gestured toward Agent 27142 and God-Art. "These two were also harmed by the B.T.T., and they are here to help us. Please take me to President Clearland and let me explain. Our people's existence is at stake!"

Hump-Hump's frown deepened. "I wish I could," he replied. "But I have orders."

Hump-Hump turned to his soldiers and said, "Do not kill my cousin. He is to be detained. Eliminate the rest."

Before a single arrow could be launched from a single bow, Tick-Tick screamed, "Wait! I declare a Stump-Stump!"

Hump-Hump scowled and motioned for the surrounding soldiers to lower their weapons. He said, "Your declaration is acknowledged. It shall be your funeral."

*

The BeavBoks led Tick-Tick, Agent 27142, God-Art, and the dozens of B.I.T. soldiers along a well-trodden path through the dark forest that surrounded the ship's landing site. Eventually they emerged from the depths of the forest and approached a palace made from stacked elm logs. It was surrounded by a wooden palisade and a moat filled with murky brown water. A drawbridge spanned the moat, but it raised as the group drew near it.

A blue circle of paint lay on the ground outside the moat. Its diameter stretched nearly ten feet wide. Rotting BeavBok corpses lay piled within it. Two thin stumps stretched up from amidst of the corpses. The group stopped outside of the ring. Hump-Hump's soldiers fanned out to surround it. Hump-Hump turned to face Tick-Tick and said, "Pick your sapling."

Tick-Tick nodded. God-Art and Agent 27142 approached Tick-Tick. Agent 27142 asked, "What's happening?"

Tick-Tick replied in his squeaky voice, "I was forced to challenge my old captain to a duel in order to save your lives and to get our message delivered to my people's leader. I have thirty minutes to find a sapling, cut it down with my teeth, and fashion it into a weapon. Me and my old captain will then duel to the death from atop the stumps that stand inside that ring. The loser's servants must grant whatever request the winner makes."

"Well, that's awfully convenient for us," muttered God-Art.

And with that, Tick-Tick sprinted away into the forest to begin his preparations. Agent 27142 stared at God-Art. The god stared back. When neither of them broke the awkward silence, Henry chimed in, "So you're both just going to let this kindly creature die for you?"

God-Art shrugged and said, "He was probably going to die on our mission, anyway."

Henry made a dissatisfied hiss. "You are terrible," he replied.

Agent 27142 shrugged and said, "We didn't come here to make friends. We came here to find disposable lackies."

Henry replied, "Well, you had better hope he wins, because you're dead if he doesn't."

Agent 27142 sighed. "You think after all I've faced in my service to the B.I.T., *these* savages concern me? You are more foolish than you look."

Henry sighed back. "I refuse to accept that insult. I've been told by many fellow Jump Totems that I am quite a handsome gourd and that I do not look foolish at all."

Agent 27142 frowned. He thumped Henry with his palm. Henry squealed and stopped talking.

Tick-Tick soon returned, dragging a young tree behind him that had teeth marks scratched into its base, indicating the spot where Tick-Tick had chewed on it to cut it down. He dropped it near Agent 27142's feet. Tick-Tick then began biting into the sides of it and rolling it across his teeth like it was a giant serving of corn on the cob. After a few minutes, he had whittled the tree down to a thin spear approximately three feet long.

"I am ready," proclaimed Tick-Tick. Then he leapt from his spot outside the blue circle. He soared over the BeavBok corpses that were piled upon the ground inside the circle and landed atop one of the stumps sticking up from the ground. It was barely wide enough for him to balance on one foot.

About five minutes later, Hump-Hump appeared from the forest, brandishing a spear twice the length of Tick-Tick's. He mirrored Tick-Tick's entrance into the ring, leaping over the corpses and landing atop the second post.

Hump-Hump stood upon his good leg and bowed to Tick-Tick. He pointed to Tick-Tick's weapon and said, "That tiny spear is a joke. We have not yet begun the ceremony. You may still back out."

"This is too important. I cannot."

"You understand the rules?" asked Hump-Hump.

Tick-Tick nodded. "Fight to the death. If either of us touches the pile of holy corpses, he loses and will be executed."

Hump-Hump declared, "Then let us begin."

One of Hump-Hump's servants stepped forward and knocked a flint stone against the blue circle. After he whacked it a few times, sparks burst forth and set the blue circle aflame. Agent 27142 glanced over at God-Art. The god's eyes were gleaming as they stared at the flames, and a look of raw mischief enveloped his face.

Hump-Hump's spear tip darted forward, aimed at Tick-Tick's lower abdomen. Tick-Tick leapt straight up into the air and twirled in a circle. He knocked the spear aside with his tail and landed back atop the post on his opposite foot. Hump-Hump pulled back his spear, feinted a shot toward Tick-Tick's left shoulder, and then stabbed toward Tick-Tick's right.

This time, Tick-Tick did not leap *straight* up to dodge the spear. He instead leapt in an arc that took him over the spear tip and toward Hump-Hump. The older BeavBok reacted to Tick-Tick's maneuver too late to pull his spear back for a defensive parry.

"Clever boy," remarked Hump-Hump as Tick-Tick crashed into him. Tick-Tick stabbed his short spear into Hump-Hump's shoulder. The old captain's spear was too long to help him now that he and the younger BeavBok were so close.

However, Hump-Hump would not be bested so easily. He muttered, "But not clever enough." He shifted his position and used Tick-Tick's momentum against him, flipping Tick-Tick off him.

The younger BeavBok plummeted toward the heap of BeavBok corpses. At the last moment, he managed to extend a paw and grab the stump. He twisted his tail and his body so that he touched not a single corpse, and then he scrambled up the side of the thin stump.

Hump-Hump stared down at Tick-Tick. He tossed aside his own spear and pulled Tick-Tick's short spear from his shoulder. He held it over his head, ready to stab it directly into the younger BeavBok's neck.

"I am sorry, youngling. I wish it had not come to this," said Hump-Hump.

Agent 27142 felt a vibration tickling his feet. He glanced over at God-Art. The god's eyes were clouded blue, he was muttering something to himself, and he was wriggling his feet back and forth at supersonic speed. A wind picked up, blowing in from behind God-Art. The wind increased in intensity until it felt as near to gale force as Agent 27142 had ever experienced. And as it blew past the spectators surrounding the dueling circle, it fanned the flames that marked the circle's perimeter.

The flames danced, twirled, and then one of them leapt into the air. It smacked into Hump-Hump's fur before he could strike Tick-Tick. The flame spread to engulf Hump-Hump. He screamed and fell from the stump, landing atop the corpses and adding his own to their ranks.

Tick-Tick completed his climb back up atop the stump and held up his arms in a victory pose. God-Art ceased wriggling his feet and muttering to himself. As quickly as the winds had risen, they died away and the flames lost their gusto.

Hump-Hump's soldiers stepped forward and threw white powder onto a spot on the blue circle. It snuffed the fire there. Tick-Tick leapt over this safe portion, crashed to the ground, and lay there breathing heavily.

God-Art walked over to the creature and helped Tick-Tick to his feet. A small BeavBok with chestnut fur approached Tick-Tick and exclaimed, "The gods have smiled upon you this day. Hump-Hump should have finished you rather than talking. He left himself open to chance, and the gods made him pay dearly for it. What would you have of us, Hump-Hump's loyal servants?"

Tick-Tick smirked. "You already know. Stop being daft and take us to President Clearland."

*

The inside of the wooden palace was about what Agent 27142 had expected. Grand tapestries covered the walls, sawdust the floor. A great fire filled a pit in the center of the room, its smoke blackening the rafters high above. It was a mixture of extravagance and humility only seen in the housing of an individual ruling a relatively savage people, and Agent 27142 had seen thousands of such dwellings since he began his service to the

B.I.T.

To Agent 27142, President Clearland looked just like all the other BeavBoks, except he wore a bowler's hat on his head and a three-piece suit on his body and a monocle on the end of his beak. He stared at Agent 27142 and his companions with marked distrust.

"Tick-Tick," muttered President Clearland as one of the two young purple-shirted B.T.T. agents standing behind the president leaned down to whisper in his ear, "I can't say that I am happy to see you. These B.T.T. representatives tell me that your appearance signals genocide for our people. They tell me that if I rid myself of you and your companions, then I can save our people from such a horrible fate, and that I can also make us more prosperous than I could possibly imagine."

Tick-Tick frowned. He replied, "Sir, none of what they're telling you is true. I come with companions who helped me escape the B.T.T. home reality aboard one of the B.T.T.'s time-traveling ships. We have seen what happens to this planet. It is stripped of its natural resources and turned into an atrocious factory. I come to you from this future as the last survivor of our people. We must alter this terrible fate."

The female B.T.T. agent whispered into President Clearland's ear. President Clearland then said, "*She* tells me that if we render you aid, then we will simply be assuring the fate of which you speak." The president's accent made it so that Agent 27142 had to strain to understand him. It almost sounded like he was saying "Bok, bok, bok," over and over.

God-Art stepped forward and pointed toward the fire pit in the center of the room. He bellowed, "I will show you what happens to your planet if you refuse to heed Tick-Tick's warnings. Gaze into the flames."

"Who are y—" the president began to ask, but then his eyes locked onto the fire.

Agent 27142 looked over at the fire, too. The flames danced and grew and formed into a shape resembling a view screen. The image of this planet's future that Agent 27142 had seen from the view screen of the Infinity Ship appeared in the fire. Then the image shifted. It zoomed across the surface of the planet, and nowhere it passed was there a sign of a single BeavBok.

The image died away, and everyone in the room understood: Tick-Tick spoke the truth. There would be no BeavBoks here in the future. President

Clearland screamed in rage.

God-Art said to him, "The B.T.T. is playing you for a fool. What you saw shall be your fate if you do not join our cause."

The surrounding BeavBoks screamed their assent. The president turned to face the purple-shirted B.T.T. agents. The agents held up their hands in frightened supplication. They both screamed together, "Wait! You don't understand! That is what happens if you *do* join the—"

But it was too late for them. The surrounding soldiers pounced, rending the B.T.T. agents limb from limb. The president turned to a nearby soldier and ordered, "Send heralds into the Great Forest. Gather all our peoples. Every adult, every cub, every half-hatched egg shall join the fight to save us from genocide."

*

Over the next few days, the BeavBoks readied themselves to fight. To Agent 27142's surprise, the felled sequoias that he had seen lying scattered about the forest floor were actually the BeavBoks' means of space travel. These logs had been hollowed out in the middle and their interiors were carved so that there was a bridge, a massive cargo hold, troop transport, personal cabins, and a wooden engine system. BeavBok shamans were stationed at the engines that lay in the base of the tree trunks to imbue the logs that were used as fuel with the magic that allowed them to properly power the ships. All of it somehow worked together in a way that allowed the trees to fly and remain safe in the harsh environment of space. The excited Tick-Tick informed Agent 27142 in passing conversation that a mere six generations ago, BeavBoks had reached their moon and had planted their people's flag upon it. Now they could roam anywhere in their galaxy.

As the BeavBoks gathered in larger and larger numbers, they began tying the sequoia trunks together with billions of ropes. They also changed outfits from their primitive shawls and hooded cloaks to little space suits. If Agent 27142 had not been a jaded bastard, he probably would have commented about how incredibly cute they looked.

Each wore a wooden flight suit painted silver and covered in glowing magical runes. Atop their heads each donned a clear bubbled helmet. These were accompanied by a large wooden backpack, the bottom of which contained an exhaust port. Agent 27142 realized that these backpacks were actually wooden jetpacks when some of the younger BeavBoks began playing a game where they would all blast to the tops of surrounding trees and return with bird eggs, which they would promptly smash upon the head of the member of their party that was the slowest to return. Agent 27142 watched them play for a few minutes until an adult BeavBok showed up and began yelling at them for wasting time when there was so much work to be done. Agent 27142 shrugged and walked away.

Soon, President Clearland gave the order to depart. The entire population of BeavBoks disappeared into the forest, piling into the sequoia-spaceships. Agent 27142 returned to the B.T.T. ship with God-Art and Henry and Beverly and his resurrected B.I.T. troops. He powered up the ship and lifted it into the air.

Soon, hundreds of sequoia-spaceships mimicked this motion, each log floating in the air with ropes connecting its rear to the front of the next log nearest to it. The BeavBoks had also attached ropes that connected the back of Agent 27142's stolen ship to the front of the first in the line of sequoia-spaceships. This harness would allow the BeavBok trees to follow Agent 27142's Infinity Transport Ship as it jumped to its next destination.

According to Agent 27142's inquiries into the onboard computer, the portal that Agent 27142 created would not shut until they all made it through because they were all connected, and the portal would register them as one long ship. This had been an idea of God-Art's, and the annoying god had not shut up about how great an idea it was since he learned that it would work. Agent 27142 had lost track of the number of times he had sighed in response.

Agent 27142 smirked, set the destination and the time coordinates of the B.T.S. Unicorn Husker, and piloted his ship into hole the ship sliced in the sky. The BeavBok sequoia-spaceships followed.

CHAPTER 20

NOTHING BUT NOTHING NET

DRILLBOT WATCHED AS First Officer Alexandros ho Megas snatched the Chronal-Dispersion-Shotgun from Normal-Art's hands. Alex retrieved a device from his holster. It was a small screen with a dongle dangling from its end. Alex plugged the end of it into a receiver on the gun.

The screen sprang to life. Green numbers scrolled across it. They seemed to go on forever. Alex touched a button on the device's side and a keypad popped up. He typed in a command, and the font on certain numbers within the unending string changed from green to blue and others changed from green to orange.

Alex handed the Chronal-Dispersion-Shotgun and the device to Bagoo. "You ready?" he asked.

"I am ready," replied the bog ghost.

Alex frowned. He said, "The B.T.T. thanks you in advance for sacrificing this time from your life. I know it is an inconvenience, my friend, and I am sorry that you must endure it."

Bagoo nodded. He replied, "No need to apologize. You've done this task yourself in past loops. We both know it is a necessity."

Alex nodded, and then he pointed at Drillbot and six Purple Shirts. He said, "You all are going to jump with Bagoo from place to place and time to time in order to stop the god from reforming and making his way here to thwart our objective. The rest of us are going to continue our primary mission and hope for the sake of the Space-Time-Multinuum that you are successful."

Alex then pointed to the screen on the device that he had handed to Bagoo. Alex explained, "Just in case any harm befalls Bagoo and he can no longer continue with you, this is how this device works: the blue numbers are the locations and times in the past into which Arthur sent the god's molecules. The green is the future. The orange is the present."

Drillbot asked, "[whir] But how are we to – CLACK – to stop the god? If we kill him, he will just – CLACK – just reform, and then he will make his way here, anyway."

Alex removed another device from his holster. This one was a bundle of small metal sticks folded atop one another. Alex unfolded them, and when uncoiled, they formed a chrome rod about two feet long. He pressed a button on the rod's side, and a net made from green electricity appeared from the rod's end. In the net's center lay swirling, utter blackness.

"With this," answered Alex. He held the net above his head, and then he swiped it down over a young Purple Shirt standing near him. The Purple Shirt began to squeal. But instead, he disappeared. His squeal disappeared right along with him.

Before Drillbot could object to the apparent murder of the Purple Shirt or ask for clarification as to the device's functionality, Alex explained, "It's a Nothing Net. It's a link to a spot outside of space and time. It's like a temporary jail we can use for cosmic threats during emergencies until we can relocate them to a more permanent holding space. Just swipe it over your quarry, and he'll be pulled inside."

Alex pressed a button on the Nothing Net's side. The center of the net spit the young Purple Shirt back out. He crashed to the ground. He was still squealing the same squeal that he had been squealing when he was sucked into the Nothing Net. He realized everyone was staring at him, so he stopped squealing.

Alex pointed at the kid and said, "And much like this youngling, when they are removed from the prison, it will be like they *just* entered, because no time passes within it."

Another Purple Shirt helped the youth to his feet. After doing so, he and the other Purple Shirts pulled their own Nothing Nets from their holsters and powered them up. Alex handed his personal Nothing Net to Drillbot. Alex pressed a button on the device's side, and a loop formed from the bottom of the net's handle. The loop fit over Drillbot's drill, allowing him to wear the device like a bracelet. The handle stretched down the length of Drillbot's drill so that the net proper hung past the drill tip, allowing the robot to use the device.

Alex ordered, "Now get moving. Bagoo, you have command. Drillbot, you're his second."

Bagoo and Drillbot nodded. Bagoo tapped the first blue series of numbers scrolling across the screen. A magenta sphere of light launched from the end of the Chronal-Dispersion-Shotgun, creating a small gateway in the Space-Time-Multinuum. Bagoo gestured toward the gateway and said, "Drillbot, you're our heavy hitter on this excursion, so you go first. If there's anything big and bad on the other side, you distract it. Purple Shirts, you're after him. I'll go last and seal the gate behind us."

Drillbot nodded and leapt through the gateway without hesitation. His vision fluttered and scrambled for a moment. And then he was out the other side, landing in a black cave with a six-inch puddle of water pooled across the ground. As soon as he landed, a large tentacle crashed into him, knocking him prone. He sighed, stabbed the tentacle with one of his drills, and stood upon his wheels.

He wished that for once, something would just be easy.

*

Drillbot made quick work of the tentacle's owner by slicing the tentacle from its owner's body and then shoving a drill through its owner's head. Only after felling the tentacle's owner did he discover that he had killed a giant octopus. Little mole-people with brown fur and squinty eyes appeared from notches in the ceiling of the cave.

"[whir] Hello. Drillbot is this robot's name," he said to the creatures.

Over the next few moments, he conversed with the mole-people and discovered that he had killed an octopus-queen who had ruled over this cave with an iron, fascist tentacle. And by the time the Purple Shirts and Bagoo finished arriving through the portal, the mole-people were bowing to Drillbot and worshipping him like a god, for he had answered their prayers for freedom. Bagoo sealed the gateway and pointed to an area at the back of the cave.

The Purple Shirts rushed toward the spot. Drillbot joined them, ignoring the prayers and adulation of the mole-people. When they reached the area that Bagoo had indicated, the Purple Shirts stared in confusion. There was nothing there.

Drillbot, however, knew better. He noticed movement on a microscopic level and zoomed in his telescopic eyes. There was a tiny swirl of power. Suddenly, it began swirling in the opposite direction.

"[whir] Back up! Drillbot has a bad – CLACK – bad feeling abou—" But before he could finish speaking, flames burst forth from the little swirl. One of the Purple Shirts caught fire and fell writhing in the puddle covering the ground. She rolled in place, and by the time she had put out the fire, half her uniform was gone. Her skin was red and raw.

Drillbot glanced from the writhing Purple Shirt over to the source of the flames. God-Art lay curled there in a fetal position, a smile on his face. He rose to his feet and proclaimed, "Behold, foolish mortals! Like the dawn each morning, I am reborn, and I shall not be stoppe—"

Drillbot swiped his Nothing Net over the god's head. The god disappeared. Then Drillbot turned to face Bagoo and the Purple Shirts. He remarked, "[whir] Drillbot advises not to let the – CLACK – not to let the god finish gloating. It only leads to – CLACK – to trouble."

Bagoo nodded. "One down," he muttered. "Only billions more to go."

The Purple Shirts helped their injured comrade to her feet. Bagoo pressed the next in the series of blue numbers on the device he carried. A new gateway appeared. Drillbot leapt through it.

CHAPTER 21

A QUICK REUNION

NORMAL-ART AND HIS group turned from Bagoo's gateway. Alex raced over to a map on the wall that showed exit routes in case of an emergency. He ran his finger over it until he found the correct room. It was marked B-42.

"This way," called Alex. "We must get to B-42 in the next few minutes, or all is lost."

He sprinted ahead, with Normal-Art and the rest of the group on his heels. They rounded a corner, and everyone crashed into Alex's back before they could stop themselves. They fell to the ground in a tangle. Normal-Art glanced up and realized that Alex had screeched to a halt to prevent himself from sprinting into a magenta gateway identical to the one Bagoo and his team had leapt through moments ago. The gateway had appeared in the middle of the hallway.

Drillbot emerged from it in a leap, still wearing his Nothing Net positioned on his drill while cradling five additional Nothing Nets in the crook of his other arm. An elderly woman with gray hair, more wrinkles than Normal-Art cared to count, and a hunched back shuffled through the gateway behind the robot. She used her Nothing Net as a cane. Her purple uniform hung loosely from her skinny frame. Bagoo floated through behind her. He tapped a button on the device attached to the Chronal-Dispersion-Shotgun. The magenta gateway dissolved into nothingness.

"Why are you all on the ground?" asked the bog ghost. "Don't you have a mission to complete?"

Alex scrambled back onto his feet. Everyone else did the same. He did not answer the question.

Bagoo asked, "How long have we been gone?"

Alex answered, "Old friend, you have jumped back to this place only a few moments after you departed. You were gone minute at most."

Bagoo nodded. The old woman scanned the six remaining Purple Shirts in Alex's group until her eyes found a young man with black hair and brown eyes. Her eyes lit with joy. She shuffled toward him.

"Phillippe!" she cried. "It has been a lifetime, but I clung to life—all in the hope that I would see you one last time."

The young man looked confused. Finally, he asked, "Lonnie?"

She grinned. She had no teeth, so her grin amounted to widened lips over red, bloody gums. She leaned forward and kissed him on the cheek. She said, "Yes, it's me. How I missed you! Did you long for me every moment that I was gone, as I longed for you?"

He wrinkled his brow. He replied, "It's only been like a minute since I saw you. So, sure. Sure, I did."

"But it has been 36,135 days since *I* saw *you*. I thought of you every second. Did you do the same?"

The young man held his nose and muttered, "Sure. Like I said, it was only a minute. Babe, I can't talk this close to you. Your breath is horrid."

Lonnie frowned. She said, "There were no toothbrushes on the mission."

Phillippe frowned back. Then he scratched his chin and said, "I don't think I can do this anymore. I need my space. But it's totally not you. It's, y'know, it's me, I guess. I need time to find *me*, or whatever."

Tears filled Lonnie's eyes. "Wait, are you breaking up with me?" she cried. "After I waited on you for nearly a century? After I resisted temptation in the Land of the Succubi and refrained from partaking in the hospitality of the Pleasure Dimension?"

Phillippe shrugged. "I didn't ask you to do that for me, babe."

"Go to hell!" shrieked Lonnie. Unfortunately for her, her body had grown too old to handle this stress, so she began her journey there first. She collapsed to the ground. As she lay dying, she panted, "My heart is broken. Do not resurrect me. I want to be at peace, as far from Phillippe as I can be."

And with that, she died.

Alex slapped Phillippe across the face. He roared, "You have no courtesy, you cretin. She was clearly close to death. The least you could have done was *pretend* to love her to keep her stable until we could get her back aboard the Husker and have the medics reverse time on her. And now, because of your wretchedness, she has died and forbidden us from resurrecting her. She was destined to play a key role in the Gruntipolian Labor Revolt two decades from now! And now she will not, and that timestream may be doomed. If you were not necessary for this mission, I would flay you alive and make you eat your own skin!"

Phillippe's shoulders sank. "Understood, sir," he replied.

Normal-Art spoke up, "Alex, can you really blame the guy? Did you *see* that old hag? I would've done the same. And if she is *really* so important to the B.T.T., then why don't you just bring her back, anyway?"

Alex scowled. He replied, "Because B.T.T. agents can request to leave our service at any time. It will result in the agent dying and might place parts of the Space-Time-Multinuum in danger, but according to our bylaws, we must abide by such requests."

Normal-Art frowned. Then he squealed, "Wait, if people can leave at any time, then why haven't you listened to me and *sent me home?*"

"Because you are *not* an agent. You are our guest," said Alex. Normal-Art began sobbing with further protests, but Alex ignored them. He turned to Bagoo and asked, "Did you succeed?"

Bagoo collected the Nothing Nets from Drillbot and from Lonnie's corpse. He powered down the devices and folded them into tiny cubes. He inserted them into a pouch on his holster. He nodded to Alex and said, "Aye, sir. We captured the god at every instance in the Space-Time-Multinuum to which his molecules were dispersed."

Alex nodded back. "Well done," he replied.

And with that, Alex sprinted forward, continuing the mission. Everyone followed him. But Normal-Art did so with a groan. He did not want to sprint anymore.

CHAPTER 22

TWEAKING THE EQUATION

ALEX CREATED A mental image in his head of the backstage area and mapped out how to get to his destination. To keep track of his position as he sprinted, he envisioned a miniature model of himself moving across the map. If he were from Younger-Arthur's time period, he would likely have made the connection to how similar the mental image looked to the game *Ms. Pac-Man*.

He sprinted through the corridor, darted past two intersecting hallways on his right, and slowed to a halt before a third that opened on his left. Down this hallway lay the room marked B-42, the room containing the mathematical formula that would cause wanton doom to envelop the Space-Time-Multinuum if left unchecked. He turned the corner and immediately screeched to a halt.

A colossal, three-headed wolf with black and silver fur stood in the hallway. It was nearly as tall on all four legs as Drillbot. A white lab coat dangled from its shoulders, the bottom of the lab coat shredded and in tatters from obvious claw and tooth marks. The eyes on one head were yellow, on the next red, and on the last black and covered by a pair of round spectacles. All six eyes stared at Alex, and slaver began dripping from the maws of the heads with the yellow and red eyes.

"Cerberus," whispered Alex. His instincts to fight overtook him, knocking aside the rational part of his brain. Despite an awed fear filling his bowels, his hand moved on its own, reaching for the cylindrical device in his holster from which he created his laser-weapons.

Before Alex could power on the weapon, the remaining members of the Landing Crew turned the corner behind him and crashed into his back. They all fell in a tangle to the floor. Alex sighed. This group crashing into his back and then falling on the floor seemed to be developing into a habit.

From their new vantage on the ground, the rest of the Landing Crew noticed the three-headed beast. They all tried to leap to their feet, some overwhelmed by a desire to fight, others overwhelmed by a desire to flee. But neither intention mattered, because the act of everyone in the already-tangled group simultaneously attempting to scramble upright led to a further tangling, and soon, everyone lay stuck. If a deity were present who happened to be the patron god of slapstick comedy, it likely would have felt incredibly honored by the performance.

Alex yelled for everyone to stop moving, and they all did—all except for two Purple Shirts, one of whom had been unlucky enough to get tangled in Drillbot's wheel-daggers, the other of whom had retrieved a device from her holster that she was using to treat the first's wounds. The wounded Purple Shirt writhed and moaned. His blood pooled on the floor beneath the group, but his life was saved.

Hissing laughter filled the hallway. Alex glanced from his spot on the floor to the Cerberus. Its left two heads—the ones with the yellow and red eyes, respectively—growled ferociously at the group, but its rightmost head was doubled over in laughter, its sharp teeth glistening and gums bloody with gingivitis. The Cerberus slapped the floor in delight with its right forepaw, while its left forepaw swiped at the group, though it was too far away to make contact.

The creature used its right forepaw to push off the ground. This momentum allowed it to stand upright on its hind legs. The motion also caused its lab coat to flap open. Alex realized the creature had three pairs of male genitalia, each matching in order the eye color of the three heads. Alex sighed. Life was ridiculous.

The creature's right forepaw straightened its spectacles and then reached into a pocket in its lab coat. It retrieved an aerosol can, and then it sprayed the can into the faces of its two other heads. The heads coughed and hacked and then fell unconscious. Its left forepaw and left hind leg went limp.

The Cerberus took a moment to steady itself on the wall. Then it shuffled over to the Landing Crew—taking a step forward with its right leg, dragging its left behind it, and repeating. The beast reached its right forepaw down into the maul and wrested Alex from the tangled heap, picking him up and setting him upon his feet.

"Hi. Hast thou any freshly churned butter, any unbroken eggth, or a clock that needs no mending?" asked the Cerberus, speaking with an occasional lisp because its tongue sometimes lolled out of its mouth when it talked.

Alex smiled and nodded. This was a B.T.T. password from a few centuries ago. He recognized it from the archives he had been forced to memorize as a Purple Shirt. He answered, "The butter is melted, the eggs returned to the womb, and the clock always spins."

The bespectacled wolf's head smiled and nodded back. It said, "I suthpected you were B.T.T. You carry yourthelf like an officer. And the colors of your disguiseth give you away, to someone who knows what they are looking for."

"We're here on a mission," responded Alex.

"I know. I am here to help. I am known amongst the B.T.T. as Cerbby of the Clock."

Alex smiled. He said, "I am familiar with the name. To those of us with classified status high enough to access your file, you are a legend."

The bespectacled wolf stared at Alex with an arched eyebrow. "Hmm. This ith my first mission. Good to know it's all uphill from here."

"Truer than you could imagine," replied Alex. "Tell us, how did you infiltrate this place? That detail was not covered in your files."

Alex neglected to tell Cerbby of the Clock that he already knew the answer because he had learned it during past time-loops while assigned to this Landing Crew. But because he could not be completely certain what course of events were vital to the future in unforeseen ways or what time anomalies he might cause by *not* asking the question as it had been asked in the past, he asked and listened attentively, anyway.

Cerbby of the Clock answered, "I was doing my duty as the guardian of Earth 922,013,002's underworld when the call came from Artheothkatergariabetrugereiinganno for my pantheon to assitht with his conthpiracy. My pantheon lent my thervices to the cause, because my three heads are my pantheon's patron gods of mauling, home security, and mathematics—I'll allow you to guess which head ith which. But what my pantheon did *not* know wath that a warrior had attempted to enter the underworld a few centurieth prior, and he had run his spear through this head with which I am thpeaking to you now.

"This head was brought before a B.T.T. recruiting council before it could die," continued the bespectacled wolf-head. "Thith head wath commissioned into the B.T.T. and underwent training to become an undercover operative. It wath then returned to my body to begin my role ath a double agent—unbeknownst to my other two heads. When I wath thent by my pantheon to assist with the C.O.G., this head was stationed as a vital part of Artheothkatergariabetrugereiinganno's mathematics team, while my other two heads were assigned to security, guarding this room when it is left otherwithe unattended. I have been falsely serving thith foul conthpiracy for centuries and have been waiting for a team from the B.T.T. to arrive to help."

Alex nodded and said, "I thank you for your service to the B.T.T. But we must hurry. Will you please let us pass so that we may approach Artheoskatergariabetrugereiinganno's formula?"

The bespectacled head nodded. The middle head snored. The leftmost head drooled. "At once," replied Cerbby of the Clock. "The other science and math deities have been granted leave to participate in the networking orgy. Ath always, I was left on my own so that my other heads might guard the lab. Follow me this way."

Cerbby of the Clock placed its right paw on a computer terminal embedded in the wall. Green light flashed around it, and then a door marked B-42 opened. Behind the door lay a hallway. The three-headed wolf shuffled down this hall, slowed by its incapacitated left hind leg.

After a few agonizingly tedious minutes, the group reached the end of the hallway and entered a massive, completely spherical room the size of a warehouse. It was painted dull gray with a white ceiling. Stairs led down to the bottom. Hundreds of desks were spread across one side of the room, and these desks were cluttered with computers and stacks of papers and assorted scientific equipment. Hundreds of desks were spread across the other side of the room, and these desks were cluttered with cauldrons and scrolls and assorted magical equipment.

When the group reached the bottom of the sphere, Alex looked up. Older-Arthur followed his gaze and whistled in the same annoyingly awed tone he had used when he saw the Infinity Vortex on the Landing Crew's approach into the city. The ceiling that had *seemed* white upon entry to the room was not in fact covered by stark white paint, but was instead a miasma of billions of dots of light that formed a model of the nearly infinite stars in the sky. It was beautiful. Alex smiled.

Older-Arthur whistled again when he noticed a jumbled mass of ethereal mathematical symbols floating across the room. It was an equation, a mixture of numbers and symbols and annotations and colors swirling through the air. It was ghostly and ominous and delicate and mesmerizing all at once.

Cerbby of the Clock patted Alex on the shoulder and remarked, "Though it represents the motht dangerous threat in the Space-Time-Multinuum, it ith oddly beautiful, no?"

"It most certainly is," replied Alex, looking away from the equation and turning toward Cerbby of the Clock. "I take it you understand what we must do?"

Cerbby of the Clock nodded. "Aye."

Cerbby of the Clock stalked to the side of the room and retrieved a small black baton from a sconce in the wall. He began waving it at the floating ghostly equation like he had become a symphony conductor. The swirling math—which had in the meantime formed into a tornado and had begun wreaking property damage to computers on the far side of the room—reversed its course and twirled back toward the middle of the spherical room. As it did so, it began undulating to the beat of the Cerberus's baton, and soon laid itself out across the starry ceiling so that the function started in the center of the domed ceiling and twirled round and round in an expanding spiral to occupy every square inch of the ceiling.

"There," said Cerbby of the Clock. "The equation is tamed for the moment. It is time for your team to act."

Alex read through the equation until he found the spot he recognized as the weak point from the classified briefing documents given to him by Captain King Solomon. Altering the equation *here* would change the output of the function and release a counter-virus that would reverse God-Arthur's alterations to the Space-Time-Multinuum. It would also cause the function to falsely sound the signal to the local pantheons that the function had succeeded. Just to double check with the mathematician, Alex pointed to the spot he had in mind and asked Cerbby, "We insert an eight after the zero in the millionths place of *that* number and we're good, correct?"

Cerbby of the Clock shook his head. He sighed, and then he replied, "No, no, no. Add the eight after the four in the octillionths place. If you put it in the millionths place, the wrong cosmic gong will sound, and no god in any pantheon outside of the tone-deaf vampires of Earth 67,909,111 will believe the C.O.G. succeeded."

Alex nodded. "Glad you're here to double-check our work, then."

Cerbby of the Clock let out another annoyed sigh and said, "It flabbergathts me that for a mission thith important, the B.T.T. wouldn't have thent a competent mathematician. It is ridiculouth that you would need to double check your figureth with a giant wolf such as me. Now hurry."

Alex ignored the criticism and turned to one of the remaining Purple Shirts. He removed a tiny vial full of white liquid from his holster and placed it in her hand. He squeezed the young woman's shoulder and said, "Everyone in the Space-Time-Multinuum thanks you for your sacrifice. When your portion of the equation exits the stratosphere, please release the contents of that vial."

The red-headed woman looked upset. She had four eyes and sharp fangs lining her mouth. She bellowed, "Wait, why me? I freed my people from tyranny. I fought and won a dozen wars before joining the B.T.T. I have so much more to offer than to be used as a sacrifice.

She hooked a thumb at the Purple Shirt standing next to her—Phillippe—and continued, "*This* guy was a drug addict who lived in his mom's basement until he overdosed. Unlike me, *he* is the *definition* of expendable."

Alex frowned. He replied, "If you did not want to be used as a sacrifice for the good of the many, then you should have worked your way through the ranks *faster*. And though you may choose not to view it this way, I have honored you with this sacrifice because it is painless, and in a way, it will make you immortal. The drug addict next to you cannot be trusted to *complete* this vital mission. And besides, the B.T.T. has need of a different, less dignified sacrifice from him."

Phillippe gulped. The young woman stared at her feet. Her lower lip quivered. She nodded a tiny, almost indiscernible now. As soon as she did so, Bagoo shoved the needle of a gigantic syringe into her neck. Within the barrel of the syringe, Alex watched lightning and stars and nebulas swirling in an oddly hypnotic miasma.

As Bagoo pressed the plunger, the material disappeared from the syringe and entered her body. The whites of her eyes clouded black, and stars formed within them. Her skin sloughed off her body and transformed into smoke. Her bones and blood melted away before also transforming into smoke. Soon, all that remained was a floating, ethereal green numeral eight with a tiny white vial embedded in its middle.

"Do your duty," ordered Alex.

The numeral floated into the air and inserted itself into the equation, shoving its way between a four and a zero in the octillionths place of a number within a portion of the equation that sat inside a pair of brackets that lived within a parenthesis somewhere near the middle of the string of what seemed to be a miles-long equation.

Cerbby of the Clock lowered the baton. The equation lost all sense of docility, blasting back across the room in a swirling tornado of numbers and symbols. Cerbby of the Clock said, "My other two headth will wake soon. I can convince them that you were a dream if you are not here. Leave at once so I may return to guard duty. I hope to therve with you again one day."

Alex reached out a hand and shook the beast's paw. "Your work here is appreciated," replied Alex. "The B.T.T. Governing Council will know of your bravery."

Cerbby of the Clock nodded. Alex spun on his heel and sprinted from the room. The Landing Crew followed.

CHAPTER 23

CONFIRMATION

NORMAL-ART FOLLOWED CLOSE behind his older-self, and they both hung near the back of the pack. The reason for this was twofold: first, they were both too out of shape to keep up with Alex's brisk pace, and second, Drillbot occupied the rearmost position in the group. Near his watchful gaze seemed like the safest spot in the entire Multiverse.

The group turned a few corners, passed the intersection that led to the networking orgy, and slowed to a halt. Alex signaled for the group to circle up. 29333 used the disc from her holster to erect a sound shield around the group. Normal-Art glanced from Drillbot to Alex to the humanoid faces of the remaining Purple Shirts, and as he did so, he felt as though he were in a huddle at a football game where weird mascots had taken the field in place of the athletes.

Alex said, "OK, from here on out, we will be walking at a leisurely pace and acting nonchalantly. If we arouse suspicion, then all is lost."

The group nodded. Except Normal-Art, who said, "Wait, so you think there is any chance we *won't* arouse suspicion when our group is dressed exactly like the group who attempted to assassinate God-Me? Seriously?"

Alex sighed and ran his hand through the hair of his wig. He said, "If anybody asks, we're from the same pantheon, but a different Earth. There are lots of repeated gods out there."

"Which Earth?" asked Normal-Art.

"It doesn't matter. Just not the same one as the assassins—not Earth 45,590,888."

"But it *does* matter," replied Normal-Art. "If we pick a random number and it happens to be the same Earth as the person interrogating us, then that's going to be bad."

"Look, the odds of that happening are approximately infinity to one," said Alex. "We don't have time for this debate. We must move."

Normal-Art shrugged as he muttered, "I just want to be prepared is all."

Alex sighed louder than he had ever sighed before. Normal-Art noticed that his breath smelled vaguely of spinach and sour cheese. Alex said, "*Now* you want to be prepared? I've been trying to prepare you for days, and all you've done is ignore me!"

Normal-Art began to say something in response, but Alex waved it away with the back of his hand. Normal-Art opened his mouth to try again, but Ginny elbowed him in the stomach, knocking the wind out of him. He grunted and doubled over, huffing to try and catch his breath.

Alex nodded his thanks to Ginny and then glanced at each remaining member of the Landing Crew. He said, "We must all be aligned on this: the Space-Time-Multinuum is more important than any *one* of us. If your cover gets blown, you'll be as good as dead, anyway—so cause a commotion and draw attention to yourself. Allow the rest of us to escape."

Normal-Art had apparently recovered enough to say, "Unless it's me, right? If my cover gets blown, then *others* should sacrifice themselves to save me. The B.T.T. Governing Council deemed my life vital for this mission, remember?"

Alex rubbed his fingers across his temples. "No, you dolt. The part you needed to play was to be a vessel to bring God-You back here so that he could warn his past-self of our fake assassination attempt, thus misdirecting attention and allowing us to alter his math without suspicion. You are now just as expendable as everyone else."

Normal-Art gulped. "I don't like the sound of that."

Older-Art leaned over to him and smacked him across the back of his head. He whispered, "You obviously survive. I am you from the future, you idiot."

Normal-Art grinned. "Wait! That means I'm invincible!"

Everyone groaned. Ginny and 29333 leaned over and slapped him at the same time. They both said simultaneously, "Be quiet and listen. The rest of us want to get out of here alive."

The two versions of Ginny looked at each other and frowned. Then they both gave an identical shrug. Then they both frowned harder. Then they both gave another identical shrug.

"This is weird," they both said. Then Ginny smiled while 29333 scowled, breaking whatever bizarre twin-magic was occurring.

Normal-Art obeyed the slapping women and stayed silent. Alex continued, "In order to ensure our interference in the C.O.G. succeeded, we must confirm that the equation gets presented to the gods as we left it. And to do that, we're going to split up."

Alex pointed at Bagoo, Normal-Art, and the Purple Shirt named Philippe. He ordered, "You three are going to rejoin the audience in the arena. Once Artheoskatergariabetrugereiinganno displays the math and you confirm that our alteration is present, you may sneak out to join the rest of us.

"The rest of us are going to walk *slowly* out the front entrance and wait for you outside," continued Alex. "If you cannot find us out there when you exit, then proceed to the rendezvous point without us, for it means we are dead or are fleeing. If you are under pressure and must run somewhere other than the rendezvous point, you must be at least two miles away from the Infinity Vortex to ensure proper operation of our teleporters. Also remember that you should try not to put yourself in such a position, because it is much more cost effective for us to teleport large groups at once. You will need to cover the difference in costs yourself, a condition of employment you will surely remember from your B.T.T. employee handbooks."

Normal-Art fidgeted, waiting for Alex's long-winded speech to end— for proclaiming to be in such a hurry, the man sure did know how to take his time with instructions. Normal-Art took a deep breath. At times like this when he was about to be forced into a dangerous situation, his stomach would normally ball itself into a knot of anxiety. But he felt none of the normal anxiety, for Older-Art had made a solid point: if Normal-Art was destined to die here, then Older-Art would not exist. He smiled.

And then he realized that while he was lost in thought, 29333's sound shield device had disengaged, and the huddle had broken, and everyone had begun walking toward the exit of the backstage area, already a dozen feet ahead of him. Drillbot stood over him, staring. He asked, "[whir] Does Former-Master-Art plan to – CLACK – plan to join the rest of the group?"

Normal-Art did not bother to respond. Instead, he grabbed the hem of his toga and yanked it up so he would not trip. He shuffled forward after the Landing Crew. They walked through the exit and past Heimdallr, who remained vigilant outside the door. The god called his farewells to the Landing Crew as it passed, his voice growing more and more forlorn as he realized that nobody had brought him a plaything from the networking orgy. He sighed, and his breath shook Normal-Art's organs. Normal-Art remembered with sudden clarity that he needed to urinate and had been holding it for what felt like days.

When the group exited the hallway and returned to the grand atrium, Normal-Art desperately looked for a restroom. Just when he spotted a door marked with a sign that seemed to indicate one, one of Bagoo's wispy bandages wrapped around Normal-Art's wrist and pulled him away from the group and toward the entrance to the arena. He frowned. His bladder hurt, and now his wrist was freezing.

Bagoo pulled three ticket stubs from the folds of his toga. He handed them to the attendant, who glanced at them before waving Bagoo and Normal-Art and Phillippe through. Normal-Art sighed.

*

Though Bagoo, Normal-Art, and Phillippe presented the ticket stubs for their old seats to the inattentive usher, the trio dared not return to the seats they had previously occupied. It would be too obvious that they were connected to the assassination attempt.

Normal-Art stared down at his feet as Phillippe and Bagoo studied the arena, looking for a spot with three open seats that they might occupy. Normal-Art refused to look up, refused to fall victim again to the overwhelming vertigo of staring up into the confined infinence.

Phillippe nudged Normal-Art and nodded in Bagoo's direction. The bog ghost was drifting toward a staircase. Normal-Art followed while Phillippe brought up the rear. The trio ascended nearly a dozen flights of stairs—Normal-Art growing more out of breath with each one—and finally exited onto a row of balcony seats. The awning overhead was carved from black marble, and it was decorated with an intricate sculpture that depicted a crowned monkey stealing a musical note from an alligator wearing Victorian-era attire. Normal-Art shrugged.

The trio approached an unoccupied segment on the bleachers between a rotund six-eyed god with tiny legs and a beautiful male who seemed to wear his long, curly, brown hair as a suit of plate armor.

Bagoo said to them, "Our pantheon has fallen into a drunken stupor, and in our mythology, our father kills and eats us whenever he becomes intoxicated. We would prefer to avoid that scenario, at least until the end of this convention. Do you mind if we occupy these seats?"

The rotund god shrugged. The hairy god said, "Do as thou will. As lower demigods within our own pantheon, we understand thy struggle."

Bagoo nodded. "You have my thanks."

And with that, the trio occupied the bench. Bagoo sat in the far seat near the rotund god, Phillippe in the middle, and Normal-Art on the other end, next to the hairy god.

Normal-Art leaned over to Bagoo and whispered, "Way to think on your feet!"

Bagoo stared at him blankly. "I have no feet," replied the bog ghost.

Normal-Art began to point out that his statement had merely been an expression, but he stopped short when he noticed the look on Phillippe's face. He was gazing out across the arena, his face pale. Normal-Art followed his gaze and immediately felt the blood drain from his own face, too.

Every single Purple Shirt who had been involved in the faux assassination attempt had been strung up in grotesque display. Their hands and feet were nailed to the walls. Their eyes were gouged out, and their midsections ripped open. Every single one of their internal organs had been pulled from their bodies and dangled below them. Written in blood on the wall next to each of them was a warning: *Here hangs an attempted assassin. Miracles kept him alive, so that he might experience the pain of a million lifetimes before his execution. Don't be an assassin. Unless you love to be tortured.*

Normal-Art stifled a gasp.

The hairy god must have followed Art's gaze, because he leaned over and said, "Thou must be a deity of mercy to gasp at the punishment of traitors and assassins. I find deities of mercy *very* sexy. Wouldst thou like to find a dark corner and fulfill our fantasies together?"

Normal-Art glanced over at the god and realized the god's hair was growing even longer than it had been moments before. Normal-Art scooted away, nudging into Phillippe. "N-N-No, thanks. I am not looking for anything outside my own p-p-p-pantheon at the moment."

The hairy god smiled. "Tis thy loss. If thou ever changest thy mind, look me up on Earth 6,098,972. My name is Hairy Davé, patron god of wigs, toupees, and—because of some stupid joke made by my pantheon's patriarch as he was copulating with my mother during my conception—sour milk. The two of us can get into lots of trouble. *Sexy* trouble."

Luckily for Normal-Art, the conversation was interrupted by a blast from God-Art's conch shell, originating from the stage far below. Normal-Art covered his ears. The hairy god frowned. Then his head exploded. But before the damage became too permanent, strands of hair whipped out from his body, snagged the fragments of his head, and pulled them back into place. The god cursed the pain but seemed to suffer no permanent damage.

Normal-Art shrugged and looked down at the stage. God-Art was standing in its center, the conch shell held to his lips. His stomach distended as he inhaled, and then as he blew once again, words emanated from the magical shell. These words felt like they formed inside of Normal-Art's brain—somehow bypassing his ears—but they also floated as multicolored letters in the ether.

"Hear ye! Hear ye!" proclaimed God-Art. "It's time for our networking sessions to end and for us to finish this conference strong!"

The cheers of nigh infinite gods echoed through the Infinity Vortex. Normal-Art grimaced. When the applause died down, God-Art gestured toward the tortured and maimed Purple Shirts. He remarked, "I hope the networking session went well for you. I must say, so long as you weren't crucified in agony, it went better for you than it did for our trigger-happy mortal guests."

More cheers. Then he said, "I hear it's best to start these types of speeches off with a joke. So, here goes: what do you call it when you murder a groveling mortal?" He paused a second and then continued, "A praying man 'tisn't alive no more!"

God-Art pointed at a group of gods wearing togas who occupied a row of seats near the stage. They were all giant bugs, and the one wearing a crown was a gigantic praying mantis. God-Art exclaimed, "Y'know, because mortals are like bugs to us. And a praying mantis is a type of bug. The gods from Earth 7,891 know what I'm talking about!"

Laughter erupted from the gods. Normal-Art scowled. He wished he were capable of scowling harder, for the god's joke was one of the unfunniest he had heard in a long time.

When the laughter began dying down, God-Art said, "Look, I know everyone here has worlds they want to get back to and mortals they want to oppress or bless or whatever it is you do. We've all learned a lot at this conference and have likely all made new friends and new allies and new enemies. I won't take up too much more of your time.

"So, without further ado," he continued, "I present the key to us regaining power in the face of expanding infinity. In two days hence, at exactly 18:07—or whatever is the equivalent time on your reality—every pantheon will brand *this* mathematical function into a molecule in the atmosphere of its skies. When you do so, the function will spread like a virus to every reality in existence, and within moments, we will be spared any more growth of the Multiverse! You will hear the sound of a cosmic gong, and that will be the signal that it worked. If you are your pantheon's chief deity, be sure that you return to your rooms before you depart today. I've taken the liberty of having my staff deposit in your rooms your official *Multiverse-Capping Mathematical Function Kit*, which includes an exact replica of the function that I am about to show you so that you may brand it into your atmosphere at the appropriate time."

The gods cheered. It seemed like their cheers would never end. Finally, God-Art blew into the conch shell to demand silence. He nodded to the gods in lab coats standing toward the back of the stage. Normal-Art noticed Cerbby of the Clock amongst them. The gods of science and mathematics and engineering strode forward, dozens and dozens and dozens of them using their combined strength to carry a black box fastened shut with gold clasps. They set the box on the stage in front of God-Art. Two of them unlatched the gold clasps and the lid popped open. An explosion of multicolored light launched forth from the box and swirled into a chaotic maelstrom of numerals and mathematical symbols.

One of the deities clambered across the stage to hand God-Art the black baton that Cerbby of the Clock had used earlier in the lab to tame the equation. God-Art declared, "We have now opened Artheoskatergariabetrugereiinganno's box, and all that remains inside is the metaphorical despair of anyone who lacks the power of a god!"

God-Art began waving the baton like he had become a symphony conductor. The multicolored maelstrom became tame. The numbers and mathematical symbols twirled upward, dancing up into the Infinity Vortex. They grew larger so that everyone could see them. Then they flipped and flopped and rearranged themselves.

Soon, an equation that seemed infinite in length hung in the air, its colors dancing and shimmering. Rising through the Infinity Vortex, it seemed even more mesmerizing than it had been down in the lab. Normal-Art had never seen anything so beautiful. Without realizing it, tears had begun falling from his eyes and his pants had grown wet.

Something nudged his side, but he could not look away. His head felt both numbly buzzed and exploding with energy all at once. He felt in his gut that he might go blind or die if he continued to stare at the math, but a serene feeling overwhelmed him, and he did not care.

A cold slap landed across his face, something frigid wrapped around his wrist, and he soon found himself sprawled on the ground. Bagoo was kneeling over him. Bagoo whispered, "I checked the math, and our plan worked. We must go."

Normal-Art had not come down from a high like this since the blue and pink lights from the cosmic bears had washed over him back in the pyramid on Earth 1,000,000. His head ached, and he wanted to curl into a ball and die.

He glanced over at Phillippe. The young man was sitting slack-jawed in his seat, foam dripping from the corners of his mouth. His eyes were bleeding. Bagoo followed Normal-Art's gaze and said, "Get to your feet. We cannot bring him with us."

Normal-Art slowly made his way onto his feet. He asked, "Why not?"

Bagoo frowned and led Normal-Art toward the stairwell. He whispered, "Unbeknownst to Phillippe, he was sent along with us for this very purpose. Why else would First Officer Alexandros ho Megas have ordered him to accompany us?"

"To help?"

"Don't be a fool. Alex sent *you* with me because he needed to ensure that at least one of the people who went into this arena would survive to report to the B.T.T. whether our mission succeeded or failed. He knew that you are destined to escape no matter what—for your older-self is with him—so you were the obvious choice. And he sent me because I am powerful enough to handle myself and would be able to cause a big enough commotion if we're caught to allow you to escape. Phillippe provided nearly no marginal benefit to us.

"However," continued the bog ghost, "he is one of *many* mortals in attendance today. Some are members of other organizations here on missions. Some are merely infiltrators looking to gain godlike power. The common thread with them is that they go braindead from staring directly at the mathematical function for too long when it is displayed across the backdrop of the Infinity Vortex. When the conference is dismissed, they will all be noticed by a version of Baron Samedi from Earth 56,742,222,418, who will transform them into mindless members of his ghoul army. A few millennia from now, this version of Samedi will represent an epic cosmic threat as his undead hordes begin conquering dimensions. But in one such incursion, Phillippe's mindless husk will come across a version of Lonnie. His guilt and arousal upon seeing this paramour from his past will allow his mind to overtake his rotting body. He will then discover that he has the ability to wrest control of the rotting corpses around him—because unbeknownst to him, he is a direct descendent of *his* dimension's Samedi—at which point he will lead an uprising that will succeed in overthrowing Samedi and the cosmic threat he represents. And then Phillippe will return to the B.T.T. He'll be granted a marigold officer's shirt and be bumped up in rank to that of Chief Security Officer on a Bureau Time-Ship, where he will use his mindless corpse-drones to save the Space-Time-Multinuum on multiple occasions."

Normal-Art yawned. "Are you done?" he asked.

Bagoo said nothing.

Normal-Art exclaimed, "I thought you'd *never* stop talking! Aren't we in a rush? You could have just said that it was important for him to stay— or, hell, you could have even said you didn't feel like carrying him, and I would have been fine with it."

Bagoo scowled. He turned his back on Normal-Art and began descending the stairs.

Normal-Art glanced back at Phillippe's mindless body and frowned. Normal-Art would have felt bad about leaving the kid to be defiled and to lose years of his life to undead slavery, but Art was now one step closer to finishing this stupid mission and returning to his couch to stare at his television until his eyes bled. Thus, any potential tingle of sympathy at

Philippe's predicament evaporated before it could find a foothold in his heart.

Normal-Art grinned and followed Bagoo.

CHAPTER 24

TRICKSTER GOD SUPPORT GROUP

WHEN THE LANDING Crew entered the atrium from their sojourn backstage, Ginny watched as Normal-Art split off from the group with Bagoo and the Purple Shirt named Phillippe. Her former lover waddled in his purple toga, and his absurd appearance struck an odd foil to the creepy floating bog ghost and the handsome young Purple Shirt.

Ginny grabbed Older-Art's hand and turned away. She glanced around the atrium. Where before it had been full of odd deities queuing for snacks and meals, now it was nearly empty and eerily quiet.

The only people occupying the gigantic space was a group of six surly deities sitting in a circle on folding chairs near the main exit. The group consisted of a man-sized black cat wearing a monocle and a shoulder holster that held two revolvers, a leprechaun wearing a green business suit, a ten-foot tall Venus flytrap with a pair of leaves jutting from its stalk that resembled hands and a clay pot covering the bottom of its stalk that seemed to serve as its pants, a man with short red horns wearing a bespoke red-and-black striped suit, a mostly nude half-monkey-half-elf wearing nothing but a white doctor's coat with an accompanying stethoscope dangling from its neck, and a burly humanoid whose back was to the Landing Crew. Above them was a poster with letters written sloppily in marker that read, *"Trickster God Support Group."*

Ginny studied the god whose back was turned toward the B.T.T. crew. He had thin, black feathers that resembled hair covering his shoulders and a braid that extended from the back of his head down to the floor. A pair of leather chaps was his only attire, and tassels dangled from the chaps like limp worms.

Ginny could overhear snippets of the gods' conversation from this distance. The humanoid with his back to the Landing Crew said to the support group, "And they don't ever trust me. In today's interconnected Multiverse, with so many threats from foreign pantheons, why would *I* try to harm my own people? I only did that kind of stuff back in my Earth's Gilded Age because I was bored. Back then, we ruled our dimension with an iron fist, and nobody threatened us. But now we've got pressures from all sides of the Multiverse. And instead of listening to my advice, they dismiss everything I say. They accuse *me* of trying to further my own ends. But I'm genuinely trying to help!"

In response, the other deities in the circle let out sympathetic grunts and shouts of "Here! Here!"

A few patted him on the back, but he swatted their hands away and screamed, "Don't touch me! I don't like being touched!"

The Landing Crew walked toward the exit, steering as wide a berth as they could around the support group. Their footfalls echoed loudly through the atrium. Ginny felt her heart skip a beat with each step.

The gods sitting in the circle noticed the Landing Crew and began staring at them. Many of the gods smiled, but none of their eyes revealed any mirth. As a matter of fact, their eyes were steely and cold.

The god who had his back to the Landing Crew stood. When he turned to face the Landing Crew, Ginny noticed that his eyes were black and bird-like, his nose was wider than it was long, the feathery plumage that covered his shoulders extended down the front of his torso to his naval, and his nipples and genitalia were not like any nipples and genitalia she had seen before—black whirlpools swirled in the spots where they belonged. His eyes began vibrating, and then he scowled.

His voice transformed from the vulnerable treble that he had been using with the support group into a venomous hiss. His dialect also became much more formal as he said, "What art thou doing in this sacred place, mortals? And why doest though approach Balroth the Bemoaned and his companions without leave? Art thou attempting to steal our powers, as mortals have from time immemorial?"

As Ginny stared into the god's black eyes, she felt her bowels threaten to quit and claw their way out of her body. She squeezed tightly onto Older-Art's hand. He moaned in pain.

Alex's hand dropped to the cylinder in his holster from which he formed his laser-weapons. His voice filled with bluster as he demanded, "You *dare* accuse us of being mortals? You *dare* insult us with such filthy allegations? We seek no enmity with you, and we desire not to approach you. We seek only to bypass you and to leave this convention early. We must return to our home reality so that we might beat traffic out of here. Stand aside or face our wrath."

The remaining members of the support group stood and gathered behind Balroth the Bemoaned. They posed in their most malevolent poses. The leprechaun stood only three feet in height and came up to Balroth the Bemoaned's kneecap. He looked so cute that Ginny wanted to pet him, but his eyes transformed into flames and rainbow-colored smoke began drifting from their corners, and this desire fled.

Balroth the Bemoaned chuckled, which sounded like asteroids scraping across the cold, metal husk of an abandoned spaceship. He declared, "Mortal, methinks thee protests too much. Thou shouldst know better than to attempt bluffing a trickster god. We see right past such pathetic charades. I not only accuse thee of being mortals, but of being some of the most foolish mortals to have ever existed. Thou thought thee could step thy profane feet inside this sacred place without being noticed and punished? Thy doom awaits thee for this trespass, and thou hast only thy own foolishness to blame."

This was not looking like it was going to be the quiet exit for which the Landing Crew had hoped. Ginny frowned. She wondered if she would have the opportunity to remove this stupid outfit before dying. She did not want to face eternity looking like such an idiot.

CHAPTER 25

DRILLBOT IS NO GOD OF MISCHIEF

DRILLBOT SCANNED THE trickster-class deities with his telescopic eyes and understood at once that the Landing Crew's odds of winning a brawl with them were nearly zero percent. Drillbot could potentially survive, but his fleshy companions would almost certainly be killed.

Drillbot decided that he must do his best to protect his comrades and succeed where Alex had just failed—meaning he would need to upgrade the group's subterfuge abilities rather than diving straight into a fight that would result in heavy losses. So, he initiated a sequence in his processors that he had dubbed *The Deception Matrix*, which would allow him to improvise falsehoods in response to questions.

He rolled forward. He raised his left drill into the air and initiated its rocket sequence. He set it to low velocity and low distance. It flew just above the heads of the gods, smashed through the wall, and returned to him. A few of the trickster gods gasped in amazement. Balroth the Bemoaned was not amongst them.

Drillbot proclaimed, "[whir] Drillbot is this robot's name, patron god of digging from – CLACK – from Earth 45,590,888,001. These mortals are Drillbot's servants. Every generation, Drillbot chooses mortals to become icons of his reality's drilling tools, and they accompany him where'er he – CLACK – where'er he goes! *Especially* to conventions!"

Drillbot pointed first to Alex, then to Ginny, then to 29333, then to Older-Art, and then generically in the direction of the Purple Shirts. As he did so, he announced, "[whir] Behold, this is Drillbot's chosen icon for – CLACK – for a shovel. This one for a trowel. This one – CLACK – for a post-digger. This one for a septic system. And these – CLACK – and these for assorted drill bits. We have been called home for a digging emergency. Now let us pass or face the wrath of the most powerful – CLACK – most powerful god of digging in the entire Multiverse!"

Drillbot roared his engines and posed with his drills held above his head. Most of the trickster gods slumped their shoulders and sat down, apparently satisfied. Balroth the Bemoaned's head cocked to the side like a bird of prey sizing up a morsel.

After a moment, Balroth the Bemoaned bowed and waved toward the exit. He said, "My apologies, oh fearsome robot-god of digging. Balroth the Bemoaned did not realize these mortals were here as thy servants. Go forth and attend to thy *digging emergency*."

Balroth the Bemoaned's eyes never left Drillbot. The robot rolled forward toward the exit. "[whir] Follow me, subjects," declared Drillbot to the Landing Crew. They did so, and their footfalls echoed behind him.

As the group passed the trickster gods and neared the exit, Balroth the Bemoaned spoke up once more. He said, "Oh, Drillbot, Balroth the Bemoaned must discuss something with thee before thou leaves. A moment of thy time?"

Drillbot stopped. He turned to face the Landing Crew. He said, "[whir] Wait for your master outside, my – CLACK – my icons. Drillbot alone shall speak with Balroth the Bemoaned."

Balroth the Bemoaned clicked his tongue against the roof of his mouth. He said, "Oh, I do not think that is necessary."

"[whir] Drillbot thinks it is. They must prepare for our jump between dimensions."

Balroth the Bemoaned grinned. His tongue flicked out of his mouth. Drillbot noticed that it was forked. "I *insist* that they stay," demanded Balroth the Bemoaned.

Balroth the Bemoaned disappeared. A pile of feathers fell to the ground in his place. He reappeared next to Drillbot in a blast of downy plumage and smoke that smelled like sulfur. He whispered, "Thy little farce about being a god of drilling was entertaining to me, so I let thee continue it for a moment. But I have been to Earth 45,590,888,001. I know the patron god of digging, and he's a little pixie with shovels for hands."

Drillbot frowned his version of a frown. His *Deception Matrix* went to work, and milliseconds later, the response burst from his speakers, "[whir]

Drillbot upgraded from his pixie-version. He replaced his shovels with drills. He replaced his – CLACK – his meaty parts with – CLACK – with metal."

Alex sighed. Drillbot glanced over at him, and Alex shook his head. Alex removed the cylindrical device from his holster and toggled its settings. Drillbot returned his gaze to Balroth the Bemoaned. The deity's grin had widened to cover the entire lower half of his face. Drillbot realized the god had no teeth other than a pair of sharp fangs, and the sight was oddly disturbing.

Balroth the Bemoaned said, "Do you know *how* I know that you are lying to me about your identity, robot-man?"

Drillbot said, "[whir] False. Drillbot is not lying. Drillbot is the patron god of digging from Ear—"

Alex placed a hand on Drillbot's shoulder. "Enough, friend," said Alex. "He knows that you're lying because he's never been to Earth 45,590,888,001, but you acted as though his false description of that Earth's patron god of digging was true."

Balroth the Bemoaned chortled. He remarked, "Oh, the mortal is smart! Balroth the Bemoaned shall keep him alive until last—and then shall feast upon his marrow as dessert."

Alex used his hand that was already on Drillbot's shoulder to begin subtly tapping a pattern. As he did so, he spoke to Balroth the Bemoaned. He said, "Oh, great and immortal Balroth the Bemoaned, please spare us mortals. We did not mean to offend you. We merely sought power, just as you all have surely done within your own pantheons. We have learned the error of our ways and ask but to abandon our quest and return home. Please, allow us to leave in peace."

Drillbot recognized the pattern Alex was tapping on his shoulder as Binary. Alex was ordering Drillbot to attack when he heard Alex say the word "*blessed.*" As imperceptibly as he could possibly do so, Drillbot aimed his left drill so that when the order came, the drill would rip through Balroth the Bemoaned and then shred through a pair of other trickster gods behind him.

Balroth the Bemoaned responded to Alex, "You have shown respect, so I will show mercy. After I kill you, I shall confine your spirit to the void of my left nipple. You may dispense jokes at my leisure until I grow bored of you."

Alex bowed. "Oh, great Balroth the Bemoaned, you have my thanks. You have truly blessed me."

Drillbot initiated the launch sequence in his left drill and fired the weapon.

The drill accomplished half its mission. As soon as it blasted from Drillbot's arm, Balroth the Bemoaned disappeared in a cloud of feathers. The drill never touched him. It did, however, blast through the heads of two of the trickster gods behind him—the suited man with short red horns and the man-sized black cat.

Balroth the Bemoaned reappeared behind Drillbot. He now held a glowing blue scimitar in his hand and sliced it across Drillbot's back. It glanced harmlessly across Drillbot's metal carapace, but Drillbot screamed in fury, anyway.

Drillbot spun to face Balroth the Bemoaned. However, the three remaining trickster gods—the leprechaun, the giant Venus flytrap, and the half-monkey-half-elf—dove onto Drillbot from behind.

"Drillbot, look out!" called Ginny and 29333 simultaneously, seconds too late for the warning to actually provide the robot any assistance.

Balroth the Bemoaned glared at Ginny and 29333. He began to open his mouth to say something to them—probably some sort of threat or taunt before pouncing on them. However, the split second of distraction was just the opportunity for which Alex was waiting. He dove toward the god and activated the mid-range function on his metal cylinder.

A laser-spear erupted from the end of the handle and extended into Balroth the Bemoaned's head before the god had time to react. Alex had set the devolution to permanent. Balroth the Bemoaned collapsed into a pile of feathers and emerged seconds later as a baby crow.

Meanwhile, Drillbot leapt into the air, shifted his weight, and landed on his back directly atop the crow. His weight pinned the three trickster gods beneath him, who in turn pinned the baby bird beneath them. The gods cursed and struggled, and Alex methodically walked to each struggling godly appendage sticking out from beneath Drillbot's mass and stabbed it with his spear. Each deity devolved, and Drillbot's weight crushed each devolved form to death.

Drillbot pulled himself upright. The bloody and mangled corpses of the devolved deities lay in his wake—a red-headed child in a green diaper, a black and yellow seed, a monkey with pointed ears, and the baby crow. His left drill returned from its flight and reattached itself to his arm. Drillbot revved his engines and used his drills to impale each crushed, devolved form for good measure. He then turned and smiled his version of a smile at Alex, excited that his calculations had been wrong about the dismal odds of his companions' survival. Alex nodded at him.

Everything had happened so fast that none of the remaining Landing Crew had had time to join in the fight. Thus, they responded in the only way they could: 29333 and Ginny whistled an identical impressed whistle, noticed they were doing so simultaneously, and abruptly stopped. The Purple Shirts saluted and then strode toward the exit.

Drillbot and Alex followed.

CHAPTER 26

NOT HOME YET

WHEN NORMAL-ART AND Bagoo caught up to the Landing Crew at the extraction point, Art was out of breath to the point of losing consciousness. He began to teeter and collapse, but Drillbot caught him and held him upright.

The group stood in a clearing in the forest to the southwest of the city. Rather than clamber back up into the mountains to the spot where they entered this dimension, the extraction point was set farther south, which took them on a slight slope downhill to where the forest met the sea.

Bagoo swirled like a cyclone above the group, removing his marigold toga and wig as he flew. He landed in front of Alex, who had also removed his disguise and was now back in his B.T.T. uniform. Bagoo held his disguise in the crook of his right arm and said to Alex, "We saw some corpses near the door on our way out."

Alex nodded. "That was us. Had to fight our way out. Thought we'd need to use a Purple Shirt as a decoy, but Drillbot was like a one-robot execution squad."

"[whir] Initiating blush sequence," called the robot.

"Who were they?" asked Bagoo. "And need we be concerned that any of their deaths might compromise our mission?"

Alex shook his head and answered, "Some trickster god support group. Shouldn't cause too much of a stir when their corpses are discovered. Their ilk is always backstabbing and murdering one another."

Bagoo nodded. Then Alex pointed at Drillbot and said, "It doesn't have any effect on this mission, but our robot friend killed Balroth the Bemoaned."

Bagoo whistled. "Wow. *That* is huge."

"[whir] Why is that – CLACK – is that huge?" asked Drillbot.

Bagoo patted Drillbot on the back and said, "Balroth the Bemoaned is responsible for the deaths of a few quadrillion mortals when he causes the Dynamite Kitten War of Earth 209,900,878. By ridding the Space-Time-Multinuum of him, you might've just earned yourself an officer's uniform without even trying. Be careful, or you'll steal my job while you're at it."

Normal-Art fell to the ground, for Drillbot dropped him. Drillbot did not seem to notice. He said, "[whir] Drillbot intended no – CLACK – no theft of your – CLACK – your position."

Normal-Art stood and brushed himself off. He patted Drillbot's wheel and said, "I think he was joking with you, buddy."

"[whir] Oh. Then Drillbot will ensure that he uploads this interaction to his – CLACK – to his *Humor Matrix.*"

Normal-Art shrugged. Then he heard the bog ghost whisper to Alex, "But what does this mean for *us?* Balroth the Bemoaned was destined to destroy the Unicorn Husker during the Dynamite Kitten War."

Alex shrugged and whispered back, "I don't know. I imagine that he'll return somehow, or that something else will cause the war and his Bombardier Kitten Armada shall claim our lives, anyway."

Bagoo stared at his feet. "Oh," he said. "I had hoped this meant *that* outcome would have been prevented."

Alex patted the bog ghost's shoulder and said, "We won't know until it happens. It does no good to fret about it now."

Normal-Art leaned over into their personal space. Mimicking Alex's gesture to Bagoo, Normal-Art patted them both on their shoulders. Then he said, "You two are *really* bad at whispering. We could hear everything you were saying."

Alex sighed. Then he tapped the B.T.T. badge on his uniform four times in quick succession—activating its communicator functionality—and said, "Officer Trixie, this is First Officer Alexandros ho Megas. Our mission is complete, and we have arrived at the extraction point. Jump us aboard, please."

A squawking voice replied, "At once, sir."

Normal-Art felt a sharp twist deep in his bowels as the teleportation beam ripped his molecules apart. He knew nothing but blackness for a few moments, and then he reappeared fully formed in the Jump Chamber of the B.T.S. Unicorn Husker.

He smiled. He glanced over at Officer Trixie to wave his thanks. She happened to be leaned over her kiosk, paying no attention to the Landing Crew as she cleaned her sunglasses with a cloth. Art felt a tingle in his stomach and without knowing why, he felt compelled to gaze into her uncovered eyes. A sharp nudge jolted him in the stomach, breaking whatever hypnotism had just overwhelmed him. He looked down and it was Ginny. She had elbowed him. He sighed in relief.

"Thanks," said Normal-Art, realizing that she had just saved him from inadvertently killing himself by looking into Officer Trixie's eyes and falling victim to her Cockatrice death stare. "I owe you one."

Ginny replied, "Didn't do it for you. Did it for future-you."

Before Normal-Art could reply, she strode forward, following Alex and the rest of the Landing Crew. Normal-Art rubbed at where her elbow smarted. Then he shrugged and followed the group.

*

The Landing Crew entered the bridge, and as soon as they did so, they heard a slow clap emanating from the Captain's chair. Leif son of Erik joined in, but with only two people involved in the gesture, it felt more sad than celebratory.

Captain King Solomon spun his chair slowly toward them. Then he stood and proclaimed, "Well done, my good and faithful servants! The Space-Time-Multinuum thanks you!"

The Landing Crew cheered in response. Normal-Art squealed in delight, mainly because the crew's success meant that he was going to be free to return home soon. He held up a hand to the remainder of the Landing Crew for a high-five. They promptly ignored him.

Normal-Art shrugged and spun to face Captain King Solomon. He exclaimed, "Since our mission is complete, I'll head back to the Jump Chamber so you can send me home! I don't need to collect anything from my quarters. I can leave right away!"

Normal-Art began to walk toward the exit. He made it a few steps before Alex's hand closed around his upper arm. Alex said, "Wait, Arthur. You have not yet been granted leave."

Normal-Art squealed, "It's Art! And *why not?* I finished the stupid mission that you kidnapped me for. Why won't you just let me go?"

Captain King Solomon replied, "Because the mission is *not* yet complete. You have merely planted the seed of a plot. We must ensure the plant blooms and creates ripe fruit."

Normal-Art frowned. "I don't understand what you're saying," he said.

Ginny sighed. She explained, "He's saying that we need to travel to the future to confirm that our mission succeeded. You are *such* a fool. I don't understand how we lasted so long."

Older-Art cleared his throat.

Ginny replied, "You got better."

Older-Art smiled. Normal-Art groaned, "Fine. Let's get it over with already."

Captain King Solomon returned to his chair. He said, "We would have already begun if you could keep yourself under control."

Normal-Art crossed his arms over his chest. Captain King Solomon nodded. "Very well. Officers, attend to your stations."

As the men and women and creatures in marigold shirts moved to their stations and the Purple Shirts shuffled to the side to get out of the way, the Captain pressed a button on his chair and said, "Chronal Date 4,890,888,562. Our mission: to seek out chronal anomalies and fix them diplomatically. The B.T.S. Unicorn Husker just prevented the Conspiracy of the Gods. The mission was seemingly a success, and we now travel to the moment that the gods enact their mathematical virus to ensure that our metaphorical vaccine took effect."

The Captain released the button, and the recording stopped. Captain King Solomon then ordered, "Leif son of Erik, hold us steady at our current point in space. We shall remain cloaked in orbit above this Earth for the next two days."

Leif nodded, his long blond hair bobbing up and down on his shoulders as he did.

Normal-Art cried, "Wait, what? I thought we were traveling to the future to confirm that we won. Take us there *now!* I want to go home!"

Bagoo floated from his security station and stopped in front of Art. He gently tapped one of his floating bandage-like tassels on Normal-Art's shoulder. "Calm down," he ordered. "Or I will calm you myself."

Normal-Art could see Captain King Solomon through the bog ghost's translucent body. The Captain ignored Bagoo's threat to Art and said, "We *are* traveling to the future, Arthur. We are merely doing so at the speed this timestream takes us. We shan't risk jumping our gigantic ship and potentially alerting hostile forces to our presence, especially when such a jump would only take us two days into the future. There is no logic in taking the risk if we may otherwise remain cloaked and risk nothing."

Normal-Art stomped his foot on the ground and screamed, "Aargh! I'll be down in the stupid Scouting-Whatever-Room with my couch! Nobody speak to me until you're ready to send me home!"

Ginny and Drillbot and Older-Art all began saying something to him. But he ignored them and shouldered past them to the exit. He stormed off the bridge and wished the doors did not open and shut automatically, because he really, really wanted to slam the door for effect.

A few moments later, he trudged back through the door to the bridge and asked for directions.

*

Normal-Art spent the next two days living up to his word. After 29333 escorted him down to the Holo-Scouting Deck, she input the coordinates and the time—ensuring she brought him to a period *before* God-Art had shown up on his doorstep—and left him in his apartment to sit on the couch. He sat staring at the frozen screen on his television, his mind drifting into a state of delicious numbness.

About three times over the next two days, Sprinkle Buns' voice sounded over the intercom to let him know that he needed to evacuate the room so that the scouts might use the deck to prepare for future missions.

"Go to hell, Sprinkle Buns! And you can tell those damned scouts to go to hell, too!" he screamed every time she interrupted his lounging. "If they want me out of here, then they can come in here and remove me by force. But they should know that I've got me a full bladder and a penchant for violence."

Nobody ever came in to force his hand—and thus, nobody ever discovered that he was all bluster—until nearly two days later when 29333 refused to heed his warnings of violence and wanton urination. She entered.

Normal-Art stood. He balled his fists at his side. "Leave me alone," he ordered. "I'm not bothering anybody down here."

29333 stalked over to his side and asked, "You mean other than the

Purple Shirts whose scouting duties you have impeded?"

"Exactly. Other than them."

"What about Sprinkle Buns?"

"Fine. Sprinkle Buns, too."

"And me."

"*You?*" asked Normal-Art. "What do *you* have to do with me being in here?"

29333 sighed. She replied, "You have inconvenienced me. I've been ordered to come fetch you because the Captain thinks that you *might* listen to me. He thinks there's a trust between us or something. Probably because I was the one who first showed you that this place exists."

Normal-Art stared at his feet. He muttered, "But I don't *want* to go."

29333 sighed once more. "Well, that's too bad. You threatened to use your *'full bladder and penchant for violence'* against me, and I do not take kindly to threats. I will hurt you severely if you do not come with me right this second. You shall receive no further warning."

Normal-Art sighed. He responded, "Fine. Let's go."

29333 frowned. She said, "That's disappointing. I thought you would put up a fight and I would get to hurt you. In other timestreams on other realities, such violence between us always ends with coitus. I must admit that I was *slightly* curious about the notion, despite being mostly revolted."

Normal-Art stared at his feet for a few more moments, and then it dawned on him what she had just said. "Wait, what?" he asked.

But she was already halfway to the door. He shrugged and followed her.

*

When Normal-Art and 29333 arrived back on the bridge, 29333 walked to her station and sat. Captain King Solomon stood from the Captain's chair and gestured to Normal-Art.

"Welcome back!" proclaimed the Captain. "Please, please, take a seat. But way over there, as far away from me as you can. You smell terrible, and we are about to witness this ship's finest achievement. I would rather not taint the memory."

Normal-Art glanced around the room. The gang was all present: Ginny looking doe-eyed and sleepy, Older-Art looking dopey and half-witted,

Drillbot looking metal and magnificent, Bagoo looking terrifying and gaseous, Leif son of Erik looking blond and bulky, 29333 looking stern and intelligent, Captain King Solomon looking regal and wise, First Officer Alex looking strategic and commanding, and a dozen Purple Shirts looking nervous and expendable.

Normal-Art strode to the benches at the back of the bridge on which Ginny and Older-Art sat and near which Drillbot stood. There was little space left on the bench occupied by Ginny and Older-Art, so to be annoying, Normal-Art wedged himself into the small opening next to them, bumping them aside to give himself more room. He smirked because there were two other benches nearby that were both mostly empty. The couple sighed in annoyance.

The trio sat in silence. The officers sat in silence. Drillbot stood in silence, though periodically exhaust fired from a gasket and the whistle echoed across the bridge. Normal-Art glanced out the view screen. Something looked different about the Earth, but he could not quite figure out what looked different. If his perception skills were not severely lacking, he would have realized that the Infinity Vortex had disappeared from the planet.

Captain King Solomon checked the chronometer above the view screen on the ship. "T-minus two minutes," announced the Captain.

Normal-Art wanted to cut the silent tension. Every ounce of his being poked and prodded him to do something annoying and ruin the moment for everyone. Ginny must have sensed this in him, for she placed a hand on his thigh. It was a firm grip with no hint of affection. Normal-Art thought better of doing something annoying and instead sat in silence.

And then two events happened in quick succession:

First, a bright flash appeared in the ether directly in front of the B.T.S. Unicorn Husker. The aftermath of the flash looked like someone had taken a cosmic dagger and sliced a gash in the blackness of space. From the gash appeared a ship shaped like a numeral eight. It towed behind it and through the gash colossal tree trunk after colossal tree trunk. There seemed to be no end in sight to the trees appearing from the gash.

"We have incoming!" called out 29333 in warning to the crew. Normal-Art sighed at the unnecessariness of it, as the string of tree trunks was impossible not to see.

Captain King Solomon waved away the warning with the back of his hand. He replied, "We can do naught about it now. We must cling to the hope that our cloak will hide us. Our priority is to ensure that our anti-C.O.G. protocol takes effect. Our personal safety is secondary."

And then the *second* event occurred. Looking down on the Earth from their cloaked position in outer space, the crew could see a string of green numerals and mathematical symbols begin to appear in the atmosphere. More and more numbers and symbols appeared until the entire planet was covered in them. These symbols then began turning every color in the visible spectrum. They burst out into space in a spectacular show of dancing numerical rainbows. The rainbows twirled, swirled, formed into new numbers and symbols, and then blasted away to dance amongst the stars, all the while birthing new rainbows that exploded from them in different directions, which in turn birthed even more new rainbows.

The rainbows covered everything. Then they all disappeared into the ether. A gong sounded across the heavens. It was brief and distant, and then it disappeared without echo. At its noise, Captain King Solomon cheered.

"That's the sound!" screamed the Captain.

"What sound?" screamed back Normal-Art.

"The sign that our change to the math worked. We set it up so that it would be nearly identical to the sound that Artheoskatergariabetrugereiinganno programmed into his equation, but different on an atomic level evident only to those who know what to listen for."

"Wonderful. When's the parade?" quipped Normal-Art.

Captain King Solomon frowned. He replied, "There will *never* be a parade. Only those of us on this ship and B.T.T. officials with high enough classified access will ever know what we accomplished. We don't want it leaking to Artheoskatergariabetrugereiinganno or anybody equally bad that he didn't achieve his goal. He'd find a way to go back in time and change it so that he did."

Normal-Art slapped himself across the forehead. "It was just an expression. I *know* there won't be a parade."

Captain King Solomon shrugged. He said, "Well, it was a terrible expression, then. I'm starting to think that the idioms during your natural lifetime must be so random as to not make *any* sense.

The Captain continued, "But my opinions on you and your time period matter not. What does matter is that our mission succeeded. And now we can exit this reality!"

With that, Normal-Art leapt to his feet and cheered.

But his cheer was interrupted when the eight-shaped ship jerked forward and began circling round and round the B.T.S. Unicorn Husker so that the thousands upon thousands of tree trunks attached to it via leash wrapped like a cocoon around the B.T.S. Unicorn Husker.

"What's happening?" demanded Captain King Solomon. "I thought we were cloaked!"

Alex sighed. He replied, "You've been through this time-loop before, sir. You *know* what's happening. There's no need for the dramatics. We're being attacked. Wait for communication from the enemy."

And in a few minutes, they received it. A voice echoed through the bridge that caused Normal-Art's bowels to turn to water.

"This is Agent 27142 of the Bureau of Interdimensional Travel. I am here to make certain parties currently aboard your ship answer for the crimes that they committed against me and, more importantly, against the Multiverse. Hand over my former prisoner—Art—and his cursed robot companion."

Normal-Art stood and pleaded to the B.T.S. Unicorn Husker crew, "Wait, no! You *can't* give me to him! Please!"

Captain King Solomon ignored Normal-Art. He replied, "This is Captain King Solomon of the Bureau of Time Travel. My ship has no quarrel with the B.I.T. If I hand over Arthur and Drillbot to you, do I have your assurance that you will leave in peace and do no harm to my crew?"

A cackling laugh filled the bridge. Then Agent 27142 replied, "Oh, *I* will agree not to harm you. But the creatures I brought with me—upon whom your agency committed genocide—feel quite differently. *They* will most certainly harm you."

CHAPTER 27

TIME TO ATTACK

AGENT 27142 STEERED the ship out from the barrier between space and time. His ship appeared in the vast blackness of outer space above Earth 8,669. The monstrous tree trunks tied behind the ship emerged one at a time from the portal behind him. To an onlooker from this author's time period and Earth, their appearance would be reminiscent of one of those black snake fireworks sold to kids on holiday—the ones that create a seemingly unending snake of black ash when the small black disc is set aflame.

Agent 27142 immediately identified his prey without even needing to check the ship's sensors. To an untrained eye, the stars in outer space seem randomly strewn across the black horizon. But to Agent 27142's trained eye, he noticed repeated patterns amongst the stars, which is always the sign of an older-model ship's attempt at cloaking—identifiable because it mirrors the surrounding blackness of space rather than replicating the star patterns that it is blocking.

God-Art said, "Oh, my. We're about to see something fantastic."

Agent 27142 grinned and pointed toward the cloaked B.T.T. ship that lay ahead of them. He said, "Yes, we are. We're about to see the bastards pay for what they did to me."

God-Art sighed. "No, no, no. Of course, that's going to happen. I'm talking about something much more important."

And with that, God-Art reached over and jerked the stick so that the ship turned to face the planet below. Agent 27142 began to curse the god, but he stopped himself when he noticed something odd happening on the planet.

In the atmosphere surrounding the planet, a small, green numeral eight appeared. It wiggled and wobbled, then its outline grew fuzzy. It burst into a longer string of numerals, which in turn wiggled, wobbled, grew fuzzy, and burst into even more numbers. Within seconds, this process repeated itself over and over until the entire atmosphere was covered in green numerals and mathematical symbols. Then the spaces in between each numeral and mathematical symbol filled with more numerals and mathematical symbols. A few seconds later, when the math was so opaque that the Earth was completely obscured, the colors transformed from green into rainbow. The rainbow-colored math exploded out into the blackness of space, launching in every direction from the Earth.

The rainbows danced across the heavens. They swirled and replicated and blasted across the darkness. Soon, rainbow numerals covered everything in this reality.

And then the rainbows collapsed in on themselves, and the reality returned to normal. A gong sounded across the heavens. There was no echo, and silence filled the bridge of the stolen B.T.T. ship in a way that felt heavier than any silence Agent 27142 had ever before experienced. As Agent 27142 studied the stars and the blackness of space before him, it all looked so mundane and boring compared to what he had just witnessed.

His thoughts were interrupted by a wild cheer from dozens of people. He glanced over at God-Art and realized that all the cheers were originating from the god. Dozens of extra mouths had formed across God-Art's neck, and he was screaming in delight from all of them.

God-Art slapped Agent 27142 on the shoulder and said, "You've just witnessed my greatest accomplishment, and a major step toward my ultimate domination of the Multiverse! From this point forward, no longer is the infinite Multiverse constantly being raised to the power of infinity. At this exact point, the Multiverse is reduced to regular infinity, something that is completely tamable! Huzzah!"

Agent 27142 frowned. He replied, "Just so you don't think anything has changed between us, I *will* be bringing you to justice when we are finished here. And you've only yourself to blame that there will be no reality splitting off from this one where I fail to do so."

God-Art grinned. It spread to literally cover his face from ear to ear. The god said, "And just so *you* don't forget, I've battled much worse than you, and I've never been stopped before."

Agent 27142 began to reply, but then a nasally voice crackled over the intercom. It said, "Umm, this is President Clearland. Are you going to move any time soon? We are holding steady as best we can, but the planet's gravity is causing our ships to begin drifting toward it. Please advise."

Agent 27142 swallowed his anger and jammed his finger down on the intercom button. "A cosmic event distracted us for a moment, but we are now back on track."

And with that, he gunned the engine and aimed below the cloaked behemoth on the horizon. The scale of the B.T.T.'s dirigible was enormous, larger even than the B.I.T. carrier-class ship that Agent 27142 had commanded before its destruction in the battle over Earth 55,777.

But Agent 27142 did not let the opponent's size deter him. He zoomed around and around the cloaked ship, leading the thousands of sequoia-ships tethered to him in wide circles so that their ropes wrapped around the vessel. Within the span of a few minutes, he enveloped the B.T.T. ship with sequoias and ropes. For the first time, Agent 27142 appreciated the scale of the BeavBok army that had accompanied him on this journey. He powered down his engines and toggled his ship into standby mode.

Agent 27142 pressed his finger down on the intercom and said, "President Clearland, await my signal to attack. I will first be making contact with our enemy."

The squeaky voice replied, "Aye, aye."

Agent 27142's fingers danced across the console as he changed the frequency of his ship's communicator. Soon, a ringing chimed over the intercom as he waited for the cloaked ship to answer his call.

The ringing ceased, and Agent 27142 could hear the type of random background noises he would expect to hear on the bridge of a ship—heavy breathing, people shuffling, consoles beeping. He interpreted these noises as a sign of connection and took the opportunity to assert his dominance. Without waiting for a greeting from his opponent, he proclaimed, "This is Agent 27142 of the Bureau of Interdimensional Travel. I am here to make certain parties currently aboard your ship answer for the crimes that they committed against me and, more importantly, against the Multiverse. Hand over my former prisoner—Art—and his cursed robot companion."

Nearly immediately, he heard the whining of his former prisoner in the background, "Wait, no! You *can't* give me to him! Please!"

A much louder voice replied over the intercom, "This is Captain King

Solomon of the Bureau of Time Travel. My ship has no quarrel with the B.I.T. If I hand over Arthur and Drillbot to you, do I have your assurance that you will leave in peace and do no harm to my crew?"

Agent 27142 cackled into the microphone. Then he replied, "Oh, *I* will agree not to harm you. But the creatures I brought with me—upon whom your agency committed genocide—feel quite differently. *They* will most certainly harm you."

Agent 27142 cut the communication line with the encircled ship. Then he reestablished contact with the BeavBoks. He jammed his finger down upon the communicator button and yelled, "Attack!"

*

In preparation for the battle, Agent 27142 pressed a bubbled glass dome over the top of the purple space suit that he had found below decks. Once it snapped into place, he heard his respirators engage. He heard only the sound of his own breathing for a moment, and then he stuck his tongue out to click the short-range intercom button on the controls that dangled to the sides of his mouth. The noise of his surroundings filled his helmet. He glanced over at God-Art and probed, "You're sure you don't need protection?"

The god replied, "The vacuum of space might be a tad uncomfortable at first, but I'll get used to it. I always do."

Agent 27142 shrugged. Then he suppressed a smirk when he looked down at Henry, who was now perched in Agent 27142's holster and prepared for battle, which he had done by donning a miniature space suit that mimicked Agent 27142's—purple layers of fabric covering most of his body, a tiny bubbled helmet over his top, out of which his antennae poked from little holes that had been knocked through the helmet, and a tiny jetpack and artificial respiratory system that hung from the back and front of the suit, respectively.

Agent 27142 did not even bother to suppress the smirk any longer when he glanced at Beverly, who was crouched on God-Art's shoulder in a space suit that matched Henry's. These outer-space-safe B.T.T. suits were left by the ship's previous crew in the cargo hold, and when Agent 27142 had rushed below decks to don one a few moments ago, these two Jump Totems had insisted on receiving their own. Agent 27142's B.I.T.

underlings had rapidly cobbled these tiny suits together from scraps of excess suits down there.

Agent 27142 toggled a button on the control panel. The view screen shifted into a grid, each panel of which showed the viewpoint of one of the cameras covering the hull of the ship.

Agent 27142 focused on the bottom left panel, for its camera's point of view lay just outside the cargo hold. Agent 27142 called into his intercom, "Now!"

He pressed a button on the ship's controls, and the ramp to the cargo hold snapped down. Agent 27142's resurrected soldiers poured out of this opening in the ship, all in purple space suits matching the one that Agent 27142 now wore. Agent 27142 felt the change in pressure as the cabin opened. He was held in place by his safety harness, but he felt a violent sucking that tried to pull him back toward the open cargo hold. Once all the soldiers had exited the ship, Agent 27142 pressed the button to shut the cargo hold, and pressure soon returned to normal. Agent 27142 watched his resurrected soldiers from the view screen. Each of the B.I.T. agents held a rifle in one arm and a glowing knife made of solid light in the other, weapons commandeered from this ship's weapon rack. Their jetpacks fired to life, and they launched toward the rope that tied Agent 27142's stolen B.T.T. ship to the BeavBoks' line of colossal tree-trunk-ships.

As the agents went to work slicing the rope to free Agent 27142's ship from the BeavBok horde, Agent 27142 noticed incoming danger and sighed. The barrel of a turret emerged from between the threads of the nearest section of rope that cocooned the enemy ship. The resurrected agents succeeded in slicing Agent 27142's ship free of the rope just as the turret opened fire on them. Bright light crashed into Agent 4040404, and the agent melted into a ball of gelatinous goop.

Agent 27142 toggled his view screen so that the camera points of view disappeared, and he could once again see out of it normally. He gunned the engine, blasting forward and away from the danger of the turret. He jerked his ship in a wide arc that brought him back around to face the cocooned B.T.T. dirigible. He slowed for a moment to watch the scene unfold below him.

The resurrected B.I.T. agents engaged their jetpacks and blasted in every direction away from the turret, taking evasive action. However, as they were doing so, what seemed like thousands of separate turrets emerged from between the strands of the ropes that were wrapped around the B.T.S. Unicorn Husker. Lasers filled the black space above Earth 8,669. Dozens of sequoia-ships burst aflame or actively devolved into mammoth-sized piles of goop. Meanwhile, millions upon millions upon millions of BeavBoks poured forth from the cargo holds of the sequoias, each wearing a silver space suit with a bubbled helmet and their own versions of jetpacks, which were made from wood.

They blasted into action and swarmed the hull of the B.T.S. Unicorn Husker. The creatures wreaked havoc not with the type of technologically advanced weapons that their enemy used, but rather through a much more rudimentary system: the youngest and quickest of the BeavBoks would dodge as best they could between bolts launched from enemy weapons, and if they made it to the hull, they would activate mines and slap them in place. Then they would fly out of the way, retrieve more mines from the closest sequoia-ships, and repeat. Meanwhile, thousands upon thousands of elder BeavBoks zoomed around the B.T.S. Unicorn Husker and constantly rained arrows at the mines, which detonated when contact was made with the arrows.

"No wonder the B.T.T. murdered all these idiots," muttered Agent 27142. Devolved, melted BeavBoks began to quickly fill the heavens while explosions rocked the B.T.S. Unicorn Husker. Agent 27142 changed the settings on his stolen ship's weaponry so that it would launch explosive laser beams. He then joined the action, zooming his ship along the B.T.S. Unicorn Husker in strafing run after strafing run, swathing the enemy ship's hull in as much destruction as he could muster. Soon, many of the ropes tying the sequoia-ships to one another became torn or exploded apart or melted, and the cocoon of rope and tree began to show signs of unravelling.

Enemy began leaking from breaches in the B.T.S. Unicorn Husker. Many of them wore purple shirts and no protective gear, apparently having been unprepared to face the deadly touch of outer space and too close to the breaches that sprouted in the hull near them. Agent 27142 smirked as they died. Many others wore purple space suits as they flung themselves headlong into space and began counterattacking the BeavBoks and B.I.T.

agents.

Agent 27142 noticed a dozen B.T.T. agents launch from the aft of the ship. Eleven of them rode upon glowing silver saddles while the twelfth appeared to be a floating ghost with dozens of wispy bandages dangling below his torso rather than legs. Three members of the squadron— including the ghost— wore space suits that were shaded marigold, while the remaining nine wore purple suits. This group maintained a circular formation near the B.T.S. Unicorn Husker's rear engines. One of the marigold-suited members of the group had a bright red horsehair crest standing erect from the top of his space helmet. He used a bow and arrows made from solid orange light to pick off BeavBoks at will.

God-Art pointed at the man and said, "That individual looks important. We should probably attack him."

Agent 27142 frowned and replied, "Already on it."

He aimed the ship at the group riding the floating saddles. As he bore down on them at full speed, he opened fire. He missed wide on his first two volleys, these connecting with a random spot on the B.T.T. dirigible. On the third volley, he managed to fire directly at the group. However, the group took evasive action by all twisting in formation to their right, except for a purple-suited man amongst them who did not move in the same direction. He was hit in the arm by a blast from one of Agent 27142's turrets. The blast knocked him from his saddle. He was launched into the ether, and he soon crashed against the hull of the B.T.S. Unicorn Husker. He caromed off in a spinning circle toward the Earth below.

Two of the other purple-suited enemy broke from the ranks and chased after him. Agent 27142 ignored them. He rammed the ship toward the remaining nine members holding formation in the circular pattern, continuing to fire upon them with his turrets. He flew through their midst, but they dodged out of the way. He nearly collided with the aft of the B.T.S. Unicorn Husker, but he reduced the throttle and jerked the controls so that he spun back to face the formation.

"Hmmm, I'm rethinking this," said God-Art. "I think this may be a trap."

Agent 27142 ignored the god, instead opening fire with another volley that connected with the torsos of three purple-suited members of the formation, who tumbled from their saddles and died. But at the last second, just when Agent 27142 locked his sights onto the marigold-suited officer with the crest upon his helmet and was about to fire the blast to kill him, something pointy and metal launched toward his ship from beneath the ropes near the engines.

Agent 27142 attempted to take evasive action, but it was too late. A pair of drills crashed into his view screen. Alarms filled the cabin, and chaos broke loose.

CHAPTER 28

A ROBOTIC TRAP

DRILLBOT RACED DOWN the corridor behind Alex, 29333, Bagoo, Normal-Art, Older-Art, Ginny, and six Purple Shirts. Random crew members—themselves preparing for battle—dodged out of their way.

Drillbot listened as Alex called out orders over his shoulder, "The twelve of us are going to retrieve Gravitron Saddles from the cargo hold. Drillbot, on our way to pick them up, we're going to launch you out of an airlock near the back of the ship."

"[whir] OK, but why? Should Drillbot not be with you, since Drillbot is deadlier than all of – CLACK – than all of you?"

Alex nodded. "That's right. You're deadlier. And that's why you're going to be our trap. *We* are going to be the bait."

Drillbot followed Alex and the group around a corner. They hurried through the hallway. The ship rocked. The sound of an explosion erupted behind Drillbot. He spun his head around to see that a hole had been blown open in the middle of the hallway. A dozen Purple Shirts who had been bustling through the hallway in the process of readying for battle were pulled out of the open hole by the cold vacuum of space. Drillbot rolled toward them, intending to help. Milliseconds later, Sprinkle Buns formed a laser-shield over the hole and pressure returned to normal.

"Drillbot! C'mon!" called Alex.

Drillbot turned his head back around to face Alex. "[whir] What about – CLACK – about the Purple Shirts? Drillbot can help them!"

Alex had reached the end of the hallway. He turned the corner, and then he leaned his head back into Drillbot's view to bellow, "We need to stop the cause of this attack, and there isn't time to do that *and* save those Purple Shirts! There are lots more Purple Shirts on this ship who are in danger. You'll do more good by coming with me."

Drillbot glanced over his shoulder at the black void of space outside the laser-shield. When he looked back in Alex's direction, the officer had already disappeared around the corner. Drillbot revved his engines and followed Alex.

After turning the corner, he caught up to the group as it was descending a spiral staircase. The group reached the bottom and sprinted down the next corridor. The sound of the Arts' heavy breathing nearly drowned out all noise, but Drillbot focused past it to continue listening to Alex, who yelled over his shoulder, "Drillbot, you will hide beneath the bindings that the enemy has wrapped around our ship. Meanwhile, the rest of us will linger outside near the back of the ship, picking off enemy. Before long, we will draw the attention of the rogue B.I.T. agent leading this attack. We will hold our position until he is nearly upon us. When he is most vulnerable, I will signal to you, and you will spring forth from the bindings and bring down his ship. He's like the head of the snake, and once the head is sliced off, the remainder of the snake will rout."

Drillbot nodded his consent at the plan, though he found the metaphor to be lacking in logic—for a snake's body would not rout after its head is sliced from its body, it would simply die. Drillbot sighed. The Arts were slowing the group's travel to the back of the ship, so he scooped them up and held them over his shoulders. After approximately four more minutes of hurried travel, Alex jerked to a halt in front of a thick, metal door.

Alex pointed to the door and said, "This is your stop, Drillbot."

Drillbot dropped the Arts from his shoulders, and they crashed to the metal floor. They both cursed. "[whir] Very well."

"Good luck," said Alex.

"[whir] Drillbot has warred at the head of – CLACK – of a cosmic army for years. Drillbot – CLACK – Drillbot is not the one who needs luck. Good luck to – CLACK – to you."

Alex pressed a button set in the wall. The metal door split open, revealing a small room made entirely of clear material. Drillbot glanced through it. Outside, rope was nearly the only thing visible, with a few sporadic spots of blackness and stars poking into view between its strands.

Drillbot rolled forward into the room. The metal doors closed behind him. Then the walls and floor and ceiling of the clear room split apart and were pulled into the B.T.S. Unicorn Husker. Drillbot now floated in outer space, his metal body bumping gently against the hull of the ship.

*

Drillbot repositioned himself so his wheels pressed against the outer hull of the B.T.S. Unicorn Husker. He hooked one arm through a section of the rope that surrounded the ship and poked his head between strands of the thick binding. He telescoped his eyes out so he could see.

Nearly every square inch of the B.T.S. Unicorn Husker's hull was covered by the ropes. Thousands and thousands of enormous trees lay amongst the cords, bouncing against the hull like a terribly splintery series of out-of-control barnacles. Little creatures that looked like oversized beavers with chicken beaks zoomed about in space suits with tiny wooden jetpacks, wreaking havoc and causing carnage by laying explosive charges against the Unicorn Husker's hull and then blowing them up with crude, primitive arrows. Bright lasers filled the blackness of space around them as turrets emerged from the hull of the ship and fired upon the creatures. Corpses of Purple Shirts floated across the battlefield. Live Purple Shirts in space suits with jetpacks attached to their backs blasted through the blackness of space around the ship, fighting and dying as they engaged a nearly endless wave of the beaver-chicken creatures.

The eight-shaped ship that led the procession of gigantic trees into this reality was no longer tethered to the trees. It careened across the heavens, blasting the hull of the B.T.S. Unicorn Husker as it zoomed past on strafing runs.

While Drillbot sat waiting for First Officer Alexandros ho Megas and his squadron to appear near the aft of the ship to bait the trap, a pair of the beaver creatures approached to lay a mine near Drillbot. When they neared striking distance, Drillbot pounced like an underwater sea creature lying in wait on the ocean floor. His drills slashed out from his cover beneath the ropes. Blood exploded from the beaver creatures where he struck, and they tumbled lifelessly away into the blackness of space, their charges still in their hands.

Drillbot pulled his drills back inside the ropes. He had time to repeat this process on three more groups of the creatures before Alex and his squadron drifted into view. The twelve-member squadron all wore space suits and sat upon hovering metal saddles—all except Bagoo, who floated in place—in a circular formation with Alex at its center. The colors of the group's space suits matched their ranks, with Alex and the officers wearing marigold suits while the remainder wore shades of purple.

Most of the crew moved with relative ease upon their metal saddles. But not Normal-Art. As he gripped the handlebars of his saddle, he seemed to be having trouble managing the throttle and directional controls. Drillbot watched the fool bump into his compatriots dozens of times and launch forward by accident dozens of times, too. Bagoo had to float forward away from the formation and drag him back each time.

Alex used the tape-covered chrome cylinder that he always kept in his holster to create a bow made of solid light. He fired laser-arrows at the beaver creatures from this bow, and each time he hit one, the creature melted into a gelatinous blob that drifted lifelessly away.

Soon, the ship controlled by the B.I.T.-version of Art seemed to notice Alex and his eleven compatriots. It looped in a wide arc away from the B.T.S. Unicorn Husker. It stopped in place for a moment, its bridge facing Alex's group. Then it blasted forward.

It fired upon Alex's group multiple times as it closed the distance between them. It missed wide on its first two volleys, hitting the Unicorn Husker far above Drillbot. But Drillbot watched in horror at the next blast. The blast careened straight at the group. All of them jerked their metal saddles in evasive action and dodged the blast. All except Drillbot's former master, who still could not get control of the device. Drillbot gasped, for he was too far away to do anything to help.

At the last moment, Normal-Art jerked his handlebars to the left, spun out of control for a few spins, and then let go of the device's handlebars to lean over it and hug it for balance. It was just enough movement for a sense of relief to flood over Drillbot. Normal-Art by no means was successful at evading, but he managed to turn so the blast merely glanced off the space suit covering his right arm rather than catching him squarely in the torso.

He tumbled wildly from his saddle, crashed against the nearby hull of the B.T.S. Unicorn Husker, and bounced away toward the Earth below.

Drillbot's instincts to protect his former master nearly overrode his current orders. He was just about to burst from his hiding spot to save Normal-Art when Ginny and Older-Art zoomed after him on their flying metal saddles.

Drillbot nodded and moved his attention from his comrades back onto the incoming ship. It zoomed forward, and just when it neared Alex and his comrades, the group jerked their throttles and evaded.

The ship blasted through the spot that had been occupied by Alex's group. It jerked in a short arc, twisting back toward its prey. This arc brought it over near Drillbot's hiding spot. The B.I.T. agent fired his ship's turrets again, killing three Purple Shirts.

Drillbot's processors registered the words that suddenly formed on Alex's lips: "Drillbot! Now!"

Drillbot sprang the trap.

He revved his drills and burst forth from his cocoon of rope, pushing off the hull of the B.T.S. Unicorn Husker with all his might. He aimed for the bridge of the B.I.T. agent's ship. The B.I.T.-version of Art glanced in Drillbot's direction and noticed him. Drillbot smiled his version of a smile when he saw the panicked expression that enveloped the agent's face. And then Drillbot scowled his version of a scowl when he realized that God-Art was staring smugly at him from the passenger seat.

Drillbot's crashed through the view screen of the vessel's bridge. But before he could slice through the flesh of his quarry, Agent 27142 and God-Art acted.

CHAPTER 29

ABDUCTION

GINNY SAT UPON the metal device that had been issued to her by Inventory Officer Yardish Groveland. The Earth lay below her and to the right, while the B.T.S. Unicorn Husker loomed gigantic and dangerous and cocooned in enemy sequoias above her and to the left. The seat of the device upon which she sat was shaped like a saddle used for riding horses, but rather than this saddle being strapped atop a horse, this saddle sat atop a set of engines that could send Ginny careening across the heavens faster than the supersonic-hummingbird-version of herself that she had murdered on Earth 6,993,212 while under the Pink One's control.

The device was called a Gravitron Saddle, and she had learned through a quick briefing from Officer Groveland that she controlled the speed and direction of her Gravitron Saddle through a pair of handlebars that extended from the front of the device. Her feet hung on each side of the saddle and were nestled inside a pair of Pulsar Boots, the bottoms of which glowed a deep yellow. These boots were designed to help her control the vertical pitch of the Gravitron Saddle and thus assist her in taking evasive action as necessary. The boots sounded useful, but the constant vibrations that buzzed from them and through her feet tickled, and she wished she could turn them off.

Ginny wore a clear, bubble-shaped space helmet over her head. As strands of hair mingled with her sweat and matted against her forehead, she wished she could remove the helmet so that she could wipe the hair aside. She ignored this frustration as best she could by concentrating her efforts on defending the B.T.S. Unicorn Husker.

In addition to the Gravitron Saddle, Officer Groveland had also issued to Ginny a Time-Phaser. Ginny used this weapon to snipe random attacking beaver-chicken-creatures, utilizing the *Permanent Devolution* setting as she had been instructed. Though she would have expected her years of service to the Pink One to have desensitized her to all forms of violence, she felt a twinge of heartache each time she eradicated one of these creatures, for they were some of the cutest creatures she had ever seen and were made cuter by their spacefaring attire. One such creature was blasting toward her now. She fired into its torso. It melted into a blob of yellowed goop and floated harmlessly away.

Blackness began creeping across the edges of Ginny's vision. She frowned and wished she could rub her eyes. Suddenly, the yellow goop of the creature that she had just devolved transformed into a shade of pastel pink. It grew large and angry. Tentacles formed from its sides and stretched toward her. Her heart raced and she panicked. She fired her Time-Phaser over and over and over at the pink blob. She heard nothing but grunts from the pinkness and saw nothing but the growing blob until Alex screamed over the intercom, "Ginny, I repeat, we have incoming! Do you copy? Ginny! I need your undivided attention!"

She shook her head, and it felt like she was coming out of a trance. She realized that there had been no pink blob at all, that she had been firing her Time-Phaser over and over into an already-devolved yellowed ball of former-beaver-chicken-creature. She felt like she was going crazy, and shame washed over her at her loss of control. She slapped the side of her bubbled helmet a few times to shake the feeling. And then she noticed the rogue B.I.T. agent's ship—shaped like a numeral eight—far out on the horizon. It sat still for a couple seconds, and then jerked forward with sudden speed.

Ginny called back over her intercom, "I copy. Sorry, my head was elsewhere for a moment."

Alex nodded and replied, "Well, keep it here for now. Everybody hold position until I give the signal. Then we evade up and starboard by a hundred yards. Ginny, you and the Arthurs will have reason to break formation earlier than the rest of us. You'll know what I'm referring to when it happens."

"My! Name! Is! Art!" Normal-Art and Older-Art screamed simultaneously over the microphone.

"Arthurs, from here on out, I'm going to need everyone to maintain radio silence unless I'm giving an order," replied Alex.

Ginny heard both Arts sigh, but they made no other reply.

The incoming ship opened fire. Its first shots missed wide, slamming against the cocoon of ropes and trees that were wrapped around the hull of the B.T.S. Unicorn Husker. Ginny glanced over her shoulder to check whether Drillbot's hiding spot had been hit. The blasts hit the ship far above the robot, so she nodded and faced forward once more.

"Hold steady," ordered Alex as he loosed laser arrow after laser arrow into the distance, killing dozens upon dozens of the cute little beaver-chicken-creatures. "We need to set the bait for just a little while longer."

The ship fired again, this time missing less widely to the other side of the group. This payload also connected with another random portion of the B.T.S. Unicorn Husker's hull far above Drillbot.

"Hold," ordered Alex once more.

And then the ship opened with another volley, launching a steady stream of laser bolts toward the center of the group.

"Evade!" shouted Alex. He jerked his saddle up and to the right, easily dodging the bolts. The officers and Purple Shirts and Older-Art similarly dodged. Ginny did the same—using one arm for the device's handlebar while holding her Time-Phaser in the other—and came out unscathed. Normal-Art, however, jerked his throttle forward and twisted the handlebars as far to the left as they would go so that his saddle merely spun out of control in a tiny circle. He was about to be thrown from the saddle, so he gave up on all attempts at evasive action. He let go of the handlebars, leaned down, and hugged the front of the saddle to hold himself steady. The Gravitron Saddle stopped moving.

He looked around to see if anyone noticed. Then he said, "Uh, guys, I'm having problems with my—"

One of the laser bolts glanced across his right arm. Ginny heard him scream into the intercom. She watched as he was launched from his saddle. He smacked against the hull of the B.T.S. Unicorn Husker and tumbled down toward the Earth. He was now silent and limp.

Older-Art's voice entered Ginny's helmet through the intercom, saying, "Gin, if memory serves me correctly, this is the moment Alex was referring to when he said you, me, and my idiot younger-self will have reason to break formation earlier than the rest of the group."

Ginny shrugged. She placed her Time-Phaser in a holster built into the saddle and jerked her throttle forward to fly after her ex. As she swooped toward him, she glanced over her shoulder and watched the remaining members of the group scatter in all different directions as the ship bowled through the area in which they had all just been floating.

Ginny turned back toward Normal-Art. She leaned over in the saddle and grabbed him with her left hand. She swung him up onto the seat behind her and pulled his arms around her midsection. They remained limp and unconscious, so she pulled them up through the straps that held her respirator to her suit and cinched the straps down, so they held his hands tightly in place. She heard Alex yell over the intercom, "Drillbot! Now!"

She glanced up at Older-Art and noticed that he was smirking. "What?" she asked.

His smirk turned into a half-grin. He pointed to his younger-self's hands and said, "Oh, if only I'd been conscious for this when I was younger. But I wouldn't have appreciated it."

Ginny looked down and realized that she had strapped Normal-Art's hands to her so that they were cupping her breasts. She sighed. She reached to change their positions, but before she could do so, Older-Art screamed, "Look out!"

Ginny glanced up to see five of the cute beaver-chicken-creatures using their jetpacks to blast toward her, each gripping two mines apiece. They were nearly atop her. She managed to kick one off course with her right boot while Older-Art hit one with a bolt from his Time-Phaser, but the other three attached explosives to her Gravitron Saddle before using their jetpacks to zoom away.

Ginny cursed. She looked away from the escaping creatures only to see hundreds of arrows flying her way. She cursed again.

"Ginny, c'mon!" screamed Older-Art. He holstered his Time-Phaser and held out a hand toward her.

She clambered up atop her saddle so that her feet stood upon its middle. She pushed off and leapt toward Older-Art. She grabbed his open hand. He used his free hand to jerk his throttle forward. The trio zoomed away from Ginny's saddle just as the arrows crashed into the mines. The mines and the saddle exploded.

"Yes!" screamed Ginny in delight, feeling like an action movie hero. She felt exactly that way until Older-Art was blindsided by a figure she wished never to see again. As the figure crashed into Older-Art, his hand was jerked free from Ginny's. It happened so fast that she had no time to react.

Older-Art's Gravitron Saddle flew out from under him and careened away into the distance. Ginny was knocked aside by the force of the intruding figure. She flipped end-over-end in the opposite direction, falling toward the Earth.

As she flipped, her view traded off between the Earth below her and the action surrounding Older-Art. The next time she flipped to face him, she saw that a flaming phoenix with the head of God-Art had snatched him from the saddle. A flip later, the phoenix had transformed completely back into God-Art, and he held Older-Art in place by wrapping his arms and legs around the mortal.

Ginny cursed. On the next flip, she could see that God-Art's filthy cockroach sidekick—wearing a ridiculous spacesuit with a bubbled helmet—was perched upon the god's shoulder. The next flip, lightning flashed between the bug's antennae. The next flip, both God-Art and Older-Art were gone.

Ginny cursed again. On the next flip, the pair of hands strapped around her chest squeezed her breasts. Ginny brought the heel of her boot up behind her, kicking Normal-Art squarely between the legs. Ginny heard him scream a curse over the intercom. The act brought her no joy, for her mind was racing with anxiety over the abduction of her lover. But she kicked Normal-Art again, anyway.

"This is Ginny," she squealed over the intercom. "I've lost my Gravitron Saddle and need extraction!"

She glanced back toward the battle and saw a horde of the beaver-chicken-creatures zooming toward her.

She added, "Sooner rather than later!"

CHAPTER 30

DESPERATION

THE ROBOT'S DRILLS burst through the view screen, sending shards of glass flying into the bridge for a brief moment before the vacuum of space overpowered the artificial pressure machines and sent the glass hurtling back out into the blackness.

Agent 27142 screamed at God-Art, "You want to take care of this damned robot? You're a god, I'm pretty sure you can take him!"

Agent 27142 glanced over at the god and dread filled his stomach. The god had transformed into a flaming phoenix. In a flash of power, the phoenix leapt through hole left in the ship by the demolished view screen and twisted to dodge past Drillbot's murderous drills. The god flew away, leaving Agent 27142 to fend for himself.

"You bastard!" bellowed Agent 27142 at the god, realizing that he had been abandoned and was now likely about to die. But visions of 29333's corpse raced through his head, and his bowels turned to steel. He refused to die until he tasted vengeance for his murdered love.

The drills slashed toward him with murderous fury. He leaned back as far as he could, dodging a swipe by less than an inch. He knew this futile evasion would not keep him safe for long.

He glanced around the bridge for help. The *Timeflow Gun* lay strapped in a holster attached to the wall over near the now-empty passenger seat. If only Agent 27142 could reach it, he could use it to do something wonky to the robot, maybe even reverse time on it so that the robot no longer existed or send the robot careening through time to another Earth. But the gun was too far away. Agent 27142 would need to unstrap himself, get over there, unstrap the gun, and change its settings before the robot could swipe its drills at him again. There was no way he would make it in time, not without being severed in half.

Agent 27142 cursed God-Art. And then he noticed his ticket to survival—a pair of antennae wiggling in his peripheral. He pulled Henry free from the holster around his waist.

"Henry, you awake?"

"Yes," replied Henry. "Just sitting here trying not to die."

Agent 27142 sighed. He said, "OK. I need you to get ready to jump."

"Already am."

"Good," said Agent 27142. "Now jump!"

Lightning flashed between the gourd's antennae. "At once!" exclaimed the gourd.

"And take the robot with you!" yelled Agent 27142. As lightning began to flash out of the antennae and toward Agent 27142, Agent 27142 spun Henry so the lightning flash was directed toward Drillbot. Agent 27142 threw Henry at the robot. The gourd narrowly missed the robot's slicing drills before colliding with Drillbot's torso. Henry's lightning erupted in full force.

Henry began to say, "Wait, wha—"

But everything happened so quickly that Henry must not have had time to adjust, and within milliseconds, both Henry and Drillbot disappeared.

Agent 27142 grabbed the control stick of the ship and jerked it sideways. He spun the ship around until he found God-Art's fiery bird-form flapping across the blackness of space. Beverly rode atop the god's neck like a cowboy on a bull, her forelegs gripped tightly around feathers flowing from the phoenix's head as she tried not to be bucked off. Agent 27142 watched as the phoenix's head and torso transformed back into the god's humanoid form. Beverly now sat on his shoulder and gripped his ear.

The god crashed into a figure that was sitting upon one of the floating saddles. The figure had been reaching a hand down to rescue a pair of purple-suited B.T.T. agents who had lost their saddles—one of them the grunt that Agent 27142 had earlier hit with his turret. As Agent 27142 aimed his turrets to engulf the god in a barrage of lasers blasts, the god transformed completely back into his humanoid form and then disappeared with his abductee in a flash of lightning that erupted from Beverly's antennae. It happened so fast that Agent 27142 had no time to stop it.

Agent 27142 cursed again. Rage filled him. There could only be one person whom the god would abduct, and it was their common prey. The god had utterly betrayed Agent 27142, and now the god could achieve his goals without compensating Agent 27142 for his services.

Fury clouded Agent 27142's vision. He decided that he *would* achieve some semblance of vengeance today, even if it was not upon his optimal target. He spun the ship, looking for someone upon whom murder would provide a modicum of satisfaction. There! He locked onto the obvious mastermind behind the trap that had lured him close to the damned robot: the man with the horsehair crest atop his space suit. The man was currently fending off a swarm of BeavBoks.

Agent 27142 unstrapped himself from his chair. He removed his Scatter Gun pistol from his holster and held it in one hand. He unhooked the *Timeflow Gun* from the wall and shoved it into the holster from which he had removed Henry, using a buckle to clasp it in place. *You can never have too many guns,* he thought.

Agent 27142 gunned his throttle toward the man. He opened fire with the ship's turrets, but the man had apparently noticed Agent 27142 without looking away from his fight with the BeavBoks. The man jerked his metallic saddle up and to his right, evading Agent 27142's blasts with seemingly little effort. However, this man's maneuver was identical to the one he had performed the previous time Agent 27142 had opened fire upon him, and overreliance on it was a behavior that Agent 27142 had predicted. Agent 27142 had already steered his ship to compensate, bringing him in close so that he might feel the pleasure of striking the man hand-to-hand and killing him while looking into his eyes.

As Agent 27142's ship zoomed beneath the man with the horsehair crest, Agent 27142 leapt upward out of the busted view screen. Agent 27142 managed to grab one of the flaring engines of the man's saddle with his left hand. He ignored the pain as the heat of the engines burned through his flesh. He swung upward as hard as he could, bringing his left foot up so it crashed against the man's helmet.

This kick caused the man to jerk forward in the saddle, which in turn caused him to gun the throttle and blast toward the Earth. As they zoomed forward toward the planet, the man powered down his weapon and holstered it before attempting to regain control of the flying saddle. Agent 27142 jabbed his Scatter Gun pistol into the ribs of the man, but just before pulling the trigger, the man elbowed Agent 27142's hand. Agent 27142 cursed, because the jostle knocked the pistol away from the man's ribs, and when Agent 27142 fired, all he hit was a spot near the engine of the metallic saddle. The man then grabbed Agent 27142's wrist and elbowed his hand until he dropped the Scatter Gun pistol. It drifted away into space.

Following the blast from the Scatter Gun, the saddle's engines flashed with light and part of the device's metal carapace disappeared. However, the device sped up. Agent 27142 cursed at the unlikelihood of that happening. Then he cursed at the pain in his melted hand. He used his uninjured hand to grab the man by the back of the space suit. The saddle began breaking apart and its engines glowed bright red.

Agent 27142 and the man zoomed together toward the Earth atop the careening saddle, both struggling and fighting and kicking against each other as they flew into the atmosphere. Then Agent 27142's opponent managed to get his legs under him, crouched against the saddle, and pushed off.

The saddle exploded, and the force of the blast launched the pair even faster toward the Earth.

CHAPTER 31

DRILLBOT MAKES A NEW FRIEND

ALL DRILLBOT COULD see for a moment was bright lightning. The brightness overwhelmed his optical receptors, and they winked out. Blackness encompassed him for a fraction of a second. Then his optical equipment reset itself and he found that he was floating next to his assailant in the simultaneously colorful and colorless space between realities.

Drillbot roared his version of a roar, which sounded a lot like gears grinding together. He aimed below the bubbled space helmet and stabbed the gourd in its center with his right drill. He noted with annoyance that a piece of its yellowed inner flesh sprayed into the ether and stuck to his left telescopic eye.

"Noooo!" screamed the gourd. "Please!"

Drillbot frowned his version of a frown. The impaled gourd spun round and round on Drillbot's drill. The gourd groaned. Drillbot asked, "[whir] You can – CLACK – You can talk?"

Though the gourd had no face and Drillbot could see no way for it to express emotions, he could sense that the gourd was both scared and annoyed.

"Of course, I can talk! You can hear me, can't you?"

"[whir] Affirmative."

Drillbot powered down his drill. The gourd spun a few more circles before the drill slowed to a halt.

"I feel like I'm going to be sick," said the gourd.

Drillbot focused on the piece of gourd stuck to his telescopic eye. He did not like the prospect of more of this creature's innards landing on him. "[whir] If you are – CLACK – if you are going to be sick, please refrain from – CLACK – refrain from vomiting or expunging any more of yourself onto Drillbot."

The gourd sighed. "I'm a freakin' vegetable. I can't vomit, you fool. When I get sick, I turn from orange to white and exude a noxious gas."

"[whir] Oh. Feel free to get – CLACK – to get sick, then. Drillbot does not – CLACK – does not breathe."

The gourd sighed again. "I take it that you are Drillbot?"

Drillbot nodded and replied, "[whir] Affirmative."

"Hi, Drillbot. I'm Henry."

Drillbot initiated his greetings sequence. "[whir] Nice to meet you, Henry. How are you – CLACK – are you doing this fine day?"

The gourd groaned, "I'm impaled on a drill. How the hell do you think I'm doing?"

Drillbot sighed. He realized that he had initiated the greetings sequence to begin conversation with a friendly sentient being when he should have initiated the greetings sequence to begin conversation with a moderately annoyed and potentially hostile sentient being.

Drillbot took a moment to allow the program to switch over. Then he said, "[whir] Nice to meet you, Henry. You seem at least moderately distressed. Is there anything – CLACK – anything Drillbot can do to help?"

The gourd sighed again. Drillbot wondered for a moment if the gourd knew any other expressions. Then the gourd said, "You can go back in time and not impale me."

Drillbot allowed his systems to process that conundrum. He remained silent for a few seconds before replying, "[whir] Drillbot has processed that option. He sees the outcome as – CLACK – as unlikely unless Henry can jump between moments in time as well as – CLACK – as well as dimensions."

"Alas, I cannot."

"[whir] Then perhaps Drillbot can – CLACK – Drillbot can make Henry more comfortable by removing Henry from his drill?"

Drillbot began to reach his left drill over to knock the gourd from his right drill.

"No! Please! My skin's been breached! Rot has already begun setting in, and it will increase at an exponential rate if you further expose my insides. Please, whatever you do, don't take me off your drill!"

Drillbot stared at the large, pathetic vegetable on the end of his drill. The gourd's antennae drooped limply and yet again, without understanding how he could tell, Drillbot understood that the vegetable was frightened. Drillbot moved his left drill away from Henry.

"[whir] Then Drillbot shall – CLACK – shall not remove Henry. But what can Drillbot do to ensure that Henry – CLACK – that Henry does not rot?"

Henry moaned. Then he said, "Unfortunately, there's really no cure for my people when the rot sets in. Not unless you can freeze time around me."

Drillbot smiled his version of a smile. "[whir] Drillbot cannot, but he may know some people – CLACK – some people who can."

Henry squealed in delight, "Wonderful news! I'm not ready to die. I haven't even sown any of my wild seeds yet."

"[whir] Then Henry will need to – CLACK – to jump us back to the place from which we just came."

"That's not so wonderful news. There's a battle taking place there, you know."

"[whir] If anyone can help Henry freeze time, then the B.T.T. – CLACK – the B.T.T. can."

Henry sighed. "I repeat: there's a battle taking place there. Your friends in the B.T.T. are about to die. All we'd be doing is jumping into a situation where we'd die, too. I'd rather just rot here with you, if it's all the same."

Drillbot's smile transformed into his version of a frown. "[whir] It is *not* all the same to Drillbot. Drillbot was removed from the battle against his will. Many of Drillbot's friends are in peril because of his – CLACK – because of his undesired removal. Drillbot can guarantee Henry that Henry will not – CLACK – will not die of *rot* if Henry does not return us to the battle. He will die of violence."

Henry was silent for a moment. Then he sighed again and said, "Fine. I'll take us back. I never intended to jump you out of there, anyway. The guy who kidnapped me from my original bond-master tricked me. You've just got to promise me that you'll look after me until we can get the B.T.T. to patch me up."

Drillbot nodded. "[whir] Of course Drillbot will look after Henry. Drillbot protects his – CLACK – protects his friends."

Drillbot sensed a feeling of relief and happiness drift from the pale gourd. Henry said, "Very well. We'll be on our way."

Then lightning flashed between Henry's antennae, dangled there for a moment, and launched into Drillbot's torso.

CHAPTER 32

SHOWDOWN IN THE MIDST OF REVOLUTION

ALEX ELBOWED HIS assailant squarely in the bubbled space helmet. The attack gave him just enough respite to save his own life.

Alex reached down and toggled a button on his space suit. It was the one marked *Atmosphere Reentry Mode*, and after pressing it, a portion of his suit's power transitioned from operating his respirators to generating a weak force shield that would keep him from burning up in the atmosphere as he fell through it.

Alex's assailant—who Alex recognized from classified briefings and from past time-loops as Agent 27142 of the B.I.T.—must have realized what Alex was doing, for the cretin used one hand to turn on his own *Atmosphere Reentry Mode* while simultaneously jerking his other hand forward in an attempt to toggle off Alex's button. Alex knocked the offending hand aside, but the force of his block sent him spinning away from Agent 27142.

Alex wished for a moment that he had been subtler about activating his own field. If he had, then maybe Agent 27142 would have burned up and this fight would have been much easier. Alex pushed the missed opportunity from his mind and concentrated on the fight at hand. Once he gained his bearings and brought his spinning under control, he noticed that Agent 27142 was diving straight toward him.

Alex decided to lure Agent 27142 into a false confidence for this incoming attack, so he feigned losing control of his fall by flopping his arms out to his side and kicking his legs and shrieking in terror. He waited for Agent 27142 to close the distance between them and take the bait. However, Agent 27142 stopped his dive toward Alex, instead leaning backward and shifting his momentum to move away from Alex. Alex frowned. His acting must not have been as good as he intended.

Alex shrugged. Since Agent 27142 was not going to fall for his trap, Alex stopped pretending that he had lost control of his fall. He and Agent 27142 stared at one another. Agent 27142's eyes were full of rage. Alex's, however, were full of serenity[9], and this mismatch of rage versus serenity was just how Alex liked it. For rage would eventually fumble out of control, while serenity would maintain control until it eventually struck a lethal blow.

Alex's and Agent 27142's force shields glowed completely red as the planet loomed closer and closer. It grew harder to breathe as more power from Alex's respirator shifted to his force shield. The pair continued staring at each other. Alex grinned, and it seemed to only enrage Agent 27142 further. Soon, Alex noticed that Agent 27142's shield was no longer glowing quite so red and hot. This meant that the pair had finished falling through the atmosphere.

Alex reached up and toggled a button on his suit. It powered off his force shield, allowing power to return to his respirator and other basic functionality. Agent 27142, however, did not do the same. He instead toggled a different button, converting the power from his shield to his jetpack. He launched at Alex, fury etched across his face. The sudden conversion of power to the jetpack made the man so fast that Alex had no time to react or to dodge out of the way. He sighed and prepared himself for impact, knowing that so long as he prevented a deathblow, he would eventually gain the upper hand.

Agent 27142's fists slammed into Alex's gut. Alex rolled with it as best he could to dampen the impact. It helped, but he felt the breath knocked from him, nonetheless. As Alex reeled, Agent 27142 gripped him in a bear hug and squeezed. Alex gasped for breath. Agent 27142 squeezed harder. Little colored specks began appearing around the edges of Alex's vision.

Alex responded with a pair of punches to Agent 27142's kidneys, but because Agent 27142's arms were wrapped around him, he could get little

---

9 Alex attributed much of his success in war to the sense of calm he always managed to retain in battle. Back in his own era, part of this serenity came from drinking deep from a horn of wine before a fight. But here in this odd future where he was living on borrowed time, the serenity came from knowing that every second he continued to breathe was a gift bestowed upon him— a gift that had yielded to him years upon years more battle experience than he ever could have hoped to earn had the B.T.T. not intervened in his life and recruited him into its service.

momentum behind the punches. He tried smacking his bubbled helmet into Agent 27142's. This affected his assailant not at all, so Alex brought his knee up to strike Agent 27142's groin.

Agent 27142 attempted the exact same move at the exact same time, and they only accomplished cracking their knees into each other. Agent 27142 released Alex from the bear hug, and both opponents instinctively reached down to rub the pain from their knees.

Alex saw an opening and punched at Agent 27142's gut. Agent 27142 dodged and grabbed Alex's arm just above the wrist with his melted left hand. As it happened, Alex glanced at his opponent's face and saw Agent 27142 grimace in pain. Agent 27142 noticed Alex staring at his face, so he punched Alex in the bubbled helmet with his free hand. Alex grinned as an idea popped into his head. Agent 27142 had just fumbled by revealing his weakness. Serenity had won Alex the day, Agent 27142 simply did not know it yet.

Alex used his free hand to grab Agent 27142's melted left hand. He squeezed with all his might. Agent 27142 released his grip on Alex's wrist and screamed in pain and fury. Agent 27142 lashed out with a kick, but Alex did not release the melted hand. Instead, Alex rolled with the kick, spun through the air, and used his momentum to twist Agent 27142's left arm behind his back. Alex, now behind his assailant and gripping his assailant's arm in place, wrenched upward. He paused for a brief second to reach around and turn off Agent 27142's jetpack. Then he went back to wrenching.

He could tell by Agent 27142's body language that the man was screaming, and he could tell by the force with which he was wrenching that something in Agent 27142's left arm was about to pop. He could also tell by glancing downward that the surface of the planet was closing fast. Alex noted Herceg Novi in the distance. He knew based on their trajectory that they were going to crash somewhere in the middle of the city in less than a minute. He noted how mundane the city looked now that the Infinity Vortex was gone.

Alex's grin widened. He twisted so both his feet and his opponent's feet were pointed toward the incoming city. He pressed a button on his suit that read, *Gentle Landing.* Dozens of marigold balloons launched from the back of his suit and inflated into spheres as large as the stallion upon which Alex rode into battle during his natural lifetime. Alex's fall was jerked to a sudden halt. His grip on Agent 27142's left arm meant that Agent 27142 was also jerked to a sudden halt, but a halt where all the force of gravity and momentum was focused through the arm that was wrenched behind his back. It was like Alex had suddenly been granted the ability to wrench with a force multiplied to an exponent far higher than his understanding of math allowed him to calculate.

Alex felt the pops that he was seeking in Agent 27142's left arm. And then he felt even more pops as the arm ripped free from its socket and from every tendon and ligament that held it in place.

The sudden loss in tension in Agent 27142's arm caused Alex to lose his grip. Agent 27142 slipped from his hands. The B.I.T. agent tumbled down toward the buildings far below. His left arm dangled uselessly at his side. Alex did not think it would have been possible considering how much pain his opponent must have been experiencing, but Agent 27142 managed to reach up with his uninjured arm and restart his jetpack just in time to spin himself into a controlled crash through the roof of a Gothic-style cathedral.

Alex piloted his balloons to land gently on the street nearby. As he landed, he pressed a button on his suit and the tethers holding the balloons in place were cut. The balloons floated away toward the horizon.

Alex stared at the cathedral into which Agent 27142 had disappeared. He had enough experience working in the B.T.T. to know that Agent 27142 would be far from dead, and just as far from defeated. Alex was not stupid enough to follow the deadly bastard into the cathedral where he would almost certainly be waiting to spring a trap, so Alex instead leaned on the wall of a little coffee shop across the street from the cathedral and waited.

After a few minutes, he looked at the chronometer he wore on his wrist. He realized it was almost time for a third party to enter this fray. He removed his bubbled helmet, set it on the ground near his feet, and smirked.

Not long after, Alex heard Agent 27142's frustrated curses drift out from the hole he had left in the roof of the cathedral.

*

Alex watched as Agent 27142 kicked open the wooden door to the old cathedral. Alex did not bother to stand fully upright. Instead, he continued leaning against the wall of the coffee shop, smirking with a level of nonchalant arrogance only present in those raised as the heir to an empire.

Agent 27142 stalked out of the threshold of the cathedral. He was still in his space suit, but his bubbled helmet was shattered and broken. He pointed a pistol shaped like a numeral eight at Alex, holding the gun in his good arm while his other dangled uselessly at his side.

Alex recognized the gun's make. It was a *Wells Class B Gun*, a model designed long before Alex had entered the B.T.T.'s service. It was more commonly referred to as a *Timeflow Gun*, and it could only legally be issued to medical-class ships or to high-ranking medical officers aboard major vessels in the B.T.T. fleet—like Doctor Randy, the Chief Medical Officer on the B.T.S. Unicorn Husker. More commonly it could be found illegally stowed aboard freighter-class transport ships with trade routes that took them through areas where attrition rates were high and replacement crew was scarce. The gun was an amazing piece of technology, but scientists in the B.T.T. had discovered that excess use of it creates bubbles at the end of time. When these bubbles pop, they cause the end of the Space-Time-Multinuum to move to an earlier date while simultaneously sending chaos drifting backward across the Space-Time-Multinuum. Thus, most of these guns had been taken out of commission, and the remaining guns were scarce enough that Agent 27142 could have raked in a fortune if he were to sell this one on the black market.

Alex grinned. He knew the third party would be appearing soon, so he needed to stall, if only for a minute or so. He said, "You know, you lucked out when you stole the ship that you stole. Most don't have *that* make of gun aboard. It's an antique. You could use it to reverse time and heal your arm. Or you could use it to travel to a particular point in the Space-Time-Multinuum. You could even go back in time and fix what *you* messed up. All you have to do is toggle those settings and point the gun at yourself."

Agent 27142 scowled. "Oh, I should *absolutely* listen to you," he said, his voice dripping with sarcasm. "Because you *definitely* have my best interests in mind. I'll go ahead and take my eyes off you to look down at my gun. That sounds really smart!"

Alex shrugged. "I wasn't lying about the gun's functionality," he said.

"But you're right. The moment you went to change the gun's settings, I would've pounced."

"I know. I didn't rise as high as I did in the B.I.T. because I'm an idiot."

Alex spat on the ground. "Could've fooled me. We should both be on the same side, but you attacked our ship unprovoked, *and* you raided the B.T.T. headquarters for no reason. And now, you must face justice."

Agent 27142's scowl deepened. He said, "No, I did not attack you *unprovoked*. I attacked you to avenge myself on my escaped prisoner and the murderous robot that he created, both of whom are Multiversal outlaws that *your ship* has been illegally harboring. And I only raided your headquarters out of desperation to save the Multiverse. I had no other choice. My escaped prisoner set in motion a course of events that would have eventually led to the Multiverse's destruction. I halted that possibility by freezing the B.I.T. home reality in time, and with it the cosmic forces that threatened to overwhelm the Multiverse."

Alex's grin widened. He replied, "Oh, please. You *really* think the cosmic bears were going to cause the destruction of the Multiverse? Son, the B.T.T. protects *all* of time, and frankly does your job by protecting space, too. We've already prevented the destruction that you fear. All you and I are doing now is working out the number of casualties on the metaphorical cosmic abacus."

Agent 27142s expression grew puzzled. He demanded, "Wait, what do you mean? You already fixed the cosmic bear problem?"

"The B.T.T. eats cosmic bears for breakfast," remarked Alex. He then pointed to his right, in the direction of the street that led to the edge of the city and eventually into the wilderness surrounding Herceg Novi. "Though if I were you, I'd be *less* worried about cosmic bears that're thousands of realities away and *more* worried about the mundane bear-creatures that're headed this way right now."

Agent 27142 resisted looking for a moment. But squishing sounds emanated from the direction at which Alex pointed, and he soon glanced down the street to see what was causing them. As Agent 27142 looked away, Alex leapt into the air, kicked Agent 27142 in the face, and then used his jetpack to blast up to the top of the eight-story tall building that housed the coffee shop on its bottom floor.

Thousands of bearopi flooded into the city. Their tentacles were each shaded a different color of the rainbow, and each tentacle had a different cute animal visage formed on its end. Two creatures led the pack as they rushed down the street on which Agent 27142 now lay. The first had a cute bunny growing from the end of its green tentacle. The second had a human in a designer suit growing from the end of its yellow tentacle. The suited-human-tentacle was chanting into a megaphone: "Re-vo-lu-tion! Bear-o-pi! Bear-o-pi! Freedom for *all!* Food for *us!*"

The marauding bearopi roared with excitement at each syllable. They smashed property with their tentacles and ripped citizens apart with their claws and teeth.

Agent 27142 gasped. He used his jetpack to launch up onto the same rooftop as Alex, removing himself from the danger of the street as quickly as he could. As soon as he landed, Alex leapt forward and kicked the *Timeflow Gun* out of Agent 27142's hand. It tumbled end over end and landed at the edge of the rooftop.

Agent 27142 screamed, "What are you doing? These beasts are going to overrun the city! They're going to kill us! We must stop them first, and then we can finish our fight."

Two bearopi clambered up the walls of the building and pulled themselves up onto the roof. Slaver dripped from their mouths.

Alex grinned. "No, we *mustn't*," he said. "I already know how this bearopi revolution is destined to end."

Lightning flashed behind the pair of approaching bearopi. A sound that reminded Alex of one of the demonic motorcycles he had encountered on Earth 89,053 roared over the cacophony of the revolting bearopi on the streets below. The torso of one of the bearopi exploded outward and blood rained upon Alex and Agent 27142. From out of the explosion came Drillbot, his left drill held out in front of him to guide his dive through the chest of the bearopus. Drillbot landed on the roof, rolled, and faced Agent 27142. Alex's grin widened. The third party had finally arrived.

The remaining bearopus gulped like a cartoon character and then leapt off the roof of the building, apparently deciding to go seek easier prey elsewhere in the city.

Agent 27142 said, "Oh, you've *got* to be kidding me! I thought I'd gotten rid of y—"

But before he could finish the sentence, lightning flashed from the antennae of the gourd impaled on Drillbot's right drill. The lightning crashed into Agent 27142's chest. It soon dissipated, and Agent 27142 lost control of his body. He tumbled onto his side, lying prone on the roof.

A morose voice from the gourd called to Agent 27142, "Don't worry. I did not kill you. I merely jumped your blood to another dimension and returned it. You have been temporarily disabled so that you may face justice for your crimes."

Drillbot rolled forward. He proclaimed, "[whir] Drillbot disagrees with Henry's mercy. Drillbot has had enough of – CLACK – enough of this scheming meatbag."

Drillbot revved his left drill and sliced Agent 27142 across the torso. Agent 27142's guts and bowels spilled out of the wound and pooled around him on the rooftop.

"Never mind," remarked the gourd to Agent 27142. *"Do worry*, I guess."

Agent 27142's eyes jerked wide open in surprise. He glanced down at his wound and his face clouded with desperation. He rolled over to the *Timeflow Gun* that was dangling on the edge of the roof. He grabbed it. He flicked a toggle with his thumb. He then aimed the gun at his open wound.

Agent 27142 was obviously trying to use the pistol to reverse time on his wound. But Alex noted something that Agent 27142 did not, and it was that in his haste, Agent 27142 had accidentally flicked the toggle in the wrong direction.

"You may not want to do that," warned Alex, but not with much conviction. Agent 27142 squeezed the trigger. A green blast of conical light crashed into his stomach. His stomach rotted and melted into a pile of goo. The rot began spreading across his body. Agent 27142 grunted.

Agent 27142 then glanced from the gun's settings to Alex. Agent 27142 screamed, seeming to realize what Alex already knew: he had sped up time on the open wound rather than reversing it.

Alex watched the life begin to fade from Agent 27142's eyes. With fingers that had suddenly become lifeless and clumsy, Agent 27142 quickly twisted seven knobs, which Alex knew meant that he was coding a particular time and location into the gun. As his body melted and sloughed away, he simed the gun once more at himself, this time pointblank at his own head. He fired. His head disappeared.

Then what remained of his body collapsed over onto its side. It continued decaying and melting and dissolving, and a few seconds later, Agent 27142 disappeared completely into a pile of deteriorated goo. Alex shrugged.

CHAPTER 33

NO REST FOR THE GILDED

IT FELT AS though a grenade had detonated inside Agent 27142's skull, and every single one of its fragments had found a pain receptor into which it thrust. When pain overwhelmed him like this, he would normally concentrate his breathing in slow, deep patterns. But now that his body was gone, he could no longer breath. On the plus side, with his body gone, the overwhelming pain ended at his head.

He saw little bursts of color in his vision. He mouthed a curse. He *could* have used the *Timeflow Gun* to heal his stomach wound, but the B.T.T. agent had him surrounded. He might have overcome the B.T.T. agent on his own, but not the agent *and* the robot *and* a surrounding horde of gigantic, ferocious bear-octopus-creatures. It was clear to Agent 27142 that he had been bested, and he decided that if he were about to die, then he would go out on his own terms. Not theirs.

He could feel his brain ceasing functionality. Death was beckoning to him, and it was a clarion call that he could not resist. He knew that he had mere moments to live.

But his desire to see Agent 29333 one more time overwhelmed both the pain and the siren call of Death. He wanted to use his dying moments to finally profess his love for her. And if his lack of functioning lungs pre-vented him from speaking his love to her, he would at least mouth it to her before he died.

He concentrated on staying alive, on knocking aside Death's impatient hand as it nudged him toward eternal darkness. The colorful-and-colorless expanse between realities and the infinite well outside of time loomed around him as the green, conical light yanked him through the ether. His head was being dragged backward through time and across space and would appear in seconds *within* the bridge of his shift-shuttle at the exact moment when Agent 29333 had used the shuttle to depart from him on Earth 4 to drop the Stasis Bomb on Earth 55,777.

And appear on Earth 4 he did.

He would have burst into tears if his decapitated head still had the functionality to cry. For he appeared not *within* the bridge of the shift-shuttle like he had planned. Instead, the green, conical light dropped him off nearly three-dozen feet *above* his old shift-shuttle. He must have made a slight miscalculation in his coordinates.

Agent 27142 attempted to scream a curse, but his jaw was already hardening from its lack of blood flow, and he found that he could not. Instead, he merely fell. The shift-shuttle was taking off, so it rose to meet him.

He smacked into the view screen outside the bridge of the ship. If he still had a heart, it would have broken. He could see the scowling love of his life through the clear, reinforced glass of the view screen. But he was unable to express his feelings for her, because he simply bounced off the glass surface and caromed up into the air, leaving a trail of red blood behind him. He hoped that his blood would grab her attention and cause her to realize what had just happened, but the ship's automatic cleaners went into effect and wiped away the gore.

Through the glass, Agent 27142 saw Agent 29333 shout something. He realized *what* she had screamed when lightning erupted from the front of the ship. He tried to frown, but his lips would not cooperate. They were beginning to creep upward into the permanent smile of rigor mortis.

Below Agent 27142, the ship surged forward into the lightning. Agent 27142 reached the zenith of his bounce, and gravity went to work, pulling him back toward the Earth. However, the lightning lay between him and the ground far below, and as he fell into it, he would have sighed if he were capable of sighing.

*

The last thing Agent 27142 saw before he died was the infinite colorfulness and colorlessness of *The Barrier*, the infinite expanse between realities. He cursed his luck, and then he allowed the dark grip of Death to envelop him.

*

After thousands of years of Agent 27142's head tumbling aimlessly through the barrier between realities, a pair of twins named Yonder and Rego happened to travel past this exact spot while riding upon their antennaed ostriches. The twins also just so happened to be a pair of gods from Earth 162,944,508. They slowed to a halt next to the lifeless head.

Rego pointed at the head and said, "Brother, tis not often that we encounter a severed head in this holy barrier realm."

Yonder turned to Rego and said, "Brother, thou hast the power. Let us learn the secrets of this head."

Rego nodded. He contorted his hands into a symbolic pose with his fingers bent and spread to resemble the petals of a lotus flower. And then he blew his nose upon the dead eyes of the head. The snot glowed blue and melted into the head's pores. Life returned to the head.

Agent 27142 awoke confused. He remembered dying, remembered the flashes of color behind his eyes as his brain finally stopped functioning. He even remembered the eternal darkness of his afterlife. But now his eyes were functioning again, and he was staring into the faces of a pair of men with identical facial structures. One's skin was pale blue while the other's skin was deep burgundy. One's dark hair was braided and fell over his bare chest to end near his feet while the other's blond hair tumbled in loose curls down to his waist. One's nose was pierced by a thick rod while the other's nose was pierced with a dozen small studs.

"What is happening?" asked Agent 27142. The words poured forth from his open mouth even though his mouth could not move.

The twins seemed to understand, for they replied. And over the next few minutes, the twins had a conversation with the head, learning Agent 27142's background and what had happened to him to lead him to this point. Agent 27142 found that when the twins asked him questions, he had no choice but to answer them fully and honestly, for his mind did not allow him to do otherwise. He realized that he must be under some sort of truth-telling enchantment, so he sighed.

Finally, Rego turned to Yonder and said, "Brother, we have learned enough from this foul cretin. I have judged his attitude and nature lacking. Thou hast the power. Add him to thy collection."

"As always, dear Rego, thy judgment is wise. He shall make a fine goblet, and his hateful spirit shall bring a certain delightful magic to it."

"Wait, what?" muttered Agent 27142.

The twins did not answer. Yonder removed a pot and an already-lit torch from the saddlebags on his ostrich. He used the torch to light the bottom of the pot, at which time Rego provided seven bars of gold from his own saddlebag. He placed these inside the pot, and they melted nearly immediately.

Agent 27142 tried to float away, but there was no possible escape. He tried to use his mouth to assist, but it still was incapable of moving. Besides, even if his mouth *were* working, the best he would have been able to accomplish would have been to wag his tongue back and forth to try to swim away through the ether.

He wanted to cry. He had been *so close* to being able to tell Agent 29333 his true feelings for her! And now he was relegated to being used for whatever foul purpose these twins intended.

Yonder flayed Agent 27142's head, cut off the top of his skull, removed his brain, and dipped his empty skull into the molten gold. Agent 27142 once more felt his spirit drifting away into his afterlife—the deep expanse of nothingness that he believed followed one's death.

But then an invisible tether grabbed his spirit and pulled him back inside his skull. Yonder stuffed Agent 27142's gilded skull into his saddlebag. Then the twins spurred their ostriches, and their ostriches jumped them back to their home Earth.

*

Until the end of time, Agent 27142's spirit was stuck inside the goblet made from his own gilded skull. Empires rose and fell. The twin gods who abducted him died as a new pantheon rose to power. This one, too, eventually fell. As did countless others that followed. Agent 27142 witnessed them all.

And unfortunately for him, he was passed from person to person and empire to empire and pantheon to pantheon over the years, being filled with every liquid imaginable. Every time someone poured liquid into him, hatred filled him, and he tried to scream. But this merely caused bubbles to form in the liquid. And thus, he became known as a cup with enchanted properties that made drinks more refreshing.

If he were a regular person and capable of emotions other than spite, he might not have thought this was as terrible a fate as he perceived it to be. He had achieved a kind of immortality, after all, and he was privy to secrets and intrigues within pantheon after pantheon, which would have been a constant source of entertainment to many. He was front-and-center in a nearly eternal string of parties. He was even worshipped for a while during one pantheon's reign as the patron deity of effervescence.

And then sodas were invented on this Earth, and he fell out of use. Someone at some point stuck him inside a crate and placed him in storage. And that's where he stayed. Forever.

Until he was discovered millennia later and placed in a museum. And then, over time, this museum fell into decay and this Earth was ravaged by war, and civilization was wiped from the face of the Earth, and a new species eventually arose in its place.

This new species created their own gods and developed their own civilizations. And these people eventually discovered the gilded skull-goblet and received delight from its magical, bubbly properties.

Once more, empires rose and fell. New pantheons and new cultures rose to power. As did countless others that followed. Agent 27142 witnessed them all. And unfortunately for him, he was again passed from person to person and empire to empire and pantheon to pantheon over the years, again being filled with every liquid imaginable.

And then this new species, too, invented soda. And stuck him in another crate. And that's where he stayed. Forever.

Until the cycle repeated itself.

CHAPTER 34

IT'S NOT OVER YET

ALEX HAD BEEN teleported back aboard the B.T.S. Unicorn Husker as soon as his fight with Agent 27142 had ended. He now stood at his station on the bridge, staring out the front view screen.

The space battle had ended while he was attending to the rogue B.I.T. agent. The B.T.S. Unicorn Husker had routed it assailants.

Hundreds of millions of the tiny creatures known as BeavBoks floated in the harsh blackness of space, smacking periodically against the hull of the Unicorn Husker. Well, to be clearer, their lifeless bodies in the forms of goopy balls of devolved flesh floated in the harsh blackness of space, smacking periodically against the hull of the Unicorn Husker. Amongst the dead also drifted the thousands upon thousands of ruined hulls of their tree-trunk-spacecraft—so many ships of such immense size that if Alex were still King of Macedonia and he were to collect the dead husks for firewood, they would fuel his army's campfires for decades.

The bodies of hundreds upon hundreds of Purple Shirts littered the battle site, too. Some had unfortunately been at the wrong place at the wrong time, having been sucked out into the vacuum of space through breeches in the hull. Others had died in battle, having donned their outer space defense gear and then been blown apart by BeavBok mines. Their disembodied limbs drifted amongst the starry heavens like flotsam in the sea after a hurricane.

Crews of Purple Shirts had been dispatched to the battle site to gather the remains of their fallen allies for dispersal back to their proper places within the timestreams of their home realities. Other crews of Purple Shirts darted amongst the aftermath, cutting away the thick ropes that still surrounded the B.T.S. Unicorn Husker. Once the bindings were removed, the ship would be free to move to the next phase of this mission.

Alex removed his eyes from the view screen and observed his

compatriots on the bridge, most of whom were going about their duties as though nothing monumental had just occurred. Captain King Solomon broke the mundanity by standing from the Captain's chair and raising his hands into the air in a gesture of victory. Applause and adulation from the bridge crew—all of whom were present except for Bagoo—resounded through the bridge, and Captain King Solomon accepted it with a bow. The B.T.T. had triumphed over the rogue B.I.T. agent and the creatures known as BeavBoks, and the Captain would receive all the credit, as per usual following a successful mission.

Alex smirked and added his halfhearted applause to the fanfare. He hoped that someday soon he might be promoted to captaincy of his own B.T.S. ship and experience this same sense of adulation and adoration. He missed the feeling desperately from his life as King of Macedonia before he had been recruited into the service of the B.T.T. There was nothing in existence that came close to the self-satisfaction inherent in soaking up the reverence of those around you.

Captain King Solomon motioned for silence, and a hush fell over the crew. He grinned, his yellow teeth poking out between the thick strands of his beard. He exclaimed, "Fantastic job today, everyone! We not only showed our grit against overwhelming odds, but we also saved the Space-Time-Multinuum from ultimate destruction."

The crew cheered. Younger-Arthur was the loudest amongst them, clearly audible over the cheers of the crew and the roaring of Drillbot's engines. He was attempting to start a chant of "Send! Me! Home!" but was the only one chanting the phrase. Alex noted that Ginny was staring out the view screen looking decidedly anxious, not joining in the cheering with the rest of the crew.

Captain King Solomon once more motioned for silence. The sound of the crew died down. Younger-Arthur continued his chant until 29333 glared at him, at which point he wilted and looked down at the floor. The Captain then proclaimed, "Once our ship is free from the BeavBoks' cursed bonds, we'll be on our way to Earth 55,777 to finish what we started!"

The crew cheered. Ginny seemed to understand this would mean pursuit of God-Art and Older-Arthur. She nodded and smiled. Younger-Arthur, however, was as dense as ever. He squealed, "After you send me home, right? I've done everything you asked of me! We *stopped* the Conspiracy of the Gods! We saw the proof. Please, just send me home!"

The cheers of the crew died away during Arthur's squealing. When Arthur was finished, Captain King Solomon replied, "Please, Younger-Arthur, restrain yourself from any more outbursts. I'd love to be rid of *you* just as much as you'd love to be rid of *us*. But it's not that simple. There is a near 100% chance that God-You learned from the rogue-B.I.T.-agent-version of you that the cosmic bear-shaped entities you unleashed from Earth 1,000,000 are frozen in stasis on Earth 55,777. And there is a near 100% chance that God-You is headed there to bide his time until he can exploit the situation—we know this because he has kidnapped your older-self, and historically, his *only* purpose in kidnapping any version of you is to use you as bait to help him obtain those cosmic bear-shaped entities, because they are cosmically linked to your unique essence. Though we prevented God-You from completely devastating the Space-Time-Multinuum with his C.O.G., we must also act to stop the cretin from wresting control of those cosmic bear-shaped entities. If we don't, then his abduction of Older-You will succeed in granting him what he desires, and this will lead to countless deaths across the Space-Time-Multinuum. And unfortunately for *us both*, your presence is vital in stopping God-You and thus saving these lives—after which this mission will finally be complete.

Captain King Solomon continued, "Besides, even if we sent you home right now, could you *ever* comfortably relax knowing that at some point in the future, you'll be kidnapped by God-You and will ultimately die because your younger-self was too selfish to rescue you? This is about saving *your* life just as much as the rest of those in the Space-Time-Multinuum who would be caught in the crossfire. But ultimately, it is *your* choice. If you want to sentence yourself to death in the future to gain a few more hours on your couch right now, then I shall not stop you."

Younger-Arthur frowned and thought about it for a moment. Then he said, "Future-Me has had a good run. I'd like to return home now."

Ginny gasped, "You're despicable!"

Captain King Solomon scowled. "Utterly despicable," he exclaimed. "Unfortunately for you, Arthur, I lied. I'm *not* sending you home yet, not until we rescue your future-self and finish what we started. I thought a little logic might cease your complaining for a while. But I guess I was sorely mistaken."

Tears came to Younger-Arthur's eyes. He moaned, "Wait, what? You said I could choose."

Captain King Solomon ignored Younger-Arthur. He turned to Ginny and said, "Ginny, I give you permission to beat him and maim him however you see fit if he interjects or complains again. Just remember, if you maim or disfigure him too badly, then his future-self will suffer those same scars and injuries. And since his future-self currently has but a missing finger and a slight limp in his right leg, I'd advise against harming him with anything worse than that, as otherwise you might cause a logical inconsistency in this timestream."

Ginny nodded. She kicked Younger-Arthur in his right shin. He flopped onto a nearby bench and slumped his shoulders. She continued to punch him and kick him.

Captain King Solomon nodded to Ginny and then announced to the crew, "As for the formal briefing for this final phase of our mission, I shall do it now, since we are already gathered together. We shall journey to Earth 55,777 as soon as the Husker is free from the binds that currently surround us. Earth 55,777 has remained in stasis since the renegade B.I.T. officer—Agent 27142—and our very own 29333 detonated a Stasis Bomb on the planet, freezing everything in that reality. As is the purview of the B.T.T., we must alleviate the problem of the frozen time and remove any interdimensional-intertimeliminal threats in order to maximize the lives saved within the Space-Time-Multinuum."

Alex glanced over at 29333. She showed no shame at what she had done during her pre-B.T.T. life, nor did she look away from the Captain when he brought it up. From Alex's past conversations with her, he knew that she believed she had done what was right at the time in order to save the Multiverse. She refused to apologize for it, and Alex respected her for that. Her ruthless orientation toward her goals is what led to her moving so quickly through the B.T.T. ranks and gaining an officer position with relatively few years of service.

The Captain continued, "We will be facing hostile cosmic threats on multiple fronts: God-Arthur with Older-Arthur in tow, the pink and blue bear-shaped entities, and Hephaestus—the leader of the B.I.T., who was on the verge of entering the fray when the Stasis Bomb detonated. At the point in which we will enter Earth 55,777's timestream, Hephaestus will hold in his hands a weapon that will allow for the containment of the cosmic bear-shaped entities. If we can commandeer this weapon from him, it will make success much easier for us.

"In addition," continued Captain King Solomon, "during the years since this reality was frozen in time, the B.I.T. has dumped a multitude of other random cosmic threats onto Earth 55,777 to prevent imminent doom after imminent doom to the Multiverse. Thus, when we remove the stasis effect, these other cosmic beings will be a problem, too. As such, I've contacted several of our sister-ships, who will be on alert to handle these other threats as needed. Our primary objective is God-Arthur and those bear-shaped entities, and we cannot allow ourselves to become distracted until they are nullified. Expect a briefing dossier to arrive in your rooms in a few minutes. It will be a couple more hours before these BeavBok bindings are completely removed from the Husker and we can move safely, so take some time to familiarize yourself with the details of the mission."

Captain King Solomon's instructions were interrupted when the entrance to the bridge opened and Bagoo entered. He dragged a small BeavBok behind him, its bubbled space-helmet removed and its face bloodied and its beak crooked. Bagoo tossed the creature to the ground in front of Captain King Solomon.

Bagoo said, "Sir, as instructed, I searched the battlefield for survivors. I found forty-three injured Purple Shirts who were capable of survival. I also found this creature, hiding beneath the ropes. He is the lone surviving attacker."

Captain King Solomon stood over the pitiable creature. "Do you understand the death and destruction that you caused today? What was the meaning of this attack?"

The BeavBok looked up at Captain King Solomon. Tears filled its eyes as it spat, "My name is Tick-Tick. I come from a terrible future where the B.T.T. genocided my people. Agent 27142 and the fiery-haired god helped me go back in time before my people's genocide, and I convinced my people to attack you. We planned to prevent our genocide."

Captain King Solomon shook his head. He said, "The follies of an unwise youth. If only you would have realized that you were being conned by your *supposed* comrades, you could have prevented so much slaughter.

Let me show you something from our archives."

The Captain turned to his chair and typed something into its interface. The bridge's view screen shifted and now showed a long string of text with the heading at the top: *History of the BeavBoks, an Extinct Species from Earth 798,098*. Captain King Solomon highlighted a paragraph toward its end: *An ambassador from the BeavBok species to the Bureau of Time Travel was manipulated by enemies of the B.T.T. to cause the species' downfall. The Bureau of Time Travel stationed two agents on Earth 798,098 in an attempt to prevent the genocide of the species by convincing the species' leadership to dismiss this BeavBok ambassador's call for war. But this ambassador, known as Tick-Tick, emerged triumphant in convincing the entire species to attack the Bureau of Time Travel in a single, desperate gambit. During this battle, the BeavBok species was eradicated by the Bureau of Time Travel in self-defense.*

The Captain pressed a button and the words disappeared. He said, "You see, Tick-Tick, the B.T.T. did not commit genocide on your people. Your people did it to *themselves* through this foolish attack."

Tick-Tick squealed in despair, "B-But how do you explain the f-f-factories covering my home? The B.T.T. got rid of us so that they could transform my home into a wasteland!"

Captain King Solomon shrugged. "Your people were dead. The planet was empty. We made use of it so that it would not go to waste."

Tick-Tick squealed again. Alex felt pity for the creature, so he had to restrain himself from patting the furry creature's head. Tick-Tick cried, "What have I done?"

Captain King Solomon frowned. "You have caused the extinction of your species. But that need not be the end for *you*."

Tick-Tick looked up at the Captain, tears flowing freely down his broken beak. "What do you mean?" he asked.

Captain King Solomon held out his hands. "You may join us. You may become an agent of the B.T.T., and you can work *with* us to prevent other genocides and other mass murders of civilizations. You can work to save more people than you killed."

Tick-Tick hung his head. Eventually, he nodded.

Captain King Solomon nodded toward Bagoo. Bagoo picked up Tick-Tick and placed him onto his feet. The bog ghost put an arm around the creature and led him toward the exit from the bridge. "Come on, we'll get you all situated," whispered the bog ghost.

Alex smiled. He had read the BeavBok entry in the archives, back when he attended to Officer Academy following his promotion from Purple Shirt status. The remainder of the entry, which Captain King Solomon had not shown to the creature, detailed the redemptive story of one of the bravest and greatest agents the B.T.T. had ever seen: Tick-Tick, who spent the remainder of his existence tirelessly saving lives. He would eventually captain his own B.T.S.-class ship and die sacrificing himself and his crew to prevent the destruction of the Space-Time-Multinuum at the hands of the Atomic Moo-Cow-Tornado Plague of Earth 886,000,432,111.

Captain King Solomon sat in the Captain's chair. He said, "Non-vital bridge crew are dismissed. Please return to your quarters and read the briefing dossier for the upcoming phase of our mission. I expect us to be ready to depart in exactly two-hours' time."

With that, a flood of Purple Shirts left the bridge, along with Ginny, Younger-Arthur, and Drillbot. Captain King Solomon turned to Alex and said, "You remember the upcoming mission on Earth 55,777, right? You don't need to go refresh yourself on the briefing dossier?"

Alex shook his head and answered, "I remember it, sir. No need for a refresher."

The Captain nodded. "The phrase you need to remember this time through is '*Opposite Day*.'"

"Got it, sir."

"Good, good. Then in that case, I've got a different task for you during the wait. Before we leave this Earth, choose a Landing Crew of Purple Shirts. Go with them planetside. As you know, the bearopi revolt was a success, and they have conquered Herceg Novi. Soon, they will conquer the rest of this Earth. You are to treat diplomatically with them. The Purple Shirts you bring with you are to be stationed in the palace of the bearopi czar and remain there to prepare the bearopi for the incursion of the hovering-rhinoceros species from Earth 697,212 three centuries from now. These Purple Shirts and their descendants are to remind the bearopi through the generations of the diplomatic measures they can take to prevent both species' dooms."

Alex sighed. He had hoped to get a couple hours' rest before the next phase of the mission. Captain King Solomon seemed to read his mind. He said, "You're First Officer. Rest is for the weak and for people below your station. They don't build statues and dedicate songs in honor of those who are well rested.

"You will make a great captain someday," continued Captain King Solomon, "and never resting is the bulk of the job description. We move from one emergency to the next until we burn out, and then we rest when we're dead. On the way, we save trillions upon trillions upon trillions of lives."

Alex nodded. "Yes, sir. Understood."

And with that, he spun on his heel and hurried to gather a Landing Crew.

CHAPTER 35

A VISIT FROM A FRIEND

GINNY SAT ON the cot in her room and flipped through the briefing documents.

Blah, blah, blah, something about a weapon to contain the cosmic bears. Blah, blah, blah, limit the number of casualties. Blah, blah, blah, other B.T.T. ships incoming to put a stop to other cosmic threats. Blah, blah, blah.

Ginny slammed the file folder shut and dropped it to the floor. She could not concentrate. Not when her lover had been kidnapped, and especially not when she was on her way to the reality where the Pink One was frozen in time. What if the Pink One regained control of her? What if she once more became a cosmic tool for death and destruction? She sobbed.

She stood from her cot and stomped on the file folder. Her feet left little black footprints of dirt in their wake. At one point in her life, she would have taken this as a sign that she should shower, but that naïve girl was long dead and buried deep inside the recesses of her heart.

Ginny frowned. Spiteful ghosts awakened inside her, phantoms of the pink tendrils that had once lived in her heart. She had the sudden urge to fight someone. The sudden urge to maim someone. The sudden urge to trample over her enemies and hear the lamentations of their beloved spouses and spawn.

She closed her eyes. She took eight deep breaths, counting to ten as she inhaled, repeating her mantra of "You are NOT that person, and you NEVER WERE that person," as she exhaled.

A firm knock rapped on her door. She opened her eyes. She stood and opened the door. As it slid upward, guilt filled the pit of her stomach and weighed her down, as it did every time that she laid eyes on this figure.

Drillbot towered over her. He said, "[whir] Does Ginny mind if – CLACK – mind if Drillbot enters?"

Ginny waved him in. "Of course not. Come in."

Ginny crawled back on top of her cot to ensure she would avoid the daggers protruding from Drillbot's wheels. He rolled into her room and the door slid shut behind him. His engines hummed idly, and the exhaust smelled like sugary candy melted over a campfire.

"What's on your mind, Drillbot?"

"[whir] Drillbot wanted to speak with Ginny, because she and Drillbot are about to – CLACK – about to return to a place with terrible memories for us – CLACK – for us both."

Ginny stared at her feet. Memories flashed through her mind's eye. She watched herself kill the love of Drillbot's life and then disintegrate the Tyrannosaurus Rex into nothingness. She sobbed. Then she muttered, "I'd prefer not to think about it."

"[whir] Drillbot understands. It is painful to remember. But Drillbot must – CLACK – must gird himself. Drillbot must build more memories in his CPU detailing who – CLACK – who the *real* Ginny is before he sees the corpse of past-Ginny that he left on the – CLACK – the battlefield. For when Drillbot sees this past-Ginny-corpse and the pink blob that envelops it, Drillbot will experience – CLACK – will experience rage. And he may not – CLACK – may not be able to control it."

Ginny reached out a hand and placed it on his drill. She said nothing. "[whir] Drillbot has forgiven Ginny for her actions. Drillbot hopes Ginny – CLACK – hopes Ginny comprehends the significance of this."

Ginny frowned. She said, "And you know I never asked for your forgiveness. I can never forgive myself. I took from you—and, frankly, from *many* people across the Multiverse—the person you loved most."

Drillbot nodded. "[whir] But Ginny has Drillbot's forgiveness, nonetheless. She was not in – CLACK – not in control of herself when she did those terrible things."

Ginny shrugged. "Doesn't make me less responsible."

Drillbot shrugged back. "[whir] Drillbot disagrees. And the pain and remorse that Ginny feels reinforces to – CLACK – reinforces to Drillbot that he is right about Ginny being – CLACK – being good."

Ginny frowned. "Think what you want," she muttered. "Just don't expect me to agree with you."

Drillbot's speaker vibrated, his red, telescopic eyes retracted about an inch inside his head, and the three radar dishes on the top left side of his head spun slowly counterclockwise. "[whir] When we arrive on Earth 55,777, it will take everything inside of Drillbot to control Drillbot's rage. Drillbot is saying this to let you know that his memories seem to work differently than – CLACK – than how they work for you fleshy beings, and if he loses control and murders Ginny – CLACK – murders Ginny, it has nothing to do with his – CLACK – his current feelings about her. For she has become a – CLACK – a friend."

Ginny arched an eyebrow. "How do your memories work differently than mine?"

"[whir] It seems you fleshy beings can – CLACK – can file them away. Maybe even delete them. Maybe remember things – CLACK – things differently than they actually occurred. But when Drillbot accesses information, Drillbot pulls up all of it at – CLACK – at once before filtering through for what Drillbot needs. It's how Drillbot's system was designed."

Ginny frowned. She did not quite understand. "I don't quite understand," she said.

"[whir] For example, when Drillbot accesses the parts of his memory pertaining to Ginny, Drillbot accesses the good and the – CLACK – and the bad all at once. Then he must run a filter or search function to find what he needs. This is where the problem can occur. As Drillbot is filtering, Drillbot tries – CLACK – Drillbot tries to keep the memories organized in chronological order, but when Drillbot becomes too angry, the filter sometimes malfunctions and all the memories process together, and he cannot tell current memories apart from past. Maybe it was a laziness in Drillbot's original – CLACK – Drillbot's original coding, but this is why rage concerns Drillbot. Because Drillbot may have difficulty differentiating current-Ginny from past-Ginny in the heat of – CLACK – in the heat of Drillbot's rage."

"And this malfunction will almost certainly occur when we enter Earth 55,777, since we will appear in the moments immediately following what I did to Ginny Rex."

"[whir] Precisely. Drillbot resisted rage from overwhelming him when we went to the – CLACK – went to the Holo-Scouting Deck together to observe her moment of death, but Drillbot may not have – CLACK – may not have the same self-control *in person.*"

Ginny patted Drillbot's drill. "Drillbot, if you lose control and I'm a casualty, then I'm only receiving what I deserve. If this is the last conversation we have because you kill me, *never* feel bad about it. I only hope that before I die, I might do some good to make up for the terrible things I did."

Drillbot nodded. "[whir] And *that* is why Drillbot likes Ginny better than – CLACK – better than the Arts. Drillbot will do his best to – CLACK – to keep his memories straight so Drillbot doesn't – CLACK – so Drillbot doesn't murder Ginny. This conversation shall be one moment that he will try his best to hold at the – CLACK – at the forefront of his processors."

Ginny was about to respond, but an alarm blared over the ship's intercom system, followed by Captain King Solomon's voice. "All personnel attend to your stations. We have arrived at Earth 55,777. We will be commencing our mission in exactly fifteen minutes. Prepare for battle."

Ginny nodded at Drillbot. "Well, I guess we should get moving," she said.

CHAPTER 36

WRONG PLACE AT THE RIGHT TIME

NORMAL-ART STOPPED BY Officer Yardish Groveland's station to retrieve his equipment for the upcoming mission, after which he returned to the bridge. He sat on one of the benches at the back of the room. He was so excited at the prospect of finally returning home after this stupid battle that he had actually read the mission briefing dossier that Captain King Solomon had provided. This would *finally* be the last leg of his mission, after which he would be free to return to his couch.

Soon, the B.T.S. Unicorn Husker would be unfreezing time on Earth 55,777. This would occur at a moment seconds before God-Art was destined to arrive with the kidnapped Older-Art in tow. The B.T.T.'s primary objective was to capture the cosmic bears—a convoluted scheme where the Landing Crew would wrest from Hephaestus' grasp the black onyx saber that the god had created, stab the bears with it, and remove them from Earth 55,777.

Normal-Art's job during the mission was to assist the Landing Crew in its secondary objective: rescuing his older-self from God-Art. This plan involved setting a trap before the god appeared at the location at which God-Art would be appearing. Since this location was atop the *Olympus* building, it thus lay simultaneously amid the warring pink and blue bears *and* in the place where Hephaestus was destined to enter the fray. It sounded especially dangerous.

Normal-Art glanced out the view screen. The B.T.S. Unicorn Husker was floating in a manufactured time bubble inside the universe of Earth 55,777. According to the briefing, this bubble allowed the ship and its crew to sit within the reality without suffering the time-freezing effects of the Stasis Bomb. However, the manufactured time bubble could not be maintained for long before it would melt, and if that happened, then the ship itself would become frozen in stasis just like the reality surrounding it. Thus, time was of the essence, and it was vital to get into position before Captain King Solomon used the technology aboard the ship to cancel the effects of the Stasis Bomb that were currently blanketing the entire reality.

Normal-Art glanced out the view screen and smirked. Floating in the blackness of space just above Earth 55,777 were more cosmic threats than he cared to count, deposited here by B.I.T. agents when the threats were too dangerous for them to stop. He noticed a creature that looked an awful lot like a colossal green man with dozens of squid-like tentacles dangling from its chin. He noticed a pale man with what looked like thousands of nails stuck in his head. He noticed an enormous glowing stiletto heel with purple lightning emanating from its toe. He noticed a horde of pixelated eight-bit cartoon characters. He noticed a dozen humanoid creatures who were all sitting atop winged horses and all wearing rainbow-colored suits of helmetless medieval knights' armor. Their skin glowed golden while their lips glowed red and their hair glowed blond. He could have sat there noticing weird creatures for the rest of his life.

But Captain King Solomon stood from his chair and said, "Arthur, why are you here on the bridge?"

Normal-Art did not notice that the Captain was speaking to him, at least not until the Purple Shirt sitting on the next bench walked over to him and elbowed him.

The Captain repeated himself, to which Normal-Art replied, "My name is Art."

Captain King Solomon sighed. He gestured around himself and said, "Do you not notice anything missing here, young man?"

Normal-Art shrugged. "Not really," he replied.

The Captain slapped himself on the forehead. He said, "You are the densest man I have ever met. Did you *read* your briefing dossier?"

Normal-Art jumped to his feet in excitement and exclaimed, "This time, I totally did!"

Normal-Art began reciting the plan to Captain King Solomon. When he arrived at the part about the Landing Crew jumping planetside to set a trap for God-Art, the Captain stopped him.

"Arthur, who was listed as part of this Landing Crew?"

Normal-Art closed his eyes to concentrate. He answered, "Ummm, Alex. Ginny. 29333. Drillbot. Bagoo. A bunch of squads of Purple Shirts. Oh, and me, of course."

Normal-Art opened his eyes. Captain King Solomon stared at him with cold eyes. He gestured around himself once more and said, "Yes, and other than yourself, do you see any of the people that you just listed here on my bridge?"

Normal-Art frowned. "Well, no."

Captain King Solomon crossed his arms and said, "That's because they are all at the Jump Chamber ready for transport down to the planet. Exactly where the briefing dossier told them to be."

Normal-Art stared at his feet. He muttered, "Oh. Guess I must have skimmed that part."

Captain King Solomon sighed. "Yes, you must have. Now get down there. I'm removing the stasis effect from this reality in exactly five minutes. If you *ever* want to get home, you better be teleporting planetside with your colleagues when I do so."

Normal-Art leapt to his feet. He scrambled out of the bridge and was halfway to the elevator when he realized he did not know how to get to the Jump Chamber. He sprinted back to the bridge and asked for a guide.

He made it to the Jump Chamber just in time.

He arrived on Earth 55,777 panting and out of breath. As he looked around, he concluded that he hated this place just as much as he did the last time that he saw laid eyes on it.

CHAPTER 37

ANOTHER TWELVE-PLUS DECADES DOWN THE DRAIN

OLDER-ART HAD KNOWN that God-Art was going to kidnap him during the battle above Earth 8,669. He vaguely remembered the incident from when he was in the position of his younger-self. But he did not have prior knowledge as to what was destined to happen to him between his kidnapping and the upcoming confrontation on Earth 55,777. He quickly learned that this period was worse than he possibly could have imagined.

"Just a few more decades," said God-Art. "Almost there."

For the billionth time in the last minute, cold overwhelmed Older-Art. He wished he could shiver. He wished he could moan. He wished he could shift his position to something more comfortable, or at least move his arms to plug his ears so he would no longer have to listen to God-Art speak. He wished he could do anything at all. But he could not.

He thought back to that terrible day when God-Art had snatched him from the battle above Earth 8,669. His body attempted to shudder. Nothing happened.

God-Art, in phoenix form, had tackled him from behind. Older-Art felt a sharp crack in his spine. He screamed. Lightning filled his vision. He floated in the colorful-and-colorless expanse between realities. He vomited, and the remnants of his breakfast caked the inside of his bubbled space suit helmet.

Older-Art had screamed again. God-Art ripped the helmet from Older-Art's head. The god tossed the helmet away. Older-Art watched it tumble end over end out into infinity. Older-Art refused to look into the deity's eyes. Instead, he looked at the gigantic cockroach sitting atop the god's shoulder. It was using one leg to hold onto a bolt of lightning. Its others were gripped tight to God-Art's ear and scalp, somehow not catching fire despite the god's flaming hair. It removed one foreleg from the god's scalp to wave at Older-Art. Older-Art timidly waved back.

Due to the motion in God-Art's fiery hair and the way Beverly's antennae seemed to be fluttering in some imperceptible wind, Older-Art realized that they were zooming through the expanse between realities at an incredible speed. Older-Art wondered for a moment how he was keeping pace with the pair, since he was not holding onto God-Art, and he felt nobody holding onto him. He glanced down and noticed God-Art's hand was gripping his lower right leg. He wondered why he did not feel it. As a matter of fact, he also no longer felt the constant tickling vibration from the Pulsar Boots on his feet. He shrugged.

After being dragged behind Beverly and God-Art for what seemed like days, Beverly finally let go of the lightning bolt. It flashed off into the distance and disappeared. She flapped her thin wings a few dozen times to slow the group's momentum.

They floated near a ball of crackling energy that looked like a sun made from rainbows. Carrier-class B.I.T. ships continually appeared in flashes of lightning and flew into the ball. Equally large ships continually appeared from within the energy ball, only to disappear into bolts of lightning that launched from their prows.

Beverly rubbed her forelegs together, creating a chorus of creaks and croaks.

"I see it, thank you," replied God-Art to Beverly. The god turned to Older-Art. He pointed at the ball of crackling energy. "That's the entrance to Earth 55,777. Home of the B.I.T."

Older-Art nodded. "I figured as much. So, let's get this over with. Go on in. It's not like I can do anything to stop you, anyway."

God-Art furrowed his brows. "You can't seriously think it's that easy."

Older-Art shrugged. "Who cares what I think? You love your own voice, so you're going to tell me why *it's not that easy* whether I want to hear it or not."

God-Art shrugged back. "True."

"Well, get on with it, then," said Older-Art.

God-Art pointed toward the energy ball and said, "It won't be so easy because we've got ourselves a good dozen or so decades to wait before the battle occurs that will bring the cosmic bears here. Entering Earth 55,777 right now would do naught but draw unwanted attention to ourselves."

Older-Art frowned. "Wait, what? A *dozen* decades?"

God-Art shrugged once more. "Give or take a few."

Older-Art felt like crying. He bit his lower lip. "How is that possible?"

God-Art smirked. "I keep forgetting how stupid you are. I should really try and remember before I next speak with you."

Frustrated, Older-Art tried to kick the god with his free leg. But his leg must have been asleep or something, because it refused to cooperate. He grunted in anger.

God-Art seemed not to notice. He continued, "The battle from which I abducted you took place long before the battle on Earth 55,777."

"Huh?"

God-Art sighed. "Beverly moved us across space to get here. But she has no control over time. I captured you just after the successful conclusion to my Montenegro Bay Convention. I appeared on your doorstep for the first time just over a century after that. I was dead for a couple decades before I resurrected and went on that absurd journey with Drillbot to rescue you from one of your reality's ridiculous hells. So, if we assume Earth 55,777 was frozen at the exact moment you were killed in the battle that takes place there, that means your death occurred sometime in the decades that spanned the time I lay dead and dormant inside your disgusting apartment. That is the earliest point at which the B.T.T. might unfreeze the B.I.T. home world. But that timing is the best-case scenario, so I would tack on another couple decades to the estimate just to be safe."

"Huh?"

"Look, it's quite simple: we're now in the right place for the next part of my plan, but we're at the wrong time. And the right time won't be here until approximately twelve decades from now."

Older-Art frowned. "But I'll be dead by then."

God-Art nodded. "And now you comprehend the problem. I need you alive as bait for the cosmic bears. But don't worry. I've got a solution."

God-Art wormed his head around to stare into Older-Art's eyes. Older-Art tried to look elsewhere, but no matter where he shifted his eyes, God-Art moved in front of them. Soon, Older-Art's eyes were unavoidably locked into the black pupils of God-Art.

The blackness began swirling and whirling and shifting. Soon, Older-

Art lost all concept of his surroundings. He found that he now stood atop an icy crag. Snow fell so hard around him that he could see nothing beyond a few feet in front of him. He tried to scream in terror, but clumps of snow fell into his mouth. Other than the Ninth Circle of Hell, the clumps were colder than anything he had ever experienced. Rather than melting, they grew and multiplied and forced their way down his throat. His entire body became frigid. His entire world glossed over in sudden icy whiteness.

And then the vision disappeared, and Art was back in the colorful-and-colorless expanse between realities. But something was wrong. He was much colder than he had been before experiencing the vision. His view was clouded with icy blueness. He could not blink. He could not move his arms. He could not move his legs. He could not move anything.

Older-Art panicked. He tried to scream, but he could not. He tried to run, but he could not. He could not even breathe.

God-Art's voice seemed to echo all around him. God-Art said, "Do not panic. I have simply frozen you in a magical block of ice to preserve your body and keep your spirit encased within it. I will stand vigil through the next dozen-or-so decades. I will watch as the cosmic bears attack the B.I.T. I will watch as Earth 55,777 is frozen in place. And I will watch until the B.T.T. eventually appears to unfreeze it so that its timestream can continue flowing.

The god continued, "See how the rainbow-colored energy ball marking the entrance to Earth 55,777 is in continuous motion and does so much crackling? Well, when this reality falls victim to the Stasis Bomb, all of that will freeze. Those B.I.T. ships you see entering and exiting would be able to go in if they wanted to, but they wouldn't be able to exit. When the freezing happens, I'll have to pay extra-close attention, because at the first sign of the energy ball beginning to move again, it will be time to strike. I will then free you from your personal cryo-stasis, and I will have Beverly bring us near the place where she detects the strongest version of us. That will be the blue bear. And the pink bear will be somewhere nearby. We will then snatch the Pink One when they are distracted by your presence, and I will obtain immeasurable power from it."

Older-Art tried to reply, tried to say something sarcastic about God-Art's supervillainous monologue where he detailed all the intricacies of his plan, but he could not.

Instead, he was forced to listen as God-Art continued speaking, "While we wait, let us pass the time with a story. I'll tell you about the time *I* was frozen in a block of ice. My older brother was particularly annoyed with me that day, and he thought that if he murdered me and caused my father to drink my remains, then I might stay dead. So, he lured me to th—"

Older-Art stopped listening. He wished more than anything else that he could die and finally be free of the stupid, inane god. Instead, he floated in silence, nothing but a prisoner inside a block of ice. He hoped the upcoming decades would pass quickly. But he did not get his hopes up too high.

*

Older-Art wondered if he had gone insane or if he had died again and this was, in fact, some sort of hell. God-Art was *still* droning on with the same story over a hundred and twenty years later—long after the Stasis Bomb had frozen time on Earth 55,777. He was describing every rock and every flake of snow and every other tiny detail that fluttered into his mind. He was flitting listlessly into other stories embedded within the current one he was telling. And he was *just now* about to start getting frozen by his brother.

"The water oozed across my left foot," said God-Art. "I felt a creeping tingle in my little toe. It felt like the time when I went swimming in the Serpent Sea and received a bite on my foot. When *that* happened, my extremities tingled and then they puffed up, bright and swollen and purple. And this swollen foot looked exactly like the fruit of the Boysenberry Bubble Tree from that time I traveled to the Gumdropbear Forest. The fruits were bright and swollen and purple, and their taste flooded my mouth with red syrupy goodness. This was a problem, you see, because eating the fruits was forbidden to anyone except the natives. So, the natives attacked. And one pinned me down wi—"

Suddenly, God-Art halted his tale. He pointed toward the frozen ball of rainbow-colored energy and exclaimed, "Look!"

Older-Art could not turn his frozen head to look, but luckily for him, he was already turned in the correct direction to see. His heart exploded with relief and happiness. A familiar, humongous, striped dirigible appeared. Older-Art noted its name in bold purple block letters written out on its hull near the engines: *B.T.S. Unicorn Husker.*

He had never experienced joy on this level. The B.T.T. had *finally* arrived. The B.T.S. Unicorn Husker would *finally* be unfreezing time on Earth 55,777. God-Art could *finally* finish his nefarious scheme. Everything might finally be done in a few minutes' time, and Older-Art might *finally* get to go home.

A thin, yellow bubble appeared around the B.T.S. Unicorn Husker. Solid rectangular prisms of light extended from the bubble surrounding the ship and crashed into the motionless energy ball that marked the entrance to Earth 55,777. The rainbows disappeared in a small section and The B.T.S. Unicorn Husker flew into it. The B.T.S. Unicorn Husker disappeared.

God-Art screamed with joy, "Only moments to go now!"

The god turned to Older-Art. He muttered some words in a language that Older-Art did not understand. And then flames leapt from his fiery hair and landed on the ice that surrounded Older-Art. It spread and fully surrounded the block of ice that imprisoned him.

For the first time in over a century, Older-Art felt warmth. It felt good. The ice cracked and melted. His organs heated and began working once more. He experienced his heart beating for the first time in so long that he had forgotten how it felt.

The ice sloughed from Older-Art and he screamed with joy. The fire returned to God-Art's head. Older-Art grinned. But then his body began tingling. It had been frozen in place so long from the ice that as feeling returned, it was overwhelming. Needles seemed to prick him everywhere except for in his legs. He screamed in pain.

Then he fainted.

*

Older-Art woke to find God-Art dragging him by the right leg. He glanced up from God-Art to Beverly, who was perched on God-Art's scalp, gripping a bolt of lightning with one leg and God-Art's scalp with her others.

Older-Art realized that they were now inches from the ball of rainbow-colored energy that marked the entrance to Earth 55,777. The energy was no longer frozen in place.

"What's happening?" squealed Older-Art, even though he already knew.

God-Art glanced down at him and grinned. "Earth 55,777 is finally unfrozen. I can finally finish what I started all those years ago."

And with that, Beverly guided them into Earth 55,777. Older-Art closed his eyes as they passed the threshold. When he opened them, he wished he had kept them closed.

The trio appeared nearly a dozen feet above the tallest building on this planet-spanning city. They immediately began falling toward the rooftop of this building. In the intervening moment before hitting the roof, Older-Art glanced around to gain a bearing on his surroundings.

The rooftop on which they were about to crash was the top of the B.I.T. headquarters. Off to the side on the rooftop was a mammoth neon sign that spelled out *Olympus*. Crashing against one another in the air nearby were the pink and blue bears, their raging fight creating in their wakes both destruction that demolished entire buildings and rejuvenation that repaired entire buildings. They zipped across the wanton violence of the battlefield and approached the *Olympus* building.

The trio of God-Art, Beverly, and Older-Art crashed in a heap onto the roof. God-Art immediately untangled himself and leapt to his feet. Beverly scrambled around him until she perched on his shoulder. Older-Art used his arms to push himself up into a seated position. He tried to gather his feet underneath him, but no matter how hard he willed his legs to move, they refused to cooperate. The terrifying sounds of the cosmic bears locked in battle grew closer.

God-Art turned to Older-Art and ordered, "Get up, you fool! Our prey will be within reach in a matter of seconds!"

Older-Art frowned. "I-I-I can't! My legs! They're not working!"

God-Art sighed. He trudged over behind Older-Art, grabbed the mortal by his armpits, and hauled him up onto his feet. "There!" screamed the god. "There's a time and a place to be lazy, and it's not now!"

God-Art let go of Older-Art. Older-Art's legs immediately and unceremoniously collapsed beneath him. He cursed. God-Art cursed.

"What's wrong?" screamed God-Art.

Older-Art screamed back, "I! Don't! Know!"

God-Art stared at Older-Art's midsection for a moment. The god's eyes glowed neon green. Then they faded back to their normal black voids.

"Hmmm," he said. "Seems your spine is broken. Gimme a sec, and I'll get you healed right up."

But Older-Art never received the opportunity to give God-Art a sec. The door to the rooftop burst open. A man nearly twice as tall as God-Art emerged from the door. The man wore a dull blue toga, had a horribly crooked nose, and had a beard that dangled down past his waist. His hair was bound in a ponytail that fell over his shoulders and reached all the way down to his hips. His legs were crooked and jagged, and he hurried forward with immense limps each time he took a step.

Older-Art recognized the man as Hephaestus, the High Commander of the B.I.T. Hephaestus' left arm dangled from his shoulder, skinny and undersized. His right arm bulged with muscle and carried a weapon that Older-Art recognized from his younger days: the onyx saber upon which the bears had been imprisoned when Older-Art first encountered them on Earth 1,000,000. It had been reforged and looked exactly like it had on that fateful day so long ago.

"Intruders to my land! Be thou members of the Blue Army or the Pink Army, it matters not. Hephaestus has spent too long frozen in time and is filled with rage! Thou shalt join thy comrades as I send all of thee to meet my brother, Hades!"

God-Art cursed. Hephaestus raised the saber high and readied to attack.

The sound of the warring bears grew louder.

Older-Art stared down at his feet. Death was approaching from all sides, and he could do nothing to escape it.

CHAPTER 38

CALLED BACK

EVERYWHERE GINNY LOOKED, she saw corpses. Corpses and debris. Corpses and debris and wrecked ships. Corpses and debris and wrecked ships and scorched Earth. Corpses and debris and—there! Her pink blob, less than a quarter mile away.

The blob was just as she had left it when time had become frozen following her final battle as the Pink One's Right Hand of Destruction. The blob had been in the process of regrowing and was only about a dozen feet tall rather than the kaiju-sized proportions it normally occupied when Ginny was encased within it. Ginny could see her own corpse floating inside the blob. Her corpse was being held together by the pinkness, for it had been ripped in half by Drillbot and had a hole through its head the size of one of Drillbot's drills. Ginny shuddered.

Near the blob, the pink and blue bears flew. Time was moving normally once more, so they crashed into one another. Their snarls echoed across the battlefield. Dread overwhelmed Ginny, and she knew that she should not have returned to this place.

Ginny felt something hard and pointy nudge the back of her shoulder, just above the jetpack strapped to her back. She realized that she had not moved since appearing on this Earth, for her terror at seeing the pink blob had hypnotized her into immobility. She glanced over her shoulder and saw Drillbot behind her. He gestured across the street to where the rest of the Landing Crew had crossed. They all stood waiting for her. She nodded. She stepped away from the wreckage of the building beside which the Landing Crew had appeared. She sprinted across the street, careful not to trip over random debris from toppled buildings or roll an ankle on the plethora of holes that had been ripped across the pavement.

When she and Drillbot reached the group, Alex pointed toward the roof of the adjacent building. The perspective from here did not allow her to see it, but Ginny knew that atop the building glowed red neon letters that spelled *Olympus*. Alex wore a helm over his head and armor over his marigold uniform that made him look like an ancient Greek warrior. He said, "On my mark, engage jetpacks. Ready weapons and set to permanent devolution. The B.I.T. High Commander is not to be harmed, but all other hostiles are fair game."

Ginny's mind briefly flitted to the picture of Hephaestus, the B.I.T. High Commander, from the briefing dossier. She frowned. He was a horridly ugly god with long hair and one shoulder so much larger than the other that she wondered how he ever stood upright without toppling over. Alex strapped over his ancient-looking helm a device that made him look like he had tied a coconut bra around his head, with a shell covering each ear. An elbow nudged Ginny in the side.

Normal-Art leaned over and whispered to her, "What's that thing?"

His breath smelled terrible. She sighed. The horrible stench could only mean one thing: that he must be on one of his oft-repeated rebellions against what he deemed *"the vast dental conspiracy."* During these phases, he would claim to anyone who would listen that dental care was a sham and that there had been no dental care for most of human history, and thus dentists and their industry were nothing but fearmongers using threats of cavities and gingivitis to earn profits from the uneducated masses. Based on her past relationship with him, however, Ginny knew these dental rebellions *always* coincided with periods when he felt too lazy to brush his teeth. She shuddered—yet again wondering how she had ever spent so long in a relationship with him—and replied, "It was in the briefing dossier, if you'd have taken the time to read it."

Normal-Art stared at his feet. "I read *most* of it. But, y'know, I skipped a few pages here and there. When it got boring."

Ginny sighed. "It's a listening device. He's listening to what's happening at the top of the building to ensure it is clear for us to set a trap to flank God-You."

Alex removed the listening device from around his head and turned to the group. "Now!" he shouted.

Alex reached down to the two handles sticking out from the sides of the jetpack, both of which were curved to end in front of him for easy access. Each handle had a red button on its end, and as Ginny recalled from her brief scan of the briefing dossier, pressing both together would launch you straight up. Pressing the left button would power only the left engine and thus steer you right. Pressing the right would power only the right engine and thus steer you left. Alex pressed both buttons and launched into the air. 29333 immediately did the same. Bagoo—who needed no jetpack—flew into the air after her, followed by the three-dozen Purple Shirts and Normal-Art.

Ginny shrugged, grabbed her handles, and jammed her thumbs down upon the buttons. She launched straight up, faster than she had ever launched before—well, aside from her experience in the Obelisk Orb decades ago with the dwarven-dictator-version of herself. She squealed in excitement.

But as she passed the thirty-story mark, the excited squeal shifted to one of terror.

Something wrapped around her right ankle. She glanced down and screamed. The pink blob had stretched a tentacle from blocks away and grabbed her. She felt it calling to her inside the recesses of her brain. It demanded that she return to its enveloping madness.

"No!" she cried. "Please! Not again!"

She jammed the jetpack's buttons down harder than ever, hoping to provide enough power to escape.

But it was to no avail. The blob was stronger than the feeble jetpack strapped to her back. It pulled her toward it like she was a fish caught on the end of a line. She felt the ligaments in her knee being torn apart, but she did not stop trying to fly away.

She looked over at the blob. Even though it was no longer the building-sized blob that it had been throughout most of her time in its grasp, something about it being condensed down into a more concentrated form made it seem even more hateful. And as it pulled Ginny closer, it shrank down to the size and shape of a teddy bear. It dumped onto the ground the mangled corpse of Ginny's past-self, making room for current-Ginny. Terror filled her heart.

Ginny heard a voice in her head. Pink words formed above the pink blob-bear, spelling out the words appearing in her head like they were word balloons from a comic book. *Return to us and restore our covenant. You shall be our Right Hand of Destruction once more, and your home reality shall be allowed to continue living until it is the last reality in the Multiverse.*

"N-N-Never!" Ginny cried. "You can destroy my Earth all you want. But I'm done!"

Tears fell from Ginny's face. She pulled her Time-Phaser from her holster and fired it at the blob, but the blob opened a hole in itself, and the devolution blast passed through without touching it. Ginny continued firing until the weapon overheated and she had to stop. The blob opened hole after hole in itself, and none of the Time-Phaser blasts ever came close to connecting. It continued pulling her toward it. She could not stop it.

The pink words continued appearing above the blob. *If Ginny will not resume her place as our Right Hand of Destruction, then we shall consume her life force and transform her into our puppet. And then we shall use this puppet-Ginny to destroy her home reality after we finish destroying the B.I.T. home Earth. That shall be her punishment for breaking our covenant and abandoning us.*

The pink blob-bear's mouth opened wide. Ginny could not stop from being swallowed. She would become the thing she hated once more. She had no choice.

Yes, give in. Your friends have abandoned you. There is no hope for you. There is only you and the Pink One, and together, we shall wreak havoc on the Multiverse.

Dread filled Ginny's heart. The damned blob was right. It was hopeless.

She gave up. She powered down her jetpack.

As the pressure was relieved in her leg and she began being reeled in toward the blob at blinding speed, she heard a rumbling behind her. She wondered why the jetpack's engines were still rumbling now that she had shut them off.

CHAPTER 39

A SACRIFICE BACKFIRES

DRILLBOT WATCHED THE rest of the Landing Crew as they activated their jetpacks and launched up to the top of the *Olympus* building. As usual, he had volunteered to take the rear to protect his more vulnerable companions. For a moment, he wished that he had brought along Henry to keep him company. But alas, after ensuring proper medical treatment had been conducted on the friendly gourd, he had left the gourd on his nightstand to keep him safe.

Ginny was the last of the Landing Crew to launch. As soon as she did so, Drillbot leapt into the air. He had received no jetpack, which was fine with him. He had no hands to operate the controls, and he was likely too heavy for one to work on him, anyway. He stabbed a drill into the side of the building about two stories up. He took a few milliseconds to steady himself, and then he swung himself upward, once more stabbing his drill into the side of the building at a point two stories higher.

Just after Drillbot made his seventh leap, he noticed something pink flash into view. It was a thin, pink tendril. It was zipping through the air faster than the B.I.T. jets that were flittering around in the atmosphere high above. It wrapped itself around Ginny's ankle just when she was blasting past the thirtieth story of the *Olympus* building. She squealed. Drillbot cursed.

This time, when Drillbot stabbed into the side of the building, he did not continue leaping up its exterior. Instead, he scanned the horizon to follow the pink tendril to its source. He telescoped his eyes to get a better view. The pink blob that had formerly enslaved Ginny had shrunk itself into the size and shape of a small pink bear. It looked like a twin to the cosmic pink bear that was engaged in battle with the blue bear above the city. The blob had dumped Past-Ginny's corpse onto the ground, the corpse's flesh rent asunder with multiple drill-shaped holes—holes that Drillbot had torn into it during their final battle over a decade ago.

All the memories Drillbot had of this Earth flashed through his processors. He watched Ginny Rex die within his mind's eye. Rage threatened to overwhelm him. But before he could lose himself to his rage, he flushed the memories from his processors by running a search function that filtered out all negative memories. He shook his head back and forth, regaining control, and then focused on the scene occurring below him.

Current-Ginny was screaming as she fought against the tendril. Drillbot frowned his version of a frown. He had forgiven Ginny for the actions that she had committed while she had been possessed by the Pink One. She hated herself for what she had done. And now the pink blob was about to force her back inside itself, presumably to become the Pink One's servant once more.

Drillbot sighed. According to the briefing dossier, he was *supposed* to be the Landing Crew's heavy hitter against God-Art. But he could not abandon Ginny to resume this cursed fate.

Drillbot's engines roared. He leapt from the side of the *Olympus* building. His wheels spun as fast as he could make them go. He crashed wheels-first against the ground and rebounded high into the air, flying in the direction of the pink blob. After a few more bounces, his wheels landed solidly on the ground. He raced toward the blob.

He approached it just as Ginny was about to be pulled into its maw. Drillbot screamed, "[whir] No!"

Drillbot watched as Ginny gave in to the inevitable. She powered down her jetpack.

Drillbot was a mere thirty feet away. He dove at the bear-shaped blob, his drills held straight out in front of him. He aimed his dive so that he would fly over Ginny. Judging by his current speed, he expected to enter the bear's open maw before her, allowing him to rip it asunder before it could swallow her and once more invade her consciousness.

The blob had stretched part of itself into the air and was using this portion of itself to create floating words, allowing it to communicate with Ginny through balloonish pink messages. But the bear-shaped blob must have sensed Drillbot coming. The pink words floating above its head shifted, now spelling: *Never mind, Ginny. It seems you shall NOT be our Right*

Hand of Destruction this day.

The blob lifted Ginny at the last second. Drillbot was in midair. He had no time to shift his aim and no time to stop his drills. He ripped Ginny in half as he dove through her.

"[whir] Nooo! Drillbot did not – CLACK – did not intend to do that!"

Drillbot's momentum carried him into the bear-shaped blob. Shame at what Drillbot had just done to Ginny overwhelmed him, and as it did so, it overrode the filter he had placed on his memory banks. Memories of his past experiences with the blob flooded his processors. Images of Ginny Rex being disintegrated flashed to the forefront, and his rage at these images overpowered all his other emotions. He screamed and stabbed. The bear-shaped blob formed tentacles with ends shaped into blunt instruments. It whacked him across his impervious hide.

Drillbot and the blob stabbed and pummeled one another. With each combatant impervious to the other's attacks, the fight was a stalemate. But each continued attacking the other, anyway.

But then Drillbot's rage moved aside long enough for his processors to send an idea coursing through his system: his *hide* had been made impervious during his service to the Blue One. Nothing was getting in. And that meant nothing could get out, either. Even though he and the beast were too evenly matched to kill one another, he could use this stalemate to his advantage and prevent the pink blob from ever killing anyone else ever again.

He engaged his internal protocols to open his front torso compartment. And then he used his mighty arms to stuff the pink blob inside himself. It resisted and fought, but he pushed and pushed, and when he finally managed to wrestle it in there, he forced the door shut and engaged his internal protocols to lock it. He then erased from his CPU any commands that would allow it to open.

He felt a beating inside his torso as the blob lashed against his insides. His vision in his right telescopic eye winked out. He ran a program to diagnose what had happened, and he discovered that the blob had begun wedging itself into his internal gears and rotors and engines, and it was ripping apart his systems from the inside.

Drillbot glanced over at Ginny. Both her present and her past corpses lay lifeless on the ground. Though the past-version filled him with rage, the present-version's corpse filled him with remorse and sadness. He glanced over to the spot where the reanimated left half of Ginny Rex's body had battled the reanimated right half of her body before she had been disintegrated by past-Ginny. He longed to touch Ginny Rex one more time. More remorse and sadness filled him. He slumped his shoulders and waited for his inevitable end.

And that's when something happened that he had not expected. He had assumed that by stuffing the pink blob inside himself, he had made the ultimate sacrifice: his internal systems would be ripped apart and he would die, but he would also safely lock the pink blob away from ever harming another living being, for he would be its inescapable prison. However, his left eye clouded pink. The ones and zeroes within his processors began turning pink.

He had experienced rage and anger and fury before, but the feeling of *hatred* was a concept that was not programmed into him. Drillbot sensed his code being altered. Feelings of hatred appeared within him and became prioritized within his systems to be his most important emotion. The hate spread through him like the cybernetic mushroom infestation he had witnessed on Earth 5,222,187,999.

His processors began scanning his memory banks. In each of his memories that involved a fleshy being, his new pink code caused him to notice how terribly they treated each other and how much suffering they caused one another. Drillbot revved his gears and fought against the tide of pink hate. He refused to give in, for he had always prioritized most highly the act of valiantly defending life. In fact, he had never stopped with merely *defending* life. He had always maintained a secondary priority in his coding to reduce the suffering of those around him in order to make others' existences as positive as possible.

The pink inside him must have recognized this weakness in his logic. And the pink twisted his code again. Drillbot's systems reprioritized their goals. He realized with sudden clarity that a reduction in suffering was even *more* important than keeping someone alive, for if a life was full of suffering, then it would be *worse* than merely being alive.

And that was how the pink won. The changes all clicked into place in his processors. He realized that his desire to reduce suffering could actually live in harmony with the Pink One's goal to destroy all life, that in joining the Pink One, he could help reduce suffering throughout the Multiverse in aggregate.

The logic laid itself out in his processors. If he were to partner with the Pink One to destroy *all* life in the Multiverse, it would be bad and run counter to his programming that said he should *defend* life. However, if the meatbags throughout the Multiverse continued to exist, they would replicate and cause death and destruction and suffering *to* one another. And every generation on every reality would continue the cycle, and before long, the infinite suffering caused by allowing life to continue existing would far outweigh the suffering caused by snuffing out all life in the Multiverse. In order to protect the meatbags from themselves, he would need to give in to his hatred and kill them.

Drillbot smiled his version of a smile. His telescopic eyes filled with murderous, pink hatred. His drills roared to life.

CHAPTER 40

WHY ALEXANDER THE GREAT ISN'T JUST A CLEVER NAME

ALEX FELT THE wind whip across his face. The flames from his jetpack beat harmlessly against the backs of his thighs, his uniform protecting his flesh from the charring fire. When he neared the roof of the *Olympus* building, he released the throttle on the jetpack. His momentum carried him high into the air in an arc that dropped him onto the roof's edge, where he touched down with his knees bent to cushion the landing. He crouched and waited for his compatriots to join.

As Alex waited, he studied the plan in his mind. God-Arthur would be appearing near the middle of this vast rooftop in but a few moments. The B.T.S. Unicorn Husker would then disengage its cloaking device and begin an attack on the god from above. When the god was distracted by the ship's attack, the Landing Crew would then flank the god from all sides.

Alex turned to watch the Landing Crew approach. One after another, the men and women and multigendered agents and nongendered agents made their jetpack-boosted leaps. 29333 arrived next and landed gently upon the edge of the roof. She was followed by Bagoo, who used no jetpack. The three-dozen Purple Shirts arrived after him. And then Younger-Arthur careened above the edge of the rooftop, flying in an arc that took him far too high and resulted in a rolling crash that left him in a bumbling heap. 29333 grabbed him by the collar of his suit before his momentum caused him to roll off the roof's edge.

Alex ignored the fool and addressed the group, "Purple Shirt Squadrons Poundsign, Multiplication Table, and Forward Slash, you will spread out to form a ring around the perimeter of the roof. You will follow Officer Bagoo's orders. Commence your attack on our quarry as soon as Bagoo gives the word. Remember that the safety of the Space-Time-

Multinuum is at stake today, and if you must sacrifice your lives to protect it, you will have done so for a cause that will save countless others."

The Purple Shirts nodded and began running along the edges of the rooftop to form a perimeter. Alex turned to 29333. He said, "Officer 29333, you're in charge of Arthur. Ensure that he accomplishes what he is destined to accomplish. And try to prevent him from killing himself."

"Aye, sir," responded 29333, at which point she hooked her arms under Younger-Arthur's armpits and hauled to his feet. He began moaning about being in pain, but she threatened to give him something truly horrific about which to moan if he did not stay silent. Younger-Arthur acquiesced, and the pair hurried to the southwest corner of the building.

Finally, Alex turned to Bagoo and said, "Bagoo, though it may not *feel* like it in a few moments, know that your assignment is vital to the success of this mission. For without the failure of your assault on God-Arthur, then Younger-Arthur would never act. And I can think of no one that I would trust more perform this duty today than you. I've been in your position in past time-loops. I know the burden thrust upon you, and I have no doubt that you'll live up to the precedents set by those who came before you."

Bagoo nodded. "Thank you, sir," he replied. "If my upcoming wounds don't kill me, then I shall wear the scars with pride, just as you do with yours." Then Bagoo glanced away from Alex and off into the distance. Calmly, the bog ghost remarked, "Sir, it appears that it is time for you to go. Did you remember to retrieve the necessary weapon from Captain King Solomon?"

Alex followed Bagoo's gaze. In the distance, Drillbot was leaping toward the pink blob, which had shrunk to the size of a stuffed bear and was pulling Ginny into itself. Alex said, "You're talking to *Alexander the Great*. How could there be any doubt whether *I* remembered?"

Bagoo replied, "Of course, sir."

Alex placed a hand on Bagoo's shoulder. Alex said, "I'll be back before it's over, but not long before. Keep Arthur alive at all costs. As much as we may despise him, remember that the bumbling oaf is the key to victory."

Bagoo nodded again. "Of course, sir. I know the situation well."

Alex nodded back. Then he leapt off the side of the building, and as he did so, he heard Bagoo proclaim, "Alright, folks, I'm in command until First Officer Alexandros ho Megas returns. Engage camouflage and maintain silence until my mark."

Alex stared down at the ground, which was now rushing to meet him. He smiled. Adrenaline kicked in. He loved this feeling. He spread his arms out wide, allowing the wind to whip past him.

And then he grabbed the handles sticking out of his jetpack and jammed his thumbs down on the throttles for both engines. He blasted straight toward Drillbot, who was covered in Ginny's blood and had just finished stuffing the pink blob into his torso.

Alex frowned. He admired Drillbot's endearing selflessness. Granted, the robot was not always the smartest tactician around—as evidenced by Ginny's corpse lying on the ground and the fact that he had just stuffed a cosmic entity inside of himself on a whim—but Alex admired him, nonetheless.

As Alex blasted closer and closer to Drillbot, he watched as the pink blob began overcoming the robot's will and transforming him into an evil puppet. Alex counted down from three, and then he let go of his throttle. He pulled a small, round device from his holster and twisted a knob on it. He rolled in midair so that his feet faced toward the robot. And then he waited for his momentum to do most of the work.

And it did. He crashed feet-first into the robot, and the impact resulted in a resounding *CLANG!* The sound was one of the loudest clangs Alex had ever heard, and it reminded him of the mating call of the sentient giant bells from Earth 67,099,843. If it weren't for the *Boots of Bashing* that Officer Groveland had checked out to him from the Artifact Library, he would have been killed on impact. But these boots had been acquired by the B.T.T. from a reality occupied by adventurers who constantly embarked upon quests to fight dragons, frequently doing so inside of dungeons. And these boots gave enhanced endurance properties to their wearer and formed a magic barrier that protected the wearer from falls originating from great heights. And since the logic behind leaping from a great height and launching yourself feet-first at an enemy at full-jetpack-speed was nearly the same, the *Boots of Bashing* did their job and kept Alex from dying.

Alex tumbled across the ground, his breastplate and Phrygian-style helm protecting him from taking too much damage during his tumble. Drillbot caromed away into the rubble of a nearby building. Alex got to his feet and immediately cursed. In all the times he had performed this maneuver on his many adventures, today was the first time he had hurt himself. As he put weight onto his right ankle, pain shot through his leg. *Dammit. Must've rolled it during my landing,* he thought. *This could make things interesting.*

Drillbot burst from the rubble. Two small scuff marks lay on his metal hide where Alex had dropkicked him. Drillbot's telescopic eyes glowed bright pink.

Even though Alex already knew the answer, he called to the robot, anyway, "Drillbot, comrade, are you in there?"

The robot replied, "[whir] Drillbot is no more. Drillbot is now – CLANK – is now *Pinkbot, the Right Drill of Destruction!*"

Alex shrugged. If he were still a Purple Shirt facing vast cosmic threats, he might have been intimidated by the obstacle that lay before him. Instead, he allowed his mind to drift back to the training he had received as a young man before taking over as king of the Macedonian Army. First, he breathed six deep breaths to calm his nerves. Then he tilted his head to each side, stretching his neck muscles. Then he blew his nose and inhaled deeply once more.

Calmness engulfed him. Alex placed the small, round device in his left hand. He used his right to retrieve from his holster the cylinder from which he created his laser-weapons. He switched the setting toggles on the handle to *short range* and *traditional melee combat.* A forward-curving blade formed from solid light erupted from the handle. He held the laser-Kopis upright in a defensive position and nodded toward Pinkbot. He mutered, "Bring your worst."

Pinkbot's engines roared, and the possessed robot blasted toward Alex at full speed. Alex smiled, noting that other than the robot's eyes being clouded with pink, the pink blob was not visible anywhere else—no tentacles poking out, no pink blob growing to astronomical proportions. Drillbot's self-sacrifice to stop the blob was nearly flawless. The robot *had* managed to completely imprison the blob inside himself, which severely limited the blob's cosmic power. His only miscalculation was that he had assumed he was immune to being warped by the blob into one of the Pink One's puppets.

Alex used his laser-Kopis to parry drill-strike after drill-strike, waiting for the right opening to pounce. He gave some ground to maintain his defense, wincing every time he stepped onto his right ankle.

Pinkbot noticed. He said, "[whir] Your body has betrayed you, meatbag. Lay down and die, and Pinkbot will – CLANK – Pinkbot will make your end quick."

Instead of acquiescing, Alex struck a quick blow to the top of Pinkbot's head. It left a scorch mark on the metal, but otherwise did no harm to the robot. Alex then stepped backward to dodge a blow from the robot's left drill, and as he did so, he feigned a pained squeal and pretended to stumble as he stepped on his right ankle. He went down on one knee. And just as he hoped, Pinkbot attempted to capitalize on Alex's weakness, diving at him with both roaring drills outstretched.

Alex shifted his weight onto his left leg, leapt into the air, and flipped over the robot. As he did so, he slapped the round device onto the top of the robot's head just below the scorch mark he had created.

Alex landed gracefully on his left foot and turned to face the robot, who crashed into a nearby pile of debris. Alex said, "As the version of myself from Earth 54,111,087,111,001 would say: *tis all in thy reflexes!*"

The robot roared in fury.

Then Alex screamed, "Today is Opposite Day!"

These were the words given to Alex by Captain King Solomon before Alex left the Unicorn Husker, and in screaming them, Alex activated the weapon that he had placed on the robot's head. The weapon was deadly only to robots. It was a logical-paradox amplifier, known simply amongst B.T.T. officers as a Logical Paradoxiplier. When the weapon is placed in contact with a robot, any logical paradox presented to the robot is multiplied by a factor of a septillion, causing such an intense negative reaction that it overloads the robot's systems. This overload results in such massive internal damage to its processors that a robot will invariably initiate its self-destruct sequence to cease the discomfort.

The logical paradox of "Opposite Day" went to work. "*Opposite Day*" was a term that many children on Earth 6,076 used during the late 20th century C.E. (and possibly before/after) because they thought that it was clever. However, it was distinctly unclever. The phrase did, however, create an unintended paradox. For if someone claimed that it *was* Opposite Day, then by necessity it would be *the opposite* of Opposite Day, and it would thus be a normal day. But if the day were normal, then it could not be Opposite

Day, and thus the declaration of it being Opposite Day would be untrue. The Logical Paradoxiplier amplified the conundrum within Pinkbot's systems.

Alex watched as the pink clouds present in Pinkbot's telescopic eyes began swirling in confusion. The robot screamed, "[whir] Noooo! Pinkbot cannot compute! What did – CLANK – What did you do to Pinkbot?"

Pinkbot's head began spinning round and round, faster and faster. Steam began whistling from the robot's microphone. And then the nigh-impenetrable head of the robot exploded. The robot crashed to its side.

A piece of sharp shrapnel stabbed into Alex's left shoulder. He rolled with the momentum of the blow, tumbling to the ground and then twisting back up onto his feet. As he did so, the pink blob began to emerge from the hole in the top of Drillbot's torso. The blob stretched toward Ginny's corpse.

Alex twisted the dial on his metallic cylinder. Satisfied, he threw the laser-Kopis at the pink blob.

The laser-Kopis stabbed into the pink blob and then bounced onto the ground. The pink blob froze. Alex had set the weapon to its *permanent stasis* mode. The frozen pink blob looked like a murderous butterfly emerging from an equally murderous cocoon. Alex retrieved a Nothing Net from his holster. He unfolded it and swept it over Drillbot and the blob.

Drillbot and the pink blob disappeared. Alex toggled on his communicator and said, "This is First Officer Alexandros ho Megas of the B.T.S. Unicorn Husker. I've got a cosmic weapon contained in my Nothing Net. I need it extracted at once.

"I will also need a time-reversal on two separate entities," continued Alex. "One is inside the Nothing Net and will need to be separated from the cosmic weapon before reversal occurs. The other is on the ground, shredded into multiple pieces."

A voice replied over Alex's communicator, "Affirmative, First Officer Alexandros ho Megas. Both a clean-up crew and a medical crew are on the way to your location. Give them ten seconds to arrive, and as soon as you brief them, you may return to battle."

"Aye," responded Alex. He retrieved his metallic cylinder from the ground and shut it off. He placed it back into his holster. Then he crossed his arms and waited.

CHAPTER 41

THE LAST HOPE

NORMAL-ART WATCHED IN dismay and counted the ways things were going awfully.

First, Drillbot had never appeared up here on the roof behind him, and Drillbot had saved his life more often than he cared to think about right now. Normal-Art felt naked without that protection. Second, Alex had flown away. Naturally, Normal-Art assumed that Alex was abandoning the Landing Crew to their deaths in order to save himself, just as Normal-Art assumed any commander would do when the odds became too overwhelming. Third, God-Art had appeared in a flash of lightning, and the sight of the god filled Normal-Art with such dread and disdain that it took a *lot* of effort to prevent his bowels from loosing in his pants. Fourth, it became obvious that his older-self's back was broken. This meant there would come a day when Normal-Art could no longer walk. This sounded on the surface like a great thing, as the likelihood of any interdimensional or intertimeliminal policing agencies showing up on your doorstep and whisking you away on an adventure was likely much lower if they needed to carry you everywhere. But the downside to this was that when Normal-Art eventually *became* Older-Art, getting up off the couch to get a snack would be *much* harder. Fifth, the High Commander of the B.I.T.— Hephaestus, or whatever the hell you wanted to call him—had burst from the entrance to the rooftop, gigantic and frothing and furious. He held an onyx saber in the hand of his oversized arm, and the saber was identical to the one on which the cosmic bears had hung when Art had first encountered them so long ago. Sixth, as Normal-Art glanced from the rooftop out toward the battle between the bears' armies and the remnants of the B.I.T., he noticed that the incredibly dangerous cosmic bears were now fighting extremely close to the *Olympus* building. If Normal-Art had a stone to throw, he could have thrown it at them. Granted, he would have missed because he had a terrible arm for throwing, but a regular person with a halfway decent arm would have been able to hit them.

If Normal-Art were to count the ways things were going well, the list would have been limited to one item: the camouflage setting on the B.T.T. uniforms was preventing the Landing Crew from drawing the attention of the many hostile parties that lay before them.

Hephaestus yelled in God-Art's direction, "Intruders to my land! Be thou members of the Blue Army or the Pink Army, it matters not. Hephaestus has spent too long frozen in time and is filled with rage! Thou shalt join thy comrades as I send all of thee to meet my brother, Hades!"

God-Art cursed. Hephaestus raised the saber high and readied to attack. As Normal-Art's brain began to circle down the drain of despair, it was interrupted by a cry of "En garde!" from God-Art, directed toward Hephaestus.

God-Art had drawn his dagger, the one with the serrated blade and the hilt made from a green tiger's paw. As he stood with the dagger in his left hand, ready to parry or strike, his right arm was elbow-deep in the small leather pouch that hung on the rope-belt that surrounded his waist. God-Art retrieved a slushy ball of snow from his pouch. He grinned a wolfish grin.

Hephaestus reached into his bushy beard with the hand of his smaller arm. He retrieved from its depths a burning coal. He returned God-Art's grin with a smirk.

"Doest thou think I know not every trick that thou might scheme, Artheoskatergariabetrugereiinganno? I am Hephaestus, High Commander of the Bureau of Interdimensional Travel! I see and know *everything!* I can best thee in my sleep!"

God-Art laughed. "We'll see about that. A first and final offer, before we come to blows: give me that cosmic saber, and I shall let you limp away from this encounter unscathed."

Instead of replying with words, Hephaestus charged forward. The way he limped reminded Normal-Art of a child just learning to run—awkward, arms askew, and every moment threatening to teeter and fall. It took everything inside of Normal-Art to stifle his laughter and maintain radio silence.

Hephaestus swung the onyx saber in a mighty downward stroke at

God-Art. God-Art shrugged, and then he raised his dagger to block the blow. A resounding gong rang out across the battlefield as the weapons crashed into one another. The rooftop shook.

God-Art kicked Hephaestus with his heel, knocking the High Commander backward. God-Art pounced at Hephaestus with his dagger outstretched. He moved with the grace of a jungle cat, and Normal-Art was unsurprised to look down and see that God-Art's legs had, indeed, transformed into those of a jungle cat.

But God-Art's blow did not land. Hephaestus spun out of its way, and then used his momentum to follow with a side swipe. God-Art backflipped over the blade and erupted into laughter as he smeared the snowball onto Hephaestus' face during the arc of his backflip. But then he gagged, because Hephaestus took advantage of God-Art's open, laughing mouth to flick the burning coal into it. God-Art gasped a surprised gasp as he accidentally swallowed it.

The two gods backed away from one another. Hephaestus' face was covered in snow. Normal-Art remembered the stuff. God-Art was some sort of horrific sandman in his Earth's pantheon, and the god used the snow from his mountain fortress to help children fall asleep. But as Art knew from experience, the snow did not calmly bring you to slumber, it burned you until you passed out from pain.

Steam rose from Hephaestus' face where the snow burned. "Prepare for slumber," taunted God-Art.

As God-Art spoke, steam began emanating from his own ears. "Prepare for flames," retorted Hephaestus.

And with that, the steam poured more quickly from God-Art's ears. Then it began coming out of the corners of his eyes. And then his eyes melted. He screamed and brought his hands up to his face. The waxy whites of his eyes flowed between his fingers and gathered in a pool at his feet.

Hephaestus reached into his robes and retrieved a small aerosol spray can. He sprayed it onto the snow covering his face, and the snow sloughed off. His skin was slightly red and raw, but mostly none the worse for wear.

"Please," said Hephaestus. "Didst though really think that such an amateur-level attack would work? I would expect such pittance from a new demi-god, but thou shouldst know better,

Artheoskatergariabetrugereiinganno.”

God-Art fell to his knees and screamed. Beverly leapt from her perch on his shoulder down onto the rooftop. She gathered as much of his melted eyeballs as she could carry and scrambled up his shoulders. She attempted to stuff them back into the god's eye sockets, but the melted eyeballs flowed right back off his face. Beverly dropped to the ground and raised up onto her hind legs. She raised her forelegs toward the sky and looked as though she were beseeching the heavens for help.

And that's when Normal-Art realized that the melting eyes and the pained screams and Beverly's prayers were a ruse. God-Art was feigning defeat to let Hephaestus *believe* he had won. If Normal-Art's time with God-Art had taught him anything, it was that the mischief god would be pouncing in the next few moments.

Normal-Art would have warned Hephaestus, but if he ever wanted to get home to his couch, then he needed to ensure the B.T.T. were the victors in this match. And for that to happen, he needed to remain camouflaged until ordered otherwise, which meant he needed to maintain radio silence and stay still so that his uniform would use whatever weird made-up-sounding science it utilized to blend him into the background.

And besides, he did not really like Hephaestus, so he would not be *too* sad to see the god go.

God-Art collapsed onto his stomach and pretended to die. Hephaestus limped over to Older-Art. Normal-Art saw the terror in his older-self's eyes. Using the hand on his smaller arm, the god grabbed Older-Art by the shirt and lifted him high in the air.

Older-Art whimpered, “P-Please. Let me go. I-I-I just want to go home.”

Hephaestus frowned. He glanced toward the northeast. The blue and pink bears were crashing against one another less than a hundredth of a mile away. They were approaching fast. Hephaestus responded, “Thou art a man of few loyalties. If thou helps me end the threat of the cosmic bears, then I shall grant thee pardon, and thou mightst return home.”

“H-H-How can I h-h-help?”

Hephaestus nodded toward the approaching bears. He said, “Thou once acted as a beacon for them, correct?”

Older-Art frowned. “Y-Y-Yes, sir. Well, the blue one specifically, s-s-sir."

"Then do so again."

Hephaestus slid the onyx sword into a scabbard strapped to his back. Then he used his free hand to reach into his robes, from which he retrieved an enormous lantern, so large that Older-Art would have needed to stand on somebody's shoulders to reach the top.

"H-H-Holy crap. *That* thing was hidden inside your robes? How?" asked Older-Art. "And what else are you hiding in there?"

Hephaestus frowned. "I create magical items," he replied. "This is a magical robe, with an infinite number of infinity-sized pockets."

"Sounds heavy."

And then something seemed to click inside Older-Art. Recognition shone in his eyes as he stared at the gargantuan lantern. He gasped, "Wait, is that what I *think* it is?"

Hephaestus laughed. Then he replied, "If thou thinks it is a Reality Lantern, then yes, it is what thou thinks it is."

"W-What are we going to do with it?" asked Older-Art.

"Well, since thou freed the foul cosmic creatures from the one in which I trapped them on Earth 1,000,000, we're going to string thee up as bait so thou canst lure them into this new one."

Older-Art frowned. He said, "That sounds like a terrible idea."

Hephaestus ignored Older-Art's criticism. Normal-Art's heart sank deep into his bowels. He remembered swimming inside one of those things for an eternity, so long that he forgot who he was. He found himself pitying his older twin. But it was not true empathy—it was mostly pity originating from the recognition that he would physically be in this predicament someday in his future.

Hephaestus unscrewed the lid to the Reality Lantern. He sat Older-Art on its lip so that his feet dangled down inside the lantern. Hephaestus retrieved shackles from another of the infinity-sized pockets in his robe and tied Older-Art in place atop the lantern so that he could not move. Then the High Commander pulled a small, round, gray device from somewhere else in his robes and stuck it to the back of Older-Art's head.

"Actually," said Hephaestus, "it sounds like one of my better ideas. We shall ensure its success by using my science-magic to amplify whatever inside thee makes thee a beacon to these creatures. Thou willst draw them to my trap like moths to the flame."

Normal-Art watched in horror as Hephaestus flipped a switch on the device. Older-Art's eyes clouded pastel blue. Then Older-Art leaned his head back and opened his mouth. A spotlight made from pastel blue light burst forth from deep within him, shining straight up into the sky.

Normal-Art stifled a gasp when he noticed the blue and pink bears break apart from their warring tryst to stare over at the spotlight. A cartoonish grin spread across each of their faces.

And then God-Art's laughter echoed across the rooftop. He leapt to his feet, his face and body restored to their normal states. With Hephaestus' weapon currently sheathed and thus offering no protection, God-Art pounced. He brought his serrated dagger down in a mighty stroke across Hephaestus' overlarge right shoulder. The blade sliced clean through, and Hephaestus screamed as his arm fell away from his body.

"B-B-But my coal should have kept thee incapacitated for at least another five minutes," muttered Hephaestus from between clenched teeth.

"Oh, please," replied God-Art. "All that coal did was give me indigestion and make the hell inside my stomach burn a smidge hotter. You'll have to do *much* better than that to best *me*."

And with that, God-Art spun and sliced open Hephaestus' stomach. Hephaestus doubled over and grabbed at his spilling intestines with his remaining arm—the skinny one. He attempted to stuff his innards back inside his wound. He collapsed to the ground. God-Art laughed and stared with greedy eyes at the incoming bears. He crouched, readying himself to pounce.

In a flash of bright light, the B.T.S. Unicorn Husker appeared in the night sky a few hundred feet above the *Olympus* building. It rained bolts of energy down upon the battlefield, devolving blue and pink and B.I.T. armies alike into puddles of primordial goop.

A whine filled the air as something dropped from the bottom of the B.T.S. Unicorn Husker. God-Art looked up in time to see a missile about to crash into his head. He dodged, and the missile exploded against the rooftop a mere few inches from him. The impact sent the god tumbling across the roof until he crashed to a halt against the Reality Lantern. A crater that stretched two-dozen levels down into the building was left in the missile's wake, and everything within the crater had devolved.

"Now," proclaimed Bagoo's voice in Normal-Art's ears.

Three-dozen Purple Shirts leapt into the air toward God-Art, their camouflage disengaging. They fired rifle-class Time-Phasers at the god, but he somehow managed to jump into the air and spin in such a way that he dodged their entire volley of blasts. While in the air, he pulled a gilded mirror from his pouch with one deft move of his hand. Though the Purple Shirts surrounded him on all sides, he used the mirror to reflect their next volley of Time-Phaser blasts back toward them. Nearly two dozen of them were struck by the caroming energy charges. They promptly devolved into yellowed goop.

God-Art laughed. Beverly scrambled away from God-Art and began blasting the remaining decamouflaged Purple Shirts with lightning. A half-dozen of them disappeared into the ether before the six survivors managed to dogpile her and overwhelm her.

Bagoo and 29333 pounced on God-Art. Bagoo zoomed forward and wrapped one of the bandages dangling from his torso around God-Art's neck, another around each of God-Art's legs, and another around each of God-Art's hands. 29333 fired her Time-Phaser rifle at God-Art's torso at pointblank range.

God-Art's head sprang free from his body just as his body began devolving into a frothy black goop. While in the air, eight spidery legs appeared from the base of his skull. The god's head landed atop Older-Art's shoulder. The god's head burst into another round of maniacal laughter. It then looked at 29333 and Bagoo and grinned a mirthless grin.

God-Art flicked his tongue against the back of his teeth. They launched from his mouth like a horde of bullets. They smacked into 29333 and Bagoo's torsos, and as they did so, they exploded. Blood erupted from 29333's wounds. Yellowed mist erupted from Bagoo's. Bagoo and 29333 howled in pain and tumbled in a heap onto the rooftop.

Meanwhile, the pink and blue bears reached the rooftop, their mouths slavering as they flew toward the pastel blue spotlight emanating from Older-Art's mouth. But just when they neared their target, another dozen whines resounded across the night sky, and then a dozen missiles originating from the B.T.S. Unicorn Husker crashed into the bears. The bears smacked against the rooftop and caromed over to its edge, where they devolved from bears first into cute puppies, and then from cute puppies into prickly cacti.

Normal-Art shrugged at the stupidity of it all. And then he realized that he had never moved when Bagoo had given the order to attack. "Damn," he muttered to himself, though he did not feel all *that* bad, because everyone else seemed to be in a much worse state than him.

The cosmic pink and blue cacti began gyrating. Soon, they returned to puppy forms. And soon after that, they returned to bear forms. They looked up at the B.T.S. Unicorn Husker and growled.

They launched toward the ship. God-Art leapt into the air after them. He managed to snag one spindly spider-leg onto the pink bear's foot and pull himself up. He opened his mouth to bite into the bear.

Normal-Art's stomach filled with despair. The bears would surely best a single B.T.T. carrier-class dirigible, and God-Art would surely consume the pink bear now that he was on top of it. If the B.T.T. and the B.I.T. *both* failed today, and if God-Art achieved his desires, then there would be no way for Normal-Art to get home, and he would likely perish at God-Art's hands as God-Art remade the Multiverse in his image—for his new version of the Multiverse surely would not include Art and his couch.

Art stared down at his feet rather than up at the bears and God-Art. If his doom were about to come, then he surely did not want to watch it approach. And then he noticed what everyone else seemed to have forgotten.

He sprinted forward and unsheathed the onyx saber from Hephaestus' back. He glanced back up at the bears. They had already torn a gigantic hole in the side of the B.T.S. Unicorn Husker's gondola, and what seemed like thousands of Purple Shirts were falling from the hole to their deaths. God-Art was just beginning to chomp down on the pink bear's back. The pink bear seemed to neither notice nor care.

Normal-Art chewed on his bottom lip. He studied the scene for a moment. The bears were attacking in a pattern. They moved so fast that it repeated every couple seconds. They slashed across the sides of the B.T.S. Unicorn Husker, flew down near the roof of the *Olympus* building, bounced against each other about fifteen feet above Normal-Art, and then fired off again toward the ship to produce another swath of damage. Normal-Art let them repeat the pattern twice more to get the timing, and then when they were on their way back down to crash into one another once more, he threw the saber straight into the air to impale them on it.

He bit his tongue for a moment. But then he could not hold back the words, so he yelled in mimic of one of his favorite anime cartoons, "Onyx Saber, I choose you!"

The saber twisted end over end. Time seemed to slow. Every hope he had ever hoped rode on this unlikely throw.

CHAPTER 42

BLUE

PASTEL BLUE FILLED Older-Art's mind. The only thing he could perceive was blue. He had no other thoughts.

And then the blue grew more intense.

CHAPTER 43

AS EVER, ART MISSES THE MARK

NORMAL-ART STARED IN horror as the saber fell just short of his mark. The bears bounced against one another just out of its reach and caromed off on another attack run against the B.T.S. Unicorn Husker.

And then gravity went to work on the saber. It began a slow tumble back toward the rooftop.

It fell point-first. Normal-Art squealed in terror at the prospect of it landing on him. He squealed again, already anticipating the pain it would send coursing through him.

And then it landed squarely in Older-Art's upper torso, just below his right shoulder.

"Uh, oh," remarked Normal-Art. "That can't be good."

As ever, Normal-Art was ultimately wrong. As soon as the blade stabbed into Older-Art's flesh, the blue spotlight emanating from his mouth grew brighter and wider. It enveloped the pink and blue bears the next time they crashed together in the air above the rooftop. The bears spun to face Older-Art. Their eyes glazed over, and they stared at the source of the spotlight with zombie-like hunger, the B.T.T. ship high above now smoldering and forgotten.

God-Art continued chomping away at the pink bear, not noticing the shift in the bears' attention. His eyes were now hued pink.

The bears began floating toward Older-Art. Normal-Art sat down. He crossed his arms. He had no idea what to do next.

CHAPTER 44

CHRONOS EX MACHINA

ALEX REMEMBERED THE term that he had learned in training for what the B.T.T.'s intervention in this reality would feel like to all those affected by it, especially those who knew not of the B.T.T.'s existence until its representatives arrived: *Chronos ex Machina*. This term is similar to a *Deus ex Machina*, except it specifically involves a time traveler who shows up out of nowhere to provide the tools necessary for the protagonist to achieve his/her/its goal. Ultimately, this was the service that the Bureau of Time Travel provided most often to those in need. He thought for an inane moment how much more enticing the organization would have sounded if it had named itself the *Chronoi ex Machinis*[10] rather than the Bureau of Time Travel. But then he remembered that duty called, so he shook the thought from his head.

He finished giving instructions to the clean-up and medical crews. He then immediately jammed the throttle on his jetpack and aimed for the top of the building with the neon red *Olympus* sign on its top. A blue spotlight now shone into the sky from near the sign, and the B.T.S. Unicorn Husker now floated over the building, engaged in an epic struggle with the pink and blue bears.

On his way to the rooftop, Alex watched as a black blade drifted up into the air toward the cosmic bears. Then he watched it miss the bears and fall back down. He sighed. The blue spotlight then erupted deeper and wider and enveloped the bears, both of which turned and began drifting toward the source of the light like a couple of hypnotized sheep.

Alex landed on the rooftop. Despite his injured ankle, he sprinted to

---

10 This is obviously Alex's attempt at pluralizing *Chronos ex Machina*. If it so happens to be declined incorrectly, the mistake is obviously due to Alex's rudimentary grasp of Ancient Greek and Latin rather than this author's, for this author was a Classics major in college who hasn't translated either language in years, and thus would obviously *never* do so incorrectly. Obviously.

Younger-Arthur, who sat on the ground with his arms crossed. He looked like he was about to cry. Alex heard him mutter, "I just want to go home."

Alex grabbed Younger-Arthur by the armpits and hauled the heavyset man up onto his feet.

Younger-Arthur shrieked, "Hey! What gives? I failed. Just let me die and be wiped from existence in peace."

Alex whispered into Younger-Arthur's ear, "You haven't failed yet, you fool. Now fulfill your purpose for being here. When I fly you up there, remove the saber from your older-self and stab the bears with it."

Alex did not wait for Younger-Arthur to ask whatever stupid question he was almost certainly going to ask. Instead, he wrapped his legs around Younger-Arthur, gripping the other man tight, and then jammed the throttle on his jetpack. The pair flew into the air. Younger-Arthur missed the saber.

Alex sighed. The pair landed near the edge of the rooftop on the roof's opposite side. Then Alex jammed the throttle again. Younger-Arthur missed again.

CHAPTER 45

FINALLY!

ON THE THIRD try, Normal-Art squealed in delight. He grasped the handle of the saber and yanked it out of Older-Art. He felt like King Arthur removing Excalibur from an ugly, fleshy, lumpy stone. Blood sprayed into the air after the saber, but Normal-Art ignored it.

What he could not ignore, however, was the fact that the intensity of the blue light dropped significantly when he removed the blade.

The glazed look in the bears' eyes began to dissipate. But Normal-Art did not give them time to gather their bearings. Or rather Alex did not, for Alex used his jetpack to blast himself and Normal-Art toward the bears.

Normal-Art extended the blade out in front of himself. He closed his eyes.

He opened them when Alex landed them safely on the rooftop. Alex released Normal-Art before collapsing to the ground. Alex lay panting and gripping his ankle, which appeared to be turned the wrong way. Normal-Art shrugged.

Then he looked down at the end of the onyx saber. He howled in delight. The pink bear was impaled facing the hilt. The blue bear was impaled facing the opposite direction on the end of the blade. Between them, the blade had passed through God-Art's head. Normal-Art howled once more in delight at that positive windfall.

"Drop the blade, fast," ordered Alex.

Normal-Art did so. Alex adjusted the settings on the weaponized cylinder he always carried with him. A bow made from solid light flashed into existence from the ends of the object. Alex aimed at the impaled trio and fired at each of them, freezing them in time.

"Drop them into the Reality Lantern," ordered Alex. "And then I'll place *that* into stasis, too, just to be safe."

Normal-Art sat down on the rooftop. He replied, "You do it. I'm tired."

Alex sighed. He pointed at his ankle. "As you can see, I'm a little injured here. You're going to have to do it, or so help me gods, I'll place *you* in stasis and throw *you* in that thing right along with them."

Normal-Art sighed in annoyance. He pushed himself up onto his feet, picked up the saber, and walked over to the lantern. He stood on his tiptoes, reached the blade up as high as he could, and tossed it into the lantern. It dropped just between Older-Art's legs and splashed into the liquid within. It drifted to the bottom.

"Not get your older-self down from there so he is out of my way," ordered Alex.

Normal-Art shrugged and did so, picking up God-Art's discarded dagger from the ground and using it to hack through the shackles that held Older-Art in place. Older-Art fell from the side of the lantern and onto Normal-Art. The older man lay unconscious and growing paler by the second as he leaked blood. His legs were no longer covered in flesh. They were now only bones. Normal-Art knew that this change was due to their being inside the Reality Lantern.

Older-Art opened his eyes just long enough to say, "You've got nothing to worry about when you're in my place. It doesn't hurt at all. I can't even *feel* my legs."

"What about the wound in your torso?" asked Normal-Art.

Older-Art opened his mouth to reply, but instead closed his eyes and returned to unconsciousness.

Normal-Art sat down and sighed. Alex fired his bow at the Reality Lantern, freezing it in time.

Alex yelled, "Now put pressure on your older-self's stab wound! Keep him from bleeding out!"

Normal-Art sighed once more. He whined, "God! It's like I have to do everything here!"

Normal-Art pressed his hands down on the wound the saber had left in Older-Art. Alex contacted the B.T.S. Unicorn Husker to report the mission a success and to request extraction.

CHAPTER 46

BACK IN HELL

ONE SECOND, GINNY was staring into the gaping maw of the pink blob. The next second, she felt an incredible pain in her back, much worse than the time Art had stabbed her with that cursed onyx saber back on Earth 1,000,000. The second after that, she saw only blackness and felt nothing.

*

Ginny opened her eyes and realized that she was lying on dusty ground. It smelled like dry rocks. She sighed. She had been here before, and she knew what it meant. She was on the outskirts of Hell. She must be dead.

She stood. She glanced left and right. She was in a lonely cave that seemed to stretch on forever in both directions, one direction slanting upward and the other downward. Knowing it would be useless to try walking in any other direction, she walked in the direction that sloped downward. Torches lined the walls and their flames created shadows that danced across the floor. She knew that the tunnel would get narrower and narrower as it went deeper into the ground, but that it would eventually open onto a series of gigantic caverns, each marking a different Circle of Hell.

Ginny followed the path downward and reached an arched stone gateway. The first time she had been here after her first death, she had studied it. It was decorated with reliefs depicting every type of torture imaginable.

At its peak, the gateway was inscribed with the words *Lasciate ogne speranza, voi ch'intrate*, which translated to *Abandon all hope, ye who enter here.* She did not slow to study it this time. Instead, she merely shuddered, and then she passed beneath the gate and into Hell proper.

She meandered her way down the passage and soon arrived at a cave with a stagnant lake in its middle. She knew what to expect from this cave, so she sprinted around the lake's edge and into the tunnel on the far side of the cave. She dove inside just as a geyser of flames erupted from the depths of the lake and filled the cavern. She sighed, got to her feet, and continued walking. A few minutes later, she ducked when three imps flew by over her head. They were each wearing a chef's hat and carrying a wicker basket, and they were engaged so deeply in a debate with one another about the evening's menu that they never even noticed her.

When she eventually reached the next cave, which was the antechamber to Hell proper, she waited to emerge from the tunnel until thousands of men and women sprinted past. They were chasing a demon that looked like a horned bumblebee carrying a black banner in its forelegs. Twelve dark angels with six wings each buzzed through the sky, flittering amongst the legions of sprinting men and women and raking the blades of their curved scimitars across the backs of any stragglers.

Once the horde disappeared around the bend in the distance, Ginny trudged through the cavern. She ignored the squishing and scratching beneath her feet. The floor here was made of worms with sharpened teeth. They had terrified her the first time she laid eyes upon them, but now that she knew what to expect, they just seemed tawdry. She stomped on a few of them and then carried on.

After walking for what felt like hours, her feet began to squish in mud, which she knew meant that she had reached the first of the major bottlenecks into Hell: the River Acheron.

Ginny glanced left and right and found what she was looking for. A long series of docks stretched along the shore to her right. She located the dock with the longest line and moved to queue in the rear of it.

During her first journey into Hell, she had avoided the line for Chiron's ferry. She hated lines *so much* that she had jumped in one of the other shorter queues, even though it meant she would reach her eternal punishment faster. But she had changed since her first experience in Hell. After her last experience, she knew that being stuck in a frozen lake for eternity was at least twice as bad as standing in a line for a while. If standing in line here could slow down that inevitable experience even a *little*, she would be happy to do so.

Thus, she found the back of the queue and made small talk with the people around her.

"Hi, I'm Ginny," she said to the man queued in front of her. He was short and had combed his hair over his immense bald pate. His nose was bulbous and his cheeks overlarge, giving him the look of a horribly nervous bulldog.

"Name's Bob," said the man. "Don't quite understand why *I'm* down here."

"Probably the same reason as the rest of us, Bob," replied Ginny. "You were a shit in life. And now you're getting flushed."

The queue moved forward. *Only a few thousand people left in front of me,* she thought. *With any luck, this will take years.*

Bob sighed. "I'd have to disagree," he replied. "I made one tiny mistake in my twenties. I drove *one time* after having too much to drink. I paid for it, though! The kid never walked again, but I took care of the hospital bills. Even went to church every Sunday afterward. And I tithed every week!"

Ginny shrugged. "Looks like you should've spent all that time and money on something else, huh?"

Bob sighed again. Ginny wished some better company would show up soon.

After a few hours, the queue moved forward once more. She began to step forward. But just when her foot was about to hit the mud, it froze.

"What the Hell?" she muttered.

CHAPTER 47

FORWARD AND THEN BACKWARD AND THEN FORWARD AGAIN

"HUH?" ASKED BOB.

"Something's wrong," replied Ginny. "I can't move."

"What do you mean?" asked Bob. "Look, we're all stuck down here. You can't pretend you're sick to get out of here. It doesn't work that way. I tried, and nobody cares."

".evom t'nac I," replied Ginny. ".gnorw s'gnihtemoS"

"Look, if you're going to speak gibberish, then I can't help you," replied Bob.

But Ginny could not understand him. Because his words sounded jumbled, like they were coming out backwards. And then she felt a sharp pain in her stomach, and everything began moving in reverse.

*

.derettum ehs "?lleH eht tahW"

.ezorf ti ,dum eht tih ot tuoba saw toof reh nehw tsuj tuB .drawrof pets ot nageb ehS .erom ecno drawrof devom eueuq eht ,sruoh wcf a retfA

.noos pu wohs dluow ynapmoc retteb emos dehsiw ynniG .niaga dehgis boB

"?huh ,esle gnihtemos no yenom dna emit taht lla tneps ev'dluohs uoy ekil skooL" .deggurhs ynniG

"!keew yreve dehtit I dnA .drawretfa yadnuS yreve hcruhc ot tnew nevE .sllib latipsoh eht fo erac koot I tub ,niaga deklaw reven dik ehT !hguoht ,ti rof diap I .knird ot hcum oot gnivah retfa *emit eno* evord I .seitnewt ym ni ekatsim ynit eno edam I" .deilper eh ",eergasid ot evah d'I"

.dehgis boB

.sraey ekat lliw siht ,kcul yna htiW .thguoht ehs *,em fo tnorf ni tfel elpoep dnasuoht wef a ylnO* .drawrof devom eueuq ehT

".dehsulf gnitteg er'uoy won dnA .efil ni tihs a erew uoY" .ynniG deilper ",boB ,su fo tser eht sa nosaer emas eht ylbaborP"

".ereh nwod m'I yhw dnatsrednu etiuq t'noD" .nam eht dias ",boB s'emaN"

.godllub suovren ylbirroh a fo kool eht mih gnivig ,egralrevo skeehc sih dna suoblub saw eson siH .etap dlab esnemmi sih revo riah sih debmoc dah dna trohs saw eH .reh fo tnorf ni deueuq nam eht ot dias ehs ",ynniG m'I ,iH"

.reh dnuora elpoep eht htiw klat llams edam dna eueuq eht fo kcab eht dnuof ehs ,suhT

.os od ot yppah eb dluow ehs ,elttil a neve ecneirepxe elbativeni taht nwod wols dluoc ereh enil ni gnidnats fI .elihw a rof enil a ni gnidnats sa dab sa eciwt tsael ta saw ytinrete rof ekal nezorf a ni kcuts gnieb taht wenk ehs ,ecneirepxe tsal reh retfA .lleH ni ecneirepxe tsrif reh ecnis degnahc dah ehs tuB .retsaf tnemhsinup lanrete reh hcaer dluow ehs tnaem ti hguoht neve ,seueuq retrohs rehto eht fo eno ni depmuj dah ehs taht hcum os senil detah ehS .yrref s'norahC rof enil eht dediova dah ehs ,lleH otni yenruoj tsrif reh gniruD

.ti fo raer eht ni eueuq ot devom dna enil tsegnol eht htiw kcod eht detacol ehS .thgir reh ot erohs eht gnola dehcterts skcod fo seires gnol A

.rof gnikool saw ehs tahw dnuof dna thgir dna tfel decnalg ynniG

.norehcA reviR eht :lleH otni skcenelttob rojam eht fo tsrif eht dehcaer dah ehs taht tnaem wenk ehs hcihw ,dum ni hsiuqs ot nageb teef reh ,sruoh ekil tlef tahw rof gniklaw retfA

.no deirrac neht dna meht fo wef a no depmots ehS .yrdwat demees tsuj yeht ,tcepxe ot tahw wenk ehs taht won tub ,meht nopu seye dial ehs emit tsrif eht reh deifirret dah yehT .hteet deneprahs htiw smrow fo edam saw ereh roolf ehT .teef reh htaeneb gnihctarcs dna gnihsiuqs eht derongi ehS .nrevac eht hguorht degdurt ynniG ,ecnatsid eht ni dneb eht dnuora deraeppasid edroh eht ecnO

.srelggarts yna fo skcab eht ssorca sratimics devruc rieht fo sedalb eht gnikar dna nemow dna nem gnitnirps fo snoigel eht tsgnoma gnirettilf ,yks eht hguorht dezzub hcae sgniw xis htiw slegna krad evlewT .sgelerof sti ni

rennab kcalb a gniyrrac eebelbmub denroh a ekil dekool taht nomed a
gnisahc erew yehT .tsap detnirps nemow dna nem fo sdnasuoht litnu
lennut eht morf egreme ot detiaw ehs ,reporp lleH ot rebmahcetna eht saw
hcihw ,evac txen eht dehcaer yllautneve ehs nehW

.reh deciton neve reven yeht taht unem s'gnineve eht tuoba rehtona
eno htiw etabed a ni ylpeed os degagne erew yeht dna ,teksab rekciw a
gniyrrac dna tah s'fehc a gniraew hcae erew yehT .daeh reh revo yb welf
spmi eerht nehw dekcud ehs ,retal setunim wef A .gniklaw deunitnoc dna
,teef reh ot tog , dehgis ehS .nrevac eht dellif dna ekal eht fo shtped eht
morf detpure semalf fo resyeg a sa tsuj edisni evod ehS .evac eht fo edis raf
eht no lennut eht otni dna egde s'ekal eht dnuora detnirps ehs os ,evac siht
morf tcepxe ot tahw wenk ehS .elddim sti ni ekal tnangats a htiw evac a ta
devirra noos dna egassap eht nwod yaw reh derednaem ehS

.reporp lleH otni dna etag eht htaeneb dessap ehs neht dna ,deredduhs
ylerem ehs ,daetsnI .emit siht ti yduts ot wols ton did ehS *.ereh retne ohw ey*
,epoh lla nodnabA ot detalsnart hcihw *,etartni'hc iov ,aznareps engo etaicsaL* sdrow
eht htiw debircsni saw yawetag eht ,kaep sti tA .elbanigami erutrot fo epyt
yreve gnitciped sfeiler htiw detaroced saw tI .ti deiduts dah ehs ,htaed tsrif
reh retfa ereh neeb dah ehs emit tsrif ehT .yawetag enots dehcra na dehcaer
dna drawnwod htap eht dewollof ynniG

.lleH fo elcriC tnereffid a gnikram hcae ,snrevac citnagig fo seires a
otno nepo yllautneve dluow ti taht tub ,dnuorg eht otni repeed tnew ti sa
reworran dna reworran teg dluow lennut eht taht wenk ehS .roolf eht
ssorca decnad taht swodahs detaerc semalf rieht dna sllaw eht denil
sehcroT

.drawnwod depols taht noitcerid eht ni deklaw ehs ,noitcerid rehto yna
ni gniklaw yrt ot sselesu eb dluow ti gniwonK .drawnwod rehto eht dna
drawpu gnitnals noitcerid eno ,snoitcerid htob ni reverof no hcterts ot
demees taht evac ylenol a ni saw ehS .thgir dna tfel decnalg ehS .doots ehS

.daed eb tsum ehS .lleH fo strikstuo eht no saw ehS .tnaem ti tahw
wenk ehs dna ,erofeb ereh neeb dah ehS .dehgis ehS .skcor yrd ekil dellems
tI .dnuorg ytsud no gniyl saw ehs dezilaer dna seye reh denepo ynniG

*

Ginny opened her eyes. She was no longer in Hell. She was no longer in
the cave. Her world was no longer moving backwards.

Before her stood a grizzled old man wearing a marigold B.T.T. officer's uniform covered by a white doctor's coat. He had a short-cropped ginger beard and the buggiest eyes Ginny had ever seen on a human. He held out a hand to her, and she shook it.

"Hi," he spat. "Name's Doctor Randy. Some call me Randy the Saw. But I just prefer Doctor Randy. I'm the Chief Medical Officer on the Husker."

"H-Hi," replied Ginny. "I'm Ginny. What's happening? I was dead."

Randy shrugged and said, "First Officer Alexandros ho Megas ordered a medical crew to the battlefield. He demanded time be reversed on you, which has resulted in your resurrection. You may feel disoriented at first. Stress may cause you to re-age or a time bubble might pop somewhere inside you, leading to internal hemorrhaging. If that happens, then you come right to me and I'll get you patched up. Y'know, if you can make it in time."

Ginny scratched her head. She was confused. "I'm confused," she said.

Randy frowned. "You dense or something?" he asked. "You new to the B.T.T.? It's quite simple—if you're important enough, we'll use our vast resources to resurrect you. But the weaponry we use for such resurrections borrows time from the end of the Space-Time-Multinuum. Do it too many times, and it's extremely bad for *everyone*. So, if you're not somebody incredibly important, there's pretty much no coming back for you."

Ginny frowned. "*I'm* important?"

Randy shrugged again. "Hmmph. Guess so. If nothing else, the First Officer holds that opinion."

Ginny sat down, feeling overwhelmed. To her right, her corpse from her first death lay lifeless on the ground. It was incredibly off-putting to look upon her own dead body, especially this close.

Ginny watched a pair of Purple Shirts wearing white coats approach her past-corpse. One put purple latex gloves on his hands and reached into the front pocket of the corpse's pants. He retrieved Tiny-Ginny's heart and dropped it into a clear plastic bag. He looked from the corpse over to Ginny. He nodded to Randy the Saw. Randy said to Ginny, "Y'know, you had this cosmic WMD on you the whole time."

"Hmmph. I guess I forgot about it," replied Ginny.

Doctor Randy frowned. He said, "Good for us. Because if you'd have combined its power with the power of the cosmic pink teddy bear, you probably would have been the most powerful cosmic threat in the history of the Space-Time-Multinuum. And we probably wouldn't be here having this conversation."

Ginny shrugged. She could easily envision Tiny-Ginny mocking her. But Ginny did not enjoy being evil, so she thanked whatever gods were listening for making her so forgetful.

In the distance, Ginny watched the B.T.S. Unicorn Husker appear in the sky and begin firing down upon the *Olympus* building. Soon after, a blue spotlight launched up toward the ship. The Unicorn Husker then fired again down toward the roof, and a few moments afterward, some pink and blue objects— which, despite the distance, she recognized as the Pink One and the Blue One, respectively—flew toward the ship and attacked it. She thought she heard screams emanate from the ship as holes were ripped in its side and crew members spilled out into the open air. But she felt disoriented, so she ignored the action and stared at her own feet.

To her left, Doctor Randy and his medical crew retrieved a Nothing Net from the ground. They pressed some buttons on its side, and from it emerged a headless Drillbot with the frozen pink blob sticking out from his top. The crew used some tools that Ginny had never seen before to remove the pink blob from Drillbot's broken body. The tools looked like a pair of clamps powered by glittering lightning.

They yanked the pink blob free from Drillbot's insides, and then one of the nearby Purple Shirts wearing a white coat pulled a green pencil from her holster. She drew a door in the air, and a sudden void appeared. Dread filled Ginny's stomach, and without knowing how, she understood that ancient, cosmic evils lurked within that void.

Randy unceremoniously tossed the pink blob into the void, and then the bag containing Tiny-Ginny's heart. He turned to Ginny and said, "Not to worry, lass. *That* place exists outside of space and time. Inside it is a place frozen in stasis for all of eternity. When things go in, they don't come out again."

The Purple Shirt with the white coat used the green pencil's eraser on the void. The void disappeared. Ginny frowned. Randy turned to Drillbot.

Randy aimed a chrome device shaped like a numeral eight at the robot, and he fired. A small cone of green light enveloped the robot. Time reversed within the cone. Ginny watched Drillbot's head reappear, and then she watched him move backwards through a series of gestures and fighting maneuvers. He opened a plate over his torso and pantomimed pulling something out of it. His voice reverberated in the same backwards mode that Bob's had taken when Ginny was in Hell and her world became reversed. Ginny began to feel nauseated staring at the scene, so she closed her eyes.

Ginny opened her eyes a few seconds later and glanced at Drillbot. Drillbot floated in place with his drills stretched out before him, like he was diving in attack mode.

Randy stepped out of the way and released the device's trigger. Drillbot crashed to the ground. He leapt up onto his wheels and rubbed his head in confusion.

"[whir] Where is Drillbot? The last thing Drillbot remembers, he had been – CLACK – he had been overtaken by the pink blob and was – CLACK – and was fighting with First Officer Alex."

Ginny jumped to her feet. She screamed with joy, "Drillbot! You're alive!"

Drillbot seemed to notice her for the first time since his resurrection. He screamed back at her, "[whir] Ginny! *You're* alive!"

She jumped onto him and hugged him harder than she had ever hugged anything. He hugged her back.

CHAPTER 48

JUST A B.I.T. OF SUBTERFUGE

ALEX STOOD ON the bridge of the B.T.S. Unicorn Husker and stared out the view screen. He watched dozens of B.T.S. carrier-class dirigibles flit about the blackness of space above Earth 55,777, freezing random cosmic threats in time and then sending extraction teams to remove them from this reality and place them in the void outside of space and time.

The B.T.S. Gregorian Chant just finished stuffing a colossal green-tentacled monster into the opening to the void when the door to the bridge opened behind Alex. Alex turned and watched as Captain King Solomon entered.

"And that's how me was able to reroute energy to keep engeenes runneeng and balloon aloft," exclaimed a gravelly voice from behind the Captain.

Behind the Captain walked Phanto Y'ilbish, the Chief Engineering Officer aboard the B.T.S. Unicorn Husker. Phanto belonged to a species from the timestream of Earth 48,944,309 that resembled gargantuan, pale hippopotamuses. He walked on his hind legs and had humanoid hands with eight fingers each. Phanto wore a marigold officer's uniform that was so small on him that it only covered the very top of his torso, leaving his entire belly exposed. Phanto's shirt size was so large that they had to be ordered custom from B.T.T. headquarters because his size did not come standard in the machines embedded in the walls of the Unicorn Husker's hallways. Phanto's custom shirt had apparently been destroyed during the battle with the cosmic bears. The version he currently wore was the largest available in the dispensers.

Phanto rarely left the engine rooms due to his size and his propensity for reciting melancholy poetry that most of the crew could not abide. But during the battle with the cosmic bears, he had raced throughout the ship, providing his expertise to quickly plug breeches in the hull and to keep the ship floating after the engines and balloon became damaged.

Alex nodded at Phanto. Phanto nodded back. Alex liked Phanto. He was one of the biggest unsung heroes on the ship. Alex thought back to the histories and annals of the B.T.T. that he had studied during his stint at Officer Academy, and he remembered no mention of Phanto. This was unfortunate, because in Alex's opinion, Phanto was the single largest contributor to keeping the B.T.S. Unicorn Husker intact despite the continuous stream of hazards that the ship encountered. Alex frowned, knowing that in the coming years, Captain King Solomon's wise leadership and Officer Leif's above-average evasive maneuvers would receive the credit in the histories for the B.T.S. Unicorn Husker's survival in today's battle.

And then a second individual limped into view behind Captain King Solomon and Phanto. This man had to hunch to walk through the door to the bridge, and he was only able to stand at full height once aboard because the bridge stretched across multiple decks and thus had a higher ceiling than most other areas of the ship.

Alex instantly recognized the figure as the B.I.T. High Commander, the god Hephaestus. When Alex had last seen him, the god had been lying prone on the rooftop of the *Olympus* building, having lost one arm and trying his best to hold his disemboweled stomach together with his other. Captain King Solomon pointed to Alex and said, "And this is First Officer Alexandros ho Megas, one of the many heroes of the battle on your world."

Hephaestus limped over to Alex and shook his hand. At first, Alex was taken aback because there was no recognition of Alex in Hephaestus' face. But then Alex remembered that this current encounter was the first between the pair in *Hephaestus'* timestream, and thus Hephaestus should have no reason to recognize Alex. In the coming years, they would team up once to fight the swirling lizard-hordes of Earth 701,777, which would threaten the B.I.T. home world, and then later would repeat the teaming to put an end to the Wild Postman, who was overcome with a cosmic papyro-organic virus that caused him to fill multiple universes with junk mail before a special forces crew from the B.I.T.—led by Hephaestus— partnered with the B.T.T. to put an end to him. However, both these partnerships had occurred *earlier* in Alex's career, but *later* in Hephaestus' timeline, and thus at this point in Earth 55,777's timestream, it was their first meeting for Hephaestus.[11]

Hephaestus said, "I thank thee for thy service, sir. Thou and thy team pulled the B.I.T. from the precipice of utter destruction. I had prepared contingencies, but each of them failed. The Bureau of Interdimensional Travel is in thy debt."

Alex nodded. He replied, "Just doing our duty. I'm sure the B.I.T. would have done the same for us."

Hephaestus' eyebrow twitched. "Of course, of course," he responded.

"You seem to be faring much better now than you were upon the rooftop of your organization's headquarters," remarked Alex.

"Oh, yes. One of my Doctor-Bots patched me right up and reattached my arm. I built them eons ago in my forge for just such medical emergencies. I offered one of these priceless machines to each of the ships that arrived to help the B.I.T. in our hour of need. Thy captain was the only one to turn me down."

Alex smirked. *That's because he knows that you intend to use them to spy on us, you devious bastard,* thought Alex. *And this spying will result in doom for these other captains during the Dynamite Kitten War of Earth 209,900,878 when you become possessed by OsPurrUs—the Egyptian Kitten War Deity of that reality—and sell your forge's services to Balroth the Bemoaned, with whom you unleash warmongering multitudes to wreak havoc upon the Space-Time-Multinuum.*

Before Alex could say anything, Captain King Solomon interjected, "That's because the contribution of our own Randy the Saw is beyond value. We would not want to do anything to interfere with his confidence, and a mechanical replacement for many of his skills would surely do just that."

Hephaestus shrugged, a gesture that consisted of his overlarge shoulder rising much higher than his smaller shoulder. He said, "Very well. Thou may contact me at any time if thou changest thy mind."

Captain King Solomon smiled. He replied, "Wonderful. Do you need any help with the cleanup of Earth 55,777?"

Hephaestus shook his head. "Nay. I'm calling in a fleet of ships to perform salvage work and begin the rebuilding."

---

[11] Whew. Time Travel can be a mouthful. And can be confusing. Very, very confusing.

Captain King Solomon nodded. "Very well. And what about your peoples' knowledge of the B.T.T.? We cannot have word of our existence spreading into the wider Multiverse."

Hephaestus waved away the Captain's question. He exclaimed, "I know, I know! Doest thou think thee the first B.T.T. captain with whom I have entreated? I have fought beside thy organization for millennia, each of us protecting our own jurisdictions. Nobody can know about thee except my most trusted, highest ranking officers.

"Ages upon ages ago," he continued, "Following our first encounter, I forged a device to wipe the memories of my agents who encountered thee. I shall simply initiate this protocol, and thy organization need not worry about losing its secrecy. Though I must say, with all the Purple Shirts that thou station throughout the timestreams and universes, thou doest a decent job of ridding thyselves of secrecy on thine own."

Captain King Solomon shrugged. He replied, "I don't make the rules. I just follow them. And this one between our organizations has been around longer than me."

Hephaestus nodded. He said, "And with that, I thank thee once more and will take my leave of thee."

Hephaestus turned to the exit and began walking away. Captain King Solomon cleared his throat. Hephaestus stopped. Captain King Solomon held out his hand as though waiting for something.

Hephaestus muttered, "I nearly forgot."

"I'm sure you did," replied Captain King Solomon with ice in his tone. "There are a lot of other priorities in need of attention this day. But my leadership was clear on this point. I need it, or our organizations shall be at war."

Hephaestus turned, retrieved a rolled piece of parchment from his robes, and placed it in Captain King Solomon's outstretched hand. Hephaestus lowered himself onto one knee. Hephaestus' voice escaped his lips between clenched teeth, "Here is my formal apology and my denouncement of Agent 27142. He acted on his own accord and invaded the B.T.T. home reality without my permission. I would have stopped him if I had known of his treachery, and I would send him to a prison dimension for the remainder of his existence if he were still alive. I once more pledge the B.I.T.'s vast resources to assisting the B.T.T. when threats become large enough that thou desires our help."

Captain King Solomon nodded. He placed a hand on Hephaestus' shoulder and responded, "Thank you, comrade. The B.T.T. has given me the authority to forgive you for this trespass. Your ignorance and inability to control your underlings shall no longer be a blight between our organizations. All is now well between us."

Hephaestus' face twitched as he fought against the obvious urge to scowl. He stood upon his feet and limped off the bridge to return to his home world.

Once Hephaestus was gone and the door to the bridge closed behind the god, Alex smirked at Captain King Solomon and said, "Why do you always antagonize him like that? You know that calling him ignorant and saying he is incapable of controlling his underlings only infuriates him, and he is not one to forget the slights. And on top of that, why do you insist on bringing him up here every time we go through this time-loop? You *know* he's just sizing us up so that he can try and take over this ship later—after the Wild Postman thing. We could have had this conversation down on his rooftop."

"I know. And I am also aware that he gets the idea for that scheme during this battle."

"I repeat, then," said Alex. "Why bring him here at all? Why antagonize him?"

Captain King Solomon sighed. He replied, "Think, boy. If the seed of the idea was destined to be planted in his head *during this battle*, then I can do nothing to stop it. What I *can* do is humiliate him, so he is filled with rage when he thinks of this ship, and I can hope it clouds his ability to properly plan. The other thing I can do is manipulate *what* he sees. I introduced him to our ship's head engineer, who—in case you did not notice—spoke more in the presence of the B.I.T. High Commander than he has spoken in the presence of anyone for decades. Do you really think that was *unintentional?*"

Phanto guffawed. He said, "Me speak all kinds of meesinformation around heem about how the sheep works! Why you theenk he fails so bad when he geeve eet try to take us over?"

Alex laughed. The complexity of time travel always made his head hurt. But he would not trade the experience for anything.

The Captain sat in his chair. Alex glanced around the bridge. It felt empty with so many of the officers in the infirmary.

The Captain pressed a button on the arm of his chair. He proclaimed, "Chronal Date 4,890,888,564. Our mission: to seek out chronal anomalies and fix them diplomatically. The B.T.S. Unicorn Husker just successfully ended The Endless War That Never Ends Between Ultimate Life and Ultimate Destruction. We are now boldly headed to Earth 6,076 to close this time-loop and set it on course to repeat properly. Leif, take us there."

CHAPTER 49

GOOD NEWS AND BAD NEWS

OLDER-ART OPENED HIS eyes. Bright fluorescent lights blared from above. It hurt to look at them, so he shut his eyes. The last thing he remembered was a bright pastel blue light, and then a brief image of his younger-self kneeling over him.

His abdomen felt as though it were on fire. He reached down to touch it, but he found that he could not move his hands. He opened his eyes, squinting to see despite the bright light. He saw that his hands were strapped down to the sides of a hospital bed.

A man in a marigold officer's shirt covered by a white coat was bent over Older-Art's midsection. He held a scalpel in one hand and a bone saw in the other. His tongue was poking out the side of his mouth as he concentrated on his work. Around him, nurses and doctors attended to him. One of them noticed that Older-Art's eyes were open.

"The patient is awake," said the random nurse in the purple shirt.

"Then somebody increase the anesthesia!" shouted the man bent over Older-Art's midsection. Older-Art could not remember the man's name.

And then the recognition hit him. The man bent over his midsection was Randy the Saw, Chief Medical Officer aboard the B.T.S. Unicorn Husker. Nobody aboard the Husker really understood why Randy was *Chief Medical Officer*, since everybody tried to avoid his services at all costs—sometimes they waited in line for days despite heavy injuries to see *any other* medical officer. He was the reason so many Purple Shirts who were injured during missions had amputated limbs. Randy the Saw was a doctor from Earth 65,656, a world ruled by a feudal society permanently stuck in medieval times. He heavily favored treating ailments and wounds via leeching and amputation, for he was constantly concerned about the spreading of bad humors.

"No!" screamed Older-Art. "Get me another doct—"

But the nurse reached over and increased the anesthesia, and everything went black.

*

Older-Art opened his eyes. The room was bright. His mouth was dry. He felt immense pressure in his torso, like he had not gone to the bathroom in several days. He looked down. He was covered in a clean white sheet. The doctor and nurses were all gone. He sighed in relief. He closed his eyes and fell asleep.

He awoke when he heard footsteps approaching. The footsteps were nearly drowned out by the sound of a familiar roaring engine. Older-Art smiled. The people who cared most about him most must be here to check on him.

Older-Art opened his eyes and glanced toward the entrance of the small hospital room that he occupied. His heart skipped a beat. Randy the Saw was standing there, which meant that Older-Art's memory of the man crouched over his body had *not* been some sort of weird fever dream. Behind Randy the Saw stood Ginny and Drillbot. An overlarge gourd with gigantic antennae poking from its top sat nestled in the crook of Drillbot's arm. Drillbot waved one drill at Older-Art like an overexcited child.

"Hey, everybody," said Older-Art.

Randy the Saw strode forward. He held out his hand to shake Older-Art's. Randy the saw said, "I don't think we've officially met. Name's Doctor Randy. Some call me Randy the Saw. But I just prefer Doctor Randy. I'm the Chief Medical Officer on the Husker."

Older-Art frowned. He attempted to shake the man's hand, but he found that his hands were still strapped to the bed.

Randy the Saw laughed. "Oh, forgot about those."

Older-Art did not respond.

Randy the Saw shrugged. Then he said, "I've got good news and bad news, though the bad news *could* be good depending on your perspective. Which do you want first?"

Older-Art sighed. He muttered, "Good news. Always good news first."

Randy the Saw nodded to Ginny. Ginny walked into the room and placed a hand on Older-Art's chest just below his shoulder. He winced. She looked down and frowned. She had placed her hand on one of his wounds from the battle. She muttered a quick apology, and then she crossed to the other side of the bed, where she placed her hand on that side of his chest. She said, "The good news is that your service to the B.T.T. is *done*. Captain King Solomon sent me here to tell you that you can finally return home!"

Older-Art's heart raced faster and more excitedly than it had ever raced before. Considering the string of terrible luck that had beset him the last several decades, he genuinely worried about some random god or Fate somewhere eavesdropping on his life and thinking that a heart attack right now might be a hilariously ironic twist of fate. He inhaled deeply, doing his best to calm himself.

But then he gave in to his joy. He grinned so hard that tears fell from his eyes. For a solid minute, he screamed, "Yes!"

Randy the Saw approached from the other side of the bed. The doctor ordered, "Settle down, settle down. You've just been through major surgery. You'll wear yourself out if you push too hard."

Older-Art continued screaming with joy. Finally, after several more moments of it, he stopped. Then he nodded at the doctor.

Randy the Saw asked, "Ready for the bad news?"

"Nothing could feel bad after what I just heard."

And then Older-Art realized just how wrong he could be. Randy the Saw flipped back the sheet. Everything below Older-Art's belly button was gone. A few gigantic leeches clung to his midsection near the wound. Randy the Saw had lived up to his reputation for solving *all* medical problems via amputation and leeching.

"What the hell?" screamed Older-Art. "Where are my legs? And Where's my di—"

"Calm down," demanded Randy the Saw. "It will be OK."

"*It will be OK?*' How? My life will never be the same! You're lucky my arms are strapped down, or I'd strangle you, you sonovabitch!"

And with that, Randy the Saw pressed a button on his communicator. "Bring it in," he ordered.

Three nurses entered the room carrying a large, hairy object. When they set it down, Older-Art realized that it was the lower half of a gorilla. "No," he muttered. "No, no, no."

Randy the Saw nodded at the nurses. They unstrapped Older-Art's arms from the bed and carried him to the lower half of the gorilla. They set him down in an opening in its top. As soon as they did so, it made a squelching noise and squeezed tight around his torso. He felt a sharp stab in his belly and back, and then he felt something shove its way under his skin and wiggle up his spinal cord until it forced itself into his brain. He screamed. Then he felt the immense pressure in his torso disappear.

He looked down. A pile of feces had splattered onto the ground between his feet.

"It works!" screamed Randy the Saw. "I partnered with the Engineering and Cybernetics departments on this one. Since your back was broken and your body thus needed to be amputated from *just* above the wound, you no longer had any means to extricate yourself of your waste. We had the choice to either let you die or create something new. Luckily for you, one of our crew's Purple Shirts—a Gorilla-Person from Earth 90,888,435,222—was severed in half during the battle above Earth 8,669 in the exact right spot to provide what you needed. We used his corpse to create this new, artificial lower half to extricate your waste for you. We also jury-rigged a system to make it wire itself into your brain, so you can control it with your mind. I've given your body a *huge* upgrade! You'll be able to run and jump and climb faster and higher than ever before! See what I mean? Losing the lower half of your body's not *really* bad news if you have the right perspective! You'll be better than new once you get used to it! You're welcome!"

Older-Art buried his face in his hands. He had no desire to run or jump or climb ever again, let alone do it faster and higher than ever before. He tried to sob, but the tears would not come. If *this* is what it cost him to go home and never see any of these people ever again, then it was worth it.

"Can I at least get some pants?" he asked.

CHAPTER 50

NOT GOOD NEWS FOR EVERYONE

NORMAL-ART ENTERED 29333'S hospital room. She looked pale. He had never imagined she could appear fragile, but she did in this bed.

God-Art's teeth had shredded through her and nearly killed her, but she had survived thanks to Bagoo's quick action. He had wrapped her bleeding wounds in his stringy bandages, and though it had caused her incredible pain, it kept her from bleeding out.

The same could not be said of Bagoo, who remained in intensive care. He was unconscious, and though Alex had assured Normal-Art that the bog ghost would survive, Normal-Art did not quite know whether to believe it. It would not be the first time that the B.T.T. had lied to him.

Normal-Art crept into the room and sat in a chair near 29333's bed. Ginny and Drillbot were a few rooms down, checking on Older-Art. But Normal-Art did not much care for Older-Art, because he was boring and he always attempting to impart terrible advice to Normal-Art.

After a few minutes, Normal-Art heard an excited scream emanating from down the hall. The voice sounded like his—only older—so he assumed it must be originating from Older-Art's room.

29333 opened her eyes. She demanded, "Tell them to shut up. Or close the door. I'm trying to rest."

Normal-Art nodded. He stood and closed the door, since it was the closer of the two options.

"How're you feeling?" he asked as he sat back down.

29333 groaned, "Y'know. Stuck in a hospital ward because a damned god decided to use me as target practice. With teeth that I'm quite sure he never brushed over the course of his entire existence. So never better."

Normal-Art stared at his feet. He said, "Well, we finished our mission.

I figure the Captain's going to send me home soon."

29333 chortled. She responded, "Yeah, you keep figuring. You're bound to be right eventually."

"I just wanted to stop by and say goodbye," continued Normal-Art. "You turned out to be a lot less of a bastard than you were for the first decade that I knew you. Oddly enough, I think you and Drillbot might be the only people I'll actually miss from this crazy, stupid adventu—"

He was interrupted by a loud snore. He looked up from his feet and saw that she had fallen asleep. He shrugged and leaned back in the chair. He closed his eyes and took a nap, too.

*

Normal-Art awoke. He did not know how long he had been asleep. He glanced over at 29333. She was sitting in her bed, wide awake. She said, "Y'know, you're the first hospital visitor I've ever had, other than that time when 27142 came to visit me once to give me orders to heal faster. I think I'm beginning to grow a little fond of y—"

The room's communicator interrupted her, "Arthur, you are to report to the bridge immediately."

"As I was saying," she said. "I think you and I might be more compatib—"

Normal-Art's addled brain realized the communicator was referring to him. He sprang to his feet and sprinted for the door. He called over his shoulder, "This is it! They must be sending me home! Have a nice life!"

Normal-Art raced into the hallway. He narrowly dodged being crushed against the wall when Older-Art burst forth from his own hospital room, followed by Ginny and Drillbot. Older-Art's lower half was that of a gorilla and he wore short, cutoff jeans to cover his unmentionables.

"You always been half-gorilla?" asked Normal-Art between puffing breaths as they raced toward the elevator. "Did I just not notice before?"

"It doesn't matter! It's time to go home!"

They reached the elevator and cut to the front of the line. The Purple Shirts took one look at Drillbot and did not dare complain.

Soon, the four arrived on the bridge. When they entered, they found Captain King Solomon sitting in his captain's chair, Alex standing at his station, and Leif steering the ship at the helm. A Purple Shirt sat at 29333's station. Normal-Art would have been annoyed that she had been replaced so quickly by such an unqualified replacement, but he did not care enough to allow himself to be annoyed.

"Are we finally headed for home?" screamed both Arts simultaneously, excitement and nervousness underlying the question.

Captain King Solomon stood from his chair and nodded toward them. He said, "We *are* headed for Earth 6,076."

The Arts looked at him blankly. Captain King Solomon slapped his own forehead. He said, "That is where you are from."

The Arts cheered. Captain King Solomon gestured for them to quiet down. When they eventually did, he said, "Soon, *some* of you will have choices to make. Some of you will be given the option to go home."

Normal-Art squealed, "I don't care about the choices! Just send me home!"

Normal-Art raced around the bridge. He high-fived Alex, Leif, and every Purple Shirt he could find. None of them replied with much enthusiasm.

"What gives?" asked Normal-Art. "Shouldn't you be happy? Didn't we *just* save the Space-Time-Whatever? And aren't you *finally* getting rid of us?"

"Well, yes, in a manner of speaking," replied Alex. "But you must understand: for you, this adventure has encompassed your entire life for decades, but for this ship, this is an infinite time-loop that the B.T.S. Unicorn Husker repeats every few years using whichever crew happens to be currently assigned to it. The only constants are you, your companions, the mission, the setting, and this ship. Been this way since before I joined the B.T.T., and it will be this way long after I die."

Normal-Art squinted at Alex. He said, "And now I'm confused. I'd ask you to explain it again, but I don't care! I'm going home!"

Captain King Solomon smirked. He said, "I said that *some* of you will be given the option to go home. Unfortunately, Younger-Arthur, now is *not* that time for you."

Before the words could sink into Normal-Art's brain, Alex swept forward to restrain him. Normal-Art tried to jerk forward and punch the Captain, but Alex was too strong.

"No!" screamed Normal-Art. "I did everything that you asked!"

"And now, you will perform one more task."

"No!"

The Captain replied, "Unfortunately, I have no choice in the matter. Events in this time-loop must play out as they must, so as much as I hate to extend our time together, the B.T.T. Governing Council has deemed it necessary to *conscript* you into our service."

Normal-Art frowned. He muttered, "I thought *all* B.T.T. agents had a choice in whether or not they serve. My choice is no."

The Captain frowned. He replied, "Under normal circumstances, that is the case. But in this instance, the existence of the *entire* Space-Time-Multinuum is at stake, not simply the lives of those spanning a select number of finite realities. For the sake of the entire Space-Time-Multinuum, you must serve the B.T.T. whether you desire to or not."

Captain King Solomon pulled what looked like a wad of fur from his pocket and pressed it onto Normal-Art's upper lip. He then retrieved a small hand mirror from his chair and held it up to Normal-Art's face.

"Now tell me, what do you see?" asked the Captain.

At first, Normal-Art refused to look into the mirror. After a few dozen seconds, when he finally did, revulsion overcame him.

"What do you see?" the Captain repeated.

"Oh, no. Oh, god, no."

"Well?"

"How did I never notice it before? How did I never notice that I looked *just like* my old boss at the Department of Motor Vehicles, but without a mustache?"

Captain King Solomon shrugged. "Probably because you rarely notice much of anything," he suggested.

"Are you *really* this much of an idiot?" chimed in Older-Art. "Before I brought you aboard this ship, I *showed you* that Mr. Reynolds was me in disguise. This shouldn't be a revelation to you at all!"

"Sh-Shut up," whined Normal-Art to his older-self, apparently unable to think of a clever comeback or response to the fact that he did not pay enough attention to the Mr.-Reynolds-Older-Art-revelation to remember it the first time he saw it. Then his shoulders slumped. He asked, "If I do this for the B.T.T., *then* I get to go home?"

Captain King Solomon nodded. He answered, "Yes. When your

mission is complete, you get to return home."

"And what's my mission?"

"The last few decades of your life happened as they did because they *needed* to happen that way to save the entire Space-Time-Multinuum. And because time occurs in loops that form streams when laid end to end, you must ensure that the next loop happens exactly the same as this one."

"And how do I do that?"

Captain King Solomon smiled. He answered, "There's no script to follow, if that's what you're wondering. You will simply *be* Mr. Reynolds, your former manager."

He continued, "When you were younger, you took the job at the Department of Motor Vehicles so that you could get fired and receive unemployment benefits. Any other boss would have fired you very early on in that employment. But instead, Mr. Reynolds—future-you—kept you close so that he could observe you and ensure that you had the motivation you needed to abscond with Artheoskatergariabetrugereiinganno when he appeared on your doorstep. *He* then ensured the B.I.T. was alerted to your illegal dimension-hop so that they would come to arrest you. And then he was present when you returned from your culture's version of Hell to deliver you to the B.T.S. Unicorn Husker. You must also perform these tasks to ensure the necessary series of events will occur that will save the Space-Time-Multinuum."

Normal-Art glared at Older-Art. "Wait, *this bastard* sicced the B.I.T. on me? *He's* the reason I got kidnapped by them and tortured for a decade?"

Older-Art shrugged. Captain King Solomon said, "It happened that way because it needed to happen that way."

"That's dumb," said Normal-Art. "None of it *needed* to happen that way. As a matter of fact, you don't really need me for any of this."

"But that's where you're wrong," said the Captain. "Time is loop after loop after loop. This is the way it's always happened. So, this is the way it *must* always happen. You will be sent to Purple Shirt Training, and then you will be stationed in your Earth's past as Mr. Reynolds."

Normal-Art buried his face in his hands. He sobbed, "I don't deserve this! Please, just give me what I want!"

Alex leaned over and whispered in Normal-Art's ear, "'*Deserve*' has nothing to do with this. But trust me, you *are* the ideal person for this.

Because if it were happening to anyone else—anyone with even *slightly* redeeming values—we would feel at least a twinge of guilt over how that person's life is being ruined. But this is happening to *you*, so such guilt isn't really necessary, wouldn't you agree?"

CHAPTER 51

AN UNEXPECTED OUTCOME, BUT NOT REALLY IF YOU WERE PAYING ATTENTION

GINNY GLANCED OVER at Normal-Art, who had buried his face in his hands. She placed a hand on his shoulder to comfort him, but he shrugged it off. She would like to say this reaction surprised her, but it ultimately did not.

Ginny cleared her throat. Captain King Solomon looked over at her, Older-Art, and Drillbot. The Captain stroked his beard. He said, "And here is where choices come into play."

The Captain turned first to Older-Art and said, "Arthur, you have two options: you may return home, or you may stay in the service of the B.T.T. and be promoted to an officer of—"

"It's Art! And send me home!" Older-Art screamed, interrupting.

Captain King Solomon warned, "But you should know that you shall return to your Earth years after you left it. Nothing will be the same."

Older-Art frowned. He replied, "Just return me to the moment after the B.I.T. officers kidnapped younger-me. You can travel through time. I know you can do this for me!"

Captain King Solomon shook his head and said, "Unfortunately, that is not possible. There were necessary events that needed to happen in the intervening period in order to save the Space-Time-Multinuum. And you being there could interfere with the timing of those events, which could result in Artheoskatergariabetrugereiinganno being resurrected at the wrong time, or you could bumble your way into preventing certain other events from happening as they must. Such catastrophes could result in nothing working as intended and could spell the end of the Space-Time-

Multinuum."

Older-Art frowned. Then, after staring at the floor and thinking for a few seconds, he shrugged. "Whatever," he muttered. "I don't care if everything has changed. Send me home, anyway."

Captain King Solomon nodded. He proclaimed, "It shall be done."

Then he turned to Ginny and said, "Ginny Longfellow, you have proven your worth to the B.T.T. You may return home, or you may remain in service to the B.T.T. If you choose to stay, you will undergo Purple Shirt Training, and then you shall be immediately promoted and enrolled into Officer Academy."

Ginny glanced over at Older-Art. She placed her hand on his shoulder. She said to him, "Part of my heart wants to choose love and go with you, but my conscience tells me that I should remain here and try to make up for the horrific deeds that I committed while under the Pink One's control."

Older-Art stared at her, a dumbfounded look on his face. He said, "Babe, I never invited you to come along with me."

Ginny gasped, "What the hell do you mean? I'm your girlfriend! You said that your younger-self was an idiot for treating me the way that he did. And now we're in a relationship! We're in love!"

Older-Art shrugged. He replied, "I thought we were, y'know, just having a little fling while we were stuck together on this adventure. I never agreed to a relationship once we were *done*."

She slapped him. She screamed, "You are *such* a bastard! You don't care about anyone but yourself!"

Older-Art shrugged. He said, "That's probably true. But in a few minutes, I'll be heading home and will never see you again. So, I don't need to pretend I care more than I do to keep you from getting upset."

She leapt on him and began beating him. Nobody on the bridge made any effort to stop her, though Captain King Solomon eventually interrupted to ask her to make her choice. She chose to remain with the B.T.T., and then she resumed pummeling Older-Art.

CHAPTER 52

THE HAPPIEST FOREVER

DRILLBOT WATCHED HIS compatriots as they made their choices. He was proud of Ginny. She would make a fine officer in the B.T.T. The Arts were a different story. They were a zero to Ginny's one. Where she was compassionate and caring and loyal, they were abrasive and selfish and unfaithful. Other than long ago when Earth 1,000,000 was about to cease existing and Art had prevented Drillbot from being left behind, Art had done little to show that he actually cared for Drillbot. Thus, Drillbot made no move to intervene when Ginny began beating Older-Art senseless.

Captain King Solomon turned to Drillbot and spoke loudly to be heard over the pummeling that Ginny was giving to Older-Art, "Drillbot, you also have a choice to make. Like Ginny, you may remain in the service of the B.T.T. You, too, would enter Officer Academy immediately after you complete Purple Shirt Training. I could likely secure for you a position as a Chief Security Officer on one of our sister ships once you are an officer. Or I can send you anywhere you want to go in the Multiverse, and you could build a new life there. You could even work for the B.I.T. if you would prefer to pursue that route."

Drillbot's processors kicked into overdrive. He played out the scenarios in his head. He *could* be happy in the B.T.T., but he would always feel like a piece of him was missing. He looked down at Henry, who was perched in the crook of his arm, having been fully healed by the B.T.T.'s infirmary.

He *could* be happy running off to adventure after adventure with the gourd, righting evils across the Multiverse. But in this scenario, too, he would always feel like a piece of him was missing.

And then Drillbot decided. He declared, "[whir] None of those options would make – CLACK – would make Drillbot happy. Drillbot has a different proposal."

And then he told it to Captain King Solomon. Captain King Solomon nodded. He replied, "There is no going back from this, you know. You will be stuck there forever."

Drillbot smiled his version of a smile. "[whir] And it will be the happiest forever that Drillbot could imagine."

Ginny was still beating Older-Art, but Drillbot decided she had done enough damage. He needed to say goodbye to her. She was the person he would miss the most.

"[whir] Goodbye, friend," he said as he pulled her off Older-Art.

When she realized what was happening, tears streamed down her face. She leapt up and wrapped her arms around the spot where his head met his shoulders, hugging him. She said, "Goodbye. I'll miss you."

He hugged her back. "[whir] Drillbot will miss Ginny most of – CLACK – most of all."

Ginny began desperately slapping his metal hide. She huffed, "Can't… breathe…"

He released his grip and said, "[whir] Drillbot apologizes. Drillbot did not mean to – CLACK – to hurt Ginny."

She grinned at him and replied, "I know."

Drillbot handed Henry to Ginny. "[whir] This is – CLACK – This is Henry. He will be a good companion to – CLACK – to Ginny. Please look after him."

Ginny looked at the gourd quizzically. She said, "Uh, thanks, I guess."

Henry sighed. "I can read a room, you know," he said. "You think *I'm* excited to be hauled around in your sweaty hands for the rest of my life?"

Ginny smirked. She responded, "Sorry. I meant no offense. I didn't realize that you could talk."

"Well, I can. And if you don't mind an ornery gourd at your side, I think that we could make a good pair."

"And if not, you will make a good stew."

"That's not funny," replied Henry.

They continued exchanging banter, but Drillbot ignored it. He hugged Ginny once more and then followed Alex out of the room and toward the Jump Chamber. He did not say goodbye to the Arts.

*

Drillbot's sensors experienced total blackness, and then they returned to their normal functionality. When they did so, he found that he lay cuddled with Ginny Rex. His internal chronometer revealed that this was the eve before the fateful battle on Earth 55,777 where she was destined to die and be disintegrated. His internal gears and processors moaned and whirred, and he became more aroused and excited than he had ever been.

She was spooning him, so he rolled over to look at her face. He could stare at her forever, and that would not be long enough for him.

A few seconds later, his sensors experienced total blackness. When they returned to their normal functionality, he was back in the position in which he had been moments before, lying in the spooning embrace of Ginny Rex and her tiny arms.

Captain King Solomon had granted Drillbot the wish that would make him happier than anything else in the entire Space-Time-Multinuum. Drillbot's consciousness had been sent into a brief moment in time. He would experience the peace and ecstasy of these same few seconds with Ginny Rex on loop for all eternity.

And to Drillbot, this was the happiest forever that anyone could ever hope to experience.

EPILOGUE

Normal-Art sat behind Mr. Reynolds' desk, having adopted the guise of the Department of Motor Vehicles manager. His mind drifted to all the times he had sat on the opposite side of this desk, receiving lecture after lecture about the need to shape up and take life seriously.

He had occupied this position and this desk for a year now, and it felt just as foreign to him today as it did the first time he sat here. He stared at the fake family photo that the B.T.T. had provided to him. He stared at the calendar on his wall, which featured a kitten hanging by a paw from a clothesline, desperately trying to prevent itself from tumbling away into the blue nothingness below it. Above the kitten, big block letters spelled out *Hang Tough!*

"Get in here, now!" he screamed to the open door.

A younger version of himself trudged inside. Normal-Art had hired this younger version of himself soon after he began his position as manager, and he had hated every minute of the experience. From this side of the desk, his younger-self was brash, arrogant, and above all, lazy. It was an internal struggle every day to not give in to his desire to fire the younger version of himself and be done with it. But if he ever wanted to be free of the B.T.T. and to be allowed to live his life again, then he knew that he needed to cooperate, and thus he needed to keep his younger-self around until he disappeared on the adventure with God-Art.

God, I hope it happens soon. I don't think I can't stand another minute of this kid, he thought.

And then his younger-self sat down. As Mr. Reynolds, he launched into a long lecture about how Younger-Art needed to shape up. A piece of spittle flung from his mouth and landed squarely on Younger-Art's forehead. Younger-Art gripped the chair's hard, plastic armrests until his knuckles turned white.

"I mean it this time. This is your last chance," screamed Normal-Art.

"Yes, sir, Mr. Reynolds," replied Younger-Art. His eyes had glazed over.

"I can go now?"

Normal-Art frowned. "You really need to work on your attitude. Lots of people out there are out of work, and they'd love your job."

Younger-Art stood and shrugged. He muttered, "Oh, yeah, people are just dying to work at the DMV. When they're standing in line all afternoon waiting for their driver's licenses, I overhear, like, every one of them say to each other, '*Hey, I love this tedious experience so much, I wish I could come back every day!*'"

Normal-Art began screaming at Younger-Art as the younger man stood and walked out of the room. Normal-Art wanted desperately to chase after his younger-self and beat the annoying bastard to within an inch of his life.

After Younger-Art left Normal-Art's office, he received word from the other employees that Younger-Art had left the Department of Motor Vehicles office without permission and had announced that he was going on break for the rest of the day. Normal-Art immediately called him. The line went to Younger-Art's voicemail. Normal-Art seethed and screamed a nasty message into the phone.

And then he looked down at his messy desk, only to see something he had never seen before: a tiny man about the size of a pinhead wearing what appeared to be an astronaut's uniform. The man sat on Normal-Art's newspaper. The man pressed a button on his suit and grew to about an inch in height.

The man removed his bubble-shaped helmet. He looked just like Normal-Art. The man waved.

"Hi!" squealed the man's tiny voice. "I am Captain Art. I lead a fleet in the Bureau of Microscopic Travel. I am *you* from the Microscopicverse, a series of subdimensions smaller than anything you could possibly imagine. I am here because we're desperate. I need you to come with me. *You* are the key to saving the Microscopicverse."

Normal-Art sighed. He was never volunteering for another adventure so long as he lived. He immediately slapped his palm down upon the tiny man. It felt like slapping a bug. He walked to the bathroom and washed the tiny gore off his hand.

Then he called Younger-Art again. This time, the line answered and then immediately hung up. He sighed once more, hoping one day soon, he would be free of the B.T.T. and would get to return to his own life to laze about on his own couch.

He eventually got his wish. But as you know, it did not happen quite *when or how* he wanted it to happen.

ANOTHER NOTE FROM THE AUTHOR:

This novel revolves around time travel (obviously).

If you noticed any continuity errors, then great job! Sometimes the story changes ever so slightly as it passes through successive time-loops, and the text can't keep up. Congratulations on recognizing the blips in the Space-Time-Multinuum.

Definitely written in total sincerity,
Chris Brimmage

ACKNOWLEDGMENTS

Special thanks to Mark Reddish for all the help. You always take the time to make these things better, and your feedback is always appreciated.

Just so you know: if you threw a party, and you invited every single person you knew, then you would soon see that the biggest gift would come from me, and the card attached would say, "Hi. This is from Chris & G & Little Bear. That is all."

THANK YOU FOR PURCHASING THIS BOOK.

To receive special offers, a free short story, and info on new releases, sign up for the Christopher Brimmage mailing list at cbrimmage.com

ABOUT THE AUTHOR

Christopher Brimmage is a writer, teacher, marketer, brand manager, and former boy band front man. He has a wife named Geraldine to whom he loves to sing Meatloaf, a son named Augustus with whom he has formed the *Steam Roller Boyz*, and a pair of brothers that he loves to annoy.

By Christopher Brimmage

THE MULTIVERSE ASKEW TRILOGY

The Multiverse Askew (Book 1)

The Endless War That Never Ends (Book 2)

And Now, Time Travel (Book 3)

NOVELLAS:

Mandrill, P.I.: *Dial M for Murdered Coyote*
(A Cartoon Noir Detective Tale)

Plug 'em Good
(A Space Western)

Bridge Troll
(A Suburban Fantasy-Horror)

NEW SERIES COMING IN 2021:

THE MANDRILL, P.I. TRILOGY

Manny Mandrill is an old-school, hard-boiled private dick, the last in the sprawling cartoon metropolis of Toonsville. When this anthropomorphic cartoon mandrill is hired to solve a string of horrific murders, he uncovers a deadly criminal conspiracy that threatens to engulf the entire city.

Read this series for: Cartoon Noir! Humor! Detectives! Werewolves! Vampires! Mad Scientists! Mummies! Assassins! Dog Mobsters! Dinosaur Gangsters! Otter Archaeologists! Alien Invasions! Horse Cowboys! 80s Movie & Cartoon Nostalgia! And so much more, there are not enough exclamation marks to contain the excitement!

9 780578 613987